A
TREASON
OF
THORNS

Also by Laura E. Weymouth:

The Light Between Worlds

A
TREASON
OF
THORNS

LAURA E. WEYMOUTH

An Imprint of HarperCollinsPublishers

Library of Congress Cataloging-in-Publication Data

Names: Weymouth, Laura E., author.
Title: A treason of thorns / Laura E. Weymouth.
Description: New York, NY : HarperTeen, 2019. | Summary: When
    seventeen-year-old Violet Sterling returns to Burleigh House after
    years in exile, Burleigh's magic is tormented, ravaging the country-
    side, and she must strive to save her house before it destroys her.
Identifiers: LCCN 2019021074 | ISBN 978-0-06-269690-8
    (hardback)
Subjects: | CYAC: Magic—Fiction. | Houses—Fiction. | Treason—
    Fiction. | Fantasy.
Classification: LCC PZ7.1.W43757 Tre 2019 | DDC [Fic]--dc23 LC
    record available at https://lccn.loc.gov/2019021074

Typography by Jessie Gang
19 20 21 22 23   PC/LSCH   10 9 8 7 6 5 4 3 2 1
❖
First Edition

For Steph, who is Caretaker of this book.
And for the Pod, who are Caretakers of me.

PROLOGUE

A LACE-TRIMMED WEDDING INVITATION SITS ON MY nightstand and I know, beyond the shadow of a doubt, that Mama is not coming back. It was inevitable, but so far in life, ignoring the inevitable has always been easy for me.

Until now.

There's no avoiding the truth anymore. There it is, stamped in gold ink, wafting the lingering traces of rose-scented eau de toilette toward me.

Curled up on my side in bed, I stare at the invitation as if it's a snake.

"Violet." Wyn, my father's ward, calls softly from the other side of the bedroom door. "Can I come in?"

He may not be able to see me nod, but the House can. There's a click as it turns back the lock and a gentle scrape of hinges as it swings the door wide. I glance over and see Wyn crossing the room carefully, holding a cup of water with two hands so as not to spill. He's always walked so since coming to Burleigh House—as if the ground beneath his feet is strewn with invisible bits of broken glass, and he might damage himself with a single wrong step.

Wyn sets the cup down on my nightstand, in front of Mama's invitation, so that the print looks strange and distorted when seen through the glass. We may both be only eight and surrounded by servants—Jed and Mira, Papa's steward and housekeeper, are never far off—but even as children this is what we do. We look after each other.

As Wyn takes a seat at my side, the comforting ivy Burleigh House has blanketed me with rustles and pulls away from him— they've never got on that well, Burleigh and Wyn. Flames flare deep purple on the hearth and the lamplight glows in the same shade. Poor old House—it hates to see me unhappy just as much as Wyn does. I sometimes forget in these moments when Burleigh's so kind and solicitous that it's one of the five Great Houses, whose vast magic governs the well-being of England. To me, my House has always been both more and less than that. Burleigh, like Wyn, is simply this: both family, and a friend.

Wyn shifts, putting a little more space between himself and Burleigh's retreating leaves. If he were anyone else, he'd ask if I'm alright. But Wyn's been a quiet child since the day Papa brought him back to Burleigh House from a Taunton foundling home. Which is just as well, if you ask me—I've never seen much use in endlessly worrying over troubles. I don't want to talk about how Papa's gone yet again, off in London on House business. I don't want to talk about how Burleigh House's fears have been seeping into me through the floors, and how sometimes they make my heart pound so fast I can hardly breathe.

I absolutely do not want to talk about Mama.

Instead, I hug my legs tighter, wishing to make myself so small I'll disappear. Wyn looks down at me, solemn and wide-eyed. I know he and the House will stay with me all night and dog my steps tomorrow. They never abandon me, at any rate. The House will wrap me in flowers and lull me to sleep with nightingale song, and Wyn—well. Wyn never sleeps in his own bed. He prefers a pile of blankets and a pillow in my airing cupboard.

I can't help but remember what Mama thought about all of this. My mother and father fought about everything, but the way I feel about Burleigh and Wyn came up often.

"She *should* put the House first, Eloise," Papa would say. "Vi will be Caretaker of this place when she's grown. Burleigh will choose her, I'll pass on the key when I'm ready, and His Majesty will certainly approve of the arrangement—you know the king's always taken an interest in Vi. This is who she's meant to be."

"She doesn't know who she is *now*, let alone who she ought to be in the future," Mama always argued back. "And how will she ever sort herself out if you keep her tethered to Burleigh House and never let her be with ordinary children?"

"Wyn keeps her company."

"He is *not* an ordinary child."

They'd go on and on like that, in endless circles, arguing behind closed doors. Perhaps they didn't know Wyn and I sat outside listening, or perhaps they were past caring.

But now all the fighting has come to an end, and Mama's off in Switzerland, planning her second wedding to some foreign baron.

"Wyn." I sit up and look at him. I need to know that all this is worth it. I need to know that no matter what I've lost, I've lost it for the greater good.

"Yes?" he says, all untidy sandy hair and serious grey eyes.

"Do you think I'll be a good Caretaker for Burleigh House?"

Wyn doesn't answer. He fixes his gaze on the blanket of ivy still covering my bed, except for the conspicuously empty space around him.

"A good Caretaker puts her House first," I say, half to myself.

"Always?" Wyn asks.

I reach out a hand and a strand of green ivy twines around my wrist, a near match for the latticework birthmark of slick pink skin that stamps me there, like a bracelet. "Always. Papa says so—a good Caretaker puts her House before king. Before country. Before family. Before her own life, even."

"But what if you change your mind?"

Now that is unthinkable. Mama may leave, I may grow up, but the one thing that will never change is my resolve to serve Burleigh House. My father, George Sterling, is a perfect Caretaker, and in the rare moments when he's at home, he sees to it that I learn my place. That one day I'll follow after him: the best Caretaker England has ever known. Under Papa's watchful tenure, Burleigh has thrived. The counties our House governs have known peace and prosperity.

"I will *never* change my mind," I tell Wyn. "I'll put Burleigh first all my life, because this place is greater than you or me or any one person."

And though I've learned this lesson by rote under the watchful eye of my stern father, my heart still swells when I repeat it. For as long as I can remember, Burleigh has been everything to me. This House is like a mother, father, comforter, and friend. I intend to repay the favor someday, when I'm able.

"We may not understand the House, we may not be able to speak with it, but Burleigh House was here watching over the West Country before you or I were born, and it will be here long after we're gone. It is my duty as a Sterling to serve this place, and to help it care for the countryside. Mama *knew* that, Wyn. She knew it. But she was always jealous of Burleigh. She couldn't see why it's worth looking after." I stop and swallow fiercely, past the heat burning in the back of my throat and behind my eyes.

Wyn stares down at the floor, looking as small and miserable as I feel.

"And what about a good House?" he asks after a long silence. I frown as he plucks an ivy leaf and shreds it to bits. "What does a good House do? Shouldn't you get something in return?"

I run a finger across the ivy, soothing the place where Wyn marred it, and the leaves turn to my touch like flowers toward sun. "I don't expect anything. A good House puts *itself* first, because the well-being of the countryside is bound up in the health of its House. And so a good House chooses its Caretaker wisely, and doesn't spare them when trouble comes."

The fire flickers on the hearth, as if to confirm my words.

"Violet."

When I glance up at Wyn, the expression in his eyes makes my stomach clench. He always looks just so—restless, ill at ease, like an animal poised for flight—before making the suggestion I know is coming. "Let's run away. You don't have to stay here, or be a

Caretaker, if you don't want to. We could go to Switzerland, to your mother. Or somewhere else—you can choose, just . . . let's leave."

Wind moans in the chimney, like a sob, and the ivy on my bed begins to recede, sliding sadly away toward the windows it crept in through. Out of habit and out of practice, all my self-pity shifts as my heart goes out to Burleigh House.

"You shouldn't say such things," I tell Wyn, my tone a reproach. "You know I'll never go, and you know even talking about leaving upsets Burleigh."

Wyn hangs his head and looks so woebegone I don't know who I feel for more—him, or my keening House.

"Oh, stop it, Burleigh," I say, and the wailing wind subsides even as I speak. "I'm not going anywhere."

But it's Wyn who I throw my arms around, and he relaxes just a little. As much as Wyn ever does, at any rate.

"I'm sorry about your mother," he whispers, and I hold him tighter.

"I'm not." The words come out so fiercely I almost believe them. "I'm not, I'm not. I've got you and Burleigh, and Papa when he's not working on House business. What more could I possibly want?"

After Wyn climbs off the bed and retreats to his makeshift cot in the cupboard, I get up. Opening the drawer in the nightstand, I pull out a letter Mama enclosed with the wedding invitation. It carries even more of her scent than the invitation itself, and I breathe in that aroma of roses, remembering the feel of her arms around me.

One sentence stands out, for the ink has run and spotted, as if tears were shed when it was written.

Come to me, my Violet—let me make a home for you here.

But I have a home. I am a Sterling—I was born on the grounds of Burleigh House, and someday, I hope to be as brilliant a Caretaker as Papa.

A good Caretaker puts her House first. Before king, before country.

Before family.

Kneeling next to the hearth, I feed Mama's letter to the sympathetic flames, which shift to blue as I scrub the sleeve of my nightgown across my eyes.

"Think about something else. Anything else. It helps," Wyn's voice says from the shadows of the cupboard.

I take a shaky breath and begin to hum. It's a song Papa always sings for me when he's at home.

> *Blood for a beginning*
> *Mortar for an end*
> *Speak out your binding*
> *Be you foe or friend*
>
> *Take up the deed*
> *Take it well in hand*
> *And bind a House's power*
> *Bind it to the land*
>
> *Blood for an ending*
> *Mortar for a start*
> *Unmake a binding*
> *At your House's heart*

Unleash a House's power
Let it all run free
Leave naught for the king
Naught for you or me

First House for a prison
Second for ladies' rest
Third for a palace
Fourth to be blessed

Fifth House holds quicksilver
The Sixth ruins all
But for blood in its mortar
But for breath in its walls

But this time it doesn't have the usual effect, not even when I fix my mind on the words.

All I see is Mama's handwriting. All I can think of is the fact that she's never coming back.

"Once upon a time there was a Great House," I begin somewhat desperately. I haven't told Wyn a story in over a year, not since he grew used to life here at Burleigh. But it grounds me, the sound of him settling in to listen, and the feeling of the immense, brooding presence that is my beloved Burleigh turning its attention in my direction. "There were the Sterlings, too, who lived and died for it. Their blood ran with its mortar. Their bones rested in its ground."

When I turn away from the fireplace, every inch of the bedroom floor is carpeted with new-sprouted daisies. Slowly, I lock up the sadness of my mother's leaving deep inside, because I know I would give anything for this place. One day, my blood will run with its mortar. One day, my bones will rest in its ground.

1

Nine Years Later

BENEATH ME, THE FLAT BOTTOM OF MY BOAT THRUMS ever so slightly as a fenland pike bumps against it. The long, gleaming creature is focused on its fishy business, and I've been motionless for near an hour, letting gentle currents in the marsh water carry me this way and that. I'm all but invisible to the pike, and an invisible fisher is a successful one.

Sun beats down on my bare head, and heats the long rope of my braid. Sweat trickles between my shoulder blades and down my raised arm, which holds a sharp-tipped fishing spear aloft. This is the one thing that affords me relief—this moment where everything comes together and all of me fixes on a single goal. I'm no longer Violet Sterling, dispossessed daughter of a treasonous nobleman, too long separated from her family home. All the aching worry over Papa and Wyn and my House recedes, and I become whole instead of fractured—Vi of the Fens, who never ends the day empty-handed.

In this moment, I distill into my most elemental self. A level head. A keen set of eyes. A pair of hands that move like quicksilver, or summer lightning. The fish turns over on its side, exposing a glistening expanse of scales.

In an explosion of spear and net and brackish water, I haul the pike aboard. It thrashes ferociously and the boat rocks, but a quick blow from the hatchet I keep under my low seat puts an end to that. Shoving my braid back over one shoulder, I finally allow myself to grin, to wipe the sweat from my forehead, and to feel that my nose has burned terribly yet again. It'll peel and freckle, and Mira will scold, but so be it. We'll eat for half a week thanks to this fish. And in this moment of clarity I've found a way to shed the creeping anxiety that's plagued me these past years. At least for a little while.

But even as I straighten and stand above my catch, the sense returns—that I am too far from home, but still bound to it by a long, taut stretch of line. It's not just Burleigh I can't get past, either.

"What do you think of that, Wyn?" I murmur. I only indulge the habit of speaking to him when I'm alone on the fens, careful to make sure no one hears. God knows who actually talks to Wyn now—who takes his silences and his moods into account, who lets him stay close when the night is too long and too dark, full of noises and shadows that remind him of things he'll never speak of. I hope it helps, that I send my voice to him when I can.

With the trackless expanse of the East Fen surrounding me, there's only a miry waste of bogs and silt deposits and tidal estuaries to hear my secret conversations. In places, the land's been shored up and laid to pasture, so that farmhouses and sheep enclosures stand out incongruously against the marshland. It's all a jumble and a maze, but I know this place better than any other save one. The currents speak a language I've learned, the seabirds call to me, and the brassy blue sky above is a map waiting to be read. The marshes are honest, if you understand them, and they always play by their own particular set of rules.

But they are not the West Country, which encompasses the five most southwesterly of England's counties, and which Burleigh House nurtures and governs. This land is wide and flat and straightforward in its wildness. It's unlike the Blackdown Hills I grew up among, which look tame at first, checkered with enclosed pastures and apple orchards, but which hide old shrines in their valleys and bone-wrought charms in their hedgerows. And nothing could compare to Burleigh's strange, enchanted grounds. The truth is, though I take up the oars and begin sculling back to shore, it doesn't feel like heading for home. It never does.

By the time I make it back to our little cottage on a raised hump of land in the middle of absolutely nowhere, the light's growing long and golden away inland. Mira has the shutters thrown open, and Jed sits on the front stoop whittling. He wasn't a whittler before our exile, but I suppose I wasn't much of a fisherwoman, either.

"Find your luck, then?" Jed asks as I tie the boat to our bit of dock. In answer, I sling the pike up, and it takes two hands for me to lift it.

Jed lets out a low whistle. He's a thickset, bearded man with a florid white complexion and close-cropped hair that long ago went grey, and though he's stood by me through good times and bad, I love him best for how he was with my father. There never was a more devoted steward, whether Papa was present or absent. When the king sentenced my father to House arrest, it took six men to hold Jed back. He shouted and struggled as they sealed George

Sterling away behind Burleigh's walls, and he never stopped fighting, not till the front gate vanished, replaced by unbreachable stone.

"Mira's waiting inside," Jed says. "She's—we—have something you need to hear."

I can feel the smile fade from my face at his words. "What—"

But before I'm able to ask, Mira's voice calls from within the cottage, cutting me off. "Bring that fish in here at once and wash the stink of it off your hands."

As I step into the close confines of the cottage, she tuts at me. "I expected you home hours ago."

Mira does rule us with a bit of an iron fist, but Jed and I would be lost without her. We're a family—an odd one, to be sure, but time and tide have bound us together and it would break my heart to lose them.

I cross the cottage's tiny downstairs room—just the one space for cooking and eating and living, with a curtain drawn across the nook that holds Jed and Mira's bed. A ladder leads up to a loft for me, and that's all there is to it.

With a weighty thud, I let my pike fall onto the kitchen table, and Mira turns. Horror writes itself across her face.

"Violet Sterling, you're a sight, and today of all days I wanted you home early."

Leaning against the table that holds my rather splendid fish, I hunch my shoulders, as if doing so can protect me from what's surely coming. If Wyn were here, he'd appear and just stand at my side, a silent ally in all things. And if we were home, the House would already have a carpet of reassuring flowers around my feet.

Will I never feel whole without them?

"Why? What's happened?" I finally summon the courage to ask.

Jed ducks into the cottage, and the whole space feels suddenly smaller. "Mira had a visitor come looking for you today. A messenger from the king."

All the air goes out of me. I drop onto my chair, ignoring the fish now lying forgotten on the table.

"His Majesty's back from Belgium and stopping at the Knight's Arms in Thiswick tonight," Mira says. "Apparently he'd be much obliged if his only goddaughter would pay him a visit tomorrow at noon, before he journeys on. The messenger said—he said there's news from Burleigh House."

"News." My voice breaks on the word. There's been no news from Burleigh House for seven years. And every sun that sets without it is a relief to me, because it means that across the country, my father and Burleigh and Wyn have survived another day of House arrest.

Jed steps up behind me and puts his enormous hands on my shoulders. "He didn't give any particulars, but I don't think we have to tell you what to expect."

I choke back questions I know Jed and Mira have no answers to, and mechanically lay the table for supper. But when we've eaten and the dishes have been cleared, I duck out of the cottage the instant Mira's back is turned. Jed watches, saying nothing as I shove our dory into the water and scramble aboard. I ship the oars and haul back on them and the boat reluctantly begins to move.

"Violet!" Mira calls through the open cottage doorway. "Just where do you think you're going so close to nightfall?"

"Away!" I answer back, sculling for all I'm worth. The dory pulls steadily forward, building momentum until I'm skimming across the water, dragging the welter of my emotions behind me like a length of tangled net. Movement is the best thing for me, I know— to still the aching of my heart, the clenching of my stomach, the furious grinding of my teeth. I scull until my arms and back ache— till sweat drips between my shoulders again and the last of the day's sun adds freckles to my freckles.

And when I've rowed for so long that each oar seems weighted with lead, I drop anchor in the middle of a tidal floodplain. Water stretches ahead of me to the very edge of the eastern sky, which has gone dark. I turn away from it, and from the vast, uneasy North Sea, looking westward instead, toward the setting sun. Beyond that blaze of splendor lies my past. Beyond it lies my future. Beyond it lies my House.

Blood and mortar, I miss it with everything in me. Every bone and every breath. I thought the end of Papa's House arrest might taint things between Burleigh and me, but even knowing what's surely happened—that my father must be dead, finally killed by the House itself—all I feel when I think of Burleigh is an agonizing desire to be with it.

So I know in the morning I'll visit His Majesty. I'll sit in front of him while he feigns pity and tells me Papa's protracted death sentence has ended, and a new Caretaker must assume his place. I'll do what must be done, choking down my hatred and fear of the king, all for the sake of Burleigh House. Because in the wake of Papa's arrest, Burleigh will need a gentle hand.

It is a wicked punishment, House arrest, designed to torment both a Caretaker and the Great House they tend. If found guilty of treason, a Caretaker is stripped of the key that allows him to channel his House's magic safely, and restricted to the grounds. The House is bound to let no one in or out until its powerless Caretaker lies dead.

But a Great House cannot keep the countryside healthy for long without a key-holding Caretaker to direct its power. Sooner or later, a good House must put itself and the land first, no matter how badly it hurts to do so.

There have been five House arrests over the years, before my father's. Two Caretakers killed themselves before their Houses had to. Three were killed by their Houses, though outside the confines of an arrest, the binding the Great Houses have been placed under expressly forbids them to take a life.

My heart aches for Burleigh, required to do what is neither in its nature or its bond. But it breaks at the thought of Wyn. Seven years after the arrest began and I still don't understand why my father was allowed to inflict a portion of his punishment on a child and keep Wyn trapped within the manor walls. I've never been able to think of it without resentment gnawing at my insides. Everything else I can fathom—Papa risking arrest and a charge of treason in his attempt to steal Burleigh's deed from the king and free our House. Indeed, all across England, there are people who support the unbinding cause in spite of its risks.

Of course I sympathize with that. Of course I want Burleigh out from under the king's thumb. The royal family has maintained control of the Great Houses since William the Deedwinner first bound them. Caretakers may manage the Houses' magic, but it's the deedwinner they must obey. I suppose it wore on Papa, watching the king make decisions for Burleigh that were not in its best interests.

Yet the price Papa paid for his attempt and subsequent failure—the choice he made to sacrifice not just his own freedom, but Wyn's—has never sat well with me. And I don't know why it had to be that way.

A good Caretaker puts her House first, I remind myself, to calm the anger that still rises in me when I think of Wyn. *Before her family. Before her friends.* Surely, that must have been what Papa was doing, whether I understand his actions or not.

The light on the horizon burns down to crimson embers. Swallows skim across the water, and far above them, bats flit here and there. Around me, the air cools and sweat dries on my skin as the sky darkens. I shiver, a salt girl alone on a salt marsh.

When the stars wake in the sky, winking to life one by one, I count them. It's an old trick Wyn and I learned together, long ago, when we'd sit out on the roof of the House. We were both of us children plagued by worries, and on the nights they kept us from sleeping, we'd count stars together until the fears faded. It used to work. It used to keep my fear at bay.

Now, though, I always lose count before the tide of my worry turns, and this night is no different from any other since my father and my friend were sealed away within Burleigh's walls. When I've lost myself among the stars, I turn inward, the way I learned to do after both heart and home were taken from me. In the labyrinth of my own mind, I count fears instead of stars.

I am afraid of memory, and the visions it brings of my father's careworn face—his stern eyes, his harried smile. Did he do right?

Will I be a worthy successor to him? Will I someday meet the same fate?

I'm afraid of never seeing home or Wyn again, of living my life in limbo here on the fens, and never wishing for better. Of never feeling whole.

I'm afraid of losing Jed and Mira as I've lost everything else. I'm afraid of hunger, which stalks us each winter as the saltfish barrels run low. I'm afraid of the sea, that gives life and then buffets the coast with storms.

Each fear surfaces and as they rise, I take them one by one, box them up and put them away on a dusty shelf in the back of my soul. I don't know what else to do with these thoughts that threaten to choke me, so I keep them locked inside, like last winter's moldering apples or a dragon's tarnished hoard.

The last fear I tuck away is this: I'm afraid of the king, desperately afraid. But for me, the good of Burleigh House will always come before that fear. It must.

"I want to go home," I whisper to myself and the night sky and the stars.

Home. The word tastes like honey and ashes, like hope and regret, and this I know: I would face the devil himself for a chance at getting back to the House I grew up in, and at finding out what fate has befallen the one friend I had as a child. The king is only a little worse than the devil, after all, and I would beg or bargain, whichever he prefers, to get back to where I belong. To be what I was born to become—the Caretaker of my beloved House.

The tide has turned, running out to sea. It pulls at my boat, tugging me eastward and away from home. For the first time in years

I ship oars and truly set myself against it.
As I scull toward the west, I hum an old, old song.

Blood for a beginning
Mortar for an end
Speak out your binding
Be you foe or friend

Fifth House holds quicksilver
The Sixth ruins all
But for blood in its mortar
But for breath in its walls

2

HIS MAJESTY IS A LATE RISER, AND I AM NOT. IN FACT, I've already been up for several hours by sunrise, on the water with a dark lamp and my fishing spear, and even delivered a catch in Thiswick. I learned long ago that there's nothing like activity to keep sorrow at bay.

But now, as the meeting time draws closer, I sit cross-legged on the pallet in the loft that serves me for a bed. Dried onions and bunches of rosemary hang only inches above my nose. Outside, the world is awash with pale light and gulls cry mournfully as they wing their way seaward. I look toward the shore, and somewhere inside me, there's a grief that can't be borne. I didn't expect it, and I'm not entirely sure who it's for—my father or Wyn or my House or myself. I can't afford to fall apart, though. Not with His Majesty waiting. Not with Burleigh's fate hanging in the balance. So I shut my eyes and tamp down the sorrow so far that all I can feel is a whisper of it. This, too, is one of my manifold fears—that someday I'll shut up my heart so securely there's no unbinding it, and I'll be left numb till the day I die.

"Come down for a bite of breakfast," Mira says from below. "Whatever's happened, I don't like to think of you facing it on an empty stomach."

I couldn't eat, though. Not for love or money. Instead, I shuffle on my knees to where a battered chest sits under the round window. A briny breeze dances in and blows cool against the back of my neck as I fumble with the chest's lock. It sticks a little, stiff with lack of use. When at last the lock gives way, I push the lid up and let out a long sigh.

We left Burleigh House in a hurry. His Majesty sentenced Papa on the front drive before a traveling court and ordered me out by day's end. I was only able to snatch a few of my things, which I've since kept tucked away, needing no reminders of home when my blood forever calls westward and anxiety churns constantly through my veins.

This morning seems a time for reminders if ever there was one, though. I push past a one-eyed china doll, a drawing of Wyn's, and a long-outgrown frock until I find a sprig of dried ivy leaves. I take it out and hold it gingerly, as if it might crumble beneath my touch.

Mira's voice drifts up to me. "Violet, I'm begging you, love."

"Not hungry," I call back, looking down at the ivy until my eyes blur and lose focus.

The smell of damp soil.

Rain running down my bedroom windows at Burleigh House.

The weight of a full valise, tugging at one arm.

Below, the king's carriage stands on the drive. I press my face to the glass, still only a child, just ten years old, not ready for any of this. It's past time to leave, and Mira's already come up to my bedroom to ask if I need help with anything. I sent her away, because I can't bear for anyone to see how broken I am at the thought of leaving Burleigh, the only constant presence in my life since the day I was born.

But the House sees, and that hurts me worst of all. I want to be brave for it, to be a good Caretaker, but I can't stop silent tears from tracking down my face. Wind moans in the chimney, rain sobs against the windows, and white funeral flowers bloom from the cracks in the wall. Hurrying toward the doorway, I stumble over one of my dolls lying abandoned on the bedroom floor. My valise falls and bursts open, scattering hastily packed clothes about the room.

Always, always, it is one last insignificant thing that finishes me. I crouch in the midst of the mess and sob, shoulders shaking, stomach aching, my heart torn to shreds. The House trembles on its foundations, but there's nothing it can do.

And then, though I didn't hear the door, Wyn is in front of me, picking up the mess I've made, pushing pinafores and stockings back into my valise. When everything is packed away once more, he holds the bag out to me. I look up and his face, too, is tearstained and pale.

"It's time to go, Violet," he says.

"I know," I tell him. "You're finally getting your wish. We're running away."

Wyn's already wretched expression grows a little more miserable. "This isn't what I wanted. You know that—I'd never want anything that hurts you so."

He reaches out and takes my hand, a rare gesture from a boy who seldom bridges the gap between himself and the rest of the world.

I swallow and look down at our intertwined fingers. "Don't let go. I can't do this all by myself."

"You can do anything you set your mind on," Wyn says fiercely. "*Anything*, Vi, don't you know that?"

But all the way down the stairs and out the door onto the drive, the only thing that keeps me from falling apart again is his hand, warm in mine.

Jed and Mira are waiting for us. We stand with them and watch as Papa emerges on the front steps of the House, flanked by half a dozen royal guards. Thunder rumbles low on the horizon and the darkened sky weeps endlessly, water pooling in low spots on the lawn and making wide puddles, rain dripping cold down the back of my neck.

When the guards bring Papa out and he catches sight of us, his jaw clenches and his gaze clouds over.

"Wyn, Violet," he says, voice rough from unnumbered sleepless nights. "Come here to me."

Wyn and I look at each other, and I see my own fear and despair mirrored in my friend's eyes. Wordlessly, I tighten my grip on his hand and he does the same. We climb the front steps together as a peal of laughter sounds from the king's carriage—His Majesty's waiting to see Papa's sentence carried out, but even today, he's brought a trio of courtiers along to make up a foursome for whist. I'd like nothing more than to snatch the cards from his hands and tear them to bits.

Papa can't put his arms around me—they're bound behind his back, but he's never been much of a one for displays of affection anyway. Nevertheless, I let go of Wyn and cling to my father for a moment, choking back tears.

"Be brave for the House, Violet," Papa whispers. I gather my scant courage and pull away, reaching for Wyn again.

But before he can take my hand, Papa shakes his head. "No. Wyn, come stand at my side."

Wyn turns toward him, wide-eyed.

"Come on now, Wyn," my father says. "You'll stay with me, just like we agreed on."

"*What?*" My voice rings loud across the front lawn, even with the rain to deaden it. Papa won't meet my eyes—he just looks at Wyn, who stares up at him and finally nods, stepping away from me.

The tears I've kept in check burn their way down my face and I feel as if something on the inside has shattered.

"Papa, don't take Wyn," I beg. "You and the House, and him now, too? It's too much—it's everything I have. I don't know how to live without any of you. You'll make a ghost of me."

"Don't be hysterical, Violet," Papa says, and there's steel in his tone. "You'll upset Burleigh."

"That's because Burleigh loves me," I stammer. "And I love the House, everyone knows it. So . . . let Wyn go free, and if someone has to stay, keep me instead. I would do it willingly. I don't care— you know I don't. Let the king seal us in together. I will stand by your side and be just what you taught me to be—a good Caretaker, who puts her House first. Please, Papa, please."

"Jed, take Violet," my father says. Indomitable as he is, Papa's voice breaks on my name.

Jed steps forward and takes me by the hand. "Miss Violet. It's time to go."

Mira appears at my other side and puts an arm around my shoulder, but I cannot tear my gaze away from Wyn, standing by Papa, his shoulders hunched in silent resignation.

"No. No!" I'm shouting now, and the king and his courtiers peer out of the carriage windows with interest. But I don't care. Let them watch me make a scene. "It isn't fair—look at Wyn. He doesn't want to stay! Let him go, and let me be with Papa and the House."

It's true Wyn's pale face is pinched and unhappy. He hurries down the steps and throws his arms around me and I hold him tight.

"Don't do this," I say tearfully. "You don't have to—they can't make you. We should be together. Wyn, *run away with me.*"

"No," Wyn answers. "I can't. Not anymore. But promise me something."

"Anything."

"Once you're gone, stay away. Don't come back."

I hardly have time to feel another stab of hurt and betrayal, because at his words, the ground bucks and heaves beneath us, jolting us apart. I stumble and nearly fall, and when I've righted myself, Wyn is at my father's side again.

"You have to go, Violet," Papa says. "Think of the House."

I am. I do. I always think of the House. So I square my shoulders and turn my back on Papa, taking the first steps down the drive and away from everything I've ever known.

"Violet Helena Sterling," my father calls after me. "I love you."

I've never heard him say those words before and I can't answer back, because if I do, they will have to drag me kicking and screaming from the grounds of Burleigh House. I carry on without a word, and when I draw up alongside the king's carriage, His Majesty looks out.

"I'm sorry, Violet," he says, though there's little in the way of remorse in his eyes. "The law is the law, and your father broke it. I never pegged him for the sort who'd be weak enough to insist a child bear his punishment as well, though. Funny about the boy."

"Shut up," I hiss, infusing the words with every ounce of venom my ten-year-old self can muster. "Just shut up. I never want to see you again."

"Now, now," the king chides. "Is that any way to speak to your own godfather? Who's going to look after you, if not me?"

I step up to his carriage window, small and furious and heartbroken. "I have one father, and you're killing him. I'd rather die than take your charity."

"Suit yourself," the king says with a shrug. "But you're still standing on my land. Burleigh, see Miss Sterling off the grounds."

A peal of thunder breaks overhead and suddenly I'm outside the front gate in the laneway, with Jed and Mira at my side. His Majesty's coach has been transported as well, along with the royal guards. Through the rain and the ironwork of the gate, I can make out Papa and Wyn still standing on the House's front steps.

The king gets down from the carriage and walks over to the wall surrounding Burleigh's grounds. When he reaches out a hand, the stonework trembles beneath his touch, but he is the deedholder—my father may be able to channel Burleigh's magic, but it's the king who truly controls it, who can bid and bind it, and the House cannot refuse him.

"Burleigh House," His Majesty says. "George Sterling has been found guilty of treason. I leave him to your care. Let no one in or out of these walls until he lies dead. No new Caretaker will be afforded you until his punishment is carried out."

The harsh, scraping sound of stone on stone grates through the air as the wall begins to fill in the space where the gate once stood. Dimly, I'm aware of Jed lurching forward and the guardsmen holding him back as he struggles toward the wall. I stare at Wyn's distant form through the narrowing gap until the last inch closes. Then I turn to the king and spit at him as he passes me by.

His Majesty pulls a clean white handkerchief from one pocket and wipes his face.

"Someday, little Violet, you will come begging to me," he says as he climbs back into the carriage. "You are your father's daughter, and I know you. George won't even be cold in his grave before you crawl back, asking for the key to Burleigh House. Sterlings never can resist this place."

"I'm a Caretaker," I snap. "I was born to look after Burleigh, and yes, I will do whatever must be done to see it safe. A good Caretaker puts her House first, even if means begging favors from a monster like you."

The king shakes his head and reaches into his pocket, dangling a skeleton key before me. My breath catches at the sight of it— there's a dull chip of grey stone set in the bow, and I'd recognize it anywhere. I've seen my father toy with it a thousand times in idle moments, and hold fast to it when he needed the protection of the guardstone while working House magic. I fight down the urge to snatch at it and run.

"You're not a Caretaker without a key, are you?" His Majesty says softly. "In fact, Burleigh House has no Caretaker now. We'll see how long that lasts. How long before the House must deal with the fact that your father stands in the way of its well-being."

He tucks the key away and I stand by, staring at him belligerently, refusing to be the first to falter.

"What a game we'll have when all this is over, and you want the key." The king smiles. "Don't doubt that I will make you dance for it. That is, if I don't give it to someone else first."

I have nothing to say to that. The idea of His Majesty giving Burleigh's key to anyone else and forcing Burleigh to accept a stranger as Caretaker pours ice through my veins. I watch as the carriage pulls away, the king's guardsmen marching in its wake. The wall surrounding Burleigh House is unbroken and impermeable stone now. Jed stands near the place where the gate used to be, shoulders slumped in defeat.

I take a few steps up onto the grassy verge and rest my forehead against Burleigh's wall, once the boundary of my world and now a prison.

"Look after him," I say to the House. I feel empty and hollow, as if there's nothing inside me but grey fog. "I know you can't do anything for Papa, and you're not meant to care for anyone but yourself. Perhaps I shouldn't even ask—maybe a good Caretaker wouldn't. But, oh, Burleigh, if you can, look after Wyn. And someday I promise I'll be back to look after you."

"Vi!"

Mira jolts me out of my remembering, appearing flushed and worried at the top of the loft's ladder.

"Child, what on earth is taking you so—" She catches sight of the open chest and softens. "I'm sorry. But you should eat something, even if you are feeling a bit out of sorts."

"Maybe just a cup of tea? I'll be down directly."

When she's gone, I glance at the sprig of ivy in my hand. Impossibly, it's flushed green once more, the leaves waxy and alive, so fresh it might have just been cut from the vine. I press the token to my lips and manage a small, mirthless smile.

"Soon, Burleigh," I murmur. "I'll be home soon."

The ivy goes grey, and I feel the faintest prickle of magic as mortar suffuses the leaves. In a moment, they've lost their shape entirely, leaving my palm gritty with dust and smelling of old stone. A little tendril of pain and fear curls through my skin.

My homegoing can't come soon enough. I won't let anyone, not even a king, stand in my way.

3

THISWICK, THE NEAREST VILLAGE TO OUR COTTAGE, WAS built near a crossroads. It sees plenty of travelers, which means the Knight's Arms is crowded at noon, my appointed meeting time with His Majesty. I push my way into the cavernous public room and cast about myself, looking for royal uniforms, or the king's familiar face.

Through a doorway that leads to the inn's private dining space, I catch a glimpse of red livery. Of course His Majesty wouldn't be out here, eating with common folk—foolish of me to think he would. Surreptitiously rubbing my damp palms against my skirt, I shove past merchants and sailors and tinkers, only to have Dex, the proprietor of the Knight's Arms, stop me at the door to the private room. He's a tall, broad-shouldered man, with an amiable smile and a purple birthmark that stands out against one white cheek.

"Are you sure you want to go in there, Vi?" Dex asks. He's known since we first arrived who I am and why I'm here, worlds away from Burleigh House. Sometimes I think all of England's party to my sad family affairs. Especially in the West Country, where they say folk keep calendars marking the days since Papa's arrest, and drink to his health every night instead of the king's.

Who will they drink to now, I wonder?

I square my shoulders. "No, I'm not sure. But I have to do it anyway—the king said he has news about the House. About my father."

Dex lets out a long breath and nods. "So it's finally come to that. I'm sorry. We all are. I'll be about if you need anything."

"Thank you, Dex." Before my nerves can fail me, I cross the threshold into the private dining hall.

The inn staff have been dispensed with in favor of the king's own liveried servants, who stand quietly along the wall, ready to step forward at the slightest indication they're wanted. A handful of courtiers sit at the table, fearfully au courant in ribbons and lace, the women wearing flimsy dresses with waistlines that nip up under their breasts, the men in frock coats and breeches and garishly colored cravats. I wonder if this is how I would look, had my life gone differently—bright and unmarked by grief, fashionable and sharp as tacks.

As it is, I'm drab and downcast by comparison, in my plain wool-spun shirt and often-patched skirt. Like a reed bunting beside kingfishers. But none of it matters. I have no pride, no position, and no place left to me. I've come to hear the worst, to ask after Burleigh House, and, as the king knew I would, to beg for a chance to go home.

His Majesty sits at the head of the table with a plate of dainties before him and a bored expression on his face. He's a lean, middle-aged man with shrewd dark eyes and a white complexion, pale from too much time spent indoors at his desk and the gaming tables.

The sight of him chills me to the bone. It is a relic of the old medieval hostage system that he's my godfather at all. Since the Great Houses were bound, Caretakers' children have been placed under the guardianship of the reigning sovereign. A pretty thought at face value—the royal family serving those who serve the Houses. Truly, it is a ploy to ensure the loyalty of the Caretakers. His Majesty took an interest in me when I was small—sent gifts, and would stop at Burleigh House whenever he passed by. He taught me to play cards, and I spent my childhood convinced he and Papa were friends.

But none of that familiarity and feigned friendship was enough to ensure mercy for my father, or clemency for me once Papa's great crime was uncovered.

I will make you dance, His Majesty said. Well, here I am. Will it be a waltz, or a gavotte?

Hiding my hands behind my back so the king won't see how they tremble, I step closer to the table and clear my throat. One of the courtiers is twittering away, and I go unnoticed.

I reach for anger rather than fear, but can't quite find it. Sterling stubbornness will have to suffice.

"Uncle Edgar," I say, loud enough that everyone in the room can hear. The courtiers fall silent, and their eyes widen at my decision to call him by the name I used when I was small. "You wanted to see me?"

A delighted smile replaces the king's look of boredom. With a loud scrape he pushes his chair back, and I will myself not to falter as he puts a hand on each of my shoulders and presses a kiss to my cheek. "Violet Sterling, *where* is the pretty child I knew? You look like an absolute fishwife. What would your father think?"

The courtiers giggle, assured that their pleasant day will carry on much as it has done, and that my intrusion will cause no trouble. But somewhere within me, music has begun. If I'm to dance for my House, I mean to lead, not to follow.

So I step past the king and drop into his chair at the head of the table. The silly laughter of the courtiers dies down. His Majesty raises a disapproving eyebrow and snaps two fingers together.

One of the waiting servants hurries up with another chair. The king takes a seat and leans forward, resting his elbows on his knees, as the courtiers pick up their silverware once more, pretending their attention isn't fixed on the head of the table, on me and His Majesty.

"Not a single kind word for your godfather?" the king chides. "Have you lost your manners out here on this bog? I didn't expect to ask for a royal visit only to find you sulking."

"I'm not sulking, Your Majesty," I say. "I'm grieving. I will always be grieving. You took everything from me, and tormented my family's House in the process."

Covert glances fly between the courtiers. Perhaps their day won't be as pleasant and dull, but it has become more interesting.

Something like remorse crosses the king's shrewd face. "Violet, do you think it brought me joy to sentence your father to House arrest, or to receive the news that his confinement had finally ended? George was a friend, and the finest Caretaker I've known. I thought the world of him until he betrayed me. The deeds to the Houses are my family's birthright—they've been so for eight hundred years, and yet he tried to steal Burleigh's from me. One cannot simply ignore that. Nevertheless, it pains me to have lost him, too."

So it is as I expected. My father is dead. I look past His Majesty, out the dining room's long bank of windows toward the fens I've come to know. Familiar in all their aspects, but never, *never* my home. I don't know who I miss more in this moment—Papa, or Wyn, or Burleigh.

"How did it happen? The end of the arrest, I mean," I ask, because there is no use arguing over the king's version of Papa's conviction. We will always be at odds about it. What Uncle Edgar calls treason, I call a Caretaker's duty to put one's House first, because Papa would never have risked trying for Burleigh's deed unless the House had need of it.

The king reaches out and pats my hand, and I resist the urge to pull away.

"You know I've been in Belgium for several months," he says. "I bound the Houses to obey the duke of Falmouth in my absence. He sent surveyors to Burleigh twice, to ensure everything was going smoothly. They found the gate had appeared in the wall again, and knew the arrest must have ended, but the House refused to let them in. Falmouth had to go down to Somersetshire himself, and even then the House tried to go against its binding to obey him. It tried to keep Falmouth out, but when he eventually got in, he found your father. Evidently George had been working House magic without the protection of the key, which is what killed him in the end. That's how he was able to prolong the arrest the way he did—anytime the House's magic built up and threatened to wreak havoc without a Caretaker to put it to good use, your father siphoned it off himself."

His Majesty tuts dramatically. "What an unpleasant way to die."

I ball my hands into fists beneath the table and press, nails digging into soft skin. I need the small pain it brings, to distract me from a larger agony blossoming inside. It's not just unpleasant, death by House magic. It's slow and messy and gruesome. And though I cannot think on it now, I can feel that a bright and vital part of me has been ruined by this news. Something young and yielding and fragile has fallen apart within my soul, crumbling into countless irreparable pieces.

A little House magic, a little mortar in your veins, is unpleasant but won't do too much harm. It'll be carried off into your blood and diluted, but never really leave you. Add a little more and perhaps it'll shorten your life—shave five or ten years off when you're weak with old age and start coughing up grey matter. It's the mortar that comes back to haunt you, settling in your lungs.

Add more magic still and you may die younger, taken with fits or with madness or with heart failure, as the leftovers of the mortar you've absorbed find their way to your heart or your brain. Take in enough at once and it will kill you outright, suffusing your veins, flooding your body with poison.

But whether you're exposed to a great deal or a little, whether you allow yourself time between doses or not, mortar stays with you. Every bit you add only brings your death nearer. That's why the Caretaker's keys were made—no one's ever explained to me how their magic works, but they allow their bearer to channel mortar without being harmed. So long as you hold a Caretaker's key, House magic passes through you without a drop of mortar staying behind. You can do wondrous things with a Caretaker's key—mend your House, mend the land, work the weather, encourage the crops.

That's why I'm here. It's not just to hear the truth of my father's death—I'm all Burleigh has left now and I need that key. There's no one but me to speak for my House, and no one else who ought to be Caretaker now Papa's gone.

But I won't let the king see how badly I need this.

"What about Wyn?" I ask instead of mentioning the key, though I'm terrified of the answer I may hear. "What's happened to my father's ward?"

The king lifts an indifferent shoulder. "They said there was no sign of the boy. What that means, only Burleigh House knows. Look, now all this is over, can't we let bygones be bygones, Vi? Chalk it up to a misunderstanding and start again?"

"Do you even hear yourself when you speak?" I ask in disbelief, voice made sharp by the grief I hide. "You sentenced my father to a living death and forced my House to carry out the punishment. The only friend I had is missing, and very probably dead because of your actions. Do any of those sound like forgivable offenses?"

I'm meant to be dancing, but here I am, intentionally treading on my partner's toes. One of the courtiers, a golden-skinned girl with a mass of loose dark curls, coughs into her handkerchief. I favor her with a vicious smile, all fen predator on the outside when inside I'm still flighty as a marsh hen.

"Did you enjoy the soup course?" I ask her. "I killed the pike myself—stabbed it through the heart this morning."

The girl dabs at her mouth and sets her kerchief aside. "Well, that explains the aftertaste of rancor. You're quite a feral thing, aren't you?"

His Majesty smiles fondly at the two of us, as if we're a pair of children sitting down to tea with our dolls. "Violet, I don't think you've had the pleasure of making my daughter and heir's acquaintance before. This is Esperanza, Princess of Wales."

Behave, Violet, I chide myself. *Behave.* But my own unspent emotions have me bitter and reckless. "Oh, there's two of you? How delightful."

"You were absolutely right about her, Father," Esperanza says, smiling affectionately at the king. "She's prickly as a hedgehog. What fun the three of us could have."

Now I know they're connected, I can see the similarities between the two of them, though the king is far paler than his daughter. They both have a habit of tilting their head to one side when contemplating a problem—in this case, me. Their dark eyes both spark with a sharp and intent curiosity. And they both seem determined to run rings around one Violet Helena Sterling.

The king beckons to a footman to bring him a pudding. "Do you hear from your mother often?" he asks me, and I'm sure to an outsider his display of interest seems genuine. "I must say, I was surprised to hear you'd taken up residence in this swamp when I turned you out of Burleigh House. I thought you'd have gone to her. Where was it she ended up after the divorce? Austria? Germany?"

"Switzerland." I can't disguise the venom in my answer. "She lives in a chateau now, and has two little boys. She writes once a year, at Christmas. I'd rather die than go to her."

The king smiles, a beatific expression that looks entirely incongruous on his clever face. "How you do hold a grudge. Fortunately Switzerland should never be necessary, as you've been blessed with a doting godfather, who intends to start taking an interest in you again."

I swallow back yet another biting retort, reminding myself that

I'm not here for my own advantage, I'm here for Burleigh. The king picks up his spoon as a footman sets a pudding in front of him. "Would you like to come to court, Violet? Be Esperanza's companion, perhaps?"

The two of them share a scheming smile.

"No, thank you." Though I'm trying to be civil, the words still sound tart. "I'd like to go back to Burleigh House."

"No one's going back to the House," His Majesty says around a mouthful of pudding. "It's completely unmanageable now—refused three new Caretakers. Fact is, the place was in disrepair when your father took it over, and without him, it appears to be dying. I've come home from Belgium expressly to put it down."

The air suddenly feels hot and close, and there's a ringing in my ears. "What do you mean, *dying*?"

For once, the king answers in absolute earnest, and there's pity in his usually well-governed voice. "Burleigh's failing, after spending so long without a proper Caretaker. It will have to be burned to the ground, like the Sixth House. You know as well as I do how dangerous the Great Houses can be if they fail without a proper channel for their magic, Violet. Yorkshire is a wasteland now because of the mistakes I made with Ripley Castle. I won't risk that in the West Country. Better to destroy Burleigh, and its pent-up mortar, before it does terrible damage."

Dex appears with an enormous tray of ices, which one of the footmen hurries to take. Once relieved of his burden, Dex lingers in the doorway, tilting his head at me as if asking a question. But no, I don't need rescuing. My House, however, surely does.

A good Caretaker puts her House first—before her own life, and far, far before her pride.

I slip from my chair and kneel before His Majesty, not even bothering to hide the angry, despairing tears that fall from my eyes at the thought of Papa's fate, of Wyn's face disappearing from view as the House arrest began, of Burleigh House in flames.

Every courtier's attention is riveted on us. Even the servants are watching.

"In seven years, I haven't asked you for anything," I say to the king. "I was content to live a small life and never trouble you, not as your goddaughter, not as a girl whose prospects you destroyed and whose heart you broke. So long as I knew my House was managing, nothing else seemed to matter. But I am *begging* you now. Let me go back to Burleigh. Give me the summer with it, and if it is not in good health again by fall, then burn it down. But at least let me have a chance first. I was born for this, and you know it."

The king gives me a narrow look. "What would you do for that chance?"

I swallow, and remember Burleigh House growing a garden of flowers in my bedroom, one winter when I lay ill with a fever wishing for spring to come. "Anything. I'd do anything you ask if you'll give me the key and let me serve as Caretaker."

Jed would be horrified if he could hear me. We crossed the country and hid away on the fens because he and Mira hoped to keep me from the king's clutches. And here I am, bargaining my independence away.

His Majesty smiles languidly and my stomach drops.

I know that look. I'm eight years old again, sitting across from the king as he prepares to win yet another hand of écarté. He always did prefer games of strategy, and all I ever managed to beat him at was Slaps.

"I will *never* give a Sterling the Caretaker's key or my trust again," the king says. "I'm no fool, to make the same mistake twice. But I will let you go home, little Violet. That is all, though."

I rock back on my heels. "But how will I help without the key? I can't work House magic without it. What do you expect me to do, *talk* Burleigh out of its ailments?"

"That's none of my concern." His Majesty shrugs. "You're a resourceful girl, and goodness knows Burleigh's always taken an uncommon interest in you. Figure something out. And if you manage to restore the House to good health, I expect you to support the Caretaker I choose. More than that, I expect you to convince *Burleigh* to support my Caretaker."

When I hesitate, the king leans forward, ready to consolidate his victory. "Either you agree to my terms, or I will do what must be done and torch the place before it makes a ruin of the West Country."

I don't like his terms, not one bit, but it will have to be enough for now, this chance to go home.

"I'll need time alone with the House, to settle it," I tell him, grasping for any scrap of advantage. "Veto power over your choice of Caretaker, too—I won't have Burleigh saddled with some incompetent fool."

The king laces his hands together behind his head, satisfaction written across his face. "Such a Sterling. I'm so glad you came to see me, little Violet. You may be just what Burleigh needs after all."

"As you say," I answer, and Esperanza's eyes narrow. Because what Uncle Edgar doesn't notice as he turns his attention back to his pudding is that when I look at him, I'm halfway to murder.

4

WHEN THE KING PLACED MY FATHER UNDER HOUSE
arrest and I was ordered out of the only home I'd ever known, the
one hope I had was Jed and Mira. I'd have been lost without them.
They'd served my family as steward and housekeeper since before I
was born, managing things through good times and bad, through
crises large and small. And in the moment after my father's sentenc-
ing, in spite of the trouble that had befallen me, they took my part,
Mira hurrying into town to sell a few valuables and Jed doing the
same with the best of the livestock, so we'd have something to start
out on as we began our new life together.

Today is no different. When I wake the morning after my visit
to the king, groggy and muddle-headed following a night of fitful
sleep, the cottage is bare and clean. Two trunks and a jumble of
satchels stand beside the doorway, holding all we own between the
three of us. Mira's few pictures have been taken down and tucked
away. The broad-brimmed hat I've never worn is off its peg. The
pile of wood shavings Jed always leaves under his chair has been
swept up. Even Jed and Mira's mezuzah is gone from the doorpost.

The last seven years are reduced to memory already.

And I haven't said a word about my plans to go home.

"He's outside," Mira volunteers before I even have to ask.

I step into the grey dawn air and find Jed sitting on the upturned dory, staring out across the marsh.

"Dex told me what I need to know," he says as I settle onto the boat at his side. "This isn't what I'd have chosen for you, Vi. Mira and I would have looked after you as long as you needed—kept you safe and away from the king. You're our family now, you know?"

"I know," I say, looking out, too, at the trackless fens I've grown so familiar with.

"You're old enough to make up your own mind," Jed tells me. "If Burleigh House is what you want, and you're willing to deal with the king to get it, then back to Somerset we'll go, and whatever happens, you'll never hear a word of reproach from me."

I shake my head. "You don't have to come. It may go badly, and I hate to see you uproot yourselves again on my behalf."

Gently, Jed bumps my shoulder with his own. "Don't talk nonsense. You're ours, Vi. We go where you go."

His Majesty's left a carriage waiting for us in Thiswick. Its doors, emblazoned with the royal crest, have drawn quite a crowd. I squint dubiously at the emblem—a lion rampant in front of the five remaining Great Houses, on a sanguine field and with the family's motto beneath: *Operibus Eorum Cognoscetis.* You Shall Know Them by Their Deeds.

"Well, that's a mercy," Mira sighs at the sight of the carriage, setting her baggage down and putting a hand to the small of her back. "At least we can make the journey in comfort."

I dislike the reminder that it's the king who has the last word about what happens to Burleigh. Eager as I am to go home, I hate the idea of climbing willingly into a gilded cage with His Majesty's heraldry sealing my fate.

"What about the public coach?" I suggest. "I know it's not as comfortable, but—"

Mira plants her feet. "If we're going back to that House, you'd best get used to being beholden to the king, Violet Sterling. He owns it, and before long he'll own you, too."

But Jed stumps forward toward the carriage as she speaks.

"Drive on," he orders the coachman gruffly. "We're taking the coach."

Mira lets out another pointed sigh as the carriage pulls away. We have lunch in the public house, and climb into the overcrowded coach when it arrives, our fares paid for by the bit of money Jed and I put aside after our last stint of thatch-cutting.

"Where are you headed?" a whey-faced curate seated across from me in the coach asks, to make conversation as the slow miles roll by.

"Burleigh House," I tell him, though I want to be quiet. I want to sit with the fact of my father's death, to let the grief wound up inside me unravel across the length of England, and sink away into the earth.

"A coach going north would have suited you better to get to Burghley," he says with a prim frown. "You're a bit out of your way."

"Not Burghley in Cambridgeshire," I answer, suppressing the urge to roll my eyes. "*Burleigh* in Somerset. Every noble with pretensions of grandeur wants a Great House, and they named that . . . edifice . . . in Peterborough after mine, when it was built. My Burleigh's much smaller, or so I've been told. But it's an actual Great House, with everything that entails."

"You're never Violet Sterling?" The curate goggles, a most unattractive expression on his already insipid face.

"In the flesh," I admit.

All at once, the curate's manner grows far more solicitous.

"Do you know, I support the cause your father died for. Unbind the Great Houses, I say. Snuff?" he asks, holding out a little box. The lid is emblazoned with keys—they've been the fashion forever, as long as there have been Caretakers to hold them. This time, I do roll my eyes, and wave dismissively at the curate and his snuffbox.

"Don't trouble yourself trying to make friends. My House isn't keen on strangers at the best of times, and nor am I. And if it's my hand you have sudden designs on now you know I've a Great House to go home to, you should also know that Burleigh's in dire straits. So I'm far too busy for nonsense, and ill-tempered, besides."

The curate withdraws his snuffbox, growing very absorbed in the passing scenery, and Mira shakes her head at me.

"Manners," she mouths, and I pretend not to understand.

It's near two weeks we spend on the road, stopping at inns by night to stay in low-ceilinged rooms filled with cots and the unfamiliar sounds of sleeping strangers. We lose time for Jed and Mira to keep Shabbat, and I know they're anxious about prying eyes, because we pass the day very quietly. It's strange not to have candles and singing, or anything more to eat than a hurried bite in the inn's public room. Even on the fens, when winter grew long and food scarce, Mira found ways to make our Shabbat meals special. And at Burleigh House, Jed and Mira's faith was never a secret, but a part of the fabric of our lives.

We have a late start on Sunday, losing another morning for me to attend service at an old Church of England. By the last afternoon of our protracted journey, Mira and I are short-tempered and Jed's fallen completely silent.

But then Mira grips my hand tight in hers and points out the window.

"Look, Vi. It's the Taunton church. We'll be home soon."

We carry on, and everything grows familiar, as if I remember it from a dream. Then at last we round a bend and the Blackdown Hills lie before us. A fierce joy twists inside me at the sight of patchwork pastureland and trees, all running up to the sky or down to valleys that hide little rivers and towns. The village of Burleigh Halt lies in just such a valley, and beyond it, up against the woods, Burleigh House.

It's true. I'm nearly home. And I didn't realize until now how at odds with myself I've been, miles away from this place. I don't know what I'll find at the House, but there is a rightness in this I can't deny.

Mira nudges my foot with her own as the coach finally stops in front of the Red Shilling, the Halt's inn and tavern.

"Stop that, Vi," she clucks at me, and I snatch a hand from my mouth, chastened, with the nail half-bitten.

Jed shoulders our small trunks, and Mira and I take the satchels. Fortunately we haven't much and the walk to the House isn't long. We trudge down a country lane together, out of the small village and into the glory of a Somersetshire springtime. Daffodils are everywhere, the trees have begun putting out leaves, the hedgerows are full of birdsong, and lambs and calves gambol across pasture-land. The abundance of pretty, domestic life is startling after the wildness of the fens—it's as if I've wandered into a painting, done all in summer-hued oils.

As I look more closely, though, I begin to see that something has gone wrong with the countryside. There's blight on the new apple leaves. The bloated corpse of a sheep lies in a field beside the lane. A man trudges past us with a hangdog look about him, pushing a handcart that I suspect is holding everything he owns.

Things were never this way in my father's time. I could begin to fill the empty space he left and make things right in the coun-tryside if I had Burleigh's key. I could heal what ails the land bit by bit, day by day, as the House's magic wells up and renews itself again. They're like springs, the Great Houses, their power con-stantly flowing. Once, that magic ran unchecked across the West Country. Now it's been bound and harnessed, and can only be used productively when a Caretaker channels and directs it. With-out a Caretaker, it builds and builds, festering and growing more destructive the longer it's pent up.

When we round a bend in the road and the first curve of my House's high stone wall comes into view, I have to stop. I set down the satchels I carry and press one hand to my mouth, the other arm to my belly.

Apple blooms show white above the wall from the orchard, and bees buzz lazily among them. The sounds are so familiar that I can hardly draw breath. I swear to myself in this moment that I will never let anything drive me away from Burleigh House again.

But as we come to the place where the front drive normally turns in through the great gate, I find Burleigh's wall is marred by a vast wound. There's no sign of the hinges or the gate itself, just a gaping hole where someone has violently blown them away. A good deal of the stone wall's been damaged, besides. Rubble still clutters the lane. Enormous brambles tangle together in the gap, completely patching the hole where the gate once stood, and mortar weeps from the thick vines.

"What did they do to you?" I whisper, stepping forward and pressing a palm to the wall. Fury courses through me at the thought of the House being treated so shamefully. I can feel something from Burleigh, too, emanating out from that thorny scar—suspicion and betrayal and hurt and fathomless exhaustion all rolled up into one bitter sensation.

"Can we have a moment?" I ask, turning to Jed and Mira. There's quiet shock on their faces at the sight of the wound where the gate once was. They nod and disappear around the bend in the lane.

Shifting closer to the wall, I rest my forehead against it, letting all my grief and concern and care for the House rise up and run beneath my skin like a rip current.

"Burleigh," I murmur. "It's Violet. I've come back, and how I've missed you, my darling."

All I feel from the House in return is mistrust, and the cold, ordinary touch of stone. My hands begin to tremble, and my eyes blur. When I speak again, the words come out thick with tears.

"Oh, Burleigh, I'm so sorry. I don't know what's happened here, but I'm back and I want to help. I'm on your side—not the king's, not the country's, not anyone else's but yours. Won't you let me in?"

The minutes stretch on and on and nothing changes. No way in opens before me. No sign is offered by my damaged House.

At last I can't contain myself any longer and stand weeping against the wall, great ugly sobs tearing my throat like thorns. I haven't cried like this since I left Burleigh, the day of my father's arrest. I didn't expect to do so again on the House's very doorstep. But it is too cruel, everything that's happened to Burleigh and me, to both of us together, and I don't know who I ache for more.

Jed and Mira reappear, but after a glance I can't look at them. Inside I'm crumbling, ruined by the death of this last hope. If I had the key, I could coax and bargain—begin at once to heal Burleigh's hurts by channeling its own vital magic. But I am not a Caretaker, and I have nothing to offer but words and a willing heart. Taking a step back, I wrap my arms around myself, not sure how to start my life over yet again.

Worse still is the king's threat, ringing in my ears as if he'd only just spoken it. *Either you find a way to restore Burleigh, or I will burn it to the ground.*

Make me a way, Burleigh. Make me a way.

A small sound cuts through the fog of my sorrow, and I look over at Jed.

"What did you say?"

He shrugs his broad shoulders. "Nothing."

Pivoting on one heel, I turn back to the House only to hear the low grumbling of stone, and see the trees beyond the walls sway violently as if struck by a sudden gale. Storm clouds darken the sky over the manor grounds and the temperature drops a few degrees.

Bitter and wild though it may have become, I've never been able to shake the impulse to help when Burleigh keens.

"Violet, don't!" Mira gasps as I move toward the brambles that are reaching for me with sharp-edged fingers.

❧ 5 ☙

THE CLOUDS OVERHEAD VANISH. THE WALL MELTS AWAY. Dimly, I feel thorns bite into my flesh, but I can't see them.

Instead, my father's room swims into focus around me, with its enormous four-poster bed and long bank of windows that look down onto Burleigh's front drive. But that is all I recognize, because the room is terribly changed. Piles of rubble sit in the corners, fallen from the ceiling overhead. Cracks seam the walls and ivy has crept in at the windows. Briars twine up the bedposts. A smell of damp and decay and rot hangs heavy on the air.

Worst is the wall the bed sits up against. A jagged, yard-long word has been slashed into the plaster with something sharp—a knife, or a letter opener, perhaps. After a glance, I can't bear to look, because the George Sterling I knew would never hurt his House so. Not even to spell out my name, *VI*, in tall capital letters.

Something stirs under the mildewed bedcovers, and I realize with a sickening jolt that I'm not alone as I'd first thought. Drawing close to the bed, I look down at my sleeping father. Papa is skeletal and unshaven, his closed eyes set in shadowed hollows. Ivy twines around his wrists and ankles, and the skin is rubbed raw where he's struggled against his living bonds. Seeing him brings the sort of pain that cuts so deep you feel it only for a moment, before your mind decides it cannot be borne and refuses to feel at all.

As I watch, his eyes open, but they're milky and unseeing, not the knowing hazel I remember.

"Burleigh House," Papa rasps.

A little tendril of ivy snakes up and brushes against his face. Papa turns his head aside and coughs. It's a terrible rattling sound, and brings up blood and mortar, which must mean he's close to his end.

"Take what you need," Papa says, as I've heard him tell Burleigh so often before, key in hand, ready to work House magic. But I don't know how there can possibly be anything left in him to give.

There's a rush of focused energy as Burleigh turns its full attention toward Papa. Mortar courses beneath his skin, giving him an inhuman grey cast. His eyes roll back and his hands seize on the bedspread.

And then there is the moment that's hung over me for seven agonizing years.

Papa goes limp. His head lolls. His chest falls still. It is ugly, and brutal, and all at once my knees buckle. I'm left with both hands pressed to my heart, which feels as if it will burst, not just with my own grief but with the House's, which pours into me in an overpowering groundswell of sorrow.

The door flies open and Wyn crosses the room, sinking to his knees beside the bed. He's changed a great deal since I last saw him, but I still know the friend of my childhood as he reaches out and shakes Papa.

"George." Wyn's voice cracks. "George, wake up."

"Oh, Wyn, he's not going to," I say, but it is the House's memory replaying the scene, for I can still feel the faint bite of thorns against my wrists. Wyn cannot see or hear me.

"I told you he'd had enough," Wyn growls at the House. "You knew it, too. How could you? *How could you?*"

By the end, he's shouting. Wyn scrambles to his feet and drives a fist into the rotten plaster of the wall, which gives way easily. Mortar weeps from the House's new wound, and Burleigh shudders beneath our feet.

Wind whips the patched fabric of my skirt around my legs as the memory fades and I'm brought back to the present. Briar thorns prick at my wrists, for I'm standing right up against the space where the gate once was, arms thrust into the brambles that fill the gap. Somewhere behind me, Jed and Mira are waiting. Above us, thunder grumbles and lightning splits the sky.

I don't know what I'm feeling. If it's heartbreak, I never expected it to be such a bodily thing. My chest aches and the back of my neck has gone hot and a rushing noise fills my ears. But there is Burleigh before me, half-wild with what it's been through, and almost the last thing Papa said to me was that I must be brave for my House.

"Burleigh," I say clearly. I force down my own pain because I was born and brought up to be a Caretaker, and a Caretaker puts her House first, no matter how it hurts. "It's alright, my love. None of this was your fault. You did what had to be done."

Perhaps my House is broken, but we are a matched set, split apart in the same place, and a broken girl is just the thing for a broken House. Without hesitation, I step forward, as if an open gate stands ahead of me rather than a thicket of briars. Not for a moment do I allow myself to doubt.

And the brambles patching Burleigh's wall unravel before me, leaving the way clear. The sky above roils and goes blue, becoming a glory of white clouds and spring sun. Gravel crunches underfoot as I step onto Burleigh's grounds.

"Mark my words," I swear to the trees, the grass, the sky. "I'll be dead before I leave you behind again. And I will never, *never* let anyone harm you. I'm going to look after you, Burleigh."

A final mutter of thunder sounds on the eastern horizon, and any last trace of the House's suspicion vanishes, replaced by a wave of relief that surges up from the earth, so strong it nearly flattens me.

As I walk down Burleigh's front drive, it's impossible to keep more tears from falling. The air is heady with the scent of flowers and grass and rich soil, and memories spring up around me. Over there on the lawn is where Wyn taught me to turn cartwheels. Beneath the oak tree is where we sat to read together, heads bent over the same book. And on the drive itself, I'd ride my pony in eager circles, waiting for Papa to appear.

I stood just there, on the gravel, waving to my father each time he made the journey to London, to fulfill his duty as a Caretaker and a member of the Home Council. But where he would always pause and turn back for one last farewell, something impossible has sprouted up. Towering from the middle of the drive is a tree I recognize only from the geography books Papa used to pore over whenever he had the time. It's a jacaranda, meant for warm southern climes, and yet here it is, boughs laden with luminous purple blooms.

Even without words, my House can sometimes speak.

Stepping up to the tree, I run a hand across its rough bark. Lavender-tinted shadows shift about me.

"He always did right by you," I murmur. "I plan to take care of things just as he did, now he's gone."

Ahead of me, the front door swings open of its own accord. It seems the House has overcome its initial reluctance, and is ready to welcome me home. It's only then that I think to glance over one shoulder and see that Jed and Mira haven't followed. The brambles have barred the way behind me and they stand in the lane, unable to enter.

I wag a finger at the House. "Don't be ridiculous. If you want me, you know you'll have to let them in, too."

A breeze tosses jacaranda petals into my face, but the brambles pull away and Jed and Mira hurry inside.

"I'd nearly forgot what this place is like," Mira says with a shake of her head. "Temperamental old barn."

Whatever it thinks about that, Burleigh House keeps its own counsel.

As we step indoors, the House's interior wraps around me like a worn blanket, or a mother's arms. Jed and Mira disappear, Mira to the kitchen and Jed to sort out our belongings. I wander the halls, calling Wyn's name at each doorway, but not really expecting to find him. After what Burleigh showed me, I wouldn't blame him for leaving and never coming back, though it's a whole new sort of pain, thinking of him on his own in the world. And of course, he might not have expected me to return—he did tell me he'd rather I never came back, though I still can't fathom why.

As I go, I run my hands across the faded wallpaper, the cracks in the plaster, the places where ivy creeps between shattered window-panes. Years without a proper Caretaker have left the House with an air of neglect, and despite the magic in its mortar, it's gone wild exactly the way one might expect a more ordinary building to do. Water spots stain the ceiling in places, and there's a vague smell of mold.

I open windows methodically, assessing damage and starting a list in my head of repairs that will need to be made and what they're likely to cost. If I had the Caretaker's key, the biggest jobs could be done by House magic—focusing the House's own energy on what needs fixing. I can feel Burleigh's magic, churning dark and dangerous beneath my feet, and in the walls. The House is on edge because of it. The West Country is on edge. But I haven't got a key, and without it, I don't dare channel the House's power.

In my father's study, I stop and sink into the leather chair behind his desk. The room is all wood paneling and bookshelves and, unlike the rest of the House, still smells faintly of tobacco and good parchment and ink. It's as if Burleigh can't let that last trace of my father go.

I tuck my knees up under my chin and wrap my arms around them, becoming as small as I can. Papa's household ledger sits open to the first page, where he wrote the terms of Burleigh's binding the day his own father died and he became Caretaker. I read the terms, though I know them by heart:

Burleigh must obey the deedwinner and all heirs of his blood in perpetuity.

Burleigh must not permit talk of the deeds to occur on its grounds.

Burleigh must not channel its own magic.

Burleigh must never take a human life, except in carrying out the first term of its binding, or in preventing itself from being unbound.

Looking down at the terms of Burleigh's binding, the responsibility of caring for such a vast, ancient place seems like an impossible burden to bear. And I haven't begun to test the truth of His Majesty's statement yet—that something has gone fundamentally wrong with Burleigh. That my House is dying.

But there's no time for the indulgence of self-pity at present. Burleigh's initial relief at my return has worn off and I can feel other things from the House—exhaustion and the low ache of long-borne pain and a sharper discomfort, like an itch that wants scratching. This place needs tending. I may not have a penny to my name or a Caretaker's key, but come hell or high water, I still intend to keep Burleigh House in good condition, just as my family's always done.

Leaving the study, I get a few paces down the corridor and then stop in my tracks. There's a familiar, intermittent sound drifting from the little-used west wing, where my parents housed guests and entertained during my earliest childhood. I wander down the hallway, following the sound back through the front entry, where the wide stairs cascade down from the second-floor gallery and a four-lamp kerosene pendant hangs from the ceiling. I keep after the noise, trailing down the opposite corridor, past long-empty rooms—the ballroom, several company parlors, the smoking room, the ladies' lounge. At the very end of the west wing is a wide dining hall, with long windows to catch the evening light. I stop at its closed door and listen. There it is. *Tap tap. Tap tap tap.*

Swinging the door open, I catch my breath and lean against the frame, weak with the same relief that poured through the House the moment I stepped onto its grounds.

Off to one side of the room, Wyn stands on a wooden stepladder, nailing boards over a shattered window.

"I saw you coming up the drive," he says, the words muffled by a mouthful of nails. "Welcome home. I'll be done in a minute."

"Take your time," I answer, trying not to sound too eager. He turns back to his work and hammer strikes ring through the room once more. My heart jumps with each report, until I can feel it racing in my chest.

I watch Wyn as he finishes the job, trying to sort out who he's become. Some of him is as I recall—that disheveled sandy hair, the way he squints when he's concentrating. But more has changed. There's a leanness and narrowness about him, not just in his profile but in his eyes and what lies behind them. It wasn't there when I left, and it speaks of hard times and storms weathered, desperation felt and darkness witnessed. Wyn's not who I remember, and yet I feel as if I've hardly changed.

At last Wyn sets his hammer aside. He climbs down from the stepladder and picks up a rucksack I hadn't noticed sitting next to the wall.

"Hello, Violet," he says with a nod. "Goodbye, Violet."

"Oh," I say. I can't keep disappointment from writing itself across my face. "I didn't even know you'd be here, and now you're leaving already? I thought we could . . . I don't know, catch up."

Wyn stuffs his hands into his pockets and hunches his shoulders. "I don't have much to say. I was only waiting for you to get back before I left. Now here you are, so I'm off. Good luck with Burleigh."

He walks past me and out into the corridor, and it's suddenly too much. My mother, my father, the knowledge that Burleigh is dying. I can't take another loss, another heartbreak. And I've never had any pride when it comes to Wyn, so I follow after him.

"Please don't go," I beg. "It's not just the House I came back for. It's you, too. I missed you, Wyn."

He stops, his back still to me. I gnaw at a hangnail as he speaks.

"You missed who I was," he says. "I'm not that person though, Vi. I doubt you're the same, either. We aren't friends anymore, we're strangers."

"But we could be friends again if you stay," I insist. "We could learn to be the way we were. Do you know, I talked to you on the fens, every day? I couldn't write, so I talked."

There's a long pause, and I bite my lip, certain he's about to leave.

"I talked to you, too," he finally admits, turning so that we're facing one another. "But think of what you're asking, Vi. Would *you* stay in a prison for me?"

"The gate is open," I say. "It's not a prison anymore."

Wyn makes a small, bitter sound. "After seven years, Burleigh will always be my prison. Answer the question. If things were the other way around right now, would you stay?"

I look into his eyes. *Who are you? Who have you become?*

"Wyn, I haven't changed," I tell him.

"Which means yes, you'd stay." He runs a hand through his untidy hair in frustration. "Blood and mortar, I should have left the moment I heard you were coming back. I never should have waited."

Nothing is as I thought it would be. All those years on the fens, I dreamt of this day. Of arriving home, grieving my father, but ready to take up his mantle as Caretaker, with Burleigh's key in hand. Wyn was always there, in my dreams—I can't imagine Burleigh House without him anymore.

But neither can I stand to see him miserable.

"Forget it," I reassure him. "It was wrong of me to ask you to stay here. Of course you aren't happy at Burleigh House anymore, how could you be? I'm being selfish—don't pay me any mind. I wish you all the luck in the world, wherever it is you're going."

I hold out a hand for him to shake, and at first he only stares at it. But then he slides the rucksack from his shoulder and lets it drop to the floor.

"I'll stay until tomorrow," Wyn says. "That's all, though. After that I'm gone, Violet. For good."

When he walks away without taking my hand, it feels like another death. I stand alone in the hallway for a long time, just trying to piece myself back together.

6

A THOUSAND QUESTIONS CROWD TOGETHER AT THE BACK of my throat as we sit down to supper in Burleigh's enormous kitchen following an afternoon of settling in. The long staff table that once sat my father's household of twenty might seem empty with only the four of us, if not for the low evening sun pouring in the kitchen windows. The light at Burleigh House has always been thick and golden as a new-minted coin, and it's as good as company in a pinch.

And then there are the things we skirted around on the fens, never speaking of, which hang heavy on the air. They can't be avoided any longer, though, not now we're back home. I gather my courage and ask the question no one's ever yet been willing to answer for me.

"I know he was looking for it, but did Papa ever actually find the location of Burleigh's deed?"

Mira freezes with her teacup halfway to her lips, and Jed sets his fork down with a clatter. A muscle works in his jaw. "What are you doing, Violet?"

"It's no secret that's why Papa was charged with treason—he'd been looking for the deed to Burleigh House, planning to set it free." I butter a piece of bread and bite into it, though there's a rumble coming up from the floor beneath my feet at the mention of deeds. It makes me nervous, but I won't show my worry in front of Jed. *Hold on, Burleigh. Keep your vines and thorns at bay, because we can't do without a kitchen.* "I'm asking all of you—did he find the deed?"

"He was killed just for looking, and that should be enough for you," Jed says. He gets up abruptly and stalks out the kitchen door into the overgrown vegetable garden. It's a sign of how upset Jed is that he forgets to touch the mezuzah he's already put up when passing by. There's a clatter as he opens the shed, and then the scratching of a hoe against unworked soil.

We sit in silence for a long while after Jed leaves. Wyn is withdrawn, not looking anywhere but at the plate in front of him.

Finally, Mira reaches out to pat my hand. "He loved your father, Jed did. Thought the sun rose and set on him. But he loves you more, Violet. We both do. And Jed's been afraid of answering that question for you since George died."

"Why?" I protest. "No one ever talks to me. Don't I have a right to know how far Papa got before—"

The rumble beneath my feet intensifies. A vine—sharp-thorned bramble, not English ivy—twines up the table leg and brushes against my hand. Absently, I run my fingers along its spiny green leaves, mindful of the thorns.

"It's not just a question you're asking," Mira says. "It's treason even to speak of taking a deed from the king. So if you want to stay in this House without ending up like your father did, you'll hold your tongue, mind your own business, and do as His Majesty bids you."

"I'll be happy like that, will I?" I ask, not bothering to hide my distaste for her suggestion. "Just rolling over like a well-mannered dog and begging the king for favors? Letting Burleigh House go to ruin?"

Mira looks straight at me, her gaze unflinching. "Happy is neither here nor there. You'll be alive, which is more important. You were happy on the fens—you could have had that life, but you chose to return here."

"I wasn't happy on the fens," I say, pushing my plate aside. Any appetite I had is gone.

"Content, then."

"Nor content. I was waiting, Mira. Biding my time, until I could come home. I'll never be happy anywhere but at Burleigh House."

"Then reconcile yourself to the way things are," Mira warns. "His Majesty won't make you Caretaker. Your father failed to get the deed. Burleigh House is falling apart—did you see the country-side? Folk around here are suffering because of this place. It might be better if—"

"Don't say it." I turn away and fiddle with the sleeve of my blouse to hide how her words pain me. Mira sighs.

"Vi, my darling girl, I'm not trying to hurt you by telling you the truth. But the fact is, I'm not sure there's a safe way of keeping this House."

Getting up from my place, I kneel at Mira's side, taking her work-worn hands in my own.

"I don't have to be safe," I tell her. "I have to do my job, as someone who's meant to be Burleigh's Caretaker. Did Papa find Burleigh's deed? *Please*, Mira, I need to know."

"What will you do with the answer to that question?"

She looks into my eyes and my gaze falters. I say nothing.

"George found where the king keeps the deed," Mira admits, "though I don't know that he ever laid hands on the thing itself."

I'm breathless. The air around me is breathless, too, as the House holds back, fighting against the restless, destructive energy I can feel through the flagstones beneath my feet. I am pushing too far, I know. But I can't stop now.

"Where, Mira? Where does His Majesty keep Burleigh's deed?"

She shakes her head. "Your father never told a soul but a friend of his called Albert Weston, and the two of them are dead and buried. I expect no one knows that secret now but the king and Burleigh House itself."

With a wrenching shriek, metal twists and a sapling bursts through the center of the kitchen's long wood-fired range stove. The tree rises to the ceiling and spreads leafy branches over us, dark flowers and darker thorns jutting from every twig.

"Oh hush, I'm sorry," I soothe, crouching to press my hands to the flagstone floor. Mira gets up and goes out to Jed, because she knows the words aren't for her.

Wyn gets up, too, wordlessly dropping his plate into the washbasin and leaving the room. As I watch him go, guilt and regret and longing all churn in my stomach. I want to be the way we were, but he'll barely look at me. And now here I sit, having done no more than speak of treason, and my words have already bred damage. Fear fills my belly, and I ruthlessly tamp it down.

* * *

After dark, I creep up to the long echoing attics at the summit of Burleigh House, drifting past old wardrobes and chests of drawers and clotheshorses. Opening a familiar window, I shimmy out onto the roof and scoot around a brick chimney only to find Wyn, lying on his back on the slate tiles, eating a wrinkled winter apple and staring up at the starry night sky.

"It's nice to see some things haven't changed," I say, a little shyly, because I don't know if I'm wanted or not. "I missed coming up here."

"Didn't they have stars in Lincolnshire?" Wyn asks, and takes a bite of his apple.

"Yes, but not like these ones. Am I interrupting? Do you want me to go?"

Wyn glances over at me. "I can't tell you to go. It's not my House."

"It's not mine, either," I point out. "It's the king's."

"But you want to change that. Tell the truth."

I settle down with my back to the brick chimney, which still holds a hint of the sun's warmth.

"What else am I supposed to do?" I ask, drawing my knees up to my chest and wrapping my arms around them. "His Majesty won't give me the key, but Burleigh needs help. I don't see a way around this, Wyn. Have you looked at the countryside, or at Burleigh? I'm afraid this House won't last the summer, and that's all the time I've got. After that, the king's sending a new Caretaker to oversee things."

"Then let His Majesty choose a new Caretaker now, and tell Burleigh you approve," Wyn says.

The House rumbles ominously underneath us. I'm not sure I could convince it to accept a new Caretaker, even if His Majesty sent me someone sympathetic. What's more, I don't think I trust anyone else to look after Burleigh. Revulsion churns in my stomach at the thought of the key in a stranger's hands. It's not just me the idea upsets, either—ill temper and distaste are creeping up through the slate tiles of the roof.

"I don't think that'll be enough," I tell Wyn. Not enough for Burleigh, and not enough for me. "I think—blood and mortar, Wyn, I think I have to finish what my father started."

There it is. The thing that's been weighing on me since we left the East Fen, and that I haven't, until this moment, fully acknowledged even to myself.

"You don't have to, though." Wyn's voice is flat, devoid of emotion, and he keeps his eyes fixed on the sky. "You're not a Caretaker. You don't have the key, like you said, and you can't work House magic without it. It's foolishness to think you can do much here, Violet, and trying for the deed will be the death of you. You don't need to end up like your father did."

On my far side, out of his view, little daisies sprout beneath my hand, their soft petals brushing the webbing between my fingers.

Don't I?

"What happened?" I ask Wyn.

"Your father kept doing his job. Working House magic after the king had taken the key. That's what killed him."

"Not that. Why did you stay?"

A muscle works in Wyn's jaw. "George asked me to."

"I still know when you're lying. That's not the truth," I chide.

Wyn sits up with a single fluid motion and fixes his eyes on me. I can *feel* restrained anger radiating from him, just as I always feel Burleigh's frame of mind.

"That is the truth," Wyn says. "Or at least as much of it as I'm willing to tell."

I rest my head against the chimney and watch the sky as Burleigh paints a mournful, pale green aurora across it. It isn't the season for such a sky. But here—magic is always in season at Burleigh House.

"Violet," Wyn says, and my heart sinks at the sound of his voice. I know what he's about to say. "Come with me when I leave tomorrow."

"I can't," I tell him regretfully. "You know I can't."

"Trying for the deed will get you killed. Better to leave Burleigh to its fate—let things run their course, and let the king put it down before it ruins the West Country. Yes, I know that's what he plans to do—gossip travels faster than horses."

The slate roofing tiles shudder and jump beneath us, making a high-pitched, chattering sound. I reach back and press a hand to the solid brick of the chimney and slowly, Burleigh calms.

"I told you I haven't changed," I say. "Burleigh still comes first for me. Before—"

"Stop," Wyn says angrily, that bad temper I sense bubbling up from beneath the surface. "Burleigh isn't human, Vi. It's not your family or your friend. It serves its own ends, and that is all. Even your father acknowledged that fact—a Great House puts itself first. This place does not deserve your loyalty or your blood or your tears. It is a monster bent on nothing but its own survival, and every pretty trick, every fire lit for you, every flower blooming at your feet, is nothing but a ploy to win your affection."

A breeze kicks up, making a sad, dissenting sound as it runs over the open mouth of the chimney.

"Well, if Burleigh's such a monster, why are you still here?" My words ring on the night air like a challenge. "You could have left weeks ago. Yet here you are, Haelwyn of Taunton. Here you are."

"I stayed for you," Wyn grits out. "To try and change your mind about this place. But I see you're right—you're no different than before. Still stubborn and pigheaded as ever when it comes to Burleigh. Do you know who had the right idea about this House? Your mother. She's the clever one. Got out while she still could."

He scrambles to his feet and swings back into the attic through the dormer window before I can reply. I'm left swallowing back tears yet again—it seems that's all I've done since coming home.

A few feet away from me, just where Wyn was sitting, a pair of ghosts spring to life. My child-self and Wyn as he once was sit side by side, shoulder to shoulder, sharing a thermos of tea back and forth between them and watching the stars. There's a strange bluish cast to them and an odd sort of ripple, as if they're lit by sun reflecting off water. It's a peculiarity of Great Houses, this dredging up of old memories that makes it look as if spirits haunt the halls and grounds.

I watch for a moment before wincing and shaking my head. "Please don't, Burleigh."

The children Wyn and I were flicker and fade away.

7

IT'S STILL FULLY DARK WHEN I WAKE THE NEXT MORNING to the sound of rooks shouting at one another in the House's eaves. For a moment I'm disoriented, not sure why the gulls sound so strange, and then I remember—*I'm home.* My head throbs with too little sleep, but I sit up anyway. The smells of stone and wood smoke and mildew wash over me, along with the fresher, cleaner scents of earth and wet grass, drifting in from the windows I forgot to shut last night.

Movement near the fireplace catches my eye, and I freeze in place. There, beside the cold hearth, is my own ghost. I can feel an urgency in the air, a sort of static hum registered by the skin and not the ears. Burleigh wants my attention. It has something to say, and this time I let its memory play on.

Little Violet must be nine, judging by the ragged patch of hair at the back of her head. I remember that—I'd caught my braid on spruce gum and had to have it cut out by Mira. My younger self, brought back to temporary life by the House, lies on the hearth rug with a well-worn copy of *Gulliver's Travels* open in her hands. Like the memories last night, Little Vi's not quite solid or real. I sit and watch as she glances at the clock on the mantelpiece, tucks the book under one arm, and skips out of the room.

As a child, I grew used to turning a corner and finding some long-dead Sterling in the corridor or beyond an open door, as the House pondered an incident in its past. But Burleigh's memories have never come with this sense of importance before—with the awareness that there's something my House is desperately trying to *say*. Curiosity piqued, I slip out of bed and follow after Little Vi.

She makes her ghostly way down the stairs, step by slow step, barefooted and sliding her hand along the banister to better feel what the House feels. I do the same, and there's restlessness under the habitual anxiety and pain creeping up from the floor. Something about this memory Burleigh wants me to see worries it, and I wish I could ask the House why.

My child-self dances down the central corridor of the east wing, heading out through the conservatory and across the rose garden. She picks up her skirts and leaps like a deer through the wildflower meadow, forcing me to hurry to keep up. Though there's enough light to see by and the sky is growing pink with dawn in this present moment, the Violet of the past is lit by full sun. It must have taken place at midmorning, this memory, though I can't recall it yet.

At the very edge of the meadow, up against the woods at the back of the grounds, Little Violet ducks into a summerhouse. I blink uncertainly—the small, glass-paned building is there, but not there. Sometimes I see a pile of rubble, sometimes the structure whole and complete. And I think I know now what it is the House is dwelling on.

The summerhouse's interior ripples with the same shifting, limpid light that strikes my ghost. I settle down on the ground to watch as my father and a gentleman, white-skinned and prosperous-looking, speak in hushed tones. Little Vi sits nearby and opens her book once more. I remember that—the book, my father's nearness. What I've never remembered is the conversation he had. All I recall is the sweet scent of the roses overgrowing the summerhouse, and Gulliver among the Houyhnhnms.

The House remembers, though. And it remembers what I didn't see at the time—Wyn as a small boy, crouching in the long grass outside the summerhouse.

"—they want answers, George. They want us to make our move," the unfamiliar gentleman says. His voice sounds distant, as if I'm standing with my ear to the keyhole of a locked door. "It's time we have this done with."

Outside the summerhouse, a stiff breeze seems to have risen up. Though I can't feel it in my present moment, the stalks and heads of ghostly wildflowers tap-tap against the panes of glass, sounding for all the world like eager fingers. It's as if a legion of Little Folk are asking to come in.

"It's no use, Bertie," Papa says. He's haggard and careworn—I can tell all of this happened not long before the king descended with his soldiers and his charges of treason. "I've found locations for all the deeds except Burleigh's. And if you think for an instant that I'll set things in motion when my own House is the one left at risk, you're a fool. There's not a chance."

My sun is fully up now, and shining cheerfully enough. But the light around Little Vi and Papa and the gentleman called Bertie has gone grey. I can hear fitful gusts of rain beating against the glass of their summerhouse. Even as a child I was quick about picking up on the moods of the House, and rainfall during daylight hours should certainly have told me something was wrong—Papa kept everything well-regulated in the Blackdown Hills, with rain falling only in late evening. But that day I found myself so absorbed in my book, I failed to notice Burleigh's growing discomfort, just as I missed a bedraggled Wyn, peering through the glass.

Papa noticed, though.

I watch as the remembered version of him glances out through the summerhouse's glass panes and shakes his head. "We shouldn't be speaking about any of this on the grounds—it's hard on Burleigh to hear us. But I'm afraid of being overheard in the village."

Papa's companion likely doesn't even notice the House's distress. To him, it seems like nothing more than the vagaries of weather. He doesn't know how good-natured Burleigh generally is.

"Couldn't you overcome your scruples and let us go ahead without Burleigh's deed?" the gentleman suggests. "This place is devoted to Sterlings. I can't imagine it ever doing you any harm, even if the king commanded it. And we could use the rest of the deeds as leverage to force His Majesty to hand Burleigh's over."

The gusts of rain turn to a flurry of hail. An anxious, stomach-churning feeling grips me, and I know it's not my own. But I can't tell if it's a part of the House's memory, or a part of my present reality, or both.

Papa's face darkens.

"Out of the question," he snaps. "I won't hear you suggest it again—not to anyone, but especially not to me. I'm not willing to hazard that, but I don't like any of this. There are too many loose ends. And not being able to find the location of Burleigh's deed, out of all of them? It feels like bad luck. I've bribed and questioned far too many people by now—I'd hoped to have this done with months ago. There are roadblocks at every turn, though."

My surroundings fall entirely still, both in the past and the present, as if the House is listening. The rain and hail stop. The light is low, and not a single bird sings. Little Vi looks up from her reading and puts her head to one side with a frown.

Papa's friend leans in, toward my father. "Do you think someone's working against you, George?"

"I don't know." Papa rubs a hand across his face. "It certainly seems like it at times. Albert, if anything were to happen to me, you'd look after Vi, wouldn't you? Give her a home at Weston Manor?"

"Of course," Albert promises. "Don't fret about it for a moment."

"Papa." My child-self's voice is high and wavering with worry. "The House—"

The sky of that remembered morning has gone a sickly green. Inside the summerhouse, there is a slithering, hissing sound as thick vines snake up the walls.

"Violet!" my father shouts, and lunges forward to shield me as glass shatters and beams snap. But he's too far off, and Wyn is faster. The boy flies through the open summerhouse door and bowls me over, the two of us landing in a tangled heap.

This I recall—the sudden worry that tore my attention away from my book, the horrible sound of breaking glass, and the shock of being knocked down. I cover my head instinctively, though the falling shards have no power to harm me now. Their touch is feather-light, barely remembered.

When the clamor fades and the summerhouse lies in ruins, both in truth and in memory, I can make out my father at the center of the chaos, bent over Wyn and Little Vi. And I see what I didn't at the time—the fragments of mortar-coated glass that have shredded the back of Wyn's shirt, the blood trickling down his neck and arms. I don't think he was hurt badly, but my heart sinks at the stricken look on my father's face.

"George, did the House—" Papa's friend begins. But Papa ignores him.

"Are you alright, Wyn?" he asks. The boy nods without speaking.

"Go on in and find Mira," Papa urges. "She'll look after you."

Without a word to me, Papa straightens, and there's anger in every line of his posture.

"We pushed the House too hard," he says to his companion. "The binding prevents it from hearing much about the deeds without trying to stop whoever's speaking of them. Burleigh, I'm so sorry."

Sun shines on the trio of ghosts once more, and distant birdsong begins again. Daisies sprout and unfurl in front of Little Vi, who sits unharmed at the center of a ring of broken glass. Papa and the strange gentleman both watch as the child I was plucks the flowers with a sad smile.

"Of course I'm alright," Little Vi says to Burleigh, because no one else has asked.

The memory fades and I'm forced to jump back from the old wreckage of the summerhouse with a yelp as enormous, thorn-studded brambles twist themselves around its sun-bleached remains with frightening speed. Before long, there's not an inch of the summerhouse left visible.

The low, nagging discomfort I've felt from the House fades, leaving only the constant strain of Burleigh trying to hold back its own magic. Out of the center of the brambles, a small wild rose sprouts. I reach for it carefully, mindful of the thorns, and pluck the blossom, inhaling its summer-sweet fragrance.

"Deeds and keys, kings and Houses," I murmur to myself. "What is it you're saying, Burleigh?"

I wish I could understand this place as instinctively as I once did. When it was as easy as breathing, knowing what Burleigh wanted—sensing how, even without a key, I could best offer help and comfort.

"You'll figure it out. That's what the Sterlings do, don't they?" Wyn's standing at the edge of the back woods, not the ghostly child version of him, but his real, all but unfamiliar self. The Wyn I'm not sure how to handle. I flush and stare at the ground. There's still tension between us in the wake of our argument last night, and I'm at a loss as to how to make things right before he leaves. I can't turn back time and undo what's gone before. All I can do is move forward.

And so I take a step in Wyn's direction. He shifts and glances up at me from beneath that untidy hair, one hand on the strap of his rucksack.

"Wyn, I'm sorry," I tell him quietly. "I'm sorry about everything. The House showed me what happened to Papa, when I first arrived. You never should have had to live through that, or any of the arrest. Whatever Papa's reasons, it was wrong of him to keep you here. I don't—I don't blame you for wanting to leave now that you can. I think you should go, and be free."

Wyn gives me a sharp look, and his jaw tenses. "The House showed that to you? Your father dying?"

"Yes. I think it wanted to make sure there were no secrets between us."

"I asked it not to make you watch," Wyn says, anger in his voice. "I'd have spared you seeing your father die. It seems Burleigh House is less merciful."

"I'm glad it showed me," I answer defensively. I've always been quick to defend Burleigh. No matter what it's been forced to do, I don't think that will ever change. My House is mother and father and home to me now—everything I have left. "I'd rather know the worst."

Taking a second step forward, I wrap my arms around myself, as if they can protect me from the rejection I'm beginning to realize is inevitable.

"Can't we part on good terms, Wyn?" I beg. "Even if we aren't the way we once were? I know that life's been unfair, and that you've had things worse than I did. But I can't help wishing you weren't leaving angry at me."

He shakes his head wearily. "Violet, I'm not angry at you, I just wish you'd done as I asked and not come back at all. The House is failing, and if it founders entirely before the king sets a torch to it, ruin will follow in its wake. I *liked* knowing you were clear of that. I'd rather you still were."

The ground trembles beneath us, the House clearly unhappy at the thought of me leaving it to its fate.

"I want you to own it to me," Wyn says. "That Burleigh might be past saving."

I press my arms tighter against myself, trying to contain the unhappiness I feel. "You sound like Mira, and I can't agree with either of you. I can't let Burleigh go without doing everything possible to keep it safe, and well, and whole. I have to try for this place, Wyn, no matter the risks."

He holds a hand out to me. "Goodbye then, Violet."

And it's me this time who doesn't reach back. Something—disappointment? resignation?—flits across Wyn's face. He turns and walks off into the woods, where, in a moment, the trees hide him completely.

8

IT'S A TESTAMENT TO THE FACT THAT WE'RE STILL SET-
tling in that Jed and Mira and I only sit down to breakfast at
midmorning the day after we arrive. I don't think we've ever eaten
so late before. It feels strange, and uncomfortable. Jed drains his
cup of black tea and gets up, pressing a kiss to the crown of Mira's
head, and then mine.

"I'm off," he says. "Don't know when I'll be back, so don't wait
supper."

"Where are you going?" I ask, a little forlornly.

"To look for work," he says. "If I'm lucky, I'll find day labor on
one of the farms."

"While you're at it, ask if anyone wants washing done," Mira
tells him. "I'll want something to keep me busy."

And then it's just Mira and me, and Burleigh.

"Where's Wyn this morning?" Mira asks.

"He left," I say. "For good. I don't want to talk about it."

Mira reaches across the table and gives my hand a quick squeeze.
"Alright. I'm sorry, love."

I linger at the table after she gets up. I'm unaccountably anxious at the thought of wandering off into the House on my own. I don't know why I should feel so nervous—perhaps it's the time apart, or how poorly things went with Wyn. But I'm suddenly terrified that in spite of my insistence that I'm meant to be a Caretaker, I may turn out to be less than Burleigh needs.

Mira clatters about, opening and shutting cupboards, taking stock of what we've got in the House and what we'll have to buy or borrow. After a while, she turns to me with a sigh.

"Violet, love, you've got to find something to do with yourself. Begin as you mean to go on, eh?"

I stand and let out a ragged breath. "You're right. Have we got a broom and a dustpan I can use?"

"Corner cupboard. Good girl."

I take them out and walk through the guest wing to the long-abandoned ballroom. The crystal chandelier's fallen and smashed, no one bothering to clear up the bits of glass. I begin sweeping, and the shards make sharp, musical sounds as they're pushed against one another. It seems like such a small thing to be doing—such an insignificant task compared to the immensity of Burleigh's discomfort, which is bleeding up through my feet and pressing in on me from all sides.

Halfway through the job, I give up and slip out of my soft-soled shoes. The moment my bare feet hit Burleigh's floors, that sense of old pain and prodigious effort intensifies. I reach out and press both hands flat against the hardwood planks in front of me.

No, not good enough.

Shifting, I lie down on my side, one ear pressed to the floor, which is chill and smooth beneath the skin of my jaw, the side of my mouth. If I could, I would sink down into the very heart of the House and lend it my strength. But brick and mortar, skin and bone, have always been at odds.

"Tell me what ails you," I whisper to Burleigh, desperate to help. "Show me where it hurts."

A ponderous groan heaves up from the floor beneath me.

"That's right," I coax. "Unburden yourself, my love. I'm here now. I'm not going anywhere."

The House is tentative. It opens up slowly at first. A few threads of pain snake through my skin and into my blood.

"There you are," I tell Burleigh. "Show it all to me. Don't be afraid."

The threads grow into ribbons that become ropes that become iron. Intractable bands of the House's pain wrap around the soft, necessary things inside me. Halfpenny nails of it stud my bones, their small, sharp points driving deeper and deeper, filling me with fractures.

I lie on the floor and gasp, tears starting in my eyes. But I will not cry out or beg the House to stop. I must know the worst and the worst is this—even darling Burleigh, ancient as the hills, greater than I can fathom, powerful beyond measure and wise in ways past human comprehension, cannot survive long in the face of so much pain.

A low, anguished sound escapes me as I'm struck by a sense of rot, of things going bad and decaying at my very core. I can no more escape this awful awareness of the House's dying than all those numerous limpid creatures could escape the razor edge of my fishing spear. It grows so great I cannot bear it—I'm just a girl, after all. A little, fragile thing made of breakable parts.

And then the cold bite of mortar begins.

It nips at my fingers to start, then gnaws at my knuckles, freezes my wrists. I watch, dully, as the veins lining my hands stand out and go grey.

You have to stop this, the fierce fen-survivor in me says. *Stop it now.*

It's all you have to give, the part of me that was born to be a Caretaker argues. *All you have. Doesn't your House come first?*

And in a way, it's reassuring. Great Houses are extremely particular about who they'll work House magic with. If Burleigh is willing to use me as an outlet for its mortar, it must see me as a true Caretaker, whether I have a key or not.

But none of that makes this any less dangerous.

Before I can decide what to do, the cold fades. Burleigh's pain vanishes as the House wrenches back, pulling its power and attention away from me with a supreme effort. There's a horrible sound of splintering wood as the floor splits and a rift opens up along the center of the ballroom. For a moment the chandelier teeters on the edge and then tips over, what's left of it smashing at the bottom of the newly opened chasm.

I sit up, somewhat unsteadily, and take a breath. What am I doing here? Wyn was right—I've no idea how to be a Caretaker. For all my father drilled it into me that someday, I'd look after Burleigh House, I'm only making things worse. But oh, Burleigh, I *want* to help.

Burying my head in my hands, I think of Papa. Of the man he

was, and of the space he left behind. Of how small I feel, when I imagine trying to follow after him as a guardian of this powerful, incomprehensible place. Of how high the stakes have risen, and how little I can do to help without the Caretaker's key, which I've held but once before in my life.

I still remember the feel of that key. The heaviness of it on my palm, the bite of its teeth against my skin when I held it tight. The way the bowstone warmed to my touch and wicked mortar from my skin as I worked magic the way a Caretaker ought to. I think of it now, as I sit and wait for the intolerable aching of House magic to fade from my limbs.

We were on holiday at the Cornish coast the day my father handed me the key to Burleigh House. We never went far from home in those days—Papa already hated leaving the House behind to travel to London for the Home Council. Mama used to beg to visit the Continent—even Scotland would do, she said, but we never left the West Country. Secretly, I was glad of it.

So we went to St. Ives the summer I was seven. Mama was moody the whole week we spent at a rented guest cottage. Papa and I did our best not to notice, making sandcastles and bathing in the surf and eating ice creams. I'd never spent so much time with him before, and it was lovely, if a bit strange. Wyn stayed at home with Jed and Mira, and I missed him every day. It was the one thing about the trip Mama insisted on—that we leave Wyn behind.

The morning we were to leave for home, dark clouds hung over the sea. Thunder grumbled from the west and lightning flared low on the horizon. Papa stood on the beach and watched, though our things had already been packed up and Mama sat waiting in the carriage. It was as if Papa knew what was coming. Perhaps he did. Perhaps the House found a way to tell him.

Mama kept me at her side until a little boat emerged from the distant storm and limped into port. When I saw Papa head for it, I flung the carriage door open and bolted.

"Violet!" Mama called after me, a note of desperation in her voice. "Vi, come back here. Stay where it's safe!"

But I tore across the sand until I reached Papa. He looked down at me, worry in his eyes.

"Now then, Vi. Let's sort out this storm," he said.

I knew well enough that Cornwall sometimes saw bad weather— not every storm could be calmed by the House's magic, and the coast was often buffeted by squalls that Burleigh did no more than tame, so that they cost less in the way of lives and property than they might have. While Burleigh could maintain perfectly clear skies at the heart of the Blackdown Hills, even a House has a hard time pitting itself against the sea.

Papa and I hurried down a nearby pier to where the little boat had pulled up alongside a vacant slip. When the weathered fisherman aboard tossed a painter to Papa, he caught it and made the vessel fast, then helped the man ashore.

"I'm George Sterling," Papa said, and even as a child it fascinated me, how he could speak his name and the tension drained out of people. The wind was rising by then, buffeting the pier and making whitecaps out to sea.

"Sir, that's a hundred-year storm out there," the fisherman shouted, raising his voice to be heard over the wind. "We never used to see them more than once a century, but they've been coming more and more often since my grandfather's day. It's blowing in fast—you'd best get you and yours inland as quick as you can, and find some place to shelter. There'll be damage done tonight, and no mistake."

"I'll stay—" Papa began, but then all three of us turned to face the sea, as with a strange rushing noise the water pulled away from shore. One moment it was there, and the next gone, receding with unnerving speed.

"Violet."

I tore my gaze away from the retreating water. Mama had left the carriage and was tugging at my hand. "Come with me. You and I will go somewhere safe. Let your father deal with this. It's what he does."

There was bitterness in her last words, and I didn't like it, not one bit. I stood at her side and watched in an agony as Papa went back down the pier and out onto the empty beach. Damp sand stretched far, far out to sea, pockmarked with shells and the little holes dug by clams. The boats moored to the pier hung from their painters, or snapped them and fell to the mud below.

"Violet Sterling, you will come back to the carriage with me at once." I could hear from the break in Mama's voice that she was near hysterical, but Papa seemed so alone, out on the sand with no one to stand beside him. I've never been able to forget the look Mama gave me as I slipped my hand from hers and ran down the pier, racing across the sand. As if drawn against her will, Mama followed in my wake.

"Eloise," Papa said as Mama arrived at his side. Silent tears pooled in her eyes—she'd learned long ago that sobbing had no effect. "I need your help. I need you to take the key. I can shift more magic without it, and you can channel some as well."

That startled me. I'd never seen Papa without the Caretaker's key, which he kept tucked into his fob pocket, secured on the end of a gold watch chain. No one was allowed to touch it—not me, not Mama, not Jed. I knew, with a child's knowing, that the key kept him safe when he worked with the House. That it let him move Burleigh's magic, directing the flow of power here and there with his own energy and attention, while ensuring the House did not leak mortar into his living blood, or take more from him than he could give.

Mama's face went very white. "I won't, George. I want nothing to do with any of that and you know it. Isn't it enough that I suffer through living under Burleigh's roof?"

Papa turned to me and two bright spots appeared on Mama's cheeks.

"No," she said, the word all resentment and sharp edges. "If you give the key to our daughter—our *child*—I swear to you, George, I will pack my bags and leave. Does nothing mean more to you than that House?"

"Violet, will you take the key?" Papa asked. I nodded solemnly and held out both hands.

Mama stifled another sob and went back up the beach, tripping and crying all the way. It hurt me to hear her, but the key fit into my hands as if it were made to rest there, warm in my grip, warmer than I'd expected. It sent a little electric thrill from my head to my toes, and I could feel the House's energy so much more clearly, running through the ground beneath my feet. That energy focused with all-consuming intensity on the horizon, and the stormhead, and a strange gleam of light that stretched across the sea. I squinted and the gleam resolved itself into a wall of water, taller than I'd imagined possible, rushing in toward the shore.

Raw fear poured through me. The key blazed hot but I refused to let it go. Papa trusted me to hold it, and whatever came, I meant to keep my word.

"Alright, Burleigh," Papa said, crouching in a familiar posture and sinking his hands into the damp sand that surrounded us. "Do what must be done. Take whatever you need."

Something like a blast of wind hit me, but I felt it inside, not outside, and knew it must be House magic surging out to sea to meet that terrifying wave. Papa dug his hands deeper into the sand and I clutched the key desperately, though it burned in my grasp.

The earth beneath me trembled with the House's effort, as it pushed against the incoming sea, striving to unmake the wall of water racing into shore. Papa trembled, too, without the key to safeguard him. He shook and shook, until I feared the House might tear him limb from limb.

"Stop, stop," I shouted, clinging to the key, but tremors still racked Papa and that dreadful wave roared closer, already halfway through the bay and taller by far than Burleigh House itself.

With nothing to guide me but the overpowering current of House magic flowing out to sea, I stepped in front of Papa, as if to shield him from the rushing wave. The roar of its coming was so loud it ate up my defiant, wordless scream as I clutched the key and fell to my knees, plunging my own hands into the sand and squeezing my eyes shut.

Noise and fury.

Fear.

The roar of the wave.

The cold touch of mortar and magic rushing through me.

I shook, and the earth shook, and then . . .

Salt water, welling gently up around my legs.

My eyes flew open. In spite of the House magic I'd worked, the protection of the Caretaker's key had let it pass through me harmlessly. My hands looked ordinary as ever, with no trace of mortar left behind. Just pale skin and the small pink bracelet around my left wrist—the mark I'd worn since birth.

The wall of water had gone, along with the stormhead and the wind. Small, docile waves lapped their way into shore, gradually moving up the beach to the high-tide mark. They were ankle-deep already when I turned and saw my father, lying crumpled on the sand, his face seamed with veins of stone grey. Stumbling to him, I pressed my warm forehead to his cold one and sobbed.

But a few brave souls were already emerging from the houses along the bay. They ran to us, and helped me pull Papa up past the high-water mark.

"Where's your mother?" the fisherman who'd warned us of the storm asked gruffly.

It was only then that I looked, and saw she'd been good to her word. The carriage was gone. I had never felt so lost as in that moment, knowing my mother had fled and my father might breathe his last at any time.

They put us up in the public house and I stayed at Papa's bedside for three nights as he alternately shook with chills and burned with fever. Mortar leaked from his pores, staining the bedsheets and filling the room with an unnatural, stony smell. I clung to Burleigh's key, never letting it go whether I woke or slept.

On the fourth day, rescue came, although it was not Mama. I never saw her face again after that day, and never really forgave her. Instead there was a great clamor outside and His Majesty the king swept into the room. I ran to him with a choking cry and he put his arms around me.

"Violet, my darling girl, I'm here to make everything alright," he said.

And he did. Uncle Edgar took care of the arrangements for us to return home and rode in a carriage with me all the way. He distracted me with card games and sleight of hand while Papa, still delirious, rode in another coach with the king's own physician.

But when we arrived at Burleigh House, Uncle Edgar stopped at the gate. At the end of the drive, the House sat forlornly. Half the shingles had been torn from the roof and littered the lawn. Every window had shattered, as if blown out by a blast of gunpowder. The front door lay on the gravel drive, torn from its hinges.

"I won't go in," Uncle Edgar said, patting my hand. "Dr. Foyle will stay with you until George is well. But the House won't want me on the grounds, not when it's like this. They're touchy about the deedholders, you know—don't like us seeing them at anything but their best."

I took him at his word, and waved as his carriage jolted back down the lane. Once he'd disappeared from view, I stepped through the gate only to be met by Wyn, hurtling across the lawn. He threw his arms around my neck, and, astonished, I hugged him back.

"Is everything alright, Wyn?" I asked.

He nodded, eyes wide. "It is now."

When Dr. Foyle helped Papa from the second coach, sweat still stood out on my father's forehead and his face was very pale. But when he looked at Wyn and me, his eyes were clear and kind.

"Violet, give me the key."

Without hesitation, I held out a hand. Since that moment on the beach, I'd gripped the key tight ever since he'd given it to me. It hadn't even gone into my pocket, not once.

Papa took the key with a sigh and settled himself down on the front doorstep, leaning against the House for support.

"Sir," Dr. Foyle protested. "You must go to bed at once."

"No," Papa said. "Not until I've helped Burleigh set itself to rights."

I sat down at his side, and he rested a hand on the top of my head. "You did very well, Violet. Very well indeed. What a Caretaker you're going to be."

Pride flooded me from head to toe, even as the vast weight of Burleigh's focus and power settled on Papa and he shut his eyes.

"Where's Mama?" I asked Wyn quietly.

He shook his head. "Oh, Violet."

"Where is she?" I asked again, my voice sharper.

Wyn fixed his eyes on the ground. "She took all of her things and left. I don't—I don't think she means to come back."

"Papa?" I turned to my father, but his face was drawn and his attention entirely absorbed by Burleigh House.

Squaring my shoulders, I stood and took Wyn's hand in mine. "Well, we'll be alright, won't we? We always are."

But the words sounded flat, and hollow.

They still do, as I mutter them under my breath in the wreckage of Burleigh's ballroom. I feel every bit as alone and unsure of myself as I did in that moment.

I told Wyn the truth—I haven't changed at all. It's only taken a day back at home for me to lose the surety I'd gained on the fens.

"What am I going to do, Papa?" I say to the air, and the earth, and the walls.

"He's not going to answer, you know," a sardonic voice says from behind me. Scrambling to my feet, I turn, and my stomach drops clear through the ruined floor.

His Majesty the king stands in the doorway, brushing an imagined fleck of dust from the snowy lace edging his sleeves. "Fortunately, I'm here to sort out your little troubles, though I must say, you're not managing the House nearly as well as I'd hoped. Shall we have a chat?"

9

"WHAT ARE YOU DOING HERE? HOW DID YOU GET IN?" I ask the king after taking him to Papa's study and settling into the chair behind the desk. I suppose I should be more formal, but old habits die hard. And then there's the matter of the bitterness that still churns in my stomach every time I look at my godfather.

Burleigh's unhappy with the king's presence, too. I can feel the House's discontent seeping up through the soles of my still-bare feet.

"I'm the deedholder," His Majesty says mildly. He takes out a pristine handkerchief and wipes at a spot of dust on the desk. "The Houses can't actually deny me without damaging themselves, you know. Though I do try to take their feelings into account whenever possible."

"Why aren't you in London?"

I knead my hands together under the desk. The mortar's faded from the surface of my skin but I can still feel its chill bite. It will never leave me, now I've let it in. Any subsequent House magic worked will only add more.

His Majesty shrugs. "I thought I'd take the waters in Bath. Spend the summer there, perhaps. I wouldn't mind being nearby, to keep an eye on you and the House as you settle in."

"Leave us alone and we'll settle in just fine."

A pair of guards stand in the hallway outside the study door, and having them in the House makes my skin crawl. The floor is fairly vibrating with Burleigh's discomfort, and a small pewter figurine rattles across the desk and nearly falls. His Majesty reaches out and catches it with one deft, long-fingered hand.

The king smiles, and I force a smile of my own in return. If I don't settle myself and Burleigh in short order, we're headed for disaster.

Calm down. Calm down, I think at my frantic House.

A thin stream of plaster dust falls from the ceiling in the far corner of the room.

"I've brought you a lovely surprise," the king says. "His name's Lord Pottsworth. I know you'd prefer to remain at Burleigh House if it pulls through all this"—he waves vaguely at our dilapidated surroundings—"so I've come up with a plan. I think Pottsworth'll do quite nicely for the new Caretaker, and a husband for you. Then you can stay on here with him, and be with Burleigh House."

The king beams at me, as if I'm a child to whom he's just handed a lolly.

"I *beg* your pardon?" I stare at the king in disbelief. "I am not getting married. Not now. Possibly not ever."

"Oh, come now," His Majesty says. "Pottsworth's entirely unobjectionable—you can overrule him about household decisions whenever you like, and as you'll be satisfied, I suspect the House will be as well. So run along, and make yourself charming. You're getting married."

I cross my arms, though my heart is pounding in my ears and my hands have started to tremble. It has less to do with my own fear, which I can feel swimming beneath the surface of my conscious mind like a starving shark, and more to do with the furious power churning through the House. "You promised you'd give me time with Burleigh. I've had barely a day. I'm not going anywhere, and certainly not to my own wedding."

His Majesty manages a regretful look. "I'm afraid you are. Burleigh?"

The floor shifts, tipping my chair and spilling me onto the floor. I bark my shin against the corner of the desk and sit for a moment in a miserable heap, fighting back tears and anger and nausea as beneath me, the House's feelings pulse through my skin.

Sorrow and rage. Sorrow and rage.

His Majesty gets up and stands over me. "Come along then, my dear. Do as you're told, and everything will go well for you. Disobey, and I will show you how incapable this House is of resisting my orders for long, whatever its sentiments may be."

Sorrow and rage.

Fear.

And the fear is what breaks me. Wordlessly, I take the king's hand and let him pull me to my feet, though his touch turns my stomach.

"Good girl." He pats me on the shoulder. "I knew you'd see reason. You've always been a clever thing—far more sensible than your father."

I say nothing because if I speak, the bitter words that spill out will surely cost both me and my House dearly.

"Go on then," His Majesty urges. "Do whatever it is young girls do on their wedding days. And smile, Violet. This is a happy occasion, for both you and the House. Soon you'll have a perfectly serviceable Caretaker to make use of."

Sorrow. Rage. Fear.

I don't want anyone else to be Caretaker. Neither does Burleigh. And blood and mortar, I do *not* want to get married.

I wander into the hall, hardly able to think through the fog of the House's feelings and the pressure of its unspent magic. One thing's clear: I need to get His Majesty off the grounds before Burleigh loses its composure.

"Uncle Edgar," I say as he joins me in the corridor. "I'm just going to need a moment to get dressed, as you say. Why don't we meet out in the lane?"

He raises an eyebrow. "Because of Burleigh?"

My face burns as I answer. "Yes. Because of Burleigh."

"Oh, very well." The king runs a finger along the study doorpost, and the whole frame shudders. "You have your work cut out for you here if you're going to stave off the inevitable, Violet. I don't think I've ever seen a House in such a state."

I swallow back a retort, reaching out and resting a comforting hand on the nearest wall instead. But as I do, the icy bite of House magic gnaws at my skin, turning my fingertips grey.

Burleigh's doleful, apologetic even, and yet here it is. My second dose of House magic since waking. I'd make a widower of Lord Pottsworth in a month, at this rate.

"Well, I'll see you shortly, Uncle Edgar," I say with half a curtsy, and hurry up the stairs. All the way to the second floor, I run my hand along the banister and watch as more mortar spreads through my veins.

What can I do, though? Burleigh needs help and it's not in me to refuse my House, whatever the cost.

By the time I shut the bedroom door, my skin is grey to the wrists and I can hardly feel my hands. Nevertheless, I sink down next to the bed and press my numb fingers to the floor.

"Peace, Burleigh," I whisper. "Peace."

But the House's anguish and rage and fear at the king's presence are all still roiling in its walls, and in my blood. I squeeze my eyes shut, because my head feels fit to burst and the light hurts me.

Cold creeps further and further up my arms.

Distantly, I hear a whine of hinges as the bedroom door opens, and then Wyn's voice cuts through the fog of Burleigh's pain or my own, I'm not entirely sure which it is anymore. But that can't be right. Wyn left.

"You've got to stop this," he says sharply, his tone all splinters and thorns.

"I'm not doing anything!" I manage to protest. My eyes fly open as Wyn settles on his knees in front of me and takes both my hands in his own. I may not be able to feel much, but I can feel that.

"Not you. The House. I'll torch it myself if it doesn't stop."

A fierce gust of rain lashes the window in response. Is it raining? The sky was clear a moment ago, unless I've been sitting here taking in mortar for longer than it seems. I'm not used to Burleigh's sudden changes anymore—they were once a matter of course, and now they take me by surprise.

"That's enough," Wyn says, and I know he's not speaking to me this time because there's something fierce and compelling about his voice, like I've never heard before.

Immediately, the pressure in my head lets up as Burleigh's focus shifts. Slowly, slowly, warm and living blood runs back through my veins. The icy touch of mortar begins to let up as its flow reverses, draining out of me and into Wyn. When I look at him, his eyes are fixed on mine, but vacant and unseeing.

"Wyn?" I breathe. "What's going on? What are you doing?"

He doesn't answer—just sits there, and it's as if his body is nothing but an empty shell.

I look down at our clasped hands. Wyn's are pale as ever, and dusted with a few freckles, but there's no sign of the mortar that's leaving me to run beneath his skin. No grey poison threading through his veins. And yet, somehow, the House magic is working in him. I can *feel* it, passing out of my body and into his.

The last of it goes, but Wyn's gaze stays blank and lightless.

I don't know what to do. A helpless rage, choking in its futility, floods me from head to toe.

Then Wyn blinks, and his eyes focus on me.

"I saw the king's coach while I was on the road to Taunton," he says, as if absolutely nothing has happened. "So I turned around to warn you, but clearly he beat me here."

"What *was* that?" I ask, ignoring what he's just said. "What did you do with the House magic? I've never seen anything like that before. Never even heard of something like it."

Wyn pulls his hands away from mine and hunches his shoulders, growing prickly and withdrawn once more. "Don't worry about it. What did His Majesty want?"

That question's the only thing that could possibly distract me from what's just happened. "He came to tell me I'm getting married."

I can't keep despair from my voice. I don't know how to get around this—though everything in me says to bolt, I can't. Burleigh is a tether I will not loose myself from. "The king has someone he wants to name Caretaker, and I know if I don't do as I'm told, he'll turn me out of Burleigh House. Congratulate me, Wyn."

"I will not." When I glance up, Wyn's scowling.

"You're not getting married," he says. "You're Violet Sterling; you've never done anything you don't want to do. So stop being a fatalist and get yourself out of it."

"I left Burleigh House. I left my father. I left you," I tell him, bristling at his tone. "So in point of fact, sometimes I am forced to do things I don't want to. And I don't *know* how to stop this."

Wyn shrugs. "We were children when you left the House. We're not children anymore. Think of something."

I let out a growl of frustration. "It's not that easy!"

Getting to his feet, Wyn makes for the door.

"I'm going down to the kitchen to talk to Mira," he says as he goes. "I'll stay for an hour. If you've found a way out of this by then, I'll stay longer—give you the fresh start you wanted. But if you let the king bully you into a marriage of convenience, I'll be gone again by the time you're back."

I scoff. "As if your presence is some great prize. I'm not sure I even want you here anymore."

Wyn turns, and gives me a long-suffering look. "I'm not the prize to be won, Violet. Your freedom is. If you win it, I'll stay awhile, because you could clearly use the help. But I won't stay on only to watch you be ground down under the heel of His Majesty's boot."

He shuts the door behind him, and as he goes, all my despair is replaced by anger and stubbornness and determination. That's always the way with us Sterlings—we fight our hardest when backed into a corner. When facing down the impossible.

I clench my fists and scowl at the door, because of course Wyn knows that. This is no different from the time I hit my head, slipping on damp rocks in the streambed at the back of the grounds. Too afraid to leave me to run for help, Wyn pulled me to my feet and jeered and bullied and cajoled until we made it back to the House. *It's not so bad, Violet, don't fuss over nothing, you're being ridiculous*, he'd said. I remember Mira shrieking at the sight of me, covered in blood, and Wyn disappearing the moment Jed took charge. It wasn't until after I'd had my head bandaged and been washed and dressed that I found Wyn, in my cupboard as always. His hands were still shaking, but he'd got me home by waking that Sterling stubbornness.

"Alright, then," I say, squaring my shoulders. "Burleigh House, I don't want to get married. You don't want a new Caretaker. What are we going to do?"

Two figures flicker to life across the room—myself, no older than six, and the king. Little Vi sits on one side of a small card table drawn up before the fire, His Majesty on the other. They're playing a game of écarté, and the king takes trick after trick before Little Vi finally pushes back her chair in frustration.

"Uncle Edgar, I don't want to play anymore," she says with a stamp of her foot. "You always win. And I had the king of trumps this round! It isn't fair."

His Majesty smiles indulgently. "Life isn't fair, my dear. Some people win and some lose. You must learn to play a better game."

Little Vi's only answer is to cross her arms stubbornly and scowl.

The king leans toward her. "I'll tell you a secret. The truth is, you're getting very good at écarté. Truly. You've improved by leaps and bounds since we first began playing. I think by now, you could beat most people."

"When will I beat you?" Little Vi squints cannily and the king throws back his head and laughs, an uproarious and unbothered sound.

"No one beats me, Violet Sterling. Do you know why? I *am* the king of trumps."

"What am I, then?"

The king reaches out and pats Little Vi on the head. "A small queen." His mouth twists. "And your father, it seems, is a knave. Now. Shall we play again?"

Little Vi holds her ground. "I said I don't want to. I'll only lose."

"Of course you will," the king says. "But it's such fun for me to watch you *try.*"

"What about Slaps?" Little Vi asks hopefully. "I can win at Slaps."

His Majesty's dark eyes spark with a clever light. "When do we play Slaps? Think carefully."

"Um." Little Vi puts her head to one side. "When Papa's here?"

"Nearly."

"When my governess is here?"

"Close."

"Oh! I know—you only let me play Slaps when there's someone else about. Isn't that funny?"

"Exactly." The king's hands are busy, dealing out another game of écarté, which Little Vi hasn't yet agreed to play. "Why do you think that might be?"

I've never been particularly deep. My younger self only stares at His Majesty.

"If I'm the king of trumps, then what does that make life?" the king prompts.

"A game?"

"Yes. Which means that when people choose to behave one way in company and another in private, they're bluffing. Fortunately for you, I am indeed the devoted godfather I make myself out to be. I just hate to lose."

"I agree with Papa," Little Vi says pragmatically, climbing back into her chair. Clearly she's resigned herself to a few more hands of écarté. "You *do* talk a lot of nonsense."

The king laughs again, and echoes of it are still ringing through the room when the memory fades.

"This is all a game to him," I say, more to myself than to my House. "I've just got home, which means we've been dealt our respective cards. And this—what if he doesn't care so much about marrying me off, he's just drawing me out, trying to see if I'll play on or fold?"

White blossoms burst jubilantly from the mantel and the sun

scuds out from behind its cover of clouds, pouring golden light through the windows.

"Well then, Burleigh," I say grimly. "We haven't got much working in our favor, so I think it's time to bluff."

His Majesty waits in the laneway, mounted and escorted by a dozen royal guards. There's a carriage waiting behind him, identical to the one he sat in the day my father's arrest began. A new tendril of fear uncurls in my belly at the sight of it. I tamp it down. Steady on, Vi. Don't let him see you're afraid.

In contrast to the king, I drift through the bramble-choked scar in the wall as light as gossamer, a scrap of gentle summer sky come to earth. I twine my fingers in my skirts as I walk down the gravel drive. I'm wearing one of Mama's old gowns. The frock is too low in the waist to be quite the thing, but it's long enough, and the forget-me-not blue makes me look harmless, which is what I want. It's fitting to do this in Mama's clothes, too, as for once it's her I need to imitate and not Papa. No matter how unhappy she was, whenever an outsider arrived at Burleigh, Mama closed ranks. She put on a dazzling smile and lied through her teeth, chattering about how lovely life in a Great House was, and how perfectly wonderful things were between her and my father. Right up until the end, she kept her misery hidden from everyone but her family.

That's who I must be now—a girl without a care, a reed that bends without breaking. Never mind the state of my House, the treason I'm planning to embark on, the fear that sometimes threatens to overwhelm me—His Majesty must not sense the slightest bit of it.

"Uncle Edgar," I say with a curtsy as I step through a gap in the mortarous briars that now serve Burleigh for a gate. "Thank you so much for waiting. I feel worlds better about this now that I've had a chance to freshen up."

I don't. After working House magic twice in one day, I feel as if I might fall over at any moment. But I'm planning to tell rather a lot of lies, so I might as well begin as I mean to go on.

"Well, you're a pretty picture now," His Majesty answers indulgently. "Shall we carry on to the village? Lord Pottsworth is waiting at the church."

I let a small sigh escape my lips, and the king raises an eyebrow. "Troubles, my dear?"

"I don't *know* Lord Pottsworth. I've never even met him. It isn't that I object to marrying a Caretaker you choose—you're Burleigh's deedholder and it's for you to appoint a new keyholder. I accept that. But it does seem hard that I don't have *any* say in the matter. And you promised me time to settle in. I'd hardly call a day generous in that regard."

Coming up alongside the king's charger, I reach out and rub a finger along the horse's embossed leather martingale. His Majesty stares down at me, a frown playing across his features.

"You could have far worse men for your husband than Lord Pottsworth," he says. "He's dull as powder, but that only means you'll be able to manage him however you like. And he has a passion for orchids—I'm sure if you bring Burleigh round, he'll do marvelous things with the greenhouse and the gardens."

I don't point out that the greenhouse has, in fact, been overtaken by brambles and that without the key, I can't restore it. Nor do I mention that my House doesn't need a Caretaker who can be managed, but one with fire and strength of will and an unflinching resolve to put Burleigh's needs first.

Instead, I glance up at the king with what I hope is a wistful expression. "It's just that everything's been taken out of my hands. And it's all so sudden. Your own marriage was a political match—were you happy before Queen Isabella had to return to Spain?"

I refuse to let my gaze falter. The words sound entirely innocent, but it's the king himself who taught me to play games of strategy, and I know as well as anyone how badly his match to Isabella went. The king gives me a searching look, but I stand my ground, wide-eyed and guileless as only a seventeen-year-old girl with ulterior motives can be.

"No one likes a forced marriage," I say, letting self-pity creep into my voice. "All I want is a bit of time, and some choice in the matter. In return, I promise to bring Burleigh around, and settle down happily once you've found someone I fancy."

For a long while the king only watches me, with that prying, hawkish gaze of his. I want to shift, to look away, but hold fast, even when I begin to suspect he's about to drag me off to be married to the faceless Lord Pottsworth by force, if necessary.

"Very well," the king concedes finally, and I think I might melt with relief. Or at least I do until I hear the rest of what he has to say. "I'll give you a choice. Marry Lord Pottsworth now, stay on here, and find a way to reconcile the House to him. Or you're welcome to spend half the summer alone with Burleigh and come August I'll give the key to Lord Falmouth, should the House still be standing. Falmouth won't want to marry you—he's got his eyes set rather higher—but I hear he's dreadfully hard on chambermaids. Perhaps he could find you a position as a servant here."

"Lord Falmouth who tore this hole in Burleigh's walls? That's hardly much of a choice," I say, keeping my voice to a petty grumble while my mind races.

"Mm, yes. He's the one who alerted me to your father's treasonous inclinations as well. But that," the king purrs, "is me raising the stakes, you vixen. How badly do you want time with the House? And what do you plan to do with it, I wonder?"

"Host a number of lawn parties," I answer lightly, though my hands, hidden in my skirts, are balled into fists. "Perhaps take up tennis. Alright, you've got a bargain, Uncle Edgar. Come August, should the House still be in need of a Caretaker, I will let it pass to your man Falmouth, without a murmur or a complaint."

Two months then, for me to succeed where my father failed.

"I still plan to summer in Bath, to keep an eye on things here," His Majesty warns me. "And I expect *unfaltering* loyalty from you until your wedding day, of course."

"That goes without saying," I answer with a smile. "You're all I have left in the way of family, Uncle Edgar. I feel far more forgiving now I'm home and you're allowing me some leeway. I think we'd better let bygones be bygones."

"You're a devious little witch," the king says affectionately, patting my head as if I'm a faithful hound. "I always did like that about you. We're far more similar than you think, Vi."

Like hell we are. "Oh, I think so, too, Uncle. We do tend to land on our feet."

"As you say." He gestures to the guardsmen and they start off down the lane, moving away from Burleigh Halt and toward Taunton.

"You know where to find me if you need me," His Majesty calls back over one shoulder. "Oh, and I'm sending someone into town, to look out for you and the House. Just in case Burleigh should unfortunately need to be—dispatched—at short notice."

So we're to have an executioner in residence while I plan my treason. Wonderful. What could possibly go wrong?

Rather than complain or answer back, I stand in the lane and wave, a dutiful girl farewelling her beloved godfather. It's only once the king's party has rounded the bend in the road and disappeared from view that I step back and lean against the House's wall for support.

"I hate him," I whisper to the sun-warmed stone. "I want you out from under his thumb, and for neither of us ever to have to answer to him again."

Mortar oozes from the wall in reply, like blood from a wound that won't heal.

10

I FIND MIRA IN THE KITCHEN, BUT THERE'S NO SIGN OF Wyn.

"Are you married, then?" Mira says, looking up from the basin full of laundering she's at work on.

"No," I tell her. "Not yet, at least."

"Good," she says with an approving nod. "Wyn told me what was going on. My first thought was to run out with the rolling pin and beat the priest over the head with it, if need be. But then I remembered you're nearly grown and set on being a Caretaker, so you need to fight your own battles."

I rest my chin on my hand and let out a sigh. "Everyone's far more confident in my capabilities than I am."

Mira smiles wickedly. "If things hadn't gone your way, I had every intention of making that lord's life utterly miserable while he was under this roof. Burleigh and Jed and Wyn all would've helped. The king's man would have been begging for an annulment after a fortnight. And there was always the rolling pin, if he tried to lay a finger on you."

I look at her, bent over the washbasin, her hair all gone iron-grey, arms red to the elbows from the sting of harsh soap. I love her. Blood and mortar, I love her and Jed so much it hurts sometimes.

"I'm sorry I was cross about the deed," I tell Mira. "I don't deserve you or Jed, truly I don't."

She rolls her eyes. "No family agrees about everything; why should we be any different? But Violet, *try* to be safe, won't you?"

"I'll do my very best," I promise, getting up and brushing a kiss to her cheek. "Wyn hasn't left yet, has he?"

"No, he said he was going to do some plastering in the dining room. He was . . . anxious . . . while you were out there with the king."

"Anxious that I'd come back within an hour, maybe, and that he'd have to speak to me again," I grumble. But I leave the kitchen and walk down the dimly lit, musty corridor that leads to the dining room. I'm still trying to learn Burleigh's new face, but it seems to me as if several more cracks have sprouted in the walls since I last came this way. Surely I would have noticed those gaping fissures, and the way they spill mortar and black-thorned brambles out over the wallpaper.

It feels like a chance at redemption, finding Wyn in the dining room yet again, this time plastering over gaping holes in the walls rather than nailing up a broken window.

"Still here, are you?" I say from the door. "I hope you've finished being angry at me. I haven't done anything, Wyn. I know other people have done things to you, but I haven't. And I want to help— not just the House, you too."

At the sound of my voice, Wyn sets his palette down and turns, visibly collecting himself.

"I'm not angry," he says. "Hello, Violet. I missed you. Welcome home."

I want to be petty. To hold on to how standoffish and harsh he's been, but I don't have it in me. It feels like everything was upside down, and now it's gone right-side up again. I'm not sure which I needed more, either—the *I missed you*, or the *welcome home*.

"Do you have another palette?" I ask.

"On the drop cloth," he says. I pick it up, and for a quite a while we work together in silence, mending some of Burleigh's hurts. It may not be House magic, but as we go, a bit of the tension singing through the floor beneath my feet fades.

Oh, Burleigh, all you want is to be looked after.

I gather my courage as we reach the last damaged section of wall, and steal a glance at Wyn. He's got his serious face on, a slight frown pulling his brows together as he smooths plaster across a seam.

"Why did you come back?" I ask.

"I don't really know," Wyn says without looking at me.

"Will you stay long?"

His frown deepens. "I don't know that, either."

"I still plan to look for the deed," I warn him. "To finish what my father started. Now more than ever—Burleigh couldn't keep itself together at the thought of a new Caretaker. So if you can't live with that . . ."

"No, it's alright." Wyn takes a step back and eyes his work critically. "I remembered something while I was on my way out to Taunton—I never could change your mind, when you were set on something. So I've changed mine, instead. You say you came back to help me, but I've come back to help you, too. Or at least to keep you from killing yourself with House magic."

This time, I'm the one who frowns. "It's that simple?"

One corner of Wyn's mouth tugs up, and he looks almost wistful. "Yes. That simple. Look, Violet, I'm sorry. I'm sorry I was hard on you, but you've been away. I've been here all along and I watched *everything* that's happened. So I know that if you're not terribly quick and clever, either Burleigh or the king will be the death of you. I don't want to see another Sterling die."

"I'm not going to die," I tell him with far more confidence than I feel. "I'm just going to . . . get ahold of Burleigh's deed, free my House, and live forever."

Wyn laughs, the sound short and dry, and possibly a little bitter.

"You were right," he says. "You haven't changed."

But I have. I realize that now. Out on the fens, I was so sure I could fix things if I just got home. But now I'm actually here, doubt runs through me, as insidious as leftover mortar.

When Wyn and I have finished with the plastering, I make a flimsy excuse and slip away. I flit through the empty, echoing halls, where an occasional ghost shimmers in a corner or a doorway. In the conservatory, I push the glass-paned doors wide and go out into the garden, where the air is thick with late afternoon sunlight. As I pass by the tangles of unpruned roses, I can't help but notice that there's something not quite right about them. They blush grey rather than pink at their soft and velvety hearts.

But it's not the garden I want. I go through the roses and the wildflower meadow to the edge of the woods at the back of Burleigh's grounds. There, hemmed in on three sides by a drystone wall and on a fourth by the forest itself, is the Sterling family cemetery.

I let myself in through the little wooden gate. The sound of it shutting behind me is horribly final, as is the sight of bare earth mounded atop my father's grave. There's a stone marker with Papa's name and the years of his birth and his death cut deep into it. The grave itself is fresh and new and raw, like a knife wound to the surface of Burleigh's good earth.

Sinking down in the grass alongside the grave, I take a handful of bare soil, still damp from the earlier rain. This, too, reminds me of how badly things have gone wrong. When my father managed Burleigh it never rained before evening. Burleigh and Papa kept the land in excellent health and the weather carefully regulated.

My father worked ceaselessly on behalf of the House. He knew everyone at court, and rode back and forth across the length of the country in what I now know was his search for Burleigh's deed. How can I possibly begin to retrace his steps, and to uncover the information he brought to light? I am just a girl, with no connections, no income, and no key with which to help my House. My resolution to save Burleigh and to complete the task Papa began is an empty one. What do I have, besides the strength of my own will?

Across the wildflower meadow, there's a shimmer of faint blue-green as the House remembers Papa and me walking hand in hand toward the back woods, fishing poles resting on our shoulders. Whenever he managed to steal an hour or two for me, that's what we liked to do—sit on the banks of the trout stream in the forest, sometimes catching something, sometimes not. We'd talk about Caretakers, about my duty to Burleigh House, and how so long as I looked after it, Burleigh would always be there for me.

But I left, and Papa is dead now. Burleigh is dying. I know, I *know* it's not my fault, yet it still feels as if I had a hand in it.

What if I'd stayed? What if Papa had kept me behind, instead of Wyn? Would things be any different now?

I scrub both hands across my face in abject frustration.

You're meant to be a Caretaker, Vi, Papa's voice says in my head. *And a Caretaker always puts her House first.*

Run away with me, Wyn counters. *We could go anywhere, let's just get away from here. Burleigh's not the friend you think it is.*

Your father never told us where the deed's hidden, Mira adds. *The only ones who know that secret now are the king and Burleigh House itself.*

I watch as the remembered versions of Papa and me reach the eaves of the forest and vanish among the trees. Then it strikes me like a bolt of lightning.

My father knew where the deed was.

Burleigh likely still knows it.

And while Burleigh can't let me speak of the deed without destroying pieces of itself, it can show me memories of my father. Of what he said, what he discovered, where he planned to go.

Blood and mortar. I think I know how I'm going to save my House.

Jed comes home at sundown, tired but pleased to have been offered a place day laboring at Longhill Farm, not far from Burleigh House. We all eat our supper at the staff table and are uncomfortably quiet—I suppose no one wants another row. I can hardly wait to excuse myself, pleading lingering exhaustion after our long days of travel.

No one mentions the king's visit to Jed, and I'm glad of that. I don't need him deciding it'd be better to whisk me back to the fens, not now I've finally got a plan.

When I leave the kitchen, Jed's whittling morosely and Mira and Wyn are at the washbasin, cleaning up the dishes. It isn't that I don't want to help—I do, and I think tomorrow I'd better go out and find a way to earn my keep—but my time tonight will be best spent on Burleigh.

Stopping in Papa's study, I scoop his enormous, leather-bound household ledger off the desk and tuck it under one arm. Then I carry on up to my room and shut the door firmly behind me. As I do, a friendly, violet-hued fire springs to life on the hearth. The wardrobe door swings open. The water in the pitcher on my washstand warms of its own accord and lets off a gentle curl of steam. It seems my new sense of purpose has lifted Burleigh's spirits, too.

Though I'm nearly vibrating with excitement at the prospect of doing something—*anything*—productive on Burleigh's behalf, I smile. You're right, House. I might as well be comfortable before I start poking around in your memories. Better for both of us, if I'm not too keyed up. So I wash with sweet-smelling soap and pull on clean nightclothes and a dressing gown. Not until I've finished that do I sit down cross-legged on the rug in front of the hearth and let out a trembling breath.

Spreading out Papa's ledger in front of me, I scan the pages. He wrote everything in here—the price of crops, the dates of repairs, the requests and troubles of tenant farms, where he traveled and when. The last is what I'm looking for.

I scan the pages. Most of his trips have a terse explanation next to them in the margins.

September 14th, 18XX: London for a fortnight. Home Council session.

February 20th, 18XX: Bristol for a week. Arranging shipment of local goods.

But some are a mystery.

October 3rd, 18XX: Poole.

April 25th, 18XX: Minehead.

August 17th, 18XX: Exmouth.

If I know my meticulous father, he couldn't resist the urge to record and document his illicit search for the deed. Here it is, spelled out in black and white. Just more trips on Burleigh's behalf—nothing truly noteworthy, unless you knew what he was up to. Then those journeys with no explanation read like a map.

Or at least, I hope to God they do.

I cannot ask Burleigh about the deed outright, for fear of pushing my beleaguered House so far it loses control of its pent-up magic. But Burleigh isn't bound to prevent talk of my father, and it certainly seems keen on remembering him. I'm not sure anyone's ever asked the House to remember something before—to dredge up a particular moment in its long and colorful history, and play it out once more.

I'm about to, though. I splay a hand across one of the ledger pages.

May 11th, 18XX: Tintagel, my father's handwriting proclaims in black ink.

"Burleigh?" I ask. "Do you remember anything about my father going to Tintagel the year I was seven? Can you show it to me, if you do?"

All I expect is conversations—I've never seen Burleigh remember something that took place off the grounds, and don't think it actually can. So I won't be able to watch Papa's excursions, but perhaps he said something of use before leaving or after returning home.

I wait. At first, nothing happens. No rippling ghosts appear from thin air. But then, everything goes suddenly and entirely dark. I wave a hand in front of my face and can't see a thing.

"Burleigh?" I repeat. My own voice sounds strange and muffled. Panic begins to rise in my throat. I can feel the House's attention churning restlessly around me, but there's no loss of control yet. No mortar seeping cold into my skin.

After a moment, the darkness begins to fade, replaced by the morning light of a grey and overcast day. An overwhelming wave of vertigo hits me as I see Papa's study, overlaid on top of my bedroom. Everything in it ripples and shimmers, until Burleigh's light-on-water memory seems like reality and the solid presence of my room like a mirage. I blink and squint until at last, my mind accepts this strange duality and settles into Burleigh's recollection even as my body remains cross-legged on the hearthrug.

The first person I see is Mama. Something in me twinges at the sight of her. She and Papa sit opposite each other on two armchairs drawn up by the study fire, but there might as well be a world between them. It's easy to see they're already at odds—she sits with her knees angled away, staring out a window. And Papa is withdrawn, closed off within himself, a map of the West Country spread out before him.

"I'll be off again next week," he says, after a long and agonizing silence.

Mama sighs. "And where are you going on the House's behalf this time, George?"

She keeps her eyes fixed on the dim sky and lush grass of the lawns outside, rendered a ghostly blue by Burleigh's memory.

Papa glances down at his map. "Tintagel first, I think. I'll carry on down the coast for a few days afterward, search everything between there and Port Isaac. It feels a bit like looking for a needle in a haystack, though, without anything more concrete to go on yet."

"Oh," Mama says, and the single word is cold as ice.

My hands involuntarily ball into fists at my sides. I hate dredging up my family's unhappiness. If it didn't serve a purpose, I would never raise these particular ghosts.

"Why don't you take the boy with you?" Mama says, and for the first time I notice Wyn. He's crouched under my father's desk with a blank book and a stub of pencil, sketching away.

Papa gives her a reproachful look. "Eloise, you know I can't."

Mama turns away from the window and her eyes are as cold as her voice. "I don't like having him here. You never should have brought him home with you."

"He won't be any trouble." There's almost a pleading note to Papa's words, and I fight the urge to stop my ears. "Mira will look after him, if you'd rather not."

"*Violet* will look after him and there will be nothing I can say to stop her," Mama answers. "She adores the boy, and I know you encourage her, but to what purpose, George? It'll end in heartbreak. Perhaps you're raising her to be a Caretaker, but she's not you. She doesn't give up the things she loves so easily."

"Eloise, please." Papa frowns at her. "He can hear you."

"Do I look as if I care?"

Mama gets to her feet and sweeps from the room.

"Wyn," Papa calls softly. "Come out, Wyn. I want to show you something."

Wyn scrambles out from his hiding place and approaches step by slow step, like a wild cat, or an anxious rabbit.

"Do you see this map?" Papa holds it up and Wyn nods. "This is the sea. And all along the coast there are caves. I'm going to search for treasure that's hidden in one of them."

"What sort of treasure?" small Wyn asks. "Gold? Diamonds?"

"Even better," Papa says. "Someday when I find it, I'll bring it home and show you, and I think you'll agree it's very nearly the most precious thing in the world."

Wyn's already lost interest in treasure, though.

"What—what does the sea look like?" He puts out a finger and traces Cornwall's coastline on the map. "Will I ever see it? Can I go with you?"

Papa's smile is sad. "It's very big, Wyn. And I hope someday you will see it, but I can't take you along this time."

A muffled thump sounds outside my bedroom door.

"Burleigh, stop," I hiss, not wanting Jed or Mira to have to see the reality of what I'm up to. It's bad enough they know I'm going after the deed—I might as well spare them having to think on it too often. Immediately, the House plunges me back into darkness and when my vision clears, there's only my room around me. The ghostly overlay of Burleigh's memory has gone.

I sit, waiting for a knock, but it never comes. So I get to my feet and peer out, only to find Wyn in the corridor. He's got a tattered blanket and moth-eaten pillow and is fussing about in the hall like a wolfhound bedding down for the night. For a moment, I can't quite reconcile the small boy I remember with who he's become. It's as disorienting as having Burleigh take over my reality.

"What are you doing?" I ask Wyn, unable to keep a disgruntled note from my voice.

"Don't worry about it," he says tersely. "I won't bother you."

"Wyn," I say again. "Answer the question. What are you doing?"

"Burleigh's restless about something," he says. It's true the House's attention is still bent on me as it continues to mull over the memory I asked for. "I don't want it getting upset and deciding you make an easy outlet for its magic again."

I bite my lip, not wanting to tell him that it's mostly my fault the House is restless. But Wyn bringing up mortar and magic reminds me of yet another of my manifold unanswered questions.

"That reminds me, I wanted to ask you about this afternoon," I say. Wyn gives me a sidelong look and settles down on the floor. He lies flat on his back and shuts his eyes. I crouch, because I feel ridiculous towering over him in my dressing gown. "What *was* that? You were working House magic, weren't you? I could feel it. But I didn't see a thing—not a bit of mortar under your skin. How is that possible?"

"I don't know," Wyn says without opening his eyes.

"Have you done it before?" I press.

"Mm. Loads of times."

"Loads of times?" I say in disbelief. "House magic's terribly dangerous. You know that—you shouldn't be doing it at all. Was this during the arrest?"

"Yes. Go to bed, Vi."

"I'm talking to you." I gnaw at a hangnail anxiously. "I just—I don't like it, Wyn. Not one bit. What if it's doing something to you that can't be seen or felt?"

He opens one eye and peers up at me. "Look, I only did House magic today because you started working it first. In fact, I was leaving Burleigh House. So can we not talk about this anymore? I'd like to go to sleep. You *ought* to go to sleep. And Burleigh needs to calm down."

Wyn says the last pointedly, at the walls and the listening air. Burleigh takes the high road, and doesn't respond.

I get to my feet and shake my head at Wyn, who turns over so that he's facing the wall.

"You don't have to sleep in the hallway, you know," I tell him. "I'm fine on my own."

"Well, I don't fit in the cupboard anymore," he mutters. "And I don't believe you."

Heaving a sigh, I retreat to the sanctuary of my own room and climb into bed, curling up on one side. I'm all mixed up, torn between elation over the progress Burleigh and I have made in only one night and discomfort over Wyn's presence outside my door. No, not his presence—the reason for it. I used to look after him, and now things seem to be the other way around. I don't like it. It makes me feel like a burden, and I've always hated to inconvenience anyone else.

And yet. There's something in me that rests easier, knowing Wyn is nearby. For almost a year after we moved to the fens, I'd wake in the middle of the night gasping, overwhelmed by an urge to look for him though I knew he was the length of the country away. If being with Burleigh feels like I'm home again, being with Wyn feels like I'm whole once more. He must feel it, too, at least a little. Why else would he have come back?

I stare at the closed door for what seems like a long time, thinking about getting up to open it. But before I can, I fall into a dark and dreamless sleep.

❧11❧

I DID NOT EXPECT TO BE OUT IN THE LANE, BRISKLY WALK-
ing away from Burleigh House after two days at home, and yet here
I am. Nothing's as I thought it would be. Not the House, with its
endless, all-encompassing pain, not Wyn, and certainly not me. I
expected some sort of instinct to take over and guide me once I got
home, letting me know exactly what Burleigh needs. It hasn't, and
so I fall back on what I know—that Burleigh likes to be looked
after in the ordinary way of houses. Paint and nails and plaster
always cheer it, but they also cost money, and I haven't got any. It's
not just Burleigh His Majesty owns—following Papa's arrest, the
Crown seized all his assets.

I need to earn, just like the rest of my odd little family. Jed's
already off to his farm labor. Mira's at her washbasin. And when I
left Burleigh, the sound of a saw was already ringing through halls,
meaning Wyn was busy, too. I'm no use at House repairs like Wyn's
clearly turned out to be, but I can keep him in supplies.

Anything to bolster Burleigh's flagging spirits.

Ripping a switch free from the hedgerow, I snap it at the

inoffensive bushes bordering the lane. Songbirds burst from the hedge in an outcry of feathers and wing their way across the fields. Watching them go sets guilt twisting in my belly. I don't know what a single one of them is called, while back on the fens, I could tell even a female reed bunting from a corn bunting on sight.

As I carry on down the lane toward the small village of Burleigh Halt, I look to the land with a Caretaker's eye, and don't like what I see. Suspiciously grey and stony leaves sprout in the hedgerows. Some of the sheep in the fields have a downcast way about them, their heads drooping and their sides rising and falling only with an effort. Half a dozen songbirds lie dead in the bottom of a ditch. Burleigh House is leaking magic and mortar into the countryside like gangrene, unable to hold back all of its festering power.

But I knew Burleigh was struggling before I came back. I doubt the king would ever have allowed me home otherwise. All I need is for my beleaguered House to hang on until I can find the deed. One day at a time, Burleigh my love. We'll take this one day at a time.

It's not just the House that's ailing this morning, though. I'm cold in spite of the warm weather, my legs weak as water and occasional chills running through me. It's the aftermath of the mortar, I know—Wyn may have managed to siphon some of it off, but he didn't get it all—and I think I'd better be discreet in how often I ask the House to show me its memories, in case I strike a nerve.

At last I round a bend in the lane and arrive at the little village of Burleigh Halt. There isn't much to it. Just a row of pretty stone houses lining the main street, a market square that's jammed with carts and wagons on Saturday mornings, a single shop that in the way of village vendors sells just about everything, and the Red Shilling.

After a moment's indecision, I walk through the tavern door.

Small windows make for a moody, dimly lit interior. Tables and booths litter the front room, and a Black woman with hair smoothed and pulled back in a tidy knot stands behind the counter, polishing glasses. My stomach's gone flighty with nerves at my sudden decision to come in here, but I walk up and perch on a stool in front of her. She crooks an eyebrow at me.

"Can I help you?"

"I hope so," I say. "I've only just arrived in town, and I'm looking for work."

The woman shakes her head. "In that case, no, I can't help. Try day labor, out on one of the bigger farms."

"Thought you might say so, but it was worth asking." I slide down off the stool. "Good day to you, ma'am."

I'm nearly at the door when she calls me back. "Girl. You look like you've been on the fens, judging by your clothes. I've got a brother out fen way."

"I lived outside Thiswick the last few years," I answer carefully. "Did some fishing, cut some thatch. Whatever would make me a bit of coin. I'm not proud, and I work hard."

I quell the urge to bite at a fingernail as I wait for her response.

"Oh, don't string her along, Frey," a strange voice says from a dim corner of the public room. I twist my head around and notice two figures I'd overlooked sitting in the shadows at a booth. There's a young man, dressed like a gentleman and impeccably tidy, but it was his companion who spoke in a girl's clear tones. She's all in black from head to toe, with her back to me.

"You know you're going to hire her," the girl says without turning around. "If only for a chance to say you had George Sterling's daughter in your employ."

Frey, the innkeeper, sets her glass and polishing rag down.

"So you're George's girl come home." There's no surprise behind the words, and I expect she knew all along. When I nod, she gives me an appraising look.

"You willing to fetch and carry? Wash and dry? I'll need you to be quick and sharp. The village lot think they're a cut above and don't like getting their hands dirty. There's no place here for you if you feel the same."

I step forward, eager to please. "I'll do anything you'll pay me for, and you won't hear a word of complaint."

She smiles and holds out a hand to shake. "Good girl. Your father would've liked that answer. I'm Frey, as her ladyship said."

I take Frey's proffered hand across the counter, and her grip is firm. "Vi. Pleased to make your acquaintance."

"Likewise. I'll need you for evenings, so your shift starts at three o'clock. That'll be your start time, every day but Sunday. And I'll want you to start today. Alright?"

I don't hesitate. "Of course. Thank you, ma'am."

Her smile broadens. "Not ma'am, just Frey. You can call that other one sitting over at the table *ma'am*. I've said all I need to, but I'm sure she's not finished with you yet."

"I am not a *ma'am*," the girl in the booth says, clearly disgruntled. I crane my neck, trying to get a look at her face, but she stays well within the shadows. "You make me sound like some hideous dowager with five grown children. Nothing could be further from the truth, isn't that so, Alfred?"

"Hm, what?" The young gentleman across the table from her glances up from the book propped in front of him and smiles. "Oh, of course. You're a pearl among women. A shining star. A veritable fountain of youth. Absolutely not a ma'am."

"Laying it on a bit thick, don't you think, Alfie?" the girl says fondly. "Frey, can we use the private dining room, and trust you'll see we're not interrupted?"

In answer, Frey tilts her head toward a doorway near the strange couple's table. I hesitate as Alfred gathers up his things and precedes us, a long-suffering stoop to his shoulders.

"Oh, come on," the girl says as I continue to hang back. "Frey's right here, and the kitchen staff are nearby. If I try to chloroform you, there are plenty of people about to hear you scream."

"I don't think that's how chloroform works," I answer dryly, but the girl doesn't respond. She simply waits for me to step into the room before her. Overcome by my own curiosity, I finally give way. I can hear the rustle of her skirts as she gets up from the table and I fight the urge to glance over one shoulder. If she doesn't want me to see who she is till we're alone, I'll wait for introductions.

The private dining room is done up far more expensively than the public room, with silver-grey damask wallpaper and a long, gleaming wood table. I'm so used to dropping off fish and clams at back doors that it seems exceedingly strange to have been in not one but two private rooms in the past month, although I hope this interlude will be less upsetting than the last one. Alfred's already settled himself back in at the head of the table, book open before him once more. The girl shuts the door behind me, and I turn, finally getting a look at her.

She's a good six inches shorter than I am, with a small round face. There's a hint of gold to her skin, like sand on a sunny day, and her eyes are deep brown, nearly black. Her hair is a mass of loose black curls bundled up on top of her head, and when she moves her hands, silver bangles make music at her wrists. I've seen her once before, and I'd know her anywhere.

"Get out of my way," I growl at Esperanza, Princess of Wales, heir to His Majesty's throne, as I make for the door to leave.

"Violet, stop." The princess stays steadfastly between me and the exit. I think wildly of knocking her down—surely she can't put up much of a fight, tiny thing that she is. "I want to help you."

"Oh, like your father helped mine into an early grave? Or like he just tried helping me into a forced marriage? No thank you. Move. Aside."

"Please." Esperanza clasps her hands together. "The king's sending someone else to keep an eye on you and Burleigh. Someone much worse. I wanted to warn you—"

"No, I don't think so, I can very plainly see he sent you, as you're standing right in front of me. Good day."

I try to edge past her and she glares, dark eyes blazing.

"What was your father, Violet Sterling?" Esperanza asks, and it's not a question but a command. She emphasizes my last name and I can feel myself grow more defiant.

"England's greatest Caretaker," I answer proudly. Everyone knew it, before Papa's arrest. Most people still know it now. How else did he and Burleigh manage to survive for seven years without a key? "No place ever prospered like the West Country while he looked after Burleigh. No one did their duty quite like him. The House came first, before king, before country, before his own life."

Esperanza leans a little closer. "So we agree it was more than odd then, that your father, the model Caretaker, should risk everything, but first and foremost, Burleigh's health and safety, on a chance at obtaining the House's deed? He's not the sort of man who'd do that for personal ambition, or the simple nobility of the goal. No, it must have been desperation instead."

Esperanza reaches out and pats the chair next to her. "Vi, he knew the truth—that Burleigh is failing. Dying. Whatever you want to call it. It's the only reason he was desperate enough to gamble on the House's freedom—because Burleigh's plight isn't the result of the House arrest. It was already sickening before it was forced to kill your father."

"I don't trust you," I tell Esperanza. She nods. "But I'm going to sit down."

The princess takes a sealed and yellowed envelope out of her reticule and hands it to me. "I know you've just got home and we've only just met, and it's an understatement to say you're on bad terms with my father. This must be difficult to hear from me and even harder to believe, but I really do want to help. And I know you don't trust me yet, but I think I know whose word you *will* trust."

I take the envelope reluctantly and break open the seal. With a little chill, I recognize the untidy scrawl that wanders across two pages of parchment. It's my father's script—I'd know it anywhere, and the faintest whiff of tobacco and starch and Burleigh House itself still clings to the pages. I'm run through by a sudden and childish longing to be at home with Papa's final words, sitting in the haven of my airing cupboard with Wyn as we used to when we were small. But Esperanza, Crown Princess of England, is watching me, so I smooth out the wrinkled pages and read.

Dear Violet,

You're still just a child as I write this, and perhaps I've kept too much from you, because I hate to burden you with the responsibilities I've been given. In my own way, I've tried to prepare you as best I know how, to look after Burleigh House when I'm gone. But I would keep that task from you for as long as possible. It has been my joy and my privilege to serve our House, Vi, but never for a day has it been easy.

The truth is that the Great Houses of England are in decline, sickening beneath the bindings they've been placed under. As best I understand it, the binding they've been placed under prevents them from ever really ridding themselves of all their magic. A Caretaker helps, to be sure, but can channel only so much of a House's power away. And as old magic lingers, it goes bad, tainting the rest of it, like poison in the blood.

Only the return of the deeds may restore the Houses' health. I say may because it is no sure thing, and all my efforts on Burleigh's behalf may be too little, too late. They call me a great Caretaker, but I am no greater than any other, and it took me far too long to see the truth, Violet. That in taking from the Great Houses and binding them to our purposes, we meddled with something we should not have, and perhaps signed their death warrant.

Should I fail to save Burleigh, it will someday fall to you to finish what I started. I know you love our House, Vi—I haven't only kept myself apart from you because the business of a Caretaker occupies me so often. Part of my reasoning for keeping a distance between us was so that you'd learn with your heart as well as your mind to put Burleigh first. Perhaps this was unkind, even cruel, of me. I've done many things for our House I would not have, under any other circumstances. Many things I'm not proud of. And I think, my dear, that if you do set both your heart and mind upon it, you will not just be a great Caretaker. You will eclipse me in every way, and do the things I could not do, be the person I could not be.

Things are coming to a head, and soon I will either succeed or fail in everything I have set my hand to. Jed and Mira will look after you, should I fare badly. There are precious few other people you can rely on—Frey at the Red Shilling, if you can win her over. The Westons and Sterlings have worked alongside each other for centuries, and it's a tie their family won't throw over lightly. I've asked Bertie Weston, a colleague of mine, to take you in should you find yourself without a home. Queen Isabella is a friend, too, and one I'd trust with your life. Beyond that, look to yourself, Vi, and our House.

I'm sorry I couldn't stay with you. You're my very heart and soul. But I am a Caretaker, and I pray I've taught you well what that means.

All my love,

Your father, George Sterling

PS Tell Wyn I'm forever grateful to him. Tell him it isn't enough, but it's all I have to offer.

When I glance up from the letter, having read through it twice, Esperanza and Alfred are both watching me.

"Where did you get this?" I ask.

"My family name is Weston," Alfred says.

I fix him with a narrow look. "Yes, the House showed me a memory of someone called Bertie. Your father, was he? And the letter says your family was to take me in if anything happened to Papa. What went wrong?"

Alfred shakes his head apologetically. "Yes, Albert Weston was my father. But he died not long after George was placed under House arrest. Heart failure. My mother couldn't bring herself to go through his things until several years after his death, and by then I was on the Continent. That letter only fell into my hands a month or two ago, along with instructions to give it to you if any trouble befell George and your House. I'd have found you and delivered it earlier if I'd known it existed."

"Well, better late than never, I suppose," I say, staring down at Papa's handwriting.

"Let me get you a raspberry tart," Esperanza offers. "It'll make you feel less grim. Alfie, would you mind?"

Alfred disappears and returns in a moment with plates of finger sandwiches and little sausage rolls and fruit tarts, which he sets out while Esperanza watches approvingly. He stops at her place last, and she catches his hand, pressing a kiss to his palm.

"Darling," Esperanza says. "I know you never thought you'd hear me say this, but I want you to talk about Great Houses."

Alfred gives her a dubious look. "Truly? What if I get carried away?"

"Well, I'll have to cut you off. But I have faith in you. Even you, Alfred Weston, can be concise."

I bite into a sausage roll, swallowing past a pained, empty feeling that's opened up in my chest since reading my father's words.

"Does he know a lot about the Great Houses?" I ask.

"He's literally writing the book on the subject." Esperanza carefully picks several blackberries off her fruit tart. "Vi, it's the most tedious thing I've ever heard. He's three volumes in and it's supposed to be eight when he's finished. I have him read it to me when I can't sleep."

"Yes, well, it's a scholarly work, Espie, not a novel," Alfred says dryly.

"That's how we met each other." The princess gives his hand a conciliatory pat. "While he was on the Continent, doing research among the ruins of the Great Houses that have failed there."

I frown. "I've never heard of any Great Houses on the Continent that failed."

"Unfortunately you have," Alfred says. "You just didn't know what you were hearing about at the time. Do you know where the first of Europe's Great Houses was bound?"

I shake my head.

"In the Italian countryside. At the foothills of a mountain named Vesuvius. They called the House Arx Oriens and made it a shrine, with an oracle in place of a Caretaker. Oriens had been bound for nearly five hundred years by the time it failed, causing the mountain to erupt. But Italy has many bound Shrine Houses now, and very few people will speak of the House that once stood outside Pompeii.

"There were others like Arx Oriens. Casa de Descans, in Catalonia, which failed in 1428 and caused an earthquake. The failure of the Dutch Zeelicht Landhuis in 1570 was followed by a tidal wave. Great Houses die as they live—with immense power."

My mind's already racing through everything I know of Europe and England's history.

"Things are different here, though," I say. "Everywhere else Houses were bound one at a time, usually a century or more apart."

"Exactly," Espie says, slicing one of her leftover berries in half with a scowl. "Nowhere's quite like England, where six Houses were bound in the span of a single year thanks to my ancestor William the Deedwinner. Five of those Houses still remain and are heading for failure due to their bindings, but Burleigh's going fastest. It's by far the oldest of the five, and the House arrest did so much additional damage, Burleigh must be dealt with first."

I press my lips together and hold my tongue. I'm inclined to believe these two, but that doesn't mean I've set aside all my suspicion. Let them share what they know and what they're planning—I'll keep my own scheming to myself.

"It would mean disaster on a national scale," Alfred says quietly. "Yorkshire's still a wasteland after an attempt to free Ripley Castle went badly and the House failed. Imagine that happening across the country. At this point, it's a matter of either freeing the Houses, or burning each of them and their mortar as they begin to fail. Espie's father favors the latter plan because it's less of a risk to the countryside, and means he can keep hold of the remaining Houses till the bitter end. He doesn't want to give up the control they allow him, you see."

There's a window nearby, in front of which a rhododendron blooms. Its crepe-like petals are luminous and unblighted, and all of this seems like a dark story meant to frighten wayward children.

"Don't fret about England," Esperanza says at last. "That isn't why we came to you, Vi. The thing is, I've got contacts and spies and money, and I'm optimistic we'll find the deeds, but . . ."

"But what?"

Esperanza looks down at her hands. "We want your help with unbinding Burleigh, obviously. No one knows the House better than you. But Burleigh's bound to destroy anyone who tries to set it free. All the Great Houses are. My forebearers were nothing if not very thorough in ensuring their power was protected. You remember what happened to Marianne Ingilby when she tried to free the Sixth House. And then there's the matter of getting to the heart of the House if you do find the deed. You know the old rhyme—*blood for an ending, mortar for a start, unmake a binding at your House's heart*. According to Alfred, only a Caretaker can find a House's heart. Burleigh doesn't have a Caretaker, though."

"Burleigh has me," I answer staunchly. "I'm its Caretaker. It doesn't want anyone else. And if Burleigh will let anybody into its secret heart, it'll be me. So if you want the House unbound, I'm the one to do it."

"Are you sure?" Esperanza asks. "It's very dangerous, Vi."

"Of course I'm sure," I say without a moment's hesitation. "But why are *you* doing this? The Houses are your birthright, and your future power. Why would you want to give that up?"

The princess's dark eyes soften. "I spent half of my childhood at Hampton Court, the royal family's Great House. You know what they're like, Vi—I loved that place with everything in me. But the king, my father—he would use the magic to keep the House in check. Would let its magic build, and build, until Hampton was beside itself, and only then would he do his duty as Caretaker. He said"—her mouth twists—"that it was important for the Houses to know we rule them, and not the other way around."

"Sounds like Uncle Edgar," I mutter.

Esperanza shakes her head, curling a stray lock of hair around one finger absently. "My father likes to hold both the deeds and the crown over my head, saying he'll disinherit me if I don't do what he wishes. As for my birthright, I spent eight years in a Great House, and every day and every night I felt its sadness through the floors and the walls, until I could not find a way to be glad."

I know the feeling. It is all too familiar, that burden of knowing your House is unhappy.

"I'm afraid, too," Esperanza admits. "There have been monarchs before, who intended to unbind the Houses. After taking the throne, they never made good on their promises. Power is a seductive thing, Violet."

"My father always said people don't give it up lightly," I reply.

Esperanza leans forward, and there's sincerity in her dark eyes and small, round face. "That's my fear. That while I feel for the Great Houses now, if once they were bound to me, I might refuse to give them up. So I want to see this done before I take the throne. And it starts with Burleigh, because Burleigh is running out of time. What do you say, then, Violet Sterling? Shall we join forces? Will you help us in this, or let us help you?"

Mira would be livid if she saw me gnawing indecisively at a

fingernail in front of the princess of Wales. Perhaps I'm signing my death warrant by trusting Espie. But after all of Jed and Mira and Wyn's reluctance to see me seek out the deed, it's heartening to find someone who will give me her absolute support.

"I don't know . . . ," I say, because while I have every intention of unbinding Burleigh, I'm still not sure of this princess.

"Espie," Alfred says quietly. "Tell her about your mother."

The corners of Esperanza's mouth turn in, and all the light leaves her eyes. "I don't like to talk about Mama, you know that, Alfred."

"I do. But you're sitting next to the one person in England who'll understand about her. Who knows what you're living with."

Esperanza turns to me, and her face is drawn and unhappy. "The thing is, do you know why my father, the king, sent my mother back to Spain, Vi?"

I frown. "I thought they didn't get on. It was a political match, and didn't go well, so she went home."

The princess shakes her head. "No. Papa sent my mother away because . . . she's dying. She couldn't bear to watch Hampton Court suffer, and since my father held the key and would not do his duty as a Caretaker, she began to do it for him. Or rather, she did it for the House. Mama worked House magic ten, perhaps twelve times. She would have worked more if my father hadn't sent her away. But she's been sickening ever since she left England, day by day, year by year. It is slow and ugly and painful. I'm so afraid to open every letter that comes from Spain, because I know it might bring the news that she's finally gone."

Esperanza falls silent. She takes the handkerchief Alfred offers her, but there are no tears swimming in her dark eyes.

I know why. You can't cry when you're waiting, when you're caught moving inevitably toward heartbreak. You can only watch it grow closer and steel yourself against the pain to come.

"How did you bear it?" Esperanza asks finally, and her voice is little more than a whisper. "How did you manage, Violet, while you were on the fens? Because sometimes I feel as if everything's frozen around me, and other times as if each day's gone in the blink of an eye."

I reach across the table on an impulse and take the princess's hand.

"I got by the same way I'm sure you're doing," I tell her. "I woke up each morning and just kept going. I found something to do. I knew it was what Papa would have wanted, more than anything else. For me to carry on. He never gave up, you see, not until the bitter end."

Esperanza nods. I squeeze her hand, and decide to take a leap of faith.

"We're in this together, then?" I ask.

The princess shuts her eyes for a moment. When she opens them, any trace of grief and fear has been carefully tucked away, replaced by a fierce determination. "We are indeed. Let's finish your father's treason. Confound the king. Unbind Burleigh House."

❊12❊

TWO IN THE MORNING HAS COME AND GONE BY THE TIME I make it home from my first shift at the Shilling. Wyn's asleep in the hall outside my bedroom, and there's a faint smell of sawdust and plaster as I slip past him. I bite back a smile. It's equal parts irritating and endearing that he's so convinced I need looking after. He turns over without waking, and I remember that about him—he's always been a restless sleeper.

Shutting myself up in my bedroom, I sink wearily into a chair next to the cold and empty hearth. A few sparks play among the waiting firewood and I shake my head.

"Don't, Burleigh. Save your strength—I want to talk to you."

A handful of white petals fall from the air and settle softly on my lap. I gather them up and hold them to my face, breathing in their honey-sweet fragrance.

"I met someone in town today," I tell the House. "The king's daughter. Have the two of you ever met before?"

A breeze rattles at the windows.

"Can you show me?"

This time, I'm prepared for the sudden darkness Burleigh draws around me like a curtain. When it fades, a watery version of the front entry has been superimposed over my bedroom.

Esperanza stands near the front door. There are brambles everywhere and mortar weeps from the window frames and the doorposts. I've never seen the House so—even in memory, a wave of its wild grief hits me.

"Oh, Burleigh," Esperanza says quietly. "I'm so sorry. You poor thing."

"Who are you?" Wyn's voice says from behind me, and he sounds as if Burleigh's agonized thorns and mortar run beneath his skin. I turn, and there he is, just coming down the last stair from the second floor. There's an ill look about him—he's winter-pale, and shadows like bruises spread below his eyes.

"I'm the princess of Wales," she says. "Esperanza will do. And you must be Wyn."

He scowls at her. "Did you come to gloat over your father's handiwork?"

"No," Esperanza answers, her voice still low, as if she's speaking to some frightened, feral creature. And truly, Wyn seems ready to bolt or lash out at any moment. He's filthy and ragged, fists clenched at his sides, something dark and broken in his eyes. My heart aches fiercely at the sight, and I press a hand to my chest.

"I'm here to look after George's remains, if they haven't been seen to yet," Esperanza continues. "I've brought gravediggers, and a coffin. I know no one likes to think about that side of things, but it has to be done."

For a moment, I think Wyn will snap at her, and refuse the offer of help. But then his shoulders slump.

"I just left him, and shut the door," he admits. "I couldn't . . ."

Esperanza steps forward and rests a gloved hand on Wyn's arm. "No one expected you to. That's why I've come."

A booted step rings in the hall, and a gentleman appears from the maze of Burleigh's corridors. He's dressed in riding clothes, his profile severe, and he looks old enough to be my father.

"Esperanza," the gentleman says sharply. "Who is this mongrel?"

She flinches at the man's words, but Wyn stays motionless.

"This is Haelwyn of Taunton, Lord Falmouth," Esperanza answers. "The boy who stayed behind with George Sterling. We're just making funeral arrangements."

Falmouth's mouth draws down into a frown. "You mean the body hasn't been dealt with yet? They're practically barbarians, these West Country rustics. Don't spend too long on it, Esperanza—I'll expect you for dinner at the Green Lion in Taunton."

He steps outside and shuts the front door behind him, still grumbling under his breath as he goes. Esperanza turns back to Wyn.

"If you don't mind, I'll have my men come in and sort things out." It's not so much a statement as a question, and Wyn nods. He's about to head up the stairs once more when Espie stops him.

"Wait," she says, her voice soft with pity. "Can I find you a room in Burleigh Halt, or Taunton perhaps? I'll pay up front for as long you'd like to stay—a few weeks, half a year even. And leave some money for personal effects, a new wardrobe. You ought to have a fresh start after this."

Wyn fixes her with a long and searching look.

"No," he says at last. "I'm staying here. I promised George I would, till Violet gets back."

"It's been a long time." If Esperanza's voice was gentle before, it's a whisper now. "She might—she might not come."

"You don't know Violet. She'll come," Wyn says with absolute certainty, and starts up the stairs.

Darkness folds around me as the memory fades. Only once it's gone do I hear a faint knocking at the door.

"Vi, are you alright in there?" Wyn's voice is rough with sleep. I get up at once, crossing the room and opening the door for him. He stands on the threshold in a nightshirt and loose linen trousers, blinking like a peevish owl. "I could hear myself talking. Bit of an unnerving way to wake up. Is Burleigh behaving?"

"It was remembering something," I say quickly, to hide the fierce wave of relief that hits me at the sight of Wyn's present self. I'm overcome by a sudden and irrational urge to stuff him into my airing cupboard in the hope that nothing dreadful will ever happen to him again. "I asked it to."

Wyn shuts his mouth, swallowing a yawn. "You *asked* it to?"

I suppose it's time to come clean. "Yes. That's how I'm hoping to find the deed. Mira said both Burleigh and Papa knew where it was, so instead of asking about it outright, I'm looking through Papa's ledger for hints as to where he'd gone looking for it, and then asking the House if it remembers anything coming up in conversation about those journeys. It's easier on Burleigh."

The floor rumbles under our feet, but no House magic nips at me. I watch as the last remnants of sleep-dullness vanish from Wyn's eyes.

"That's very clever, Violet," he says. "And it's working?"

I shrug. "So far. That's what I'm doing now. I just wish I knew this isn't a fool's errand, though—who's to say the king hasn't moved Burleigh's deed since Papa found where he'd hidden it?"

Three things happen at once as I ask the question. Everything goes dark. The crushing weight of the House's full attention fixes on us. And mortar freezes my fingertips.

"Oh, Burleigh, no," I beg. "I wasn't asking you to show me anything, I was just wondering out loud."

But the House, eager to please now it's found a way to communicate with me, plunges us into a wavering version of Papa's study. The only solid things in the world are Wyn and me.

"Vi, give me your hands," Wyn says, sounding half panicked.

"Not yet," I say, and step forward, because my father is sitting in one of the study's wingback chairs, with shackles around his ankles. It must be the night before his House arrest began—the traveling court arrived at midmorning, and Papa had been found guilty of treason by early afternoon. Now all that remains is for His Majesty to carry out the sentence.

A few days' stubble shadows my father's jaw and there's a pale, haggard look about him. I cross this ghostly version of the study, barely noticing the silent guards standing by the door.

"Papa," I whisper, kneeling at his side. "I'm here. Look at me."

But he can't hear a word I say. That is, perhaps, the cruelest cut of all—knowing my father can be remembered so perfectly by the House, yet never live again. I will never have a chance to tell him what I couldn't the day I left—that I loved him. That he was, in spite of the distance between us, everything I've ever wanted to be.

"A game, George?" the king's laconic voice asks, and it's only then that I notice him sitting in the shadows behind Papa's desk. "Something to while away the hours until dawn, and the beginning of your sentence?"

My father says nothing, only keeps his eyes fixed on the floor, and the spark of fear in his gaze puts a dreadful tightness in my throat, even as mortar creeps through my veins.

The king sits forward. Lamplight picks out the lean contours of his face. "Perhaps you need the right stakes to stir your enthusiasm. We could play for . . . your freedom?"

When Papa glances up, there's vain hope written across every line of him.

"Don't let him bait you," I say, tears pricking at my eyes.

"Vi, *please*." Wyn's two steps behind me, holding out his hands. "Don't let Burleigh hurt you."

"You and Violet," the king offers my father, "safe together on a ship to anywhere you'd like to go, so long as you leave England behind. I can't very well have a treasonous Caretaker running around the island, now can I? But you could make a new life for yourself and your daughter."

Papa nods. "Deal the cards."

They play écarté, as there's only two of them, and my heart sinks. It's never been Papa's best game. The Sterlings have always been stronger on sacrifice than strategy. But Papa's attention is fixed on the game and he takes several tricks when the king's focus drifts. I can't look away, even as I feel Wyn take my hands in his own, and the mortar running into me turns toward him.

And then, though I can hardly credit it, my father has won. He looks down at the cards with the same disbelief I feel.

"Well, there you have it." The king is genial, as if he'd just lost a sovereign or a meaningless trinket. "We'll pack you up come morning light and get you to a port. Where will it be? Spain? Portugal? Or Sweden, perhaps. Hot or cold?"

Papa hesitates. The fire crackling in the grate flares blue, the way it always did for him. His shoulders droop.

"Once more," he rasps. "For a pardon. So Violet and I can stay with Burleigh."

His Majesty's face remains carefully neutral, but I know him, the devil, and the way his attention suddenly fixes on my father when before it seemed to wander can mean only one thing.

He knew their game would come to this. He knew George Sterling could never resist grasping at any straw that might let us remain with our House.

"Are you certain, George?" the king asks, and the feigned kindness in his voice is like splinters inside me. I hate him worse than anyone else in all this world, I think. Most wicked men are at least straightforward—unwieldy clubs that bludgeon you with their ill will and brute strength. But His Majesty the king is a dagger in the night, wielded with a smile.

From that point on it's like watching a cat toy with its prey, as the king languidly lets Papa take a few tricks before soundly beating him. My father just sits afterward. He's very quiet, and when I look down, his hands are trembling.

I glance over at Wyn beside me, too. He seems alright, but that vacant look I saw last time he did House magic has clouded his eyes. I gnaw at my lower lip, torn between wanting to end this memory for Wyn's sake, and needing to see it through till the end.

"Burleigh, are you sure about showing me this?" I whisper. A wave of insistence hits me. "Very well, but *hurry*, please."

"I would have let you go, if you hadn't wanted what isn't yours," the king tells Papa. "I'm good for my word, and we both know it."

"Yet I am who I am, and we both know that as well," Papa answers. "I can never help but try for this House."

His Majesty holds out his hand. "The key, if you will, George. They call me a game player, but you're the one who staked what you most value on something larger, only to lose in the end. Pity about that. I thought you might actually get the best of me and unbind the old place."

Papa pulls the Caretaker's key from his pocket and looks down at it. The greyish-brown bowstone gleams dully in the firelight. At last he surrenders it to the king, and a great, muttering groan of stone and timber rises from the House.

I can feel Burleigh's bereavement, even in memory, creeping through the soles of my feet and into my lungs with the air I breathe. Though my father still sits across from the king, the House knows—this is the beginning of the end.

From our present time I sense Burleigh struggling to see the memory through to its conclusion. The force of its attention is oppressive, and Wyn's eyes aren't just blank now, they're opaque and grey, marked by the mortar that doesn't show beneath his skin. I can't stand to see him so.

"Burleigh, that's enough!" I snap, but the House pays me no mind, pushing through to the end of this memory.

"I'm curious, George—how far did you get?" His Majesty asks offhandedly. "How close did you actually come to laying hold of the deed?"

"I stood exactly where Falmouth told me to," Papa says, and his eyes never leave the key. "And I couldn't find it. But I suppose, if Falmouth played me false, you sent me on a fool's errand in the first place."

"No." The king toys with the key, passing it from hand to hand, and the bowstone glimmers as it moves. "Joss Falmouth may be loyal to the crown, but he told you the deed's location. You were an arm's length from your heart's desire, George, and didn't have the wit to find it."

Papa says nothing. He tears his gaze away from the key and fixes it on the floor, as the king leans forward with an infuriating smile.

"Do you know how little you've truly accomplished?" His Majesty asks my father. "Nothing's changed for the better because of you, George. I don't even plan to move the deed—it's safe enough where it is. And your House is worse off having had you as a Caretaker than it was when you took charge."

Pitch-colored brambles snake up the arms of the king's chair, crumbling in places and weeping mortar. They're not part of the memory, though—they're a piece of my present time. The House trembles, an earth-deep sense of unease, of anguish, and darkness falls.

When it clears, I'm sitting on the rug in my room. Blighted vines tangle around my crossed legs, and around Wyn's, but he has his hands to the floor and his eyes are still that unseeing grey. Sweat beads on his forehead and his mouth moves soundlessly. I wait, jittering with nerves and impatience, until I feel the House's attention finally shift away from us. Even as the sickly vines loosen and burst into radiant flowers, and a rain of petals falls from the ceiling, I snatch Wyn's hands and chafe them between both of my own.

"That's enough," I tell him. "You can stop now."

Wyn's mouth moves, near soundlessly, and I lean forward to try and catch what it is he's saying over and over.

Blood in the mortar. Breath in the walls. Blood in the mortar. Breath in the walls.

It gives me an unpleasant, creeping sensation, hearing him speak the words when the rest of him seems to have gone somewhere else entirely.

"Wyn," I whisper. "Haelwyn of Taunton, come back to me."

He blinks. Suddenly he's there again, within himself once more. I draw in a shaking breath and throw my arms around him, because fear has turned my heart to a wild thing.

"I'm sorry, I'm so sorry," I tell Wyn. "I didn't mean for that to happen."

"It's alright," he says, the words warm and comforting. "No harm done. And better me than you, eh?"

"No." I shake my head. "Not better."

I let go of him and sit back, pressing both hands to my face. They're pink-skinned and perfect, no trace of the mortar Wyn drew out of me left behind.

"Wyn, I'm afraid," I tell him.

"Of what?" he asks.

"I don't know." There are too many things to name, and I can't bring myself to say that I'm afraid of Burleigh House. Afraid of its magic, afraid of its power, afraid of its future without a proper Caretaker.

"I'll meet you on the roof," Wyn says practically. "Bring up some blankets. I'll go fix us a flask of tea."

It's cold outside, at the top of my world in the silent, empty hour before dawn. I wrap a woolen blanket around my shoulders and shiver, but the stars are already working their own particular magic. The fear that endlessly swims in my veins is calmer, quieter, and I can think past it.

There's a little whine of hinges as the attic window swings open and Wyn scrambles out onto the slate tiles.

"Here." He hands me a warm flask of tea and settles in, so that we're side by side with our backs to the brick chimney. I steal a glance at him, and I can almost see who he was, his child-self super-imposed over this sullen, half-familiar boy, like one of Burleigh's memories.

"Well then," Wyn says with the ghost of a smile. "What seems to be the problem, Violet Sterling?"

I'm not even sure I know. I just feel, by turns, like the only person who can possibly save Burleigh, and like I'm abjectly, woefully inadequate for the job. But instead, what comes out of my mouth is this:

"*You're* the problem," I answer, wrinkling my nose. "What are you doing with the House magic, Wyn? I don't like it—it's danger-ous, and I don't want you getting hurt."

I pass him the flask, and he takes a mouthful of tea before answering.

"Would you believe me if I said I know exactly what I'm doing?"

"Oh, I believe you," I answer. "But knowing what you're doing and not deliberately putting yourself in harm's way are two entirely different things."

"Canny," Wyn says with a shake of his head. "Just like you've always been. A canny and relentless creature."

I reclaim the flask and frown. "Don't change the subject. I'm serious."

Wyn looks out across the grounds, and the shadowy smudge of the back woods. His eyes are very far away—not vacant, as when he works House magic, but distant, seeing something I can't.

"I'll promise you this," he says. "I won't touch Burleigh's magic unless it's losing control and channeling mortar into you. But I won't promise more than that, don't ask me to."

"I can—" I begin, and he raises a hand, cutting me off.

"Do you have to make me say it, Vi?" Frustration laces Wyn's words. "It would *ruin* me to watch another Sterling die for this House. To watch you die. I need you to let me help."

I don't want to agree. I want to forbid him to ever meddle with Burleigh's magic again, because I've felt it inside me and seen what it did to my father. I hate the idea of mortar touching Wyn, much as I love Burleigh and would do anything in my power to save it.

The House itself is oddly quiet in the wake of remembering Papa's last night and funneling magic into Wyn. A faint breeze tangles in my hair. Little marsh lights flicker between the trees in the forest. That's all, though—no vines, no petals, no wind in the chimney to whisper Burleigh's unspoken words.

Poor voiceless House. What am I for in this life, if not to speak on your behalf?

"I'm sorry," I tell Wyn, though I feel caught between him and Burleigh. "And I can live with that, if you can. But I wish you'd be more straightforward with me. I wish you'd tell me the truth about all this."

"I want to," Wyn says. "And I will. I swear, Violet, I just—have to find the right words."

"Where do you *go* when you work the magic? Because it's like you've left yourself behind. Am I allowed to ask that?"

Wyn turns away from the horizon and gives me a puzzled look.

"I don't know. It's like walking down a corridor that's endlessly long. It has no start and no end, and all the doors are shut. But when I open them, there's nothing behind them."

"Nothing? You mean the rooms are empty?"

"No." A worried crease forms between his eyebrows as he tries to explain. "There are no rooms. I open the doors and there's nothing. No darkness, no floors, no ceilings, no walls. Just—nothing. I don't know, I'm not explaining very well, am I?"

A shiver runs through me, from the crown of my head to the base of my spine. "No, but it sounds terrifying."

"Maybe it was at first, but I'm used to it now."

"Wyn?" I say.

"Violet?"

I swallow. The words I'm about to speak rest dry and sharp-edged in my throat. "I think you should go away after all. Away from Burleigh House, I mean. It isn't safe here."

"Are you going?"

I bite anxiously at one already mangled fingernail. "You know I can't."

"Then I can't, either. I thought I could, but I can't."

The sky out beyond the back woods is flushing pink behind the trees and Wyn shuts his eyes.

"What did you do while you were on the fens, Vi?" he asks, and there's something a little desperate in his voice. "Tell me about it."

"I went fishing every day," I say with a smile. "Not with a pole like we used in the stream, but with nets and spears. I dug for clams and cut peat and thatch with Jed. I salted fish with Mira and learned to make ginger biscuits when it stormed. Or at least, she tried to teach me to make ginger biscuits, but I was never very good at it."

Wyn laughs. "She tried to teach me to make ginger biscuits before all of you left, but I wasn't any good at it, either."

"What did you do while I was gone?" I ask. "Not the bad things, just the ordinary ones."

"Fixed up the House. Read some books. Grew parsnips," Wyn says. "We were alright the first few years—the House kept the gardens going for us, but the last couple they needed a great deal of coaxing. Almost everything failed except the parsnips."

"Oh dear," I say. "You never really liked parsnips."

Wyn opens his eyes and looks at me wryly. "I hate them now."

I bite my lip in an attempt to keep a straight face, but can't quite manage it.

"It's alright," Wyn says. "It is a bit funny. Of all the things, it had to be parsnips."

The first few rays of sunlight spill over the trees and across Wyn's face. For a moment I'm breathless, because I know him. I know that half-bashful, quietly pleased expression. Without thinking, I reach out and put a finger to his chin, just as I would have done when we were children.

"Hello," I say. "I recognize you."

Burleigh rumbles ominously beneath us, and at once, Wyn's face grows severe and closed off again.

"I've got work to do downstairs," he mutters, and with a clatter of tiles, disappears back into the House.

❧13❧

"AND THEN I SAYS TO HIM I SAYS, WHERE'LL I FIND A RAM to cover the flock at this time of year?"

I will admit, I'm not listening to a word Old John Howard has to say as I hurry back and forth behind the counter at the Shilling, pulling pints and setting them down before uncommonly thirsty county folk. To begin with, there's the matter of my head, which is spinning after missing a night of sleep out on the roof with Wyn. And—well, that's the end of it. I'm worn to tatters, and everything around me is a blur.

"George Sterling's girl! Another round over here!"

Heaving a sigh, I grab a tray and fill it with mugs, edging my way across the room to a table where half a dozen tenant farmers are playing at dice. Esperanza and Alfred are in a booth up against the wall, sitting side by side rather than opposite one another, and poring over stacks of old documents. I don't know how they can possibly think with all the noise down here, but neither of them seems to mind.

The thought of Wyn and his strange way of working House

magic is still plaguing me, like the beginnings of a headache I'm pushing through but can't quite shake, so I stop at Alfred and Espie's table for a moment.

"Any progress?" I ask.

Alfred squints up at me. "Hm. Not particularly."

Esperanza drops her chin onto one hand and gives me a pleading look. "Violet, I'm bored. This is so dull. Save me. I'm worlds better at digging up information by flirting at parties."

"Just be a little more methodical," Alfred suggests. "When you find references to—"

"No." Esperanza holds a finger to his lips, shaking her head. "No, Alfred. We're not all librarians at heart."

"You can wait tables if you're really that bored," I tell Espie. "We could certainly use the help."

She brightens considerably at the suggestion until Alfred puts a warning hand on her sleeve. "Espie. Darling. You're the princess of Wales. If you start serving ale in a backwater inn, it'll be front page news across England by the day after tomorrow and then your father will come down to lecture you. Is that really what you want?"

Esperanza slumps, defeated. "No, you're right. Sorry, Vi."

"It's fine. But I wanted to ask Alfred something."

Alfred takes off his spectacles and tucks them into his breast pocket, looking up at me. "I'm entirely at your disposal."

"Another pint, George Sterling's girl!" someone shouts from the counter. I pointedly ignore them.

"Have you ever heard of a person working House magic without a key, but it doesn't cause them any harm? Or perhaps it does but it starts with their mind rather than their body?" I ask.

Espie sits bolt upright. "Violet Sterling, are you doing things at Burleigh House that you shouldn't? I swear, if you're working House magic, I'll strangle you with my best jet beads; you know how dangerous that is."

"No," I say quickly. "Or at least, not on purpose. A little by accident, but that's all."

"It doesn't ring any bells, but I'll take a look," Alfred promises.

I turn aside to head back to the counter but the door swings open and a party of travelers strides in. There's a gentleman and two liveried menservants, and one of the servants goes at once to the counter to have a private word with Frey. In the heat of the common room, the gentleman sheds his long riding coat and holds it out to me.

"Here, tavern girl. Take this for me and see it's kept somewhere safe."

He looks familiar. There's something niggling at the back of my mind, half memory, half warning. And then I glance at Alfred and Espie.

Alfred's gone, vanished like smoke on a windy day. I catch sight of him at the edge of my vision, suddenly tucked in among the dice-playing farmers at a nearby table. Esperanza, meanwhile, is pale beneath the golden hue of her skin, a fixed smile on her face.

The gentleman walks over to her at once, and Espie holds out a hand.

"Lord Falmouth," she says as he kisses her offered fingertips. "What a surprise. I wasn't expecting you till next week. Papa said you were in Bournemouth, or somewhere, and that you couldn't possibly be here till June to keep an eye on things."

"I left early," Falmouth says, his voice low and gravelly as he slides into the booth across from Espie. I dislike him at once. It's Falmouth who blew a hole in Burleigh's wall, Falmouth who spoke so dismissively of Wyn in Burleigh's memory. What's more, he's looking at Esperanza as if she's a frosted cake and he hasn't eaten since morning.

I step closer to the table and look pointedly at the princess, letting my voice go decidedly West Country. "Is there anything I can get for you, Miss? Another cup of tea, perhaps?"

A muzzle for the wolf who just walked in?

Espie gathers up the papers she and Alfred were looking over and hands them to me. "Just take those upstairs, won't you?"

I drop a curtsy for good measure. "If you need anything, Miss, I'll be over at the counter. Just give a shout."

"I meant it when I said be careful with the coat," Falmouth warns me. "It had better make it up to my room without incident or I'll take its worth out of you."

"Are we having a problem over here? I'm the proprietress of the Shilling, and if there's trouble, I'm the one who ought to know about it," Frey says smoothly, appearing out of the ether. She gives Falmouth a thin smile—the sort I already know she reserves for patrons who are bad news.

"None at all," Falmouth says. "I was just asking your serving girl to take extra care with my things."

"Go on then." Frey gives me a look and jerks her head toward the stairs. "I'll take care of these gentlefolk tonight."

Falmouth's footmen are already arranging things in one of the private rooms upstairs. They start like frightened rabbits when I enter the room.

"It's not him, it's just me," I say.

One of them takes the coat and I carry on to Alfred and Esperanza's room. Alfred's abandoned the dice players and is inside already, looking peaked and sitting on the edge of the bed with his head in his hands.

"What the hell is going on?" I ask. "Who's Falmouth to Esperanza? Who are you to Esperanza, for that matter? Why did you run off like that, and what are you doing up here?"

"I'm nobly hiding," Alfred says. "Falmouth is Espie's fiancé. They've been engaged for years, ever since her fifteenth birthday. As for what I am, I think she'd better tell you that herself. I'll take those papers, though."

I hand them over and head back downstairs, rolling my eyes as I go. Nobility and their entanglements. It's like a Gothic novel in the West Country these days, between Burleigh and the princess and her assorted lovers.

At least I'm awake now.

Frey positively hovers over Esperanza and Falmouth for the rest of the evening, leaving me to man the counter and listen to John Howard's litany of wrongs done unto him. It's past midnight by the time Falmouth retreats to the private gaming room and Espie goes slowly up the stairs.

"Can I take five minutes?" I ask Frey as she joins me.

She eyes the common room, which is starting to empty out. "Yes, but be quick about it. I've got tables for you to clear up."

I slip up the stairs in Esperanza's wake and knock softly at her door.

"Come in," she says, her voice muffled.

Espie's lying on her side on the bed, her head on Alfred's lap, but when I shut the door behind me, she sits up and wipes at her eyes with the back of one hand.

"Hello, Violet."

"Should I go?" I ask. "I just wanted to make sure you're alright, not to intrude."

"No, it's fine. And thank you."

"So," I begin, a little awkwardly. "You're engaged to Lord Falmouth?"

Esperanza rolls her eyes. "I am, in a manner of speaking."

"Your father seems to like forcing girls into unwanted marriages," I say. "Are we the only ones he's tried it with, or does he do it often?"

This time, Esperanza pulls a face. "He's always matchmaking. He likes controlling people—we're just game pieces to him."

"You'll find a way out of it, though, won't you?" I ask, shifting my weight anxiously from one foot to the other. "That Falmouth, he's . . ."

"An absolute brute," Esperanza says. "The fact that he's here to keep an eye on things will be nothing but trouble for you and Burleigh House, Vi. I'm going to see if I can convince him that Burleigh Halt's too much of a backwater for him to stay more than a night. At least if he lodges in Taunton, you'll have a little space. And God forbid he find out anything about Alfred. That conversation's meant to happen in public, in front of my father, not out here with no witnesses, or it'll be pistols at dawn and widow's weeds for me."

I open my mouth and shut it. "I'm sorry, did you say widow's weeds?"

"I did." Esperanza beams. "Alfie's my trump card. We were married in secret last year at Spanish court, in front of several unassailably credible witnesses. At first it was just convenience for me—Alfie said he'd do it, and that I could divorce him once I'm queen if I liked. But then I started to like him. He's just so decent, you know? Now I quite worship the ground he walks on."

Esperanza kisses the tip of Alfred's nose, and he goes bright red, rather flustered by his flamboyant, affectionate bride.

"I adored her from the start, of course," Alfred admits. "But we both decided it would be best to keep this quiet and let Falmouth continue to believe she'll marry him. No one's more in the king's confidence, and Espie hopes to get information out of him, about the deeds."

Looking at the two of them sitting tucked together on the bed, I decide all at once that it's time to lay my suspicions to rest.

"So you're working on Falmouth, and have contacts at court, and Alfred's looking into the history of the Houses to see if he can find anything useful there?" I ask.

"Exactly so. Pass me that box of chocolate creams?" Esperanza points to a gold foil box on the chifforobe. I hand it to her and she pops one into her mouth.

"I can help," I say. Time for some honesty. "My father knew where Burleigh's deed was, and I think the House still knows. I can't ask Burleigh outright, though—the binding would wreak havoc on it if I did. So I'm using Papa's ledger as a guide, to watch old memories that might point us in the right direction."

"Oh, well done, you." Esperanza holds the chocolate box out to me. "Have one, you quite deserve it."

"No, I can't," I say with a shake of my head. "I've stayed far too long already, Frey's waiting for me."

But I stop at the door and turn. "Espie? Thank you for being kind to Wyn, when you were at the House after the arrest ended. The House showed me."

She's got her head on Alfred's shoulder, and smiles at me. "Of course, darling. I can't abide to see a suffering creature, and that boy certainly suffered. But he's got a great deal of faith in you."

"More than I deserve, I think."

Esperanza's smile broadens. "Doubtful."

The last I see of them as I shut the door is Esperanza popping a chocolate cream into Alfred's mouth as he tries to carry on with his reading, a look of bemused resignation on his face.

14

I DREAM OF ENGLAND'S INFAMOUS SIXTH HOUSE. OR rather, of the night Mama told me about the Sixth House for the very first time.

In sleep, my memories take on the same watery cast as Burleigh's. I lie tucked up in bed, not Little Vi but my own self, tall and leggy and nearly grown. Mama smooths the hair back from my forehead and I look past her, to the airing cupboard door. It's been left ajar. Wyn must be listening from his secret retreat.

"Tell me a story," I beg Mama, and though my body may be the one I've grown into, my voice is still a child's. "Papa always tells me a story if he's at home. Where did he go this time?"

"A castle by the sea," Mama says. She puts a cup of honeyed milk in my hands and I sip at it. "Shall I tell you a story about a castle?"

"Yes, please," I answer.

"Once upon a time, there was a Great House called Ripley Castle."

Mama's voice sounds very far away. Burleigh's evening rain begins as she speaks, drumming against the roof, running down the windows.

"Is this a made-up story, Mama?" I ask. "There are only five Houses. Burleigh, Hampton Court, the Tower of London, Salisbury Cathedral, and Plas Newydd, though they've sometimes changed their shapes and their names. You see, I've been studying."

"You're very clever," my mother says. "But once there were six Houses, and they called Ripley Castle the Sixth House. Ripley—"

"What happened to it?" I interrupt.

Mama wrinkles her nose at me. "I'm getting to that, if you'll just listen."

"Sorry." I sink further into bed and pull the covers up to my shoulders. "I'll be quiet."

"Ripley Castle was very much like Burleigh House. A family called Ingilby looked after it. Just as the Sterlings have been at Burleigh for a very long time, the Ingilbys had been at Ripley for hundreds of years."

I listen, wide-eyed. There's nothing I love better than stories of the Great Houses.

"Before you were born, there was a girl who lived at Ripley Castle—Marianne Ingilby—and when her father died unexpectedly just after the girl's eighteenth birthday, she wanted to become Caretaker in his stead. She wanted it and Ripley Castle wanted it, but your uncle Edgar did not."

"Why not?" I ask, sipping my milk.

A frown mars Mama's beautiful face. "Who knows with your uncle Edgar? But he is the king, and he wanted to give Ripley Castle as a prize to one of his noblemen. Marianne hated the idea. The House hated the idea, too, and chafed against its bindings, refusing to accept the king's chosen Caretaker."

I lie with my hands laced together under my chin, enthralled. All of Papa's stories contain a moment of darkness or an instant of despair, when it seems all will be lost. But then comes the turning point, when House and Caretaker work together in perfect unison, two souls with one purpose, and save the day. I'm sure Mama's will be the same.

"It broke Marianne Ingilby's heart to see her House in distress," my mother continues. She reaches out and runs a gentle hand over my hair. "And she trusted Ripley Castle more than anything else in this world. So she did what no one had yet dared to. She stole the deed to her House, and tried to set it free."

Outside, there is a sinuous, rustling sound along the walls. Ivy, newly grown, begins to tap-tap at the windows. Green sparks snap from the fire.

"You won't have heard this story yet, Violet. It's something your father doesn't like spoken of here. But secretly, he hopes to follow in Marianne's footsteps, and to try to set Burleigh free. It's a dangerous undertaking, though—in order to set a Great House free, you must take its deed to the House's heart, and there unbind it with blood and mortar, as it was bound."

"Why should that be dangerous?" I ask. Outside, the ivy is waving at me, creeping across the window glass.

Behind Mama, the door to the airing cupboard swings open another few inches. Wyn's face is pale in the gloom—he's his child-self in this dream, not the Wyn I've come to know, and even in sleep I feel a stab of disappointment.

"Vi, I know your father loves Burleigh House more than anything," Mama says, and I ignore the hint of bitterness in her voice.

"I know he's teaching you to love it, too. But every House, no matter how biddable it may seem—no matter how devoted to its Caretaker it may be—must obey its binding in the end. And the Houses are bound to kill anyone who attempts to return their deeds."

A tendril of vine snakes through a crack in one of the window frames and lifts the latch. When the window swings open, ivy creeps in, spilling silently across the window seats, pouring onto the floors.

"Burleigh isn't like that," I answer with unshakable confidence. "Burleigh would never hurt anyone."

"I'm sure Marianne Ingilby thought the same of Ripley Castle." Mama glances over her shoulder at the oncoming ivy and shivers. "But that House killed her, Violet. Ripley strangled her in obedience to its bond. It was not freed by blood and mortar as Marianne had planned. Killing her was too much for the House to bear, though. It went wild, and unleashed every bit of its destructive magic on the countryside. What is it your father always says? A Caretaker puts his House first, but a House puts itself first. Well, Ripley Castle did just that. Then in the aftermath, caught up in its own grief, it destroyed Yorkshire."

I look down at my hands, and they're a child's now. I've shrunken, folded into my former self, and I can feel tears slipping down my face.

Mama is relentless. She continues speaking, and the ivy creeps inch by slow inch toward her. With every word and every rustle, I feel as if the axis of my world is shifting.

"In the wake of Marianne's death, Ripley Castle turned the north to a wasteland. Its magic became a dark and twisted thing that spilled out into the surrounding countryside. The damage was so severe that even after His Majesty finally dealt with the House, people fled the county, and it still lies uninhabited."

Mama takes my hands in hers, and I'm too shocked by her story to pull away.

"Houses don't love us, Violet. They obey or disobey, and they use us to their own ends."

She startles with a quick intake of breath as the ivy brushes against her ankle.

"Burleigh, stop it," I snap, and in an instant, the vines crumble to ash. I look at the black smudges they've left on my bedroom floor, because I can't look at my mother.

"You needed to know," Mama says. She presses a kiss to my forehead. Her lips are cool against my skin and I catch a hint of rosewater as she stands and moves to the door.

I stop her with a word. "Wait. What happened to Ripley Castle, after it went wild?"

"The king had it burned. Every stone and every timber."

Once she's taken the lamp away and shut the door behind her, I crawl out of bed and pad across the floor to the airing cupboard. I sit down next to Wyn and shut the door behind us, so that we're shoulder to shoulder, alone together in the quiet dark.

"Violet, I'm afraid," Wyn says. "What if it's true, about the Houses?"

"I'm afraid, too," I tell him. "What would I do, if Burleigh were to burn?"

And in the way of dreams, everything shifts. I'm no longer sitting in the dark with Wyn—I'm standing at the front gate, which is once more iron-wrought bars rather than brambles. Wyn stands on the other side, within the grounds, and he's the boy I know— sandy-haired and reticent, familiar and unfamiliar all at once. He clutches the gate's iron bars, and I cover his hands with my own.

"Go on then, Violet," Wyn says. "Find your own way."

Beside me in the hedgerow, a little bird opens its beak to sing, and the voice that comes out is Mama's clear, sweet soprano.

Burleigh holds quicksilver
Burleigh ruins all
Without blood in its mortar
Breath in its walls

As it sings, I watch Wyn go down the gravel drive and into the House, where he shuts the door behind him. Smoke billows from the windows. Flames lick at the stonework, glass shatters and timbers groan. Burleigh House collapses in on itself, with Wyn inside, and it feels as if I've caught fire myself, and my own insides must surely crumble.

When I wake, that pain is still with me, crushing my chest like a vise, pushing the breath from my lungs. I gasp, and gasp, and gasp.

⇥15↤

IT IS A FINE MAY MORNING—THE LAST MAY MORNING OF this year, in fact—and Burleigh looks lovely on the cusp of summer. I sit out in the kitchen garden, on a bench in the sun with my back against one of the walls. The air is warm, and while the garden may be mostly weeds at this point, bees buzz drowsily among their blossoms. Finches flit between the green thistles. I am happy in this brief moment, and Burleigh is happy because I'm happy. Though I can still feel pain emanating from the bricks, and the immense strain of the House holding in its unspent magic, there's also contentment, benevolence, and a vast sense of fondness.

I smile and run one thumb across the bricks behind me. In response, Burleigh unfurls tendrils of honeysuckle and their flowers open, spilling sweet fragrance onto the breeze.

"Show-off," Wyn grumbles from where he's splitting and stacking firewood in front of the woodshed. "You were insufferable when we were small, you know. Always flaunting the House's preference for you."

He sets the ax aside and straightens up, wiping the back of one hand across his damp forehead. I gnaw at a fingernail and try not to look too long or too hard. Wyn's so . . . competent now. He never was before. And while I don't like to dwell on why he had to become so, the result can be a little distracting. Especially when I've got Papa's ledger open on my lap and am supposed to be looking through it for anything useful.

"The House is a fusty old building that plays favorites and doesn't appreciate the people who do the most for it," I tell Wyn. "Look at Jed and Mira—they oversaw all the upkeep during Papa's time, and when has Burleigh ever even acknowledged them?"

A skein of honeysuckle pokes me in the ear, and I bat it away.

"You love it, though." Wyn's voice is carefully empty, devoid of emotion. He might be speaking of the weather. "No matter how selfish or unfair it is. No matter what it's done to your family, or what they've done for it. That's why you came back."

I frown at him as he stacks split logs beneath the overhang of the woodshed. "There were a lot of reasons why I came back."

"Have you found anything new today?" Wyn asks, gesturing at the ledger with a stick of kindling. I know he's changing the subject, but let it slide. Instead, I squint down at the pages of the ledger.

"Actually, I think I have. I've been charting the locations of all my father's journeys, and during the last year before his arrest, he kept going to Cornwall. Over and over, without recording why. So either he had a lover there I knew nothing about—"

"Unlikely," Wyn says.

"—or he'd found out the deed was somewhere in Cornwall. Somewhere along the coast, in a sea cave."

Wyn glances over at me and he's almost smiling. "And you used to tell me you weren't clever enough for riddles."

"I am who Burleigh needs me to be," I answer, looking at the weed-choked gardens, the crumbling walls, and the low places in the ground where wet mortar has pooled.

Wyn's just about to speak again when the air grows deathly still. The sky clouds over and shifts to a sickly green. A sudden gust of chill rain falls, followed by eerie calm.

"Burleigh?" I ask. "What's wrong?"

The House, of course, does not answer, but Wyn squints around the corner of the building.

"I think there's someone at the gate," he says. "It's storming out in the lane. And the brambles patching the wall look especially thorny."

Closing Papa's ledger, I heave a sigh. "I expect it's Lord Falmouth. He came into the Shilling yesterday—the king sent him to keep an eye on me and the House."

"That'll be trouble," Wyn says with a shake of his head. "Burleigh loathes Falmouth. And I can't say as I was particularly taken by him, either, though we only met the once."

Getting to my feet, I walk over to Wyn and hold out the ledger. "Will you take this for me? I've got to go play charming hostess. I do wish Burleigh would be charming, too—the last thing we need is for a poor report to get back to the king."

Wyn takes the ledger as I've asked him to, but I don't let go. For a moment we're caught with all that's left of my father between us.

"Don't go, Violet," Wyn says without looking at me. "Don't let Falmouth in. It'll end badly."

"Oh, Wyn." It pains me to tell him no, but if I don't follow the king's rules, it'll be a torch and a quick end for Burleigh. "I have to."

"I still don't like it," Wyn says. This time he glances up at me and there's a bleakness in his grey gaze that cuts me to the quick.

"I'll try to get rid of him as soon as possible," I promise, and at last I let the ledger go. Pulling myself together, I gather up my worn fen skirts and hurry toward the front grounds, and the bramble gate beyond.

At the head of the drive, I peer through the mess of thorns that patch the hole in Burleigh's wall. A stiff, cold breeze is whipping at me on this side of the bramble gate, but on the other side, it's pouring rain. Falmouth is sitting astride a black charger and scowling over the weather. His menservants flank him with hunched shoulders, seemingly resigned to their fate of ending up soaked to the skin.

"Hello," I call out. "What can I do for you?"

"I'm here to see your mistress," Falmouth calls back, his voice terse and clipped. "Is she at home?"

I smile grimly, and oh, I should know better, but I can't resist baiting him. "She was last I checked."

Falmouth's horse dances in place and it saws at the bit in frustration. "Let me in at once, then."

"I'm not permitted to allow strangers onto the grounds," I tell him. "And I didn't know you were coming."

He mutters something under his breath. "Look, girl, I'm here on His Majesty's business, and I expect you to let me in, or the king will hear of it."

I don't want to. The House doesn't want me to. Wyn doesn't want me to. But if I don't, and Falmouth takes word back to the king that I'm being uncooperative, there'll be hell to pay.

"Burleigh," I whisper, resting my hand on a thornless length of bramble. "It's alright. I know he's hurt you before, but I'm here, and I won't let anything happen to you."

Reluctance pulses through the palm of my hand.

"Go on, then," I coax. "You're fine, I promise."

Slowly, the brambles begin to pull apart, and I can feel the House's ill humor in the ground beneath me. At last, there's enough space for a single horse to pass through, and Burleigh stops there, refusing to yield any further. I give the wall a disappointed look.

But Lord Falmouth urges his charger forward. The horse shies a little in the gap, as the House reaches out to it with thorny fingers.

"Behave, this is for your own good," I hiss at the air and the grass and the gravel of the drive. There's a distant grumble of thunder in answer.

At close quarters, Lord Falmouth appears to be a good thirty years my senior, with an unforgiving jawline and eyes that don't miss a thing.

"You're the tavern girl from last night," he says as he dismounts. "Does your mistress know how you spend your evenings?"

"Oh yes," I answer. "She doesn't mind at all."

Falmouth's scowl grows more pronounced. "Well. That's no way to run a household. Things will be a damn sight different here once I'm Caretaker, mark my words."

I say nothing, because I refuse to countenance the idea of this boorish nobleman as Caretaker of Burleigh House.

"Have a groom take my horse away and water him," Falmouth orders abruptly. "And fetch your mistress for me. I want to discuss

Burleigh's management with her—this House is a disgrace."

Behind Falmouth, a length of bramble snakes out from the wall, running across the ground toward his horse's rear hooves.

"Sir"—I reach out for the charger's reins and lead it forward a few steps, out of harm's way—"I'm afraid there's no groom at present, so you'll have to make do with me. The staff isn't what it was when my—when Master Sterling was alive."

"You mean before he was sentenced to death for betraying the king."

I paste on a thin smile, more for the benefit of Burleigh than this odious nobleman. Thunder rumbles again, and half a dozen slate tiles slide from Burleigh's roof and smash on the drive in front of the House. "Just so. Would you like to walk with me to the stables, or go on inside and wait?"

"I'll join you. Burleigh was hardly congenial the last time I was here, and it would be nice to see a bit of the grounds."

I lead the horse and Lord Falmouth falls into stride next to me.

"Did you visit during the old master's time, then?" I ask, both to make conversation and to keep him from looking toward the House. From this angle, you can see the wide cracks in the exterior walls of the guest wing, and I don't want him knowing Burleigh's in such dire straits.

"No, I never visited while George Sterling was alive, though we were well acquainted. But I serve as the king's proxy in his absences. He binds the Houses to obey me while he travels overseas. He was away in Belgium when George's House arrest ended, so I was the one who had to retrieve the body, though Burleigh House did fuss about it. I ended up having to force the gate."

The ground beneath us shifts a little. I stop dead in my tracks and turn to face him. "I'll thank you not to speak so lightly of the damage you did."

Falmouth reddens. "Who are you to speak to me in such a fashion, girl? I'll have you beaten for your impertinence."

Burleigh's livid. Every stone on the gravel drive begins to chatter, like the sound of small malevolent teeth.

Peace, Burleigh, peace, I think desperately at the House.

I can't keep this up.

"I'm Violet Sterling," I say. "George's daughter and the current mistress of this House. As I said, I don't appreciate any mention of what you did last time you were here. To do such a thing to a House under a binding is unconscionable."

"Of course you are. George's get would be working as a barmaid—he always spent too much time at the Shilling himself." Falmouth rolls his eyes. "And don't be dramatic. The House did it to itself. What was I supposed to do? Leave your father decaying on his deathbed while this place festered and went bad? Did you know that the boy George kept under arrest with him never even dealt with the corpse—just left it lying out to rot. All that was left by the time I made the House open up was bones. I had the trouble of a burial and a headstone to deal with myself."

I concentrate on nothing but the rhythm of my breath and my own footsteps, because his words are poison, and more than that, a lie. I saw Burleigh's memory. I know it was Esperanza who came and did the decent thing after my father's death.

Breathe in, and out. In and out. One foot forward. Now the next.

The sound of Wyn's ax splits the air every few moments, like gunfire. I find it oddly comforting, knowing he's nearby. Knowing I have an unquestioning ally, should I need him.

As we walk to the empty and derelict stables, daisies sprout and spring up through the gravel along my path. Light beams through the threatening clouds and follows me, so that I move in a halo of gold, like a saint or a Madonna. I'm glad of Burleigh's obvious attention, just as I'm glad of the sound of Wyn's ax. It's a reassurance, that forceful as Lord Falmouth may be, I'm not entirely alone. I tend to the horse while Falmouth watches. His men are entirely silent, never making eye contact or speaking a word. They're more skittish than the horse is, and I can only imagine what sort of master the duke must be to make them seem so wary.

Falmouth orders his servants to remain in the stable, and the two of us hurry into the conservatory as fat raindrops begin to fall from the sky. They drum against the glass, and the sound lulls me. When I shiver, a fire springs to life in the grate and I draw closer to warm my hands. We'd be warmer in the study, but brambles are beginning to take over the corners, and the conservatory is still unmarked by Burleigh's malaise.

"His Majesty did say the House is oddly attentive to you," Falmouth remarks from where he stands looking out at the rainy grounds. "And I'm prepared to let you stay here permanently in some capacity. As a scullery maid, perhaps."

The fire leaps higher, licking at the chimney in a sudden flare of flame.

"Do you have much experience with Great Houses?" I ask, because he must think I plan to step aside at summer's end.

"Burleigh will need a great deal of attention and a very deft touch if it's to recover from its present state."

Lord Falmouth turns and looks me up and down. The back of my neck prickles. I don't like his proprietary air at all—standing there, you'd think he owns everything around him. "Miss Sterling, the king and I are of one mind in this. Burleigh's been coddled by your family for centuries. What it needs is to be broken. A firm hand would do wonders for this place, and if it's really that obstinate, well. It's only one House. There are others, should Burleigh choose to go down in flames."

"It's not a matter of choice," I tell him sharply. "Burleigh is ailing because of the binding that was placed on it. It was ailing before my father's arrest, and would still be sickening even if I had the key in hand at this moment."

I'm not sure if Burleigh is feeding off my agitation, or if I'm channeling the House's anger. But the fire snaps and roars and rain lashes at the windows.

Please, Burleigh, I beg silently. *Calm yourself.*

But inside my own chest, my heart beats at a furious pace.

Falmouth pays the House no mind. Instead, he crosses the room and stands next to me at the hearth, far closer than I'd like. I grip the mantel with one hand, both Burleigh and I needing the gesture of support.

"Then perhaps," Falmouth says softly, "I'd better go back to His Majesty tomorrow, and tell him a torch is all Burleigh House is good for."

Outside, wind shrieks in the eaves of the House, and the ground trembles beneath our feet. Fool that he is, Falmouth ignores it.

"Hush, Burleigh," I murmur beneath my breath, running a hand along the mantel. "Settle yourself, my love."

But the House's distress builds and builds, until I want to crawl out of my skin. Lord Falmouth, who can obviously feel nothing of it, looks at me as if I'm about to fall into hysterics. Perhaps I am.

"Burleigh, you mustn't—" I begin, but the words are drowned out by shattering glass as vines burst into the conservatory from outside. They twine around the Duke of Falmouth's wrists and ankles, pinning him fast and driving him to his knees. I stumble under the sudden weight of the House's full attention bearing down on the two of us.

"The king will hear of this," the duke chokes out furiously as Burleigh drags him away, back through the garden and toward the front gate. It's raining still, and before long Lord Falmouth is plastered in mud. I follow along, pleading with Burleigh to stop, but the House rages on. Falmouth's servants run out of the stable, drawn by the commotion. They stop a few paces back, not wanting to interfere.

"Do you think for a moment that His Majesty will let you stay on once he hears Burleigh has gone wild?" Lord Falmouth carries on. "The king's army will be here in three days, with torches and kerosene."

The duke's words are like a knife in my heart as Burleigh dumps him in the roadway. But then, in an instant, Burleigh's attention swings away from us and toward something else. The knife twists.

"Go!" I bark at Falmouth's servants, who scurry out just before the brambles twine shut, thorny vines sealing the House's grounds more securely than any lock ever could.

"What about my horse?" Falmouth calls after me.

"You'll have to do without him," I shout back over one shoulder. "I've got more pressing things to take care of."

The clouds above have grown darker since Burleigh's fit of temper, and rain continues to pour down. Something hits the back of my neck with an unpleasant spatter, and when I reach instinctively to wipe at it, my hand comes away gritty and coated in wet mortar. The sound and substance of the rainfall changes, growing softer, fuller, more sinister, as mortar begins to coat the grass and clog the puddles. I've never seen such a thing, not in all my father's time as Caretaker, and fear eats away at my insides as I hurry around the House.

Even as I run through the overgrown vegetable garden, my fear turns to a sickening premonition. There's nothing to be heard but the damp, thick plashing of falling mortar. Wyn's ax has gone silent.

He's still near the woodshed, propped against a mound of neatly stacked logs. Wyn looks for all the world as if he could be sleeping. But when I shake him frantically by the shoulders, he doesn't wake.

"Wyn. Come on, Wyn. Open your eyes."

The full weight of Burleigh's attention is still bent on him, and the unnatural rain hasn't slackened yet. I sink my hands into a slurry of mud and mortar.

"Burleigh House," I plead, "please stop. Please let him be."

Resistance and frustration leak up through my skin.

"I'm begging you," I say to my House. "If you've ever loved me, turn away from him now."

Ever so slowly, Burleigh's focus begins to shift. The clouds thin little by little, bit by bit, and finally dissipate.

"Wyn?"

His hands are cold. I chafe them between my own, but he still doesn't wake. Glancing over one shoulder in an agony, I calculate the distance to the kitchen door. It's a hundred yards away, and though I hate to leave Wyn, I can't move him on my own.

"Don't move," I breathe. "I'm coming back for you straightaway. Burleigh, if you touch him again, I'll never forgive you."

The House rumbles, but a single beam of sunlight cuts through the cloud cover and spills over Wyn's unconscious form.

Scrambling to my feet, I bolt across the kitchen garden and in through the door.

"Mira?" I shout. "Mira, where are you?"

There's no sign of her. I rattle through the halls, calling her name as I go. At last I hear a faint answer and hurry toward the sound of her voice.

Mira's in the conservatory and, as soon as I enter the room, descends upon me, taking my face in her hands and looking me over as if I'm likely to have lost an arm.

"Violet, are you alright?" she asks in a panic. "What happened in here?"

"His Majesty sent the Duke of Falmouth to look in on the House," I say mechanically. "He was awful, and Burleigh lost its temper. The House dragged him off the grounds, but then it started losing control of its magic. There was mortar, raining from the sky, and Wyn tried to stop it—he did House magic, but now I can't wake him. Mira, please, I need your help."

It's only as I speak of what's happened that the true horror of it strikes me. Brutish Lord Falmouth and Burleigh's rage and Wyn, still where I left him.

"Where's Wyn?" Mira asks as I press a hand to my mouth and tears spill from my eyes. "Vi. Where is he?"

"Out by the woodshed," I say, pulling myself together. "We've got to get him inside."

Puddles of mortar are already drying out along the garden path. The weeds are flattened by it, borne down by the weight of that unnatural rain. Everything smells like damp, cold stone.

And when we come out in front of the woodshed, my heart jackknifes in my chest. There's no sign of Wyn.

"He was just here," I say, casting about us. "I swear, Mira. Where could he have gone?"

Mira has two fingers to her temple, as if her head aches.

"Has Wyn done House magic before?" she asks slowly.

I bite my lip and look down at the mortar-slick ground. "Yes."

"Have *you* done House magic since we got back? Violet Helena Sterling, I expect the truth from you."

I've never seen Mira so stern before.

". . . Not on purpose," I answer weakly.

"Which is a yes. Get inside and pack your bag, young lady. We're leaving."

"What?" I gasp. "Mira, you can't—"

"I can think of two things that might have happened to that boy," she says, cutting me off. "Either he realized this place is a danger to him, and left like he planned to at first, or—"

"Or what?" I cross my arms and scowl.

"You said yourself Burleigh dragged Falmouth off the grounds. This House isn't right anymore. What if it did the same to Wyn? What if it broke its bond and did away with him?"

"*Did away with him?*" The anger that courses through me is a hot and electric thing. "Are you calling Burleigh a murderer? My House would never."

Mira looks profoundly weary. "Violet, my love. Your House already has. And I know what your father taught you to be. What you've always thought was your role. But can you, Violet Sterling, really put this House before anything else when it comes down to it? Before *anyone*? Think on that. Think long and hard. And do it while you're packing—I can't, in good conscience, let you stay in a place that constantly puts you in harm's way."

For a moment, I think of stamping my feet or raging at her, but my anger's already collapsing into grief. If Mira looks weary, I feel as if I've lived on this Earth for a thousand years.

"It doesn't matter if you don't want me to stay," I tell her, and my voice breaks on the words because I love Jed and Mira with my whole heart. I'd be lost without them. "I can't go. Not until I've unbound this House or it lies in ashes."

Violets spread around my feet like ripples as I speak.

"Why?" Mira asks. "Help me to understand, Vi. Why can't you just leave this place behind?"

I sniff, and give her a long look through my tears. "Who else does Burleigh House have to speak on its behalf? No one, Mira. No one. Without me, it would be entirely alone."

"Where are you going?" she calls after me as I stumble off.

"To look for Wyn. He can't have got far."

❧16❧

WYN IS WELL AND TRULY GONE.

I search the House from top to bottom. I scour the gardens, and the meadow, and the graveyard. I look in every outbuilding. At last, I have to leave for the Shilling, but going without having found Wyn tears me to pieces. The knowledge that either he left or came to some sort of harm sits inside me, cold and poisonous as mortar.

At the Shilling, there's no sign of Esperanza and Alfred— presumably they're in hiding, avoiding an encounter with Falmouth, who's still in residence at the inn. But he's sequestered in the gentlemen's gaming room so I see nothing of him until late in the evening. Then a clatter sounds from the kitchen. At the end of the bar, Frey glances over her shoulder toward the corridor.

"Here, Vi." She hands me a tray of glasses filled with strong, expensive whiskey. "You take this into the gaming room while I see what's going on out back."

I do as I'm bid. As I go, I repeat over and over to myself, *You will not lose your temper you will not lose your temper you will not lose your temper.*

But as I walk into the smoky, lamplit room, I can feel my shoulders tense and my stomach tie itself up into knots. Falmouth sits at the farthest table, intent on a hand of what looks to be whist. I weave through the tables, replacing empty whiskey glasses and ignoring the bawdier comments from traveling merchant men— the folk of the Halt who frequent the public room never pester me so. As I work, I watch Falmouth. I watch him win his hand and smile, as if he expects the world to hand him whatever he wishes for. I think of him forcing his way through Burleigh House's wall, leaving a wound that even now hasn't really healed. I recall my House's rage at his presence. And I think of the fact that when I go home tonight, barring some miracle, there'll be no Wyn faithfully keeping watch over my bedroom door. All because of Lord Falmouth.

"Well, here she is, the Caretaker turned barmaid," Falmouth drawls as I freshen the table. "I was just telling these gentlemen that I'm off to Bath first thing in the morning, to recommend His Majesty torch your foul-tempered House. No one wants another Ripley Castle, now do they?"

I grit my teeth and silently replace his glass.

But the Duke of Falmouth keeps speaking, his voice low and his words insidious. "Did you know I was acquainted with Marianne Ingilby, too? Yes. The girl who brought down the Sixth House and ruined all of Yorkshire. We were thick as thieves back in the day, Marianne and your father and me. I rather think George fancied Marianne, until Ripley Castle finished her off and he had to settle for your mother."

Everyone's attention is fixed on us, and I keep my face a careful blank.

"You don't like hearing about the Sixth House, do you?" Falmouth taunts. "It always struck a nerve with your father, too. And isn't it odd how history seems to be repeating itself? Another failing House. Another desperate girl. Another county on its way to ruin."

A discontented murmur runs between the listening travelers, and I swallow. Of all the things I'm risking, trying to set Burleigh free, the good of the West Country weighs heaviest on my shoulders.

"Burleigh is nothing like Ripley," I answer sharply. "For eight hundred years it's guarded this piece of the country, and been only gentle."

With slow, deliberate motions, Falmouth rolls up his shirtsleeves, revealing the angry red welts at his wrists where Burleigh's vines caught and dragged him. "Is this how your House deals gently with people?"

The murmurs among those watching grow louder.

"You deliberately provoked my House!" I say. "You walked onto its grounds and did nothing but bluster and threaten and speak of its death as if it can't hear or feel a thing."

"It isn't human, Miss Sterling." Falmouth shakes his head, as if I've taken leave of my senses. Blood and mortar, I think I hate him worse than the king.

"No. No, it isn't. But Burleigh is alive," I insist. "It can think and it has a will of its own and it knows what everyone's saying about it—that it's not worth saving. That it would be better to just let it burn. So yes, of course my House is on edge. It's suffering."

"And what is the kindest thing to do for a suffering creature?" Falmouth purrs smoothly. "Put it down. The greatest impediment to the well-being of the West Country right now is not Burleigh House, Miss Sterling. In point of fact, it's you, and your foolish insistence on attempting the impossible. If your father, a Caretaker in good standing, was unable to save Burleigh, what makes you think you have the slightest chance? What *exactly* is it you're doing to try and restore Burleigh House?"

I clamp my jaws together and glare at him wordlessly. I've said too much already, but I'm not foolish enough to let this arrogant nobleman goad me into acknowledging my own treason.

Falmouth drops a handful of banknotes onto the table and gets to his feet.

"I'll bid you good night, gentlemen," he says to all those listening in. "The company's been fine, but the staff here leave something to be desired."

I let him go. I stuff my anger down so deep inside my very bones ache, but I let him go.

The last few hours of my shift are a blur. At the end of them, I step out into the cool night air and draw in a long breath. I don't know how much time I've got left with Burleigh, but every moment I have I plan to spend working on its behalf.

And come morning, I'll search again for Wyn, though I'm beginning to suspect he's gone. Perhaps this last brush with Burleigh's magic brought him to his senses—made him see how desperately dangerous all this is. In the interest of self-preservation, perhaps he finally left me and my beleaguered House behind.

For now, though, it's time to go home, and scour Papa's ledger for a question about the deed my House can bear to answer.

As I step away from the Shilling, rough hands pull me back

into the shadows and shove me up against the tavern wall. Though I wriggle like a landed fish, the Duke of Falmouth's grip on my wrists is sure and cruel.

"You dare to disrespect me in company, Miss Sterling?" he mutters hot in my ear, and I am all at once blindingly afraid and so furious I can't speak. "I will teach you to still that rebellious tongue."

He presses one arm across my throat, choking me, and my field of vision narrows.

"Tell me you're sorry for answering back," Falmouth growls. "And use my title while you do it."

But I can't speak. Falmouth leans forward, putting more weight on my throat. My eyelids flutter as everything begins to go dark.

The sharp click of the hammer on a flintlock pistol rings through the night.

"Step away from my serving girl," Frey says coolly, standing on the threshold of the Shilling's back door.

The duke hesitates, but his weight shifts and I gasp hungrily for air. Frey takes a step forward.

"Walk on," she orders, her pistol still trained on Falmouth. "Keep walking until you've left this village, and don't come back."

The duke gives Frey a killing look. "I will run your little tavern out of business, once I've seen Burleigh House burned to the ground. I'll ensure that no one reputable ever stops here again."

Frey only shakes her head. "Do you think you're the first disgruntled gentleman I've chased off for getting rough with a serving girl? Not the first and not the last. I've heard the same threats a dozen times, and they never come to anything. No, folk recognize a devil in fine clothes when they see one."

Falmouth stalks off toward the inn's front door, swearing under his breath.

"Not that way," Frey snaps. "You won't be staying under my roof tonight, so just you walk on. The Green Lion in Taunton might take you. I'll send your menservants along come morning."

Falmouth stops for a moment and his shoulders go stiff, as if he's about to protest, or turn and threaten Frey, but she speaks once more and there's a deadly seriousness to her words.

"Walk. On."

At last, Falmouth does as he's told. It's not until he's half a mile down the lane that Frey turns to me.

"Alright, Violet?"

I nod shakily.

"Good." Frey tucks her pistol into the band of her apron and sets her hands on her hips. "Now listen closely, because I'll tell you this once, and you'd do well to remember. There are some men in this world you can play against and win—who'll keep to the rules and grumble if you best them, but do no more. There are others you will only ever lose to, even if it seems like you've won for a moment. Learn to see them coming, and keep out of their way."

"Thank you, Frey," I tell her. "I'm not sure what he would have done if you hadn't come along."

She shrugs. "I've got a sense for trouble, and I generally turn up when I'm needed. You go straight home, then, Vi."

Frey stands in the shadow of the doorway and watches as I walk down the lane, in the opposite direction from that the Duke of Falmouth was forced to take. But my hands tremble and my throat aches and I don't feel truly safe until brambles twine shut behind me and I'm back on the grounds of my beloved House.

I make it to the jacaranda before I stumble and fall to my knees and sob. Burleigh wraps me in arms of ivy and grows a bed of moss beneath me, while the wind whispers wordless, comforting things in the branches overhead. When my tears are spent, a pale aurora paints itself across the sky. I lie still as a stone and watch it for a very long time, and I have never felt so hopeless or, in spite of Burleigh's presence, so alone.

❊17❊

IT'S NOT EVEN DAWN YET WHEN I WAKE TO SOMEONE knocking determinedly at my door. My heart leaps—Jed's left the House by this time of day and Mira never knocks.

I tumble out of bed, pulling my dressing gown on as I go.

"Wyn—"

But his name dies on my lips. It's Esperanza standing in the hallway, neat as a fashion plate in her riding habit.

"I'm off to Bath," she tells me, everything about her brisk and businesslike. "Somebody's going to have to convince my father that Falmouth's being an absolute boor about Burleigh, and I'm the best person for the job. But I'm leaving you Alfred, in case you need anything, and in case anything new comes up. I think we're close, though, darling—we've got a list of two dozen port towns in Cornwall that my father apparently visits every time he's about to leave England. And maybe I can winkle something out of Falmouth while I'm in Bath."

She kisses my cheek and I catch a breath of her jasmine scent.

"Espie," I say. "Be careful, won't you? Falmouth, he's—"

"Oh, believe me, I know," Esperanza answers. "But I'm quite

clever, as it turns out, and I know the most *shocking* things about that hideous man. Secrets that would severely dent his reputation if they came to light."

I shake my head. I don't know how she manages, in her world of espionage and underhanded dealings and perpetual gossip. I'd wither and die if I had to live that way.

"Where on earth do you get your information?" I ask.

Esperanza waves a dismissive hand. "From all the girls at court, of course. No one takes us girls seriously, so we make the most wonderful spies. Now I've got to be going if I'm to beat Falmouth into Bath. Be good. Don't do anything I wouldn't."

And then she's gone, as quickly as she came.

I walk over to the window seat and pull Papa's ledger onto my lap, not so much because I intend to look through it at the moment but from force of habit. Though I leaf through the pages, I can't concentrate. The eastern sky is growing grey, and after a few minutes of restless fidgeting I dress hastily, then slip out of the House.

The back woods are misty and green, though patches of mortar pockmark the forest floor. Birds sing in the trees overhead and a few bluebells still hold their bloom.

"Wyn?" I call as I wander here and there, not bothering to keep to the path. "Are you there, Wyn?"

I don't really hope to find him. The truth is, he's been on his way out since I got home—I think I just delayed the process. But I can't reconcile myself to his absence until I've looked everywhere, and left no stone unturned. If something terrible *has* happened, and he hasn't simply left, I'd never forgive myself for not keeping up the search.

"Wyn?"

Somewhere overhead, a robin begins to sing, the liquid notes of its song carrying through the wood. There's a flash of russet as a red squirrel hurries up a tree. I shut my eyes for a moment, breathing in the smell and sounds of the forest. I can almost imagine the past seven years away. Can almost picture a better life.

Mama is still with us. Wyn is down by the stream, and presently Mira will call us in for breakfast. Papa is Caretaker—

But no. Even if Papa was still Caretaker, Burleigh would still be slowly dying, sickening a little more every day thanks to the binding placed upon it.

I open my eyes, and when I do, Wyn is standing not ten yards away from me on the forest path. I squint, to make sure he's real and solid, not a memory of the House's, but there's no watery cast of light playing over him, just sun through the leaves.

Wyn seems well. Better than he has in days, now that I think about it. The hollows are gone from beneath his eyes, and his untidy hair curls damp around his collar, as if he's just washed up in the stream.

All the worry on his account that I forced endlessly down for seven years, and that I could not really feel last night for fear of falling apart, hits me like a storm surge. My hands shake, and I feel as if I'm going to be sick. Suddenly I can't bear to look at him. I turn on my heel and rush blindly through the woods, though I can hear him following after me.

"Violet!" Wyn calls. "Vi, stop a moment!"

But I don't, not till I've got out of the cover of the woods and stand in the middle of the wildflower meadow. The blossoms have taken on strange, twisted shapes, and as I clench my fists together and try to catch my breath, a hedge of brambles rises up around me, waist-high and bristling with thorns.

Wyn stops short.

"Look, I'm sorry," he says, his voice low and strained. "I wouldn't have left if I could have helped it."

I shake my head, desperate not to feel the things I'm feeling, or to remember what it was like being left behind by Mama and then made a homeless orphan by Papa. But to my heart, it doesn't matter why Wyn left. All that matters is that he went. That without warning, I found him gone. Yet I know my heart to be relentless and unfair, so with a supreme effort, I force down every scrap of loneliness and hurt.

"No," I tell Wyn. "It's alright. I shouldn't expect what you can't give; you made it clear from the beginning that you're not planning to stay for long. I'm being foolish. Don't mind me."

Wyn takes a step forward, heedless of the brambles. They retreat a little, making way for him. "Violet. Say what you mean, for once. Tell me the truth. You're upset with me, aren't you?"

"No. Yes. You *left*. I am so tired of people leaving me, Wyn. So tired. My mother, my father, you—"

"I came back," he offers, though there's no defensiveness in his voice.

"It's not just this time, though," I say. "Why wouldn't you go with me? When Papa was put under arrest, why did you stay? I needed you, Wyn. Mama always put herself first and Papa had Burleigh to think of. You were the only person I felt safe with, and you turned your back on me to stay here of all places, and I can't understand why."

"Blood and mortar," Wyn mutters under his breath as he runs a hand across his face. "Violet. Can I show you something?"

"Oh, very well," I answer flatly, because now I've said my piece, all I feel is sad and empty.

The brambles pull back and wither away as I step forward.

"It's this way," Wyn says, and leads me back into the woods. I hesitate at the edge of the forest. Part of me wants to stay out in the sunlight, in sight of Burleigh House, which has never let me down. But Wyn stops and waits for me, and at last I follow.

We go just about as far as you can get in the little forest while still remaining on Burleigh's grounds. And in a back corner, in a thicket near the edge of the wood, we come upon something I've never seen before.

There's a small shepherd's hut in among the trees, built of odd, mismatched boards and roofed with a thin layer of thatch. It has no windows, and only one door.

"What is this?" I ask Wyn. "Where did it come from?"

"I made it," he says, stuffing his hands into his pockets. "The year after the arrest began. You can go in—I think then you'll see why."

I open the door and stop on the threshold. "Will you come with me?"

Wyn joins me at once. It's reassuring, having him at my back, and I step into the close, dim interior. At first the only light is whatever filters through the chinks in the walls and the bare patches on the roof. But then Wyn strikes a sulfur match and lights a lamp, and it's like we're alone together in a small golden bubble, when everywhere else on the grounds it's impossible to escape the pervasive presence of Burleigh House.

In here, though, my sense of Burleigh's consciousness is dampened. I let out a small, audible sigh of relief as the House's pain and exhaustion fade from the edges of my mind. They don't vanish entirely, but quiet to a bare whisper.

"It's because nothing in here is part of Burleigh," Wyn explains, without me having to say what I've felt. "I found the boards in the old barn, and all the nails and the thatch—they'd been brought in from the village and were just sitting there, gathering dust. So I built this myself. The House had no part of it. When the arrest started, Burleigh was always . . . looking at me. You know the way it is, when all of its attention is focused on you, and it's hard to keep upright? It'd be like that for days at a time, and I got so tired of it I could hardly see straight. I just wanted somewhere of my own, somewhere to hide. And this is it."

I settle down, sitting cross-legged on the rough planks of the floor. Wyn sits, too, facing me, and sets the lamp down between us.

"It helps when I've done House magic, to come out here," he says, an apology written across his face. "If I've done a lot of it, I can't think of anything else. I didn't mean to let you down, Vi. Are you still angry?"

"Have I ever been able to stay angry with you?"

Wyn smiles, and it's a half-broken, wistful thing. "No. I suppose not."

"Can I look?" I ask, gesturing to the confined space around us. Wyn shrugs. "Alright. There's not much to see."

He's not being entirely truthful, though. I take the lamp and hold it up, and find charcoal drawings on every wall. They're of an achingly familiar landscape—wide, flat expanses of water and grass, with seabirds skimming the air overhead. I can almost hear the sea. Almost taste the salt. Almost smell the brine.

"It's the fens," I say, turning back to Wyn. "You drew the fens. How did you know that's where we went?"

"Jed told me, just before you left." He gets to his feet, ducking a little to avoid hitting his head on an arrangement of carved wooden birds suspended from the ceiling. I look at them, squinting a little in the low light, and I know every one of them. There's a teal, a marsh harrier, a common crane, a grey shrike with a tiny hooked beak. They're fen birds.

"I found some books in Burleigh's library, and read about where you'd gone," Wyn says.

Suddenly, hot tears burn at my eyes and my throat aches. Even while I was away, Wyn and I were still together in a sense. Sometimes, I feel as tied to him as I do to Burleigh House. And the panic I felt before dissipates, because he hasn't left, he's still here.

He's still here.

"Wyn?" I say. He looks down at me, a question in his eyes. "Please don't do House magic anymore. It's not safe, and I hate watching what it does to you."

"I know," he says. "I know I shouldn't. And I know I promised you that I'd stop. But if I'd let all that mortar out into the countryside . . ."

We both fall silent. Burleigh is failing, and someone must stand in the breach until I manage to find the deed.

If I manage to find the deed.

I turn my attention back to Wyn's drawings on the walls. There's one of gulls flying over the shore that catches my eye. When I step closer to it, I notice odd marks on the waves and the gulls' wings. Not marks, handwriting done in ink, on the opposite side of the paper.

"Do you mind?" I ask, gesturing to the picture.

"Look all you want," Wyn says.

Removing the pins that hold the page to the wall, I flip it over.

There's verse scrawled across it in an unfamiliar hand. The way they scan and flow reminds me of something—of the old House rhyme Papa used to sing to me as a little girl. But the words are all wrong. They're more like instructions, and the back of my neck prickles as I read.

> *First, speak a binding*
> *Second, wield a knife*
> *Third, give your spirit*
> *Fourth, give your life*
> *Fifth, take in power*
> *Sixth, take it all*
> *Till your blood runs with mortar*
> *Till your breath fills the walls*

"Do you know what this is?" I ask Wyn, holding out the page. For a long moment, he's absolutely silent, staring down at the paper.

"No," he says, and I know he's lying from the way he won't meet my eyes. He's never been able to bluff.

"What is it?" I press.

"I told you I don't know. Just some old nonsense, on a scrap of paper I found years ago. Put it back."

I frown at him. "I want to keep it. It could be important."

"Suit yourself," Wyn says.

But on our way back through the woods, there's tension between us. It stretches on and on until we leave the forest and I push the sleeves of my rough fen blouse up, because the day is already warm and muggy. As I do, I hear Wyn take in a sharp breath.

"Violet Sterling, what happened to you?"

I glance at him in confusion. "What?"

In answer, he takes one of my hands and holds it up. It's the first time he's touched me when neither of us is working House magic, and even though we're not entirely getting on, the feeling of Wyn's skin on mine sends a shock through me.

But I see at once what he's bothered about. Dark blue bruises have blossomed around my wrists, angry against the white of my skin. The slick pink mark that rings my arm just below my left hand is more prominent than ever.

"Oh," I say, trying for lightness and sounding a little forced. "Falmouth wasn't pleased with how things went here. We had a very . . . animated conversation, last night when I was leaving the Red Shilling."

I've never seen Wyn look so fierce. "Is he still there?"

"No, he's gone to Bath, don't worry about it," I say.

"Are you certain?" Wyn asks.

I give him a thin smile. "Frey ran him off with a pistol. I don't expect he'll be back anytime soon."

My assurances sound hollow and unconvincing, even to me. I haven't told Wyn about the deal I struck with the king—that if Burleigh survives the summer but I'm unable to find the deed, Falmouth will take over the House. And I'm certainly not about to bring it up now, when I've no idea what I'll do if things come to that.

We walk inside, through the ruins of the conservatory, shattered glass crunching like gravel under our feet. I ought to clear this up—being in disrepair is hard on Burleigh. But there are so many things that need doing. The slate tiles on the guest wing roof are so sparse it looks as if my House has contracted some sort of architectural mange. In spite of Wyn's best efforts, the dining hall is still growing cracks like a tree grows leaves. The ballroom's still split down the middle in the wake of my unfortunate accident with Burleigh's House magic. And everywhere, ivy creeps in at the windows and rooflines. The damage weighs on me constantly.

"When do you finish at the Shilling tonight?" Wyn asks, putting a hand on my elbow to steady me as I nearly trip on an overturned ottoman.

"Usually a bit after two."

"I'll be there at two, then, to walk you home."

"Oh, Wyn," I protest. "Don't be ridiculous. Falmouth is gone, and I don't—"

"Let me do this," he says. "You may not mind now, but you'll probably want company tonight. Just trust me, won't you? I know."

I relent. "Alright, have it your way."

Wyn holds the conservatory door open and looks back at the shambles behind us as I walk through.

"Got my work cut out for me today," he says. "But first let's find Mira and see if she'll feed us. I'm starving—haven't had anything to eat since yesterday morning."

Wyn grins at me, and for a brief moment, seems like an ordinary boy—the sort of person he might have become if he weren't tied to my family and my House.

"I'm fighting with Mira," I say, moping a bit because I like it when Wyn pities me. "I expect I'd be fighting with Jed, too, if he didn't leave before dawn and go to bed while I'm still out. They don't agree with me about Burleigh."

"Well, I'm not fighting with you," Wyn says.

"Really?" I ask hopefully. Perhaps he's already forgotten about the strange scrap of verse tucked away in my pocket.

"Really." Wyn tries and fails to hide a smile. "I don't ever fight with you. I just have temporary differences of opinion."

"That's the same thing," I mutter.

"No, it isn't. If I were fighting with you, I'd be cross. I'm never cross with you."

"I'm cross with *you* sometimes," I point out. "What makes you so much nicer than I am?"

I slow my pace, and Wyn walks on a few steps.

"I've always been nicer than you are," he says. "Everyone knows that."

When Wyn notices I'm not keeping up, he stops and turns, waiting patiently. I put my head a little to one side and look at him. At first when I came home, seeing Wyn was a bit of a wrench. I kept expecting to see the child I grew up with. But it's not like that anymore. Right now, I don't want to see anyone else, just him, as he is in this moment.

And blood and mortar, I'm glad he came back.

"What are you looking at?" Wyn asks with a puzzled frown.

"Nothing," I say, catching up with him. "Nothing at all."

❧18❧

MIDWAY THROUGH MY SHIFT AT THE SHILLING, ALFRED comes downstairs, looking gloomy and a bit at a loose end without Esperanza. He occupies their usual table, covering every inch of its surface with papers and notebooks, ledgers and ancient-looking texts.

Alfred only ever takes tea, I know that by now, and the second time I stop at the table to freshen his pot, I sit down opposite him for a moment.

"Have you ever seen this bit of verse before?" I ask, taking Wyn's drawing from my pocket and sliding it across the table wrong-side up so Alfred can see the handwriting on the back.

He squints down at the page through his spectacles and goes suddenly pale. "Where did you get this?"

"I found it at the House," I say.

"Forget about it," Alfred says, burying his nose in a book once more.

I reach across the table and pull the book downward, so he can't hide behind it. "You and Wyn are both being very cagey about this, and it's really not accomplishing what you intend. It's my House, Alfred. I have a right to know what this means."

He gives me a pained look. "Esperanza would kill me if she found out I told you."

"Then she never has to know," I say.

"I don't like keeping secrets from Espie." Alfred sounds disgruntled, and I give him my firmest look.

"I don't like having a House that's *dying.*"

"Oh, very well." Alfred rifles through his assortment of documents and pulls an extremely old book toward us. As he leafs through it, I can see that all the pages are hand-lettered in faded ink, and the binding made of some sort of cured animal skin. Though I can make out most of the spellings, the language is unfamiliar.

Alfred gestures to a section of text and I shake my head. "I can't read it. What is it?"

"Oh, sorry. It's an Anglo-Saxon text, from my namesake, Alfred the Great's, reign. That dates it to nearly two hundred years before the Great Houses were bound. Do you see this?" He points to a few indented lines. "That's your verse, more or less. More, really; it's almost identical. It's a set of instructions that explain how a person can be bound to a Great House. We call it a binding rhyme, those of us who've made a study of the Houses."

I frown. "Why would anyone need to bind themselves to a Great House, especially if the Houses hadn't even been bound by William the Deedwinner yet?"

"There are two stories here," Alfred says, overcoming the reluctance that's obviously warring with his chronic desire to discuss obscure points of House history. "One's about a House in the Scottish Highlands—it's not called a House in the text, though; they call it a witchcroft. According to this book, it was incredibly old, older than anything else in those parts, and began to fail. It needed new land, and a fresh start. So the man who tended it at the time—call him what you like, a priest, a shaman, a Caretaker—bound himself to the croft. He gave it his blood and bones and breath and brought it to Yorkshire, where it eventually became Ripley Castle. Fascinating."

"And the other story?" I ask.

"Hold up." Alfred turns a few pages. "Alright, here it is. The chronicler talks about a place in Exmoor, near Withypool. He says there was a strange village called Burglæcan, or 'the town that springs up.' And the people who lived there? They were called Stiorlings—from *stioran*, meaning to guide and direct. Burglæcan had been around for ages, too, but seemed to be alright until a group of Danes came inland and tried to raid the village. The raiders just . . . died, suddenly, without warning or violence, and the chronicler says a grey substance sprang from their ears and their eyes and their noses. After that, Burglæcan goes into a swift decline, until one of the Stiorlings binds herself to the place and relocates it."

"To the Blackdown Hills," I say.

"That's right," Alfred says. "To the Blackdown Hills, where I would assume it became Burleigh House."

"And we became the Sterlings."

"Exactly."

"What happened to the woman who moved Burleigh?" I ask, leaning forward. "And to the man who moved the Scottish House?" Excitement thrums through me. "Could I move Burleigh again, to give it a new beginning?"

Perhaps I won't have any need to find the elusive deed after all.

Perhaps there's a simpler answer to all my problems.

Alfred looks down at the book in front of him. "They died. There are other stories from the Continent and it's always the same. You can save a Great House by binding yourself to it, but it's a death sentence."

"Oh," I say, my voice small. "That's why Esperanza wouldn't want you to tell me. She thinks I'd—"

"Yes," Alfred answers. "That's what she's afraid of."

He takes his spectacles off and pinches two fingers to the bridge of his nose, as if his head aches. "I can't tell you what to do, Violet. I suppose it really comes down to this—is Burleigh the thing you love most in this world? Espie's that for me, and if I really had to, I'd die for her in a heartbeat. Would you die for Burleigh?"

I ought to be just as sure as Alfred is. After all, I spent my entire childhood learning my place, my duty, my calling. I am the Caretaker of Burleigh House, and a good Caretaker puts her House before anything, even her own life.

But oh, it feels as if I have only just started to live.

I was once so certain of myself and what would be required of me in this world. As a child, everything seemed clear—I would look after Burleigh, and Burleigh would look after me. Even on the fens, I knew that if I could just get home, everything would be alright again.

It isn't, though. It's all falling apart.

"Thank you, Alfred." I stuff the binding rhyme back into my pocket. "I'm glad you told me the truth."

"What are you going to do?" he asks.

"I don't know yet," I answer truthfully. "I'll have to think about it."

And I do think about it. Consequently, I make a muddle of everything for the rest of the evening, until Frey takes me aside and asks me if I'm feeling quite well. I'm not, though there's nothing wrong with me in body, only in spirit. Everything's tangled up inside me, a mess of fear and anxiety about what's to come. As I walk to the door at closing time and remember Falmouth's hands on my wrists and my throat, fear over what's already passed hits me as well. The moment I set my hand on the knob, I can feel his arm pressed up against my neck again, and his fingers digging into my flesh.

Shaking my head to clear it, I step out into the damp night air. I will not do this. I will not let one arrogant, entitled nobleman make me afraid of the place I was born to. I've enough fears already, and no desire to add to that collection.

Looking up at the stars, I start to count. But I'm interrupted before I number a dozen of them.

"Forget I was coming?" Wyn's leaning against the inn wall in a patch of moonlight. And suddenly, inexplicably, at the sight of him all my fears vanish.

"I did," I admit a little shamefacedly. "But you were right earlier—I'm glad you're here."

Wyn grins, and we fall into stride with one another, walking down the lane toward home. Though it's June, the closer we get to Burleigh House the colder it becomes. By the time we're half a mile away, frost rimes the hedgerows. The stars shine cold and clear overhead, and my breath smokes on the air. I shiver, and wrap my arms around myself.

"This can't be a good sign," I say to Wyn.

"No. Vi, about that—something happened to the House today,

while you were at the Shilling."

I stop short. "*Something happened?* What do you mean?"

Wyn winces and shakes his head. "You'll see soon enough."

All my fears spring to life once more, swimming in endless circles through my veins. As we turn in at the bramble gate, I can sense something at once—Burleigh's pain, which I'm always conscious of on the grounds, is no longer a dull throb. It's sharp and immediate and impossible to ignore. I gasp as it hits me.

Ivy slithers along the drive the moment I step through the gate and snakes up to twine around my hand. Tiny white flowers unfold along the length of it, and I can feel Burleigh's pathetic eagerness to have me home.

"Poor darling," I whisper. "What's happened here?"

Then I look up at the House itself and a sob rises in my throat.

The roof of the guest wing has collapsed in on itself. Mortar seeps from torn timbers and shattered stone, and blackened brambles are already climbing up the walls. I gather up my skirts and run down the drive, bursting into the House where Burleigh's pain hits me afresh, blazing like a beacon.

When I open the door to the guest wing, a cloud of dust pours out, choking me. Once it settles, I stare at the wreckage beyond in horror.

A massive two-story hole gapes above us, open to the night sky, and what's left of the rooms are strewn with mountains of wreckage. There's mortar everywhere, the lifeblood of my House leaking out from within it, and I press a hand to my mouth at the sight.

"Vi," Wyn says quietly, appearing at my side as I stand motionless. "Are you alright?"

No. Seeing my House in distress makes me feel as if I'm crumbling on the inside as well. I could serve food and drink and clean tables at the Shilling for five hundred years and never earn enough to repair the damage I'm looking at. Not to mention the deed. A single summer, to attempt what my father couldn't manage in years, with the full resources of the West Country and the Sterlings' ancestral lands at his disposal.

I am penniless, keyless, and woefully inexperienced by comparison. I am not enough. I will go down in history as the first and last Sterling to fail Burleigh House.

All of this roils beneath my skin, but if there's one thing Burleigh and I have in common, it's a capacity to keep our darkness and unpleasantness locked up inside. I will not break down. I will not let this panic pour out.

But I feel so very small and helpless. I want, more than anything, for Wyn to reach out and take my hand. For him to promise me everything will come out right in the end. I'm not sure it will, but I think if he said it, I'd believe him. And yet I know it's wrong to expect that of him. Burleigh is my burden to bear.

So Wyn and I stand silently, side by side, looking at the beginning of Burleigh's end.

"Would you die for something you love?" I ask finally. "If it was the only way for you to keep it from harm?"

Wyn hesitates.

"I would," he says after a moment. And then Wyn turns to me.

"Violet?" he says. "Come away with me. I promise I won't ask again, but let's just go."

There's no hope in his voice. He's asking out of habit, not

because he thinks there's a chance.

I reach out and press a hand to one of Burleigh's failing walls. Fear seeps into my skin. Panic. Loneliness.

I've never wanted so badly to say yes to Wyn, and to leave this all behind me, but I can't.

So I turn to him, too. We face each other until I bridge the gap between us. I run a thumb along the line of his jaw, my fingers in the unkempt hair at the back of his neck. Wyn's skin against mine feels like magic without the mortar. It feels like electricity and possibility, and because of what I'm about to say, like the beginning of our end.

Wyn draws in a ragged breath and looks at me, and I can see everything he wants written plain across his face.

Me, alone, away from Burleigh House. The two of us together.

And the truth is, sometimes I want that, too.

"Who would I be if I left, Wyn?" I ask, ruthlessly tamping my own wanting down. "Who would I be?"

Alone in my room, I settle myself on the window seat. I feel bruised on the inside, but I take the binding rhyme from my pocket and spread it out on the cushion in front of me.

"Burleigh," I whisper. "I know you've had a hard day. I know you're tired. But will you show me what you can about this?"

Everything grows dim, until darkness falls around me.

Papa's room wavers to life as the dark fades. My father stands beside the bed looking very young—no more than a few years older than I am now—and there's someone else lying under the covers. An older gentleman, who I recognize after a moment. I've seen his portrait before, in what is now the ruins of the dining hall. My grandfather, Henry Sterling, who died years before I was born. He looks ill, and presses a sheet of folded paper into Papa's hand.

"This is for you, boy," my grandfather says. "You'll have the key soon enough. And I hope you'll live a long life and be an admirable Caretaker. But should things go badly in your time—should the House begin to fail, as some have done on the Continent, and as the Sixth House did—know there's always something that can be done, if you have the courage for it."

Papa's young self opens the page and scans the lines of verse. "What is it?"

"A reminder," my grandfather tells him. "That just as William the Deedwinner and all his heirs have bound the Great Houses to themselves with blood and mortar, so you can bind yourself to Burleigh House."

"Bind myself to the House?" Papa frowns. "I've never heard of such a thing."

Henry Sterling struggles to sit up in bed, and Papa moves to help him.

"It's not often spoken of," my grandfather says. "Most Caretakers have chosen to forget such a thing can be done. They've let the memory of it fade from their families. But we remember."

"Alright. If you want me to do it, and it's for Burleigh's good, then tell me what must be done," Papa says without hesitation.

"No." My grandfather places a warning hand on his arm. "It's only for the very end of things, George. If Burleigh falls into dire straits and the House itself should begin to fail, then you, as Caretaker, can be bound to it—given in service to the House, to be used as a vessel to carry Burleigh elsewhere, so that it can begin again, away from its own ruins."

"And then?"

Henry Sterling, the grandfather I never knew, shakes his head. "There is no *and then*, George. The House would consume you entirely, in order to start anew. It would take you over, and leave you lifeless when it goes back into the earth."

Papa is pale and wide-eyed, and I know exactly how he feels. Exactly how the reality and responsibility of life as a Caretaker must have weighed upon him in that moment.

"How is it done," Papa asks after a moment, "should I have need of it?"

"It's quite a simple matter. Speak your intent—of giving yourself up for Burleigh—and let your blood mingle with its mortar. You'll be able to feel everything the House feels then, even without a key. Burleigh will bend to you. It is like . . . a union of souls, or so my great-grandfather said he'd been told. Should you lose your nerve, you'll have one last chance to walk away, because you must work House magic after the binding, if you're to absorb what Burleigh is. Anytime you take in Burleigh's power, it will eclipse you a little more, until it finally reaches your very heart. Then you'll be over-shadowed, the last true servant of our House, who allows it to be reborn, free and unbound."

Papa takes his father's hands in his own. "I swear to you I'll do it, should Burleigh require it of me."

Henry Sterling nods, and smiles, and a little of the tension drains from his face.

"You're very certain, my boy. And certainty is what's required.

A willingness to give of yourself. Make sure you're just as certain if the time comes when a binding is needed, because once bound to a House, you cannot be freed unless someone else takes your place. Even then, you'd have to be absent from the House entirely, in order for it to accept a new bearer and to set you free."

The memory fades, leaving me sitting cross-legged on the window seat, staring down at my grandfather's handwriting in the moonlight. But his words are still ringing in my ears.

You will be able to feel everything the House feels, even without a key. It will bend to you. It is like a union of souls.

It will eclipse you.

You will be overshadowed.

It will take you over, and leave you lifeless when it goes back into the earth.

I pull my knees to my chest, wrapping my arms around them and making myself as small as I can. I know my duty, but that doesn't keep all of this from feeling like more than I should have to bear. And it doesn't make me any less afraid.

❦19❦

EACH MORNING, I THROW MYSELF INTO THE HERCULEAN
task of cleaning up the rubble in the guest wing. Every afternoon, I
walk into the Shilling and ask Alfred if there's been any progress in
the search he and Esperanza are making for the deed. There hasn't
been. Espie's managing to hold off her father and the dreadful Lord
Falmouth, and that's about it. With anxiety eating holes inside me,
I wait tables and go home in the summer dark and plumb Burleigh's
memories, conducting my own peculiar search.

Nothing turns up. I read Papa's ledger from cover to cover. Then
I read it again. I ask for memories of a hundred inconsequential
days. I watch Papa fight with Mama. I watch him leave, and leave,
and leave. I watch *her* leave. I watch Papa drink. I watch him enter-
tain the king, and see the tension in his shoulders, the wariness in
his eyes I never noticed as a child.

But none of the family history I watch is helpful, and every
day, there are more signs that Burleigh is slowly dying. Owls roost
in the kerosene pendants. Brambles and dead leaves drift in the
corners. Mortar oozes from cracks growing in the walls. More and

more often, Burleigh becomes lost in its own memories. Where the ghosts that haunt its halls were once an infrequent and unobtrusive occurrence, they're increasingly present. Sometimes I round a corner and find myself plunged into an alternate, light-on-water world of Burleigh's remembering. Other times, I can't sleep because of the ghosts in the corners of my room.

And then one morning, I wake before dawn to voices outside my door.

I'm disoriented for a moment, sure they're just one of Burleigh's memories, but then the confusion fades and I recognize who's speaking.

". . . Longhill Farm's been hit worst," Jed says quietly. I have to listen intently to catch his words. "You know, Sam Worthing's place, east of the back woods. I've been day laboring there, and it's in a sorry state. Mortar everywhere, dead livestock, and half the orchard ruined."

"What can be done?" Wyn asks.

"Nothing." I can hear the resignation in Jed's voice, and I wrap my arms around myself. "At least not without a proper Caretaker for Burleigh House, or a quick end to the House itself, before more magic can leak out into the countryside."

A proper Caretaker. A quick end to the House. I wince at the words.

"Let me come out this evening, while Violet's at the Shilling," Wyn offers. "I did some House magic during the arrest, when things were particularly bad with George. Maybe I can help."

Blood and mortar, Wyn. Don't you dare.

"I don't like asking it of you," Jed says. "I don't like it one bit.

But even if our Vi doesn't find what she's looking for, and His Majesty burns the House, it'll be too late for the Worthings and Longhill. Something's got to be done soon before all that mortar sours the earth."

Wyn sounds tired. Perhaps Jed can't hear it, but I do. "I know. And if you have to risk someone, better me than her."

"I wouldn't have put it that way, lad," Jed protests.

"No one ever does." Wyn's voice is matter-of-fact, free of rancor. "But I only went into the arrest with George because he finally told me why I'm here, at Burleigh House. It's for Vi, to make sure Burleigh never brings her to any harm. She's to put the House first and I'm to put her first. I don't mind, Jed, truly I don't. I thought I did for a little while, just after you all came back, but it didn't last."

His words remind me of what my father said to me when he brought Wyn home. *Here's someone for you to look after, Vi. Think of it as practice for looking after the House.* None of this makes any sense.

"It was a lucky day when George brought you back to Burleigh," Jed says.

"That wasn't luck," Wyn answers. "It was design. George Sterling knew exactly what he was doing when he brought me home."

A few more words pass between them, too muffled for me to hear. And then,

"I'm off to look for another position," Jed says. "Don't know as I'll find one, with things being as they are, but I'll try. The Worthings are packing up—they mean to go to a cousin in Sheffield, if you can't sort things out for them."

Jed's and Wyn's footsteps retreat down the hall and I squeeze my eyes shut.

I don't want to do this.

It's my job to do this.

I can't let Wyn do this.

I was born to do this.

Tumbling out of bed, I grab a satchel. Into it go long stockings and a pair of Mama's old riding gloves. My patched blouse and fen skirt I pull on at once. Then I add a thin scarf and a hand mirror to the bag for good measure.

Downstairs, I pause in the foyer. There are brambles everywhere, and the soft, feathery sound of birds comes from the kerosene fixtures overhead. The corridor to the kitchen lies ahead of me, and the door to the grounds behind. For just a moment, I'm tempted to walk forward. To step into the kitchen and to pretend, for yet another morning, that I can save my House without it costing me anything more than I've already given.

Instead, I turn and step out the front door, into a dry and unbearably hot summer day. Whether I have the protection of a Caretaker's key or not, I am Violet Helena Sterling. I was born to look after this land, and to care for Burleigh House.

No matter the cost. No matter the risks involved.

I remember Longhill Farm from my childhood. Every so often, Wyn managed to coax me off the grounds of the House and through the wicket gate in the back woods. Beyond them lay Longhill, and the Worthings' good-natured, half-wild children. We would run through the fields with them, teasing placid cows and picking ripe apples off the branches in the orchard. It was like a little paradise.

But things have changed. Burleigh's back woods are no longer sunny and inviting. As I walk through them, dark brambles slither in the hollows and rooks shout ominously from the trees, which have twisted and show mortarous patches on their trunks where the bark has sloughed away.

When I let myself out at the back gate, the sky is low and grey overhead. The temperature drops precipitously outside Burleigh's grounds, and a wind that smells of cold earth whips across the barren fields. Well. At least the long stockings and gloves and scarf I've brought along won't look out of place beyond Burleigh's walls.

The gate at the end of Longhill's lane won't open. I peer at the hinges in the dim light, and realize they're coated with a layer of thick, dry mortar. The earth is grey with it, too, and as I scramble over the gate and make my way toward the farmhouse, signs of Burleigh's rampant magic are everywhere I look.

Several acres of apple trees have cracked at the base and fallen to the ground under the weight of leaves and branches plastered with mortar. The cows in the fields are streaked with it, only their faces showing the russet and dun of their fur below.

Sam Worthing is out front of the farmhouse, sitting on a chair in the ruined garden and brooding. There's mortar dust showing pale in the creases of his deeply lined and sunburned face, and caught in his greying brown hair. Papa was fond of telling me that Sam Worthing's family had lived on this land for centuries, and were as much a fixture of Burleigh Halt as we Sterlings. If they're forced to leave, I can only imagine what will become of us.

"Hello, Mr. Worthing," I say sadly. "It's been a long time, hasn't it?"

"Now then, Miss Violet," Sam says, and his expression remains unreadable. "Have you come to see what your House is doing?"

"I have," I say, swallowing back shame. I've been so caught up in looking after Burleigh I've neglected the countryside. Though how I'd manage to tend to the whole of the West Country and my dying House, and do it all without a key is a bit beyond me.

"I want to help," I tell Sam Worthing.

He shrugs. "You can't. Not without being a proper Caretaker. And even then, we all know the House is failing. You'd only ever be buying time. Miss Violet, Burleigh's done well by us in the West Country. We had our days of plenty, but now I reckon it's time to let it go before it does more damage."

A good Caretaker puts her House first and the land it oversees, I remind myself. Before her king. Before her country. Before her own life.

"Whether I have a key or not, I've come to do a Caretaker's job," I tell him. "Will you show me your farm and your land?"

He gives me a narrow look. "I'm not wanting any trouble, Miss. Not from you or the House. What is it you intend?"

"I'm trying to set things right." I gnaw at a hangnail and glance around us, at all the ruin my House has wrought. Oh, Burleigh. What are we going to do?

"Well, then you'd better follow me."

Sam leads me into the cow byre and a match flares as he lights a lantern in the gloom. I follow him down to the very end of the long row of stalls to where a heifer's been quarantined as much as space allows. Sam holds the lamp high as I step closer to the ailing cow.

She lies on her side, breathing heavily, and when I approach, the whites of her eyes show as she follows my every move.

"Sssshhh," I say to her. "There's a love. I'm not going to hurt you."

I run a hand over her side but it's easy to see where the problem's coming from. Above her heart, veins of mortar spread, marring her russet fur, and a bit of that all-too-familiar grey substance runs from one of her nostrils.

"Livestock have been taking ill like that for months now," Sam tells me. "We say they've been mortarstruck."

I straighten up. "Can we go out to the orchard?"

The trees look even worse up close. Bark peels from the trunks, revealing damp grey patches, and banks of withered leaves lie on the grass, brambles tangled in among them. There will be no fall harvest here. This farm, once a place of peace and productivity, has become a wasteland, holding nothing but a promise of starvation for those who stay on it.

Burleigh is trying, it truly is. I can feel the effort my House spends trying to hold its tainted magic in when I stand on the grounds. The focus and energy required. But all that power must go somewhere, unless Burleigh is burned, and its magic, along with its stone and timber, goes up in smoke. Until then, or until I find the deed and unbind my House, it will continue to poison this land, even if it doesn't mean to do it.

All this suffering, of people and places and Houses, and it could all be undone if the king would just loosen his grip on the reins of power.

"I'm sorry, Mr. Worthing," I say. "But I can fix this."

I hope I can, at any rate. But whatever the dangers, I could hardly call myself a Sterling if I didn't try.

Sam Worthing seems less than certain, now we've come down to it.

"Miss Violet, if you can't—" he begins with an anguished expression, but I cut him off.

"I can. I already told you. But turn your back—House magic worked without a key isn't a pretty sight. I don't want you to look."

When he's turned away from me, I kneel, hitching my skirts up so that I'll feel the earth and the House's power through the tops of my bare feet, my shins, my knees. Then I sink both hands into what was once rich Somerset soil and smile. Wherever I am, so long as I'm in the West Country, I know my House can see.

"Burleigh House," I murmur. "Take what you need."

There's no slow, careful doling out of power. No understanding of my human frailty. Instead I'm hit by a wall of dark, sickly energy and everything in me freezes as mortar pours through my veins.

At first I can't think, can't breathe, can't move. All I can do is crouch, transfixed by pain, like an insect pinned to a card or a fish speared to the riverbed.

But I have my pride, and Sam Worthing, who I've known from my childhood, still stands not ten yards away. I will not let the tremors take me. I will not cry out. I will not move my hands from the earth until this magic is done. Until every bit of darkness that has leached into this soil runs into me and leaves the land full of life again.

Overhead, the sun inches along the sky. The apple leaves shake in a warming summer breeze. And finally I watch as the brambles wither away. As the mortar on every surface crumbles and turns to dust, and that dust is consumed by the earth.

It is enough.

It will have to be. I have nothing left to give.

Sitting back, I pull my hands from the soil. Earth stains them, hiding the mortar that runs beneath my skin, but I can still feel its cold, sluggish poison. It will never leave me. It will rest within my body until someday, perhaps ten, perhaps twenty, perhaps thirty years from now, I sicken from it, and die. Sam looks at me, and it's as if he's aged a decade in this last half hour.

"There you are, then," I tell him, wiping at the mortar that weeps from my eyes. "I'm sorry on Burleigh's behalf. I promise you, I'm doing everything in my power to fix what's gone wrong in the West Country. And I pray I'll have Burleigh restored, or it will be burned, before your farm gets in such a state again."

"I'm glad to have the land back," he says with a shake of his head. All the bitterness has drained from him, as surely as the mortar is gone from the soil he works. "But I'm not sure in the end that it's worth the price, Miss Violet. Can I help you home?"

"No. Your family's waiting, and I'll be alright."

I sit in the middle of Longhill Farm's restored orchard. Some of the trees have fallen, and that can't be helped, but the rest have shaken the mortar dust from their boughs and sprouted a dozen or more pinkening apples on every single branch. Away toward the byre, I hear a clang and a joyous lowing, as Sam lets the penned heifer loose. She kicks up her heels on her way to join her companions, entirely well once more.

My father's old watchword churns around and around in my mind. A good Caretaker puts her House first. Before king, before country, before her own life.

How long will mine be, I wonder?

I pull on the long stockings I've brought, and the riding gloves, and tie the scarf around my neck, to hide the grey magic running under my skin. When I've finished, I look into the little hand mirror I tucked into the satchel as well.

Though there are shadows beneath my eyes and an ill look about me, you'd never guess the root of it. You'd never look at me and say, "There goes Violet Sterling, a girl with mortar in her veins." And by the time I get home tonight, the mortar in me will have become invisible, swimming quietly in my blood, just waiting.

Someday, I will die for Burleigh House. It's only become a matter of when.

✣20✣

"YOU LOOK ABSOLUTELY APPALLING, VI. WHAT HAVE YOU been doing?"

I turn around, nearly dropping my tray of cider mugs, and find Esperanza standing in the doorway of the Red Shilling. She's in riding clothes, smelling of horse and looking exhausted herself.

"You were gone a whole month," I mumble. "I've done a lot, and you're not exactly a fashion plate yourself, now are you?"

I've come straight here from the Worthings' farm—it's still the mortar that has me looking like death warmed over, but I'm not about to own to that.

"I suppose not," Espie sighs. "Did you know I was the best-dressed girl at the Spanish court? My, how the mighty have fallen. I'm absolutely worn-out, too. Almost as tired as you look."

"Oh, stop it," I say.

Alfred glances up from his omnipresent book and fixes Esperanza with a withering glare, as if they were never apart. "I beg your pardon; you're as ravishing as ever from where I'm sitting. Don't disparage the love of my life."

"I smell like the back end of a horse, Alfie," she grumbles. "Even you can't possibly be attracted to that."

He waves a dismissive hand at her. "Eau de cheval is my favorite fragrance, but only on you."

"I do love you, darling." Esperanza sighs. I roll my eyes, but blood and mortar, it's good to have her back.

"How did it go?" I ask, because I've got to get back to my tables and they'll be carrying on all night if I let them.

Espie rolls her eyes. "Ugh. A solid month of managing absolutely impossible men. The two of you are a sight for sore eyes, I can tell you that much."

"You didn't hear anything promising about the deed, did you?" I try not to hope, but I can't help it.

"No," Esperanza answers. "I wish I had better news for you. I was hoping you'd found something out."

"Nothing on my end." I look down at the floor. "And we're running out of time. Burleigh's—not doing well."

"We're still trying," Alfred reassures me. "We won't stop looking until, one way or another, there's no need to look anymore. It's as frustrating for us as for you that none of this is going well. We'd hoped for better, Vi."

I force a smile, though I sincerely doubt either of them has been frustrated enough to risk their lives over Burleigh's plight as I have. "I know. And I think the world of you both for helping."

"I'm not leaving again, not unless we find the deed," Espie says. She reaches out to squeeze my hand and I swallow around a suspicious lump in my throat. "We're in this with you till the end. Though my father—well, he told me to remind you that you've only got until the beginning of August, and that you're not doing very well so far."

"Wonderful," I say. "As if I didn't already know."

"How can I possibly compensate for my appalling family?" Espie asks. "Here, let's start with exorbitant tips."

She takes an enormous wad of banknotes from her pocket and pushes it toward me, but I push it back with a roll of my eyes.

"An odd princess," Alfred mutters. "Spending your allowance on tavern girls and treason, rather than gloves and fans."

"Well, *someone's* got to spend their money on the poor tavern girls, Alfie, since you're not doing it and it's usually a gentleman's prerogative," Esperanza answers.

When I get back to the counter, Frey's out front for the first time this evening. She's had meetings with merchants and greengrocers and kitchen staff, and gives me a sharp look as I take a fresh tray of mugs from her.

"A word with you in my office, Violet Sterling."

Reluctantly, I follow her down the Shilling's narrow back corridor, to a tiny room where she keeps the books and does the ordering. Frey's a fair employer, and more than good to her people, but I've been preoccupied of late and wonder if I'm about to get a dressing down.

Instead, she taps the back of one of my gloved hands.

"What are you hiding under there?"

"Nothing," I lie again. "It's cold for July, that's all."

"Then take your gloves off."

Slowly, with a nervous fluttering in the pit of my stomach, I peel them off, willing the mortar in my blood to have faded. But it hasn't. It's still there, running under my skin. I've been deathly cold all evening, with an intolerable aching and heaviness in my limbs.

"May I?" Frey asks.

"Oh, go ahead," I mutter. "Since you knew anyway."

She pushes my sleeve up and takes in a quick breath at the sight of yet more mortar veining my arm to the elbow. "Violet, you didn't."

"Oh, I'm afraid I did. Burleigh's been getting worse and worse, and Longhill Farm's borne the brunt of it. I couldn't just let my House ruin the Worthings like that. They've been in the county forever. But how did you know I've worked House magic for them?"

Frey sits down at her desk, which nearly fills the room, and gestures to the one other piece of furniture, a small wooden chair. "Your father started channeling mortar without the protection of a key before his arrest began, during the last year he had his freedom. He said he could shift more of Burleigh's power that way, get more of the magic that had gone bad out of its system. I saw the signs on him often enough."

It doesn't surprise me. Burleigh was everything to Papa. He must have been wild over its distress, though he never let it show.

"Papa mentioned you in a letter he left me," I say. "Said you were someone I could trust. Were you very well acquainted?"

Frey smiles. "That's one way of putting it. We worked together, trying to find the deeds. I'd ask leading questions of patrons in their cups, whenever we had any nobility and their help passing through, and then give useful information to your father. I do the same now, for your friends out front."

Frey pauses for a moment before speaking again. "Then awhile after your mother left, your father and I didn't just work together anymore."

"Oh. *Oh*," I say. "I'm sorry, Frey. I never stop to think that I'm not the only one who lost him."

"He was like the sun, your father," Frey says. "When he was in a room, it felt warmer. There's not a soul in Burleigh Halt that didn't grieve when he died, Violet Sterling, and don't you forget that. He was everything a Caretaker ought to be. But I'll tell you something—now he's gone, everyone who lives on your House's doorstep is just hoping to get through Burleigh's end in one piece. I know the countryside does better with Burleigh to quicken it, but remember the Sixth House. It's a terrible risk you're taking, trying to set that place free."

"I know." I twist one of Mama's gloves in my mortar-marred hands. "But what else can I do, Frey? I'm a Sterling. This is everything I've been born and bred for."

"You can break the mold," Frey says firmly. "Walk away. Let nature and the king run their course. And then, when the dust has settled and your heart's mended, I'd be happy to have my serving girl back. Maybe make you a partner someday."

It's a very generous offer. But the mere thought of living on magicless land, so close to what was once my beloved House, works in me worse than mortar.

"I'll think on it," I say. "And I don't take the well-being of the West Country lightly, I promise you that."

"You can choose your own fate, Violet," Frey tells me. "Your own priorities. Burleigh doesn't have to be your beginning and end."

But I've never imagined a world like that. I've never believed I could.

* * *

Burleigh's ghosts haunt me. They whisper and murmur in the corners of my room at all hours. I toss and turn at night, and whenever I open my eyes, all I can see in the dark is glowing figures, wavering in the moonlight. The House feels tense and frustrated, as if it knows its own end is drawing nearer. I roll over in bed and static sparks snap from the sheets.

Another week has gone by, without any new information about Burleigh's deed. In less than a month, His Majesty will descend with torches, to burn my House and send its magic up in smoke.

I've begun to steel myself for the inevitable.

For a binding. For a death.

And I wonder, sitting up in bed and watching Burleigh's memories play out around me, if it will remember me once my body has brought it to new land. Will my ghost haunt the halls of Burleigh House reborn? Or will I be forgotten once my sacrifice is made?

Panic rises in my throat at the thought. I push away the covers and pad into the hall, crouching at Wyn's side.

"Psst," I whisper to him. "Wyn. Wake up."

He rolls over and sleeps on.

"Wyn." I reach out and nudge him. He's warm with sleep and the corridor is far quieter than my room. Briefly, I'm tempted to slide under the blanket next to him. I sincerely doubt I'd drop off with Wyn so close, though. Of late, there's not just tension and sparks between Burleigh and me.

At last, Wyn stirs.

"Vi?" His voice is hoarse and he clears his throat, still barely awake as he squints up at me. "Is something wrong?"

"I can't sleep."

"Oh." Wyn's eyes drift shut again. "Well, try counting sheep."

"My room's full of ghosts. They're too loud. I can't hear myself counting."

Wyn shifts himself closer to the wall and folds the blanket back without opening his eyes. "Here. Now go to sleep."

Oh dear.

I slip carefully under the blanket, taking great pains not to touch him. Then I lie flat on my back and stare straight up at the ceiling. Mercy, it's not particularly comfortable on this floor. He's a bit of a glutton for punishment, Wyn is.

I don't allow myself to turn onto one side until I'm certain he must have dozed back off. But when I finally do turn over, I let out a startled yelp, because Wyn's awake and staring right at me.

"Blood and mortar, Wyn, what are you doing?"

"I've remembered something," he says, narrowing his eyes. "You used to sleep through anything. There was that winter I fell down your bedroom chimney, looking for Father Christmas—you never even woke up."

"Not one of your best ideas, that." I shake my head.

"Why are you really awake, Vi? What's the matter?"

We're only inches from each other. It's too warm and too close and I think I might stifle. I throw off the blanket and sit up. But Wyn follows suit, and though I'm less warm now, we're side by side and I'm acutely aware of his arm pressed against mine.

I put a finger to my mouth to gnaw at a nail, but they've all been bitten down to the bloody quick.

"That bit of verse I found, in your shepherd's hut in the back woods—you know what it is." It's not a question, it's a statement.

Wyn rests the back of his head against the wall. "Of course I do. And you've found out, haven't you?"

"Yes. Wyn, I don't know what else to do. I'm running out of time to find the deed—in a few days, even if I can sort out where it is, it'll be too late. I wouldn't be able to get to it and back again before the king arrives. I think . . . I think I have to bind myself to Burleigh House."

It sits like a cold weight in my gut, the knowledge that I will die for Burleigh. If only I could save the House any other way.

Wyn reaches out and takes my hand. He laces his fingers through mine and a little thrill runs through me.

"Vi?" Wyn asks. "What did your father love most in this world?"

"Burleigh," I answer without hesitation. "And he always put the House first."

"Did he?" Wyn lifts our joined hands. The mortar has faded from under my skin and the bruises have gone from my wrists, leaving only the faint pink ring that circles my left arm still visible. "Where did this come from?"

"I was born with it," I say. "You know that, though."

He winces. "Violet, I haven't always been honest with you. But I'm going tell you the truth now, about everything. About how I came to be at Burleigh House, and about why I stayed behind with your father, and about some other things besides."

My breath catches. I've been waiting for him to tell me the truth, but now it's come, I'm not sure I want to hear what Wyn's going to say.

"The first thing you should know is this," he tells me. "That's not a mark you were born with. It's a scar. You got it a week before

I came to the House, and every night for a year, I listened to your father tell you a story, about how you'd been born with it. At the beginning you laughed, and by the end, you believed him. It's easy to forget things when you're only six years old, but I remember, Violet. I remember."

I don't understand why Wyn would say such a thing, and I pull my hand away from his. "What are you talking about? My father wouldn't lie to me."

Wyn gives me a pained look. "You're not going to like any of this, Vi. Maybe I should just stop. Maybe I shouldn't tell you."

But I have one unimpeachable witness to everything that's gone on within these walls, who will show me the truth of any matter.

"Burleigh," I say, rubbing a finger against the mark on my wrist. "Show me the day I got this."

The corridor wavers with an overlay of memory—the image of my own bedroom. A little ghost springs to life on the braided rug nearby—Violet Helena Sterling, age five, playing with her dolls and their house. It's a replica of Burleigh Papa had made for me, though a year after Wyn joined us, Mama had the toy house taken away. *You've outgrown it, Vi*, she said, even though I still played with it every morning before she took it from me.

Little Vi plays on her own for a minute, and then fixes her eyes on the armchair behind me. I turn, and find my father's ghost has joined us as well, sitting by the hearth with a stack of correspondence.

"Papa?" Little Vi asks. "Will you play with me?"

"Not just yet," he answers, without looking up from his letters. "You know I only promised to sit up here with you so long as you didn't interrupt my work."

Little Violet sighs and turns back to her dolls, but her disappointment quickly turns to delight. Because all around the dollhouse, Burleigh has laid out a garden, just like our own grounds. There are miniature roses growing from the floorboards outside the conservatory, little grasses and wildflowers beyond them, and even a row of seedling trees to represent the back woods.

"Burleigh," I watch myself whisper. "Don't tell anyone, but I love you the most. I'd do anything for you, you know? Anything."

A green vine, marked with patches of grey mortar, snakes up from the floor and twines itself around Little Vi's wrist. She smiles, then winces and goes very still as thorns spring out from the vine. Blood beads onto my child-self's skin like a bracelet, but it isn't crimson, it's gone pink, mingling with the mortar in the vine and on its thorns.

Papa glances up, and then he's out of the chair and kneeling at Little Violet's side, tearing the vine from her wrist. Tears pool in her eyes.

"You're hurting," she says reproachfully. "Stop it, Papa."

I watch as my father takes my chin in his hand and his eyes rove over my face.

"What have you done, Burleigh?" he says.

"Burleigh hasn't done anything wrong," Little Vi answers irritably. "It's sorry, and didn't mean anything by it."

Papa wraps a handkerchief around my bleeding wrist, his gaze never leaving me. "What do you mean, Burleigh's sorry? That's very specific, Vi."

Little Vi shrugs and turns back to her dolls as soon as he lets her go. "I mean it's sorry you're angry, but thinks you shouldn't be. Don't you *feel* it, Papa?"

He shuts his eyes and the ghosts around me waver and rearrange.

In this new vision of Burleigh House, Little Vi's tucked up in bed, and it must be later on the same day, for the handkerchief still binds her wrist. Mama and Papa stand at her bedside and are in the middle of speaking in strained tones as the girl I was sleeps peacefully.

"I wanted you to know, Eloise," Papa says. "I want to be honest with you. I didn't expect it of Burleigh, but I'm going to take care of everything, and it won't matter, I promise. It won't ever come to anything, because I'm going to sort out the House, and it will never have need of Violet in that way."

Mama's face is a mask of shock and horror. "George, there is nothing you can tell me that will make things better. This House is a danger to Violet. It marked her for death. Perhaps you can live with that, but I can't."

Papa grows defensive. "It doesn't matter so long as she's not working House magic. And Burleigh only marked her because I don't think anyone's ever loved a Great House the way Vi does. She's willing. She'd give the breath out of her lungs for this place. The Houses don't understand about age or childhood, anyway—Burleigh's been here for thousands of years."

There's venom in Mama's voice. "That doesn't change the fact that Violet is five years old. She still thinks fairies live under the rosebushes. Of course she loves her magic House. But when she gets older, she'll come to realize the devil is in it. Fix this, George Sterling. Make it. Right."

"I can't." Papa spreads his hands helplessly. "There's nothing I can do. I can only try to ensure that Burleigh never needs her."

Mama turns on her heel.

"You're a smart man. A brilliant Caretaker, they say. So figure something else out," she hisses over one shoulder as she leaves the room.

The memory fades, leaving Wyn and me sitting side by side once more in the dim hallway. A little vine springs up at my side and twines around my wrist, brushing velvet petals against the place where thorns bit at me. I swallow, and tamp down an urge to pull away from Burleigh's touch.

"The House bound you to itself when you were five years old, Violet," Wyn says softly. "Burleigh's always loved you best, I'm only sorry that this is what it led to."

I sit in silence, trying not to think how the vine resting soft against my wrist suddenly feels like a shackle.

I love Burleigh. Burleigh loves me. I would choose Burleigh. Burleigh chose me.

Then why does this still seem so much like betrayal?

As always, I force my hurt feelings down inside. It doesn't matter. I have a job to do, and was intent on this path anyway. Burleigh House has just made my life easier. All that remains now is to open myself to its magic. To let it overtake me.

To become the last Caretaker, who saves her beloved House.

"I'm glad you told me," I say to Wyn, though the words sound forced. "I would have chosen Burleigh anyway, so at least the House and I are in accord."

"No, Violet. That's not all of it," he says.

⚜ 21 ⚜

FEAR GNAWS AT MY INSIDES AS WYN LOOKS UP AT THE ceiling.

"Burleigh," he says. "Show us the day I came here."

Somewhere within the walls, timbers groan.

"Burleigh," Wyn presses. And darkness falls.

A phantom image of the front drive appears around us, on a fresh afternoon in early spring. I know this day at once, because there I am, with a bandage around my left wrist. I stand waiting for Papa in my braids and my pinafore, bouncing up and down in place. He left for Taunton before dawn on an errand, which he said was partly for the House and partly for me. I remember my excitement over that—most of his trips were strictly on Burleigh's behalf. At last the gate swings open and Papa's horse appears on the drive. I bolt toward him, only to freeze in place.

Because there's a boy with my father, sitting in front of him and looking absurdly small and timid. He's pale and hunched, and I don't know what's filthier—the boy himself or his clothes.

"Papa," I call to my father as soon as he's within earshot. I'm so brazen—so certain of myself and my place. "Who's that with you? He looks a frightful mess."

Papa reins in his horse and dismounts, then helps the strange boy down. The boy stands in the shadow of my father's quiet gelding and trembles, like a frightened dog. I give him a dubious look. Never a compassionate child at best, I funnel what empathy I do possess toward Burleigh House, leaving little behind for others.

"What's wrong with him?" I ask flatly.

"There's nothing wrong with him, Vi," Papa says. "He's from the foundling home in Taunton. Was left there three years ago. But they're at their wits' end with him, because he keeps running away, and then a well-meaning someone or other finds him and brings him back."

I stare daggers at the boy. This is my House. There's little enough of Mama and Papa to go around, and Burleigh especially belongs to me. I will brook no rival in its affections.

"Why's he here?"

"To be company for you," Papa answers, taking his riding gloves off, one after the other. "You know your mother always says you shouldn't be alone so much. Well, here's a friend. And he needed a home anyhow. It should work out well for everyone."

I watch as Little Vi steps forward, not even bothering to hide the doubt that etches itself across her face. I can still remember that visceral sense of suspicion and mistrust the first time I saw Wyn. How quickly things changed between us, though.

"Boy," Little Vi asks Wyn. "Do you speak?"

He nods.

"Are you *going* to speak?"

He shakes his head.

"Why not?"

Wyn shrugs.

"Are you afraid?"

Another nod.

Little Vi frowns at him for several moments.

"Why don't you take it upon yourself to look after him?" Papa says at last. "Consider it practice, for looking after Burleigh someday."

The girl I was brightens. How well Papa knew me—if I thought something would benefit the House, I always gave it my very best.

"What do you think, Burleigh?" Little Vi asks the air around us. "Is Papa's idea a good one?"

A thunderclap sounds directly overhead, though it's a clear day. Wyn's eyes go wide as saucers.

"Do you like that?" Little Vi says, solicitous now she's been assured Wyn's presence is in the House's best interest. "That's just Burleigh. It can do lots more. I'll show you."

She reaches out a hand, but when Wyn flinches, draws back. "Don't you want to be touched? I won't, then. Not unless it's alright."

He shifts his weight from one foot to the other, and then finally holds out his own hand. I watch with a smile as Little Vi takes it in hers. "What's your name, then?"

"Haelwyn," Papa answers on his behalf. "Haelwyn of Taunton."

"What about Wyn?" Little Vi asks the boy. "That's easier, isn't it?"

He nods vigorously, and she leads him off toward the House. "I'm Violet Sterling. Did you know I'm going to be Burleigh's Caretaker someday? So I suppose it's a good thing, if I can practice on you. I think you maybe need a bath. And probably something to eat. We've got lots of rooms, and I'm sure they'll give you one . . ." The voice grows fainter as Wyn and Little Vi go down the drive. ". . . but if you promise to keep it a secret, I'll make you a bed in my cupboard. Only the House is very big, and it likes to remember, and it can be frightening at night if you're not used to it."

The very last thing I hear before the memory fades is my six-year-old self's voice, speaking to Wyn.

"We're probably better off if we stick together, you and I."

After a moment of darkness, Wyn and I are alone in the corridor once more.

"Papa brought you home to be company for me," I say a bit defiantly, because a dreadful possibility is dawning in my mind and I hate—*I hate*—even the barest hint of it.

"Come here," Wyn says. He gets to his feet and crosses the hallway to the door that leads into my father's bedroom. I haven't been able to bring myself to enter that particular room of the House—not after seeing Burleigh's memory of Papa dying. It's been shut up since I got home, because I haven't wanted to think about everything that happened inside.

"I thought that I'd come here as your companion, too." Wyn stands with a hand on the doorknob. "I thought it until the night before your father's arrest began. And then he took me aside and explained. It wasn't charity that led George to give me a home. He needed me. There was one thing he loved more than Burleigh House, you see. One thing he wasn't willing to sacrifice in his role as Caretaker."

"Wyn, don't." My voice is a small and broken thing, but Wyn goes on.

"It was you, Violet. He couldn't die knowing the House would one day take your life, as well as his. So he asked me to stay when the arrest began."

Wyn turns the knob and pushes the door open.

The room beyond is much changed. Not a stick of furniture remains, except for a pile of old bedding in one corner. Dust and dead flies lie thick on the windowsills. Carved into the far wall, the jagged letters of my name are still visible by moonlight.

VI.

Wyn crosses the room, and I follow after him like a moth drawn to flame. He reaches out and touches the place where Papa cut into Burleigh House.

"Blood and mortar," Wyn says. "It can undo one binding and make another. But Burleigh didn't want me—it wanted you. So we needed a lot of blood, and a lot of mortar. We waited as long as we could, but a year before the end of the arrest, your father was less and less himself, and there was nothing for it but to . . ."

His voice trails off. I can hardly breathe, thinking of what's been done to both Wyn and my House. Of all the ways they have been bound and broken.

"Show me the rest," I whisper, the words barely audible even in the absolute silence of this cursed room.

Wyn hesitates. Then, with a single decided motion, he pulls his nightshirt up over his head and drops it to the floor. He stands with his back to me, in only his loose linen trousers, and I can see what my father has done.

From the top of Wyn's shoulders to the small of his back, my name is written in thick lines of scar tissue. *VI*—a copy in flesh of what's been carved into Burleigh's wall.

I take in a sharp breath that's already halfway to a sob. The sound rings loud in the emptiness of Papa's room. "Oh, Wyn."

I will *never* forgive my father for this. For damaging the two things I love most in this world just to keep me safe. And while my desire to defend Burleigh is a determined constant, wishing I could undo the past for Wyn sets a fire in me.

"May I?" I ask. Wyn shrugs without turning around.

Stepping forward, I trace the tall capitals of my name with one finger. I put all of my heart into that gentle touch, as if I could heal with the strength of everything that lies between Wyn and me, and with the warmth of skin against skin. Wyn shivers, but doesn't pull away.

"Why did you do it?" My voice breaks a little on the words, and I rest the flat of my hand against Wyn's back. "Why did you agree to this?"

"I felt brave that day," he confesses. "I haven't often, since then."

And I can't bear it anymore—the things that have happened under this roof, the time we spent apart, the people we've become, the small distance that still exists between us.

"You are brave every day, Haelwyn of Taunton," I tell him. "Again and again, you've stayed here for me, and Wyn—I never would have asked you to if I'd known."

"I know," he says, still without turning. "But I never could refuse you, Vi."

"I'm sorry," I tell him. "I'm so sorry."

Drawing closer to him, I press my lips to the hollow between his shoulders. Wyn's breath catches and he turns to face me. The only time I've seen him look so bleak before was in Burleigh's memory of my father's death.

"Haelwyn. That's not even my name," Wyn says. "I had another, before I came here. I can remember that much, but I can't recall what it was. The House magic—it works differently in me than in anyone else, because of the binding. Your father lost his health first and then his mind. But I'm losing my memory. I can hardly remember anything from before I was brought to Burleigh House. And half of what I remember from after, I only know because Burleigh was a witness to it. I can see it in my mind's eye, but it's from outside myself. And I don't feel those memories, not the way I would if I was the one recalling them."

"Why didn't you say?" Hot tears spill from my eyes and I ignore them. "Wyn, let's leave now. You and me together, just like you've always wanted. Run away with me."

He smiles, but there's bitterness behind it. "I can't. Not any-more. I tried to get off the grounds after Falmouth was here and I did all that magic. Not to leave for good, mind you, just to clear my head. But the binding's gone too far and I can't. It's as if I'm walking into an invisible wall, and if I keep pushing it feels like . . . like dying."

"Blood and mortar, I should have let you go while you still could."

I bury my face in my hands, because I think I'm about to fall apart. Wyn's touch, gentle on the crown of my head, only makes things worse.

"I decided to stay, Violet," he says. "I could've left. I decided to stay for the arrest, too. And to be bound to Burleigh. None of it is your fault—I chose it all, for you."

My mind is reeling. Burleigh and Papa are everything I believed was good and upright in this world, and to find that both of them bound *children*—

Yet tempering the bitterness of that revelation is Wyn's admission that he's done all this for me. Knowing it is a weight and a burden, but it kindles heat and light inside me, where the similar burden of looking after Burleigh leaves only cold resolve.

All that warmth crumbles to ash, though, as Wyn speaks again.

"In a few days, everything will be alright," he says, though there's a note of uncertainty in his voice. "Just before His Majesty arrives, I'll do what I've been bound for. Burleigh will have a fresh start. You will have a fresh start. You're going to be fine, Violet. I promise."

I drop my hands and stare at him. "Wyn, I don't want a new start without you. *Nothing's* going to be alright if you don't make it through this. Do you really think I could stand by and watch you make the sacrifice I was meant for? What if—why can't I bind myself to the House again, in your place?"

"I'd have to go away for that to happen," Wyn answers simply. "I can't be replaced unless I'm absent from the House. But the binding's gone too far, and I can't leave. So I'm afraid this is how things have got to be. But you're a Caretaker, Vi. What does a Caretaker do? She puts her House first. Before king, before country, before—"

"*Stop*," I say. "I don't want to hear it."

Wyn bends and picks up his nightshirt, pulling it back over his head. When he faces me again, he's all maddening practicality.

"Why don't you want to hear it?" Wyn asks. "Being a Caretaker is everything you've ever wanted. Everything your father taught you to be. I can bring about what you've hoped for since we were children."

He stands there, with his hands at his sides, next to the place where Papa cut my name into Burleigh's walls and bound Wyn to the House. And Wyn seems so small and breakable next to Burleigh's thorns and mortar.

The House will eclipse him.

He will be overshadowed.

Burleigh will take him over, and leave him lifeless when it goes back into the earth.

Panic wells up inside me, setting my hands to shaking and tears to burning at my eyes. This is not what I wanted.

"I'm not a good Caretaker," I own to Wyn. "I'm never going to be a good Caretaker. I don't want to put the House first, not like this. I don't . . ." I swallow. "Wyn, I don't want Burleigh without you."

He heaves a sigh. "Well, that's unfortunate. Because I'm afraid it looks like you're going to get it."

And then I'm crying in earnest, not bothering to hide my face or turn away, because Wyn already knows the best of me, and the worst.

"Come on now," he says. "Don't do that, Vi. You really will be fine, you know."

Wyn steps forward and puts his arms around me. For a moment, I feel an overwhelming sense of safety, until the awareness that it's Wyn who will die for Burleigh strikes me all over again. I tremble in his arms and he pulls me closer.

"It's alright," Wyn says, his voice low and comforting. "It's alright."

He presses a kiss to the top of my head, but I turn my face up to his and we're caught, looking at one another and knowing that in this moment, something's irrevocably changed between us.

Then my hands are on his skin beneath his nightshirt, tracing those scars once more, and his are on my waist. My mouth meets Wyn's, and in spite of all this blood and mortar, in spite of what feels like the end of the world, everything in me sings. I kiss him as if a kiss could break a binding, and he kisses me as if it could mend a broken heart.

When we finally draw apart, I know it will never again do me any good to count the stars, or to count my fears. Because as Wyn runs a hand through his untidy hair and gives me a look that says *Well, Violet, what are we going to do now?* I can feel it with every bone in my body: he is the center upon which all my fears, at last, converge.

☙ 22 ❧

EVER SINCE WYN'S MIDNIGHT CONFESSION, BURLEIGH IS on edge. I'm on edge. Wyn seems quietly resolved, and that only sharpens the fear inside me.

I beg Alfred and Esperanza to redouble their efforts on Burleigh's behalf, though I can't bring myself to explain why. They write a flood of letters to their contacts throughout the country, asking if anyone's found even the vaguest hint as to the location of Burleigh's deed. For my part, every night I watch Burleigh's memories until I can't stay awake any longer, and fall asleep with the House's whole sad history playing out around me.

I know in my bones that this is the only chance I have—if I can succeed in finding the deed, if I can manage to unbind my House, perhaps I won't have to choose between home and heart.

Because everything has shifted between Wyn and me. Though we're careful with each other, lips and hands never meeting, our eyes meet often. Every time, my pulse goes wild. And every time, I see it in him as he looks back at me—panic, raw and wild, forced down so deep that only the merest glimmer is visible. But I am a master of keeping my emotions tightly in check and know exactly what to look for.

Wyn is like a rabbit in a snare. Whatever he may say, however he may insist he's ready to die to give me a chance at happiness and Burleigh an opportunity to start over, it's not what he wants. And it works like mortar and thorns in me, seeing him unhappy. I think that's why he's maintaining this new and scrupulous distance between us, too—because to be close is to be honest, and Wyn doesn't want me to see the truth.

Then, three nights after Wyn tells me the truth, I wake to a memory I've never seen before.

I haven't asked Burleigh to show me anything about Papa's arrest, beyond what it's volunteered. I've been wary of pushing the House to show me things that might be painful. But I open my eyes in the small, dark hours between evening and morning, and find myself looking at the dining hall.

Or rather, at the ghost of the dining hall, which now lies in ruins.

In this vision of Burleigh House, a fire crackles on the hearth and rain beads down the dining hall's long windows, though it looks to be midday. Fitful gusts of wind creep through wide cracks in the walls, and ivy twines its way up toward the ceiling.

Papa sits at the head of the table. I've never seen him look so ill—he's gaunt and hollow-eyed, with a sickly grey pallor to his skin, and when he reaches for his water glass his trembling hand knocks it over. For a long while he sits, watching the damp patch spread across the tablecloth. Then slowly, methodically, in a way that chills me to the bone because there's no passion in it, just a fixed and emotionless intent, he picks up the glass and hurls it across the room.

Shards explode out from where it hits, with a sharp, unmistakable shattering sound. Papa takes the pitcher next and sends it flying after the glass. Then his plate, his teacup, his saucer, his silverware.

It's not until the last object has gone from the table that he yanks off the tablecloth itself and balls it up, stuffing it into the fire, which backs up and smokes. By this point, mingled blood and mortar run from Papa's nose and weep from his eyes. He stops to wipe at his face with one sleeve before stalking from the room.

Once he's gone, I finally notice Wyn, perhaps a year or two younger than he is now. He's perched on the edge of a chair next to the fireplace, and so still he's nearly invisible. An untouched plate of colorless stewed parsnips rests on Wyn's knees and I watch as he sits for a moment, his throat working. Then he sets his plate aside, takes a broom and dustpan from one of the cupboards, and begins to sweep away Papa's mess.

But halfway through tidying up, Wyn stops and looks about himself, as if to ensure he's alone. He sets down the broom and dustpan and spreads his hands flat against the golden parquet floor.

All around us, the House hums, with something halfway between anxiety and anticipation.

"Go on, then," Wyn's younger self says, his voice unsteady with fear.

And as suddenly and viciously as my father flung his glass against the wall, Burleigh pours magic into Wyn. All around us the House trembles and groans. The ivy that's crept in and covers the dining room walls withers and dies, leaf after leaf going black.

Beneath its skeletal remains, great cracks knit back together in the dining room walls, dust blossoming out to hang on the air. On the hearth, the fire sparks and then roars high, consuming the damp and half-burned tablecloth.

Finally, the House lets Wyn go. He topples over and lies on his side, taking great ragged breaths. But he's there, within himself, and not an inch of his skin that I can see is stained by mortar.

"Well, that's a start," Papa says from the doorway. He stands leaning against the lintel, a frightful contrast to Wyn, with dried mortar still caught in the seams around his eyes and the lines around his mouth. "I've been wondering when you'd finally find the nerve to try it. Took you long enough, boy."

He turns and leaves Wyn sitting among splinters of china, surrounded by walls that once more keep out the rain.

I slip out of bed and crouch in front of Wyn's ghost. As I watch, his face goes blank. His eyes become vacant. He's gone from within himself, wandering that endless corridor he described to me, as Burleigh House eats away at his memories.

I can't watch any longer. Going to the door, I leave Burleigh's memory behind. My Wyn is fast asleep in the hall, a constant and faithful guardian, though at least he's not on the ground now that I've helped him drag a feather bolster out from one of the abandoned guest rooms.

Bending down, I rest a hand briefly on his untidy hair, then slip past without a sound—just another one of Burleigh's ghosts. In the silent, moonlit kitchen, I slide my feet into a pair of galoshes. Jed and Mira's door is shut, and I know at this hour they're fast asleep. I miss them—all summer we've been ships passing in the night. I feel agonizingly on the brink of something, as if I've outgrown the old life we had together and haven't yet found the next place where I'll belong.

It doesn't help that I'm planning to do something no self-respecting Caretaker would. If I were the person who Burleigh needs me to be, I would go upstairs, wake the boy sleeping outside my bedroom door, and tell him there's no place for him in my heart or my life. Tell him that it's in his power to give me everything I've ever wanted, and that I'll remember him kindly if he does.

But just the thought of speaking those words to Wyn is like splinters inside me. So I leave the kitchen and go out through the garden, where dead and dried rose canes rattle in a scorching breeze. I pass through the meadow, leave the family cemetery behind, and enter the shadow world of Burleigh's back woods. I cannot risk Wyn, and so I'm going to do something dangerous and desperate instead.

Ominous noises enliven the dark. More than once, I step into a puddle of thick and viscous mortar, and am glad I thought to put on boots. Brambles creep slowly across the footpath, too slow to trip me, but slithering toward my ankles nonetheless. Marsh lights and memories glimmer between the trees, an otherworldly blue-green. But whatever guise they wear, I know the shape of these woods and the paths that run through them. I'd know them in daylight or darkness, and whether they appear sunny or sinister, it's not in me to fear a piece of Burleigh House.

As I get farther into the woods, the air becomes cold and damp. Misting rain beads on my hair and the fabric of my dressing gown. I come to a place where a winding trail branches off through the trees and veer down it, toward the little valley where the manor's trout stream rushes and laughs over rapids, rain dimpling its surface.

Scrambling down the muddy, leaf-strewn embankment, I settle beside the stream, trying to ignore the chill that's growing more bitter with each passing minute. Blinking rainwater from my eyes, I sink my hands into the gravelly soil of the stream bank. It's an invitation to Burleigh—if anything goes wrong, here I am. A conduit, a channel, a ready vessel for your power. I may not have the key, or a Caretaker's pure intentions, but I am all you've got, House of mine, so set mortar in my blood if you must.

"Burleigh," I say. "I'm going to ask you a question. And I think you know what it is."

The wind gusts overhead, moaning in the treetops. Cold rain runs down the back of my neck and I shiver. For weeks we've danced around this. For weeks I've coddled Burleigh, mindful of its binding and failing health, never wanting to hurt my House even if doing so might save it. But I haven't the time or the patience or the goodwill left to coddle Burleigh anymore.

"Burleigh," I ask. "*Where is your deed?*"

In answer the trout stream bubbles higher, rising against its banks until water laps over the top of my boots. I pull them off and I swallow back frustration.

"Show me, Burleigh. Help me set you free."

The stream rises again, insistently, and I'm forced further up the bank. But then, darkness falls, so complete that even the shadowy forms of the trees and the occasional glimmer of water from the stream are swallowed up. I pass a hand before my eyes, but it's as if I've shut them. I can't see a thing.

A smell rises around me, out of place yet still familiar. It's not the scent of damp earth or rotting wood or forest mosses, but a wild and briny odor—the tang of seawater. My stomach ties itself up in knots, because Burleigh has never shown me anything outside its grounds before. I didn't even know that it could.

Sounds grow at the edge of my hearing. Waves, crashing against the shore. Gulls, shrieking overhead. And a hollow drip, drip, drip.

This isn't just a memory the House has for me. Burleigh, desperate to please, is showing me the location of its deed.

I strain to see in the overwhelming darkness and gradually, the air around me grows grey. Indistinct forms begin to take shape—they're not recognizable yet, but any moment they will be. Hope bursts to joyous life inside me, even as I feel cold creek water against my feet, and the icier bite of mortar leaching into my hands, still buried in forest earth.

The light grows. I see a rocky cavern floor, and beyond the cave mouth the blue, blue Cornish sea. A bit of rock rises from the water offshore.

The image holds. I try to move forward, but it's as if my feet have been cemented to the ground. This is all Burleigh can give—this picture of the Cornish coast. And it's not much to go on.

"Burleigh," I beg. "I don't know where we are. Can't you tell me? Find a way."

The sun sinks low on the western horizon. And as it does, a long, ominous wave rises out of the sea. It rushes on toward the shore, terrifyingly tall and ready to consume everything in its path.

And I know exactly where I am.

Not just a sea cave.

A cave along the coast west of St. Ives, where I stood and watched just such a wave as a child.

Abruptly, the vision shatters. The nighttime woods behind

Burleigh House reappear with a suddenness that makes my head spin. Beneath me, the ground lurches. Water is rising in the stream at an alarming rate—it's already reached my knees, but when I struggle to get to my feet, everything in me is horribly, overwhelmingly heavy. I look down, and my bare arms and legs aren't just veined with grey—they're the color of stone, and I can hardly feel them, they've grown so cold.

With a supreme effort, I force myself upright and climb the treacherous stream bank. The leaves and mud are slick underfoot, and I lose my balance several times, coming out plastered in muck. All the while, the earth beneath me groans and trembles.

At the top of the embankment, I reach out to a nearby tree trunk to steady myself. But I snatch my hand back at once with a hiss. Vines thick with razor-edged thorns are slithering across the forest floor and up the trees, and have torn my palm open. Blood and mortar ooze sluggishly from my skin.

I don't dare stop. I don't dare offer to help my keening House, for fear that it will kill me by mistake.

"Burleigh, stop. Calm yourself," I shout at the House as the ground shakes and distant crashes echo through the forest. But my voice is already thick with mortar and the trees around me are losing branches or toppling over entirely, even as more magic churns into me, bubbling up from the earth, carrying the wild, tainted power of the House. I tremble and freeze as the hiss of vines grows to a fever pitch.

Dark spots are already dancing at the edge of my vision when the first bramble tightens around my ankle.

❧ 23 ❧

THE BITE OF THORNS DRIVES BACK THE DARKNESS SWIM-ming across my line of sight, and I cry out as the vine pulls tight, its fierce teeth sinking into my skin. Something, somewhere, catches Burleigh's attention and the immense weight of the House's focus lifts from me. Clarity floods my mind, and I plunge a hand into my dressing gown pocket, pulling out a gutting knife I haven't yet shaken the habit of carrying. Sliding it from its leather sheath, I saw at the grasping vine with the knife's serrated spine, rather than its curved cutting edge, and finally pull free.

Once I'm loose, I panic. The House only ever shifts its attention like that for one person, and I can't bear to think of him taking in its cursed power.

"Burleigh," I choke. "Don't. Look at me. *Look at me.*"

But the House's attention does not return. Knife still in hand, I limp toward the wildflower meadow at the forest's edge. The woods are alive with destructive energy, though, and I watch in dismay as briars thicker than my arms begin to weave themselves through the trees bordering the meadow.

I grit my teeth, hobbling faster. If that hedge of thorns closes before I reach it, my little blade won't be enough to cut through.

Just then, Wyn appears and stands in the gap between forest and field. I fix my eyes on him, and push myself to move faster.

"Wyn, stop," I call as he reaches out to the trees on either side of him.

"Just hurry," he shouts, and I do my level best. Tremor after tremor throws me to the ground, but I push myself back up each time, closing the distance between us. Wyn holds out a hand and I reach for it.

The earth shakes angrily. Enormous brambles snake toward us. But Wyn pulls me forward with so much force that we tumble into the wildflower meadow together as only inches behind us, the forest is sealed off behind an impenetrable wall of thorns.

An eerie calm falls. Overhead, the sky clears and the moon comes out, bathing field and forest in silver light. But I can't feel relief, or pain, though I'm sure I ought to. All I feel is abominable cold, spreading up my arms and legs, creeping across my chest toward my heart.

"Violet, give me your hands," Wyn says distantly. I try to pull away, because I don't want him to hurt himself, but I can't focus on his voice or seem to move at all. Wyn's face wavers and fades from my vision as everything turns to cold and stone.

I wake on my back, still in the wildflower meadow, and the stars overhead are only just beginning to fade as dawn lightens the eastern sky. There is pain pulsing through me, from where thorns cut at the skin on my hands, and from where brambles tore at my ankle.

But I can feel it, at least. There's no cold left in me. No life-stealing mortar.

Wyn sits a short distance away, head buried in his arms. When I shift and the dry grass rustles, he looks up, and his face is so pale and drawn it breaks my heart. Yet I'm glad that there's no blankness in him—that he's fully present within himself. Whatever the mortar did to him, whatever piece of Wyn it stole, its work is already finished.

"Are you alright?" I ask as I sit up with a groan.

Wyn shakes his head, and when he speaks, his voice is rough with emotion. "What were you *thinking*, Violet? You could have killed yourself."

"I was thinking that I could do this without you working House magic again," I tell him. "That you wouldn't find out until it was done."

"I feel everything Burleigh feels now," Wyn says. "I woke up knowing you were pushing at its bond and that the House was about to lose control, with you in harm's way. Blood and mortar, Vi, why put yourself at risk when you don't have to? When I can end all of this? I should do it now, while I've got the nerve."

Wyn presses his hands to the earth, as if he's about to invite Burleigh's magic to steal yet more of him from me.

"Stop," I gasp, the words all terror and sharp edges. "Wyn, don't even say such things. Promise me, right here and right now, that you won't give yourself over to the House. That you'll hold out to the bitter end, and give me a chance to try and save you. Just a chance, that's all I'm asking for."

He looks at me wearily. "You've asked for a lot of promises since coming home."

"And you've made a lot of needlessly self-sacrificing decisions since I came back; what do you expect me to do?" I answer.

Wyn lowers himself down a little, leaning back on his elbows. "To let me finish the job I'm meant for. Do you know what I am, Vi? I'm a Caretaker. That's what your father intended for me to be. But where you look after the House, I look after you. And so you're meant to come first. Before Burleigh. Before the countryside. Before my own life."

A creeping chill runs down my spine and I shudder. "No one ever asked me if I *want* that."

Wyn shrugs. "No one ever asked any of us if we want to be in this mess. Not you, not me, not your father, not this ruin of a House—sorry, Burleigh," he adds as the ground rumbles beneath us. "Not even your mother. We're just . . . in it. And we've got to make the best of the hands we've been dealt."

"Wyn, *I'm* asking you," I say. "Do you want this?"

He stares off at the dark and twisted back woods and stays silent.

"Look at me," I press, edging a bit closer. "Answer the question."

At last Wyn turns his face toward me, and the restrained fear I've seen glimpses of in his eyes is burning there like a torch.

"I don't want to die, Violet," Wyn confesses, his voice low and raw. "I'm a coward at heart. Your father—the thing is, I could have saved him, couldn't I? If I'd just finished the binding with Burleigh and let the House overtake me, the arrest would've ended. George could have walked out of here alive. In a way, I'm as guilty of his death as the king."

I shake my head. "Is that what you think? I would never blame you for what happened to my father. You were a child when all this began—we both were. Listen to me now: none of this is your fault.

And you're not going to die. I'm going to save you."

The sound of Wyn's laugh is short and sharp on the night air. He gestures to the tortured ruins of the back woods. "Like you're saving Burleigh?"

The words cut deep, but I know it's his fear speaking, and so I let it go. Instead I meet Wyn's eyes and hold his gaze, refusing to look away.

"This didn't happen because I'm trying to save Burleigh," I tell him. "This happened because I'm trying to save you. I asked the House to show me where the deed is. Asked it directly."

A great creaking of timber rises up from the back woods as I own what I've done to Wyn. The enormous brambles twining through the trees writhe and twist like wicked black snakes.

"I found it," I blurt out. "Wyn, I found what I've been looking for. Burleigh showed me. I know where the—where *it* is. You don't have to end anything. I can do this. I can unbind the House, and free you both from each other, and from the king."

For the first time since seeing Burleigh's vision of the Cornish coast, elation swells within me. I found the deed. Or I've as good as found it. Everything is going to be alright.

But Wyn looks unconvinced. In fact, there's more anguish in the lines of his face than ever.

"It's not dying I'm most afraid of," he says. "I don't want that, but it isn't what I can't get out of my head. The House is bound to kill you if you do what you're set on, Violet. And what if I have a chance to save you by giving myself up, and in the moment, I haven't got the courage to do it? I never did, with George." Wyn runs a hand across his face. "Stay here. Don't go after the deed and put yourself in harm's way. Let things run their course. Let Burleigh get to the point where it can't afford to take my will into account any longer—where it has to make the decision for me, without any danger to you."

My desire to see Wyn safe and well and in a place where he can put all this behind him is so fierce it sets a consuming ache in my chest and throat.

"You know I can't do that," I say, taking care to keep my words soft and reassuring. But Wyn still shuts his eyes as if he's been struck, and his jaw tightens.

"I'm not going to fail, and I'm not going to die," I promise. "You're the one who said that you think I can do anything I set my mind to. Well, I've never wanted something more than I want this—not just because it's for Burleigh, but because I hope unbinding the House will unbind you, too. I need you to have enough faith in me to let me try, and to swear that you won't do anything rash until I've had my chance."

As certain as I sound, I'm desperately afraid. But I refuse to let it show.

Wyn looks at me for a long time. I don't know what he's thinking, but I look back, because I want to memorize his face in this moment.

"Very well," he says at last, his voice toneless. "I promise I will not finish giving myself to Burleigh unless you're in mortal danger, or the House forces it. Can you live with that?"

"I'll have to," I say. I inch closer to him until he puts his arm around me and I rest my head on his shoulder. As I do, I realize the only thing that makes me feel safe anymore is being close to Wyn.

I cannot and will not lose him again.

"Do you think we'll ever just be ordinary?" I ask after a long silence passes between us. We sit together, staring sadly at the ruins of the back woods. "Just Violet and Wyn, a girl and a boy, who can sort out who they are, both apart and together?"

"I don't know, Vi," Wyn says. He kisses the top of my head and I sigh. "I really don't know."

⋇24⋇

I WAKE FROM A SCANT TWO HOURS OF TROUBLED SLEEP, the smell of old leaves and river mud still clinging to my skin, and find myself plunged into memory.

Burleigh's wintry woods are all around me, and the wicket gate at the edge of the grounds is within arm's length. But its frame of twining branches does not show views of the countryside beyond, as it did when I was a child. Instead, it's filled in with honey-colored stone, as if a bit of the House's wall has come out to the woods to bar anyone from entering and exiting by the back way. As I sit and watch, Wyn appears.

It's the Wyn I've come to know through Burleigh's eyes, the boy I never knew who spent seven years locked within these grounds. He wears a moth-eaten, cast-off coat of Papa's, and snowflakes have gathered on his shoulders and in his hair. He walks down the woodland path, hands shoved deep in his pockets, and often glances back worriedly, as if expecting something to stop him.

Wyn draws abreast of me, and his breath smokes on the cold air. He holds out a hand and presses it to the unyielding stone that fills the wicket gate.

"Open," he says, and his voice cracks on the word. "Open, please. Let me be free of this place."

There's a grinding of stone and Wyn's eyes light. But the bricks split only a little, and he jumps back with a shout as black spiders pour out over his hand.

Wyn brushes frantically at his sleeve and stumbles backward, tripping over a raised tree root and falling to the ground. It's then that I notice Papa, slinking down the forest path.

He's unshaven, with a thin, snarled beard, and wearing ragged, filthy clothes. Even from a distance, I can see the grey pallor of his skin and unnatural sunkenness of his eyes, which glitter darkly in the winter light. Mortar weeps from them constantly, so that every minute or two, he's forced to raise a hand and wipe it from his face.

"It's no good," Papa says, his voice dry and hollow. "You can't get out that way. I've tried."

Wyn scrabbles around to look at my father, and I see naked fear on his face. "George, what are you doing out here?"

Papa crouches in front of Wyn. "The House let me out. Because it doesn't like what you're trying to do."

"Let me go," Wyn begs again, this time of Papa. "I've had enough. Please."

My father puts his head to one side, considering, and the gesture is strange, for I never saw him do so as a child. "Where will you run, if I set you free? Would you go to her? Would you bring her back, to take your place so that you can walk away unbound?"

"I would never," Wyn says, and there's ferocity behind the words. "I'd keep her away from here altogether."

Papa glances up, at the branches, the sky, the air.

"And Burleigh would have no one," he says. Then his attention returns to Wyn with a fixed intensity that makes me shudder.

"Why the gate?" Papa gestures to the trees, and the open spaces between them, through which hedgerows and sloping hills are just visible. "You've lived here for too long, boy. You're so fixed on the idea of needing a doorway to come and go. If you want your freedom, steal it. Creep out through the trees, like a fox, like a stoat, like a beast of the fields." The whites of his eyes gleam, and he waves a hand wildly. "What you covet is before you. Reach out and take it."

Wyn gets to his feet, casting an uncertain glance at the forest's edge. "But the House—"

"But the House," Papa mimics. "Do you trust me, or not?"

Looking down, Wyn mumbles something.

"What? Speak up!" my father snaps.

When Wyn looks up, there's defiance in his eyes. "I said I trust the man you were."

"Well, there it is, then." Papa wipes mortar from his face with one sleeve. "You'll just have to stay here and rot, because you wouldn't believe what I had to say. The House will likely kill us both, you know, when it can't take any more. You feel it, don't you, boy? Its suffering, creeping up from the earth. I know you do—I can see it on your face every morning and every night. Before long, it's going to snap, and that will be the end of you and me."

Wyn takes a step toward the wood's edge, and then another.

"Go on," Papa jeers. "Show some spine, for once in your life."

I draw my knees up to my chest and wrap my arms around them, trying to hold in how badly it hurts, seeing my father so. Hearing him hurt Wyn.

Wyn takes a breath and strides forward, but at the tree line, he comes up short and shakes his head, as if to clear it, or to banish a ringing in his ears. He stands in place for a moment, then takes a few steps back and does the same thing.

"It's no good," he says. "I can't . . . I can't make myself go any farther."

Behind him, Papa throws his head back and laughs, a bitter, unwholesome sound. "What, did you think I haven't tried leaving before? Because a good Caretaker always puts his House first? I would have left a thousand times over in the last year." He wipes mortar from his face once more.

Wyn walks back, putting twenty or thirty paces between himself and the forest's edge. Then he hurtles across the leaf mold, running for all he's worth.

A thunderclap sounds, directly overhead, and Wyn is thrown back by the power of the House. My father grins, and moves to crouch at his side once more. Wyn blinks, dazed by the fall.

"I'll tell you a secret," Papa says. He puts a hand on Wyn's chest, but it's not to help or reassure, it's to hold him down. "The only thing keeping us here is each other. If you kill me, you can walk away. If you let the House take you, I can. Which would you rather be, boy? A murderer or a martyr?"

Wyn turns his head aside to avoid my father's gaze, and although I know it's only memory, it's as if our eyes are locked on one another. The despair I see in him is all-consuming, and silent tears track down my face.

Papa's hand creeps up to Wyn's throat. His fingers rest gently, curled beneath Wyn's jaw.

"I'll make it easy on you," Papa mutters. "Push you to the point of self-defense or no return."

There's a bitingly cold gale rising in the wood—the House isn't happy about what Papa's doing, and I'm furious and sick over who he's become.

My father's hand tightens.

The earth roars and shakes beneath us. Brambles burst from the ground, tearing Papa away from Wyn, vicious thorns piercing his wrists and ankles. The vines drag Papa back toward the House itself and Wyn follows unsteadily, pleading with Burleigh to stop.

"It's a Great House," Papa rages at the boy. "It puts itself first, and you're just a broken piece of it, now I've bound the two of you together. Sooner or later, it'll take all of you for itself. And I want you to remember until then that you could have chosen your time. You could've kept me alive, or at very least given me a more merciful death."

The two of them are hidden by trees, and the earth stops its shaking as mortar begins to rain from the sky. I'm left alone in Burleigh's memory of the winter woods, and for a moment, I wish I could stay here forever. Alone. Forgotten. Until the cold leaches into my bones and numbs my aching legs and I fall into a sleep that never ends.

But the forest fades and my room swims back into view. I slip out of bed and into the hallway, where Wyn lies sleeping, shadows like bruises beneath his eyes. Sliding under the blanket, I curl up beside him. He shifts a little without waking, and his arm goes around me. But I don't sleep again. I lie still and wait for dawn, knowing I won't truly rest until all this is over and done with.

❧25❧

IN THE PALE LIGHT OF EARLY MORNING, I BREAK THE news that I've found the deed's location to my coconspirators. Esperanza descends upon the House in full state to pack me up for the journey to Cornwall, while Alfred goes off to see about post-horses and stopping places and the like. Frey grants me a leave of absence. Mira kneads bread fiercely, looking wan and disapproving. Jed's taken a rare morning at home, and he sits whittling in silence, though he's wistful where Mira is fierce.

Wyn's nowhere to be found. I've given up trying to understand him, but I can't blame him for disappearing—our last parting weighs heavy on me. It tore me in two, that last goodbye when we were children, and found ourselves separated for such a long time. I try to assure myself that I'll be back soon, and we'll be together again. It wears on me, though, thinking of leaving him behind. I worry that he lied and that while I'm gone, he may find the strength to give himself to Burleigh entirely. That he may be doing it right now. I want him by my side, to watch over as carefully as he's watched over me. I steal time away from the others to look for him, but he's nowhere in the House, and his shepherd's hut is empty, the woods around it malicious and brooding, though there are gaps in the wall of thorns now.

During a moment of solitude, when I'm left in my bedroom with a half-packed bag, I glare at the walls around me.

"So help me, Burleigh," I mutter, "if you let Wyn do anything foolish, I will set a match to you myself."

A cloud of old smoke billows out from the fireplace, and the walls groan sadly.

In a matter of hours, everything's ready. A dreary rain falls out of doors as if to mirror the way I feel, and again I'm reminded, with a heart-stopping pang, of the last time I left Burleigh behind.

This time, it won't be for seven years. It'll barely be seven days. Yet there's a painful lump in my throat as I hug Jed and Mira tightly on the doorstep.

"Look after yourself in Cornwall," Jed says, his voice a bass rumble. "We want our girl home safe when all this is over."

Mira presses a paper bag full of ginger biscuits into my hands. "For the road."

"I love you both," I say, kissing her worn cheek. "And I'll be back before you know it."

The words sound far more cheerful than I feel.

"You'll take care of Wyn for me, won't you? Find him once I'm past the gate and don't let him out of your sight. Tell him I said goodbye, and that I won't be gone any longer than I have to." I can't keep a pleading note from creeping into my voice. They assure me they will, and then there's nothing for it. I hurry down to the waiting carriage, ducking my head against the rain.

"You're so pale," Espie fusses as I climb inside. "It's a good thing we're going on a trip to the seaside."

"It's not a holiday," Alfred reminds her, and she rolls her eyes at him.

"Can't it be both?"

But I ignore their bickering, pressing a hand to the carriage window instead as white flowers bloom among the ivy that covers Burleigh from ground to roofline. It does nothing to dampen my sorrow over Wyn's refusal to appear, knowing that at least Burleigh can bear to say goodbye.

We jolt down the drive toward the lane. Rain drums against the carriage roof and I stare forlornly out the foggy window until we're nearly to the bramble gate. But just shy of the gap, I let out a gasp and throw the carriage door open, tumbling out while it's still in motion.

I can hear Espie's startled shriek, but I scramble upright and there's Wyn, waiting near the wall, soaked to his skin. Rain plasters his hair to his forehead. He stands in that familiar way, shoulders hunched, hands in pockets, and the relief I feel at the sight of him is a sharp and burning thing.

"Where were you?" I ask. In answer, Wyn steps forward and puts his arms around me and I can hardly think for missing him, though we're still together. It was bad enough, being apart when I went to the fens. But since I returned, Wyn's quiet presence has become essential to me.

"I don't want to leave you," I tell him. "But I have to go."

"I want you to leave," he says. "And I'd be lying if I said I don't still wish you wouldn't come back."

His words should sting. I know what he means by them, though.

"It's only for a little while," I promise, putting a hand to the side of his face. "I'll be back, and everything will be fine, once Burleigh's free. I'm a Caretaker, aren't I? Who's to say I can't take care of you both?"

Wyn gives me the ghost of a smile, but he doesn't meet my eyes.

This feels all wrong. It feels like goodbye forever, not just for a week, but if I stay much longer, I won't have the heart to go. Choking back a sob, I pull away from Wyn and walk the few steps to the carriage. Esperanza helps me up with a shake of her head.

"All sorted?" Alfred asks.

"For now," I say bleakly. "Drive on."

We jolt our way through the gate, and it's as if I've left half of myself behind. I huddle in a corner of the carriage, a few feet between Esperanza and me, and I can't understand why this feels so like dying. It should feel like victory, like moving toward hope, and yet here I sit, with my heart in tatters.

It's not till we've left Burleigh Halt and are rattling along the southern road that Esperanza speaks, her voice uncharacteristically soft.

"Violet?" she says. "I know it's hard to be parted. But you were right—it's not going to be for long. You don't have to fret on Wyn's account."

"My father bound Wyn to the House," I tell her. "To die on its behalf, if I can't manage to save it. Papa took the two things I care for most in this world and put their survival at odds with one another. And I'm afraid—I'm afraid Wyn may give himself over to Burleigh while I'm gone, to keep me from becoming another

Marianne Ingilby, and Burleigh from becoming another Sixth House. He's worried the House may kill me, and I'm terrified he'll let it kill him, to stop that from happening."

"Oh, Vi," Espie says, and there's a world of pity in her eyes.

"But what can I do?" I ask, my voice beginning to break. "If I stay, he'll be dead within a fortnight, when the king comes to burn Burleigh and the House . . . inhabits him. The only chance for him, not just Burleigh, is for me to go."

"I'm so sorry, darling," Esperanza murmurs as I swallow back tears and panic. "So sorry."

Alfred offers no empty words of comfort. He sits on the bench across from us and his face, as he stares out at the rainy countryside, has a haunted look. After a while, Espie drops off to sleep, and we travel on in silence.

❋26❊

EVEN MILES AND MILES AWAY FROM BURLEIGH HOUSE, IN Cornwall, the weather is bleak. It rains all throughout our journey, and rains as we arrive at St. Ives in late afternoon. I pay the weather no mind, and walk down to the abandoned beach below the town. A stiff breeze whips the waves into whitecaps. I fill my lungs with the good clean smell of brine, as if it could drive the last traces of mortar from my bones, the last vestiges of fear and doubt from my veins.

And it startles me to find that after years on the fens, standing on the shore and hearing the cry of the mournful gulls feels as much like coming home as going back to Burleigh did.

"Violet!" Esperanza calls, coming down the beach wrapped in an enormous and cumbersome oilskin cloak. "Come inside, it's nearly nightfall. What are you doing out here in the rain?"

I take her by the arm and point to the vast, restless ocean. "Isn't it beautiful? When I look at it, everything seems simpler. No matter what happens, that will still be there. The waves will still come and go. The tides will still rise and fall."

"Yes, it's lovely, but won't you come in?" Esperanza asks again. "You ought to have something to eat and turn in early, if we're to track down the deed tomorrow."

"Not just yet," I tell her. The sky is clearing on the western horizon, and the rain is beginning to let up. "I want to stay out and count the stars."

The thing is, I wonder if Wyn might be up on the roof of Burleigh House, numbering the stars and waiting for me. So I sit on the damp sand, and wait until all the sky is a wide, night-blue vault above me, spangled with the light of innumerable, immeasurably distant suns. I count them until I get lost in the dark places between, and then turn inward, to the dark places there, and manage my fears instead.

But they are oh so many, and I lose myself among them as well.

By the time I return, the inn's public room is nearly empty. Only Alfred still sits up in a corner near the hearth, bent over his ever-present books and papers. As I cross the room, he glances up.

"Violet Sterling, are you alright?" Alfred asks kindly. "I mean, not alright, but coping? How can we help?"

I shake my head. "I've no idea. I'm just—what if we don't find the deed? What if we do, and Burleigh kills me, like the Sixth House did to Marianne Ingilby? What if I can't find Burleigh's heart to complete the unbinding—they say only a Caretaker can do that. Or what if I free the House, and it doesn't fix Burleigh the way we thought it would, but lets all that magic out into the countryside? What if everything goes well but the king decides to burn Burleigh anyway? What if Wyn—"

I stop, because I can't bring myself to speak that particular what-if into being.

Alfred leans back in his chair. "Just do the next thing. Don't focus on anything else. That's how I cope with all this." He waves a hand vaguely at our surroundings. "The living in inns, the bribery, the underhanded dealings. I just make do, because Espie wants to see the Great Houses freed in her lifetime, and if she wants something, she brings it about. If I hadn't met her, I'd either be alone, poking through ruins in Europe on some abandoned hillside, or home at Weston Manor, buried among my books. Instead I am as you see me. A reluctant traitor to the crown."

"You do know when she's queen, you'll be prince consort?" I point out. "You'll never really be settled then, or alone."

"I know," he says. "But the thing is, Violet, some people are worth it. They're worth giving up everything you thought you wanted. And Espie's not just the princess of Wales to me, or even the girl I love. She's home."

Blood and mortar, how can he be so certain when I'm so muddled? I love Burleigh and I loved the fens, and I'm not entirely sure yet what sort of love I have for Wyn; I only know I sleep better when he's in earshot and I burn like a torch when he touches me.

A good Caretaker puts her House first. Papa's voice echoes in my head as I climb the stairs to the rented room Espie and I are sharing. *Before king. Before country. Before her own life. Before her heart.*

I believed him once, with all my heart. But now I'm not sure I can live that way anymore.

"You should have slept later," Esperanza chides when I appear in the inn's public room before sunrise. "The sea cave will still be there."

"I couldn't." I sit down across from her at a small side table and she clears a pile of correspondence away to make room. A serving girl appears next to us with a bob of her head.

"Just a muffin and some tea," I say, and the girl disappears. "Where's Alfred?"

"Still sleeping, like you should be," Espie answers, never one to let a chance at driving home her point pass her by. "He's always late to bed and late to rise when he has his choice."

"Why aren't you still sleeping, then?" I ask.

Esperanza cuts a sausage into dainty slices and pops one in her mouth, chewing meditatively. "I suppose I never feel as if I should have the luxury. If I'm to be queen someday, I ought to rise when my subjects do, and the fishermen set out to sea an hour ago. The farmers have already milked their cattle. The tin miners are at their pitches. Who am I to lie abed?"

I rest my chin on one hand and gaze at her, so full of life and so certain of herself. "Espie, do you ever think we want too much? Me wanting to save Burleigh, you wanting to take the throne, all of us wanting a new fate for the Great Houses? Maybe . . . maybe it's just more than we're meant to have."

Esperanza wipes her mouth on a napkin, sets it down, and wags a finger at me. "Don't be a fatalist. It's too early, and it doesn't become you. Who's ever said we should have less?"

"Your father, for one," I point out.

"My father, and all of my forefathers back to William the Deed-winner, sat on the throne of this country because they wanted something that didn't belong to them. The world is full of men who want things, and never question their right to go after them." Esperanza's eyes spark, and she leans forward in her chair. "Why should we feel any less worthy than they do, so long as what we want does no harm?"

For the first time, I'm struck by the thought that my friend, with whom circumstances have thrown me together, will make an excellent queen.

"Are you talking about the Deedwinner?" Alfred says, appearing beside us and drawing another chair up to the table. "I've nearly got to his chapter in my monograph."

He's impeccably tidy as always, and Espie favors him with an approving smile.

"You're up early."

"Turning over a new leaf. I can't let you feel smug about greeting the dawn all the time, can I? And I had a feeling Violet would want to make an early start. So I'll go talk to the staff about packing us a lunch, because whether we find the deed or not, we'll likely be hungry after clambering around in a cave."

"Why don't you pace or something?" Espie tells me when he's gone. "You look like a caged bear."

I push out of my seat. It's true—nervous energy is coursing through me, now we're so close to our goal. "What if I walk to the harbor? Can we meet there?"

"Of course. Go gaze at your sea."

There's an unseasonably cold wind coming in from offshore, but at least the sky is clear. Small clouds scud across it, like a mirror image of the whitecapped Atlantic. I walk and walk, from one end of the sandy harbor beach to another, and though the fishermen have taken the boats from their slips, a few people linger at the harbor's edge, mending nets or crab pots. But for the most part, St.

Ives is shockingly empty. When I was last here, holidaymakers lined the sand, children laughed on the carousel, and little carts stood out on the beach, from which hawkers sold lemonade and ice creams. Even a hundred miles from Burleigh House, the proof of its decay is everywhere I look.

Alfred and Esperanza join me, and we hike through town and out onto the rugged green cliffs of the Cornish coast. The wind is even stronger up here, away from the protection of the harbor. We walk in silence. I take the lead, traveling westward, remembering Burleigh's vision of a setting sun. The tang of the salt air and the *boom, hush* of the surf and the knowledge that I am about to reach the end I've been working toward have my head spinning.

At last we reach a jutting piece of headland that looks eerily familiar. The beach here is no longer sand—it's stony shingle, and the cliffs have jagged edges. The water below is inky blue where vegetation grows from the ocean floor, and lighter in the sandy spots where sea plants cannot thrive. It's all just as Burleigh showed me.

"Over here!" Esperanza shouts, beckoning to Alfred and me. She points to a worn trail, hidden behind a clump of gorse, and the three of us slip and scramble down it to the shingle below. Once we're at sea level, it's easy to see the thing we've come for—a yawning cave mouth, halfway up the cliff, safe beyond the high-water mark.

Espie clasps my hand in her own and squeezes. "We're nearly there, Violet. Look what you and Burleigh have managed."

I bite my lip and nod. The ascent to the cave looks daunting. There's been an attempt made at hewing a stairway into the rock, but it's a rudimentary effort, somewhere between stone steps and rough handholds.

Without a word, I begin the climb, not needing to look back to know Alfred and Espie are following. Halfway up, I'm forced to stop a minute, clinging to the rock face like a barnacle or a bit of cliff grass as my head spins.

"Alright, Vi?" Alfred asks from beneath and behind.

There's something strange about this place—something deeply right and wrong all at once. It feels like Burleigh, though my House is miles and miles away. By the time I pull myself up into the cave, my legs won't stop shaking.

"It's got to be here," I tell Esperanza breathlessly as she pulls herself up into the cavern. "I can feel it."

The cave isn't very large. Perhaps the size of my bedroom at home, its interior is almost entirely bare. A few stalactites cling to the ceiling, and loose stones rest in the sunken areas of the uneven cave floor. I don't know what I expected, to be honest—perhaps something with an entrance submerged at high tide, that bored deep into the cliffs, full of passageways and twists and turns, rife with places to hide a chest containing one of the things I most desire in this world.

This is little more than a hollow in the hillside. A place for a handful of bats to take refuge and for swifts to nest. It is not a place for hidden treasure—indeed, there's nowhere to hide it.

"It doesn't look like much, does it?" Esperanza says uncertainly.

I stand at the cave mouth and peer out. There's no mistaking this bit of headland, the small rocky island just off the coast that's barely large enough for three people to stand on. I am where Burleigh wanted me to be.

And there's the spinning of my head, the trembling of my legs, the sense that Burleigh is very near, to confirm the House's directions.

"Let's spread out," I tell Alfred and Espie. "I want every inch of this cavern combed over."

They take the walls, running their fingers carefully over the damp stone, searching for any cracks or seams that might hold an oilskin-wrapped package containing the deed. I get down on my hands and knees and travel foot by slow foot across the cave floor, feeling for patches of soil or indentations in the rock, and turning over the loose stones.

We go over the cave once, and by the time we've finished, the sun is high overhead, casting much of the cavern into shadow.

"Again," I say.

Alfred and Esperanza are pale with worry, but they don't protest. We search every nook and cranny a second time, and then a third. By the end my stomach is an empty pit and I'm weak as water.

"Vi." Espie rests a hand on my shoulder. "It's not here."

"How can that be?" I protest. "Burleigh House showed me this spot. And I can *feel* it here. We're in the right place."

"Your father thought he'd discovered the deed's whereabouts," Alfred says. "And yet never found the deed itself. Perhaps it's a mistake."

"I don't understand where we keep going wrong." I bury my face in my hands. "This can't be happening. Not again."

"You should eat a sandwich," Esperanza says. "It'll make you feel better."

"Espie, I can't."

We climb back down the cliff face, and twice I nearly fall,

overwhelmed by Burleigh, by regret and sorrow and magic pulsing through the earth. By time we get off the beach and to the top of the trail, we're losing daylight. I have to stop for quite some time beside the gorse bush, legs trembling beneath me. But by far the worst is my heart. I can't feel it at all—it's as if someone's cut it out of my chest with surgical precision, leaving me no more than a shell of the girl I was.

I have failed in my purpose. I have failed my House.

I've failed Wyn.

How can I go back and let Burleigh have its way? How can I do what I've been raised for, be the Caretaker I was brought up to be, when it means watching the friend of my childhood, who is much more than that to me now, give his life to save my House?

✴27✴

NO SOONER DO WE GET TO THE INN IN ST. IVES THAN THE sky opens up and pours. Rain lashes at the windows, the fire backs up and smokes, and there's no possibility of us starting for home until tomorrow at the earliest.

I chafe at the enforced confinement, and feel as if at any moment, I might fly apart.

"Do you want to talk about anything, Vi?" Espie offers.

"No," I answer sharply. "No, I don't want to talk at all."

Alfred buries himself in his books, receding so far into a stack of them that only the top of his head remains visible. Esperanza sits at the counter and strikes up a rather desperate conversation with the barmaid, about St. Ives and Cornwall and fisheries and what could be done to ease the burdens of local tin miners.

I don't have a bent for reading to distract me, or the good of England to bother with, so I stand at a window and brood, staring out into the dark of the storm. In all my life, I have never felt so low. And with nothing to occupy me, all I can do is wait for ungovernable fear to rise up, for heartbreak to blossom in my chest like a physical pain.

While I wait, I think of Burleigh House, marking me as a child. Of Mama's insistence that Papa find a way to undo what had been done. Of my father bringing a foundling boy home not a week later, when he'd never shown much of a bent for charity before.

I think of Mama's refusal to welcome Wyn into the family, to make him one of us. Of Wyn's unease throughout our childhood—his furtive requests for the two of us to run away together. Of Papa taking him, a blameless boy, into the living prison of House arrest. And I think of Wyn at home, steeling himself to do something that should not be required of him.

Suddenly, I find I am not fearful, or heartbroken.

I'm furious.

Before either Alfred or Esperanza can protest, I burst back out into the storm, grabbing a lantern that hangs by the inn door as I go. I don't care that the cliffs are slippery and treacherous, or that in the darkness the boom and crash of the surf is near overwhelming. I don't care that the rain has me soaked through in a moment, either. All I care about is getting back to that sea cave, because I can no longer tolerate failure. Perhaps I will die for Burleigh yet. But I will not go home and watch Wyn do it in my stead. I'm not just Violet Sterling, Caretaker of a failing House. I am the sum of everywhere and everything I've been. And I am still, in my deepest parts, Vi of the Fens, who never goes home empty-handed.

In the dark and the rain, I nearly pass the gorse bush that marks the head of the trail down to the little beach below the cave, where I felt Burleigh's presence so strongly. But my skirt snags on its reaching branches and I start down the rain-slick path.

The climb up to the cave is a nightmare, with unseen water frothing below as I grasp for purchase on the wet rocks, forced to leave my lantern behind. But at last I haul myself up into the cavern's scant shelter and draw a breath.

Well done, Violet, I think to myself. *You've really thought this through. Sitting in a cave during a rainstorm when you can't see your hand in front of your face will absolutely save Wyn and Burleigh.*

But do I need to see? We searched this whole place over with our eyes in broad daylight, and not a sign of the deed turned up. Perhaps it isn't sight I'm wanting. With sight, I saw nothing worth noticing. But even now, that part of me that recognizes Burleigh, that's always recognized Burleigh, can feel magic, and the familiar presence of my own House.

So in the darkness, racked with shivers, I get down on my hands and knees and reach, with the piece of me that is always reaching for either Burleigh or Wyn; the bit of Violet Sterling who sees them as family, and home.

As I do, thoughts of Wyn being bound to Burleigh rise up, and are soon met by grim imaginings of the House being put to the torch by His Majesty, and of Burleigh overtaking Wyn entirely in order to survive. I force those bleak visions down ruthlessly, all my practice at holding things in check coming to good use as I creep along the cavern floor. I don't want to live in a world where either Wyn or Burleigh does not exist—I want them both, and I refuse to trade one for the other, whatever my father was willing to do.

So I move inch by slow inch through the cave, feeling for my House. Toward the back of the cavern my awareness of Burleigh grows ever so slightly stronger. And then again as I shift a few paces to the left. And again. Then a little weaker, so I hastily backtrack. At the place where I can feel Burleigh most strongly, I meticulously run my hands across the cave floor, touching every bit of rock, and then up along the wall. Little by little I go, all of me bent on sensing my House.

When my searching fingers slide over a slight lip of rock just higher than my head and brush against a small stone, I'm shoved three steps back by the force of what I feel.

Despair, darkness, calamity. Brokenness, heartbreak, agony.

And once that subsides, I realize cold mortar is dripping from my hand. It hasn't gone into me—there was no sense of magic crawling under my skin, no, this is leftover mortar—the last vestiges of it that remain in my blood from the times Burleigh couldn't hold its power back. Whatever I've just touched, it's pulling the lingering bits of poison from me like a magnet draws metal. I've never seen the like, and never known such a thing to be possible. As the mortar goes, I feel suddenly flush with health, like waking up from a long illness you've grown used to, only to find yourself well again.

Bending, I tear a wide strip off the bottom of my already ragged fen skirt. Folding it double and wrapping it around my hand, I reach up once more and grasp at the stone resting on the rock ledge overhead. I can't see it in the darkness, but even through layers of fabric I can still feel that wild anguish, that sense of brokenness, of unbelonging, and of separation.

No wonder my father stood in this cave and never found what he was looking for. It's not deeds that bind the Great Houses—it's missing pieces of their own selves. How devilishly clever of the king and all his predecessors, to never speak a word of this truth. To ensure for eight hundred years that anyone who sought to free the Houses would always be searching for the wrong thing.

And how well Marianne Ingilby must have known Ripley Castle, to find its missing piece.

I carefully wrap up this lost bit of Burleigh and tuck it into one of my deep pockets, where its constant thrumming of loneliness and desolation immediately sets an ache in my thigh. Fear uncurls in my belly at the thought of the journey back down the cliff face, but when I turn to the cavern's mouth, the clouds have parted. A sickle moon gleams overhead, casting diamonds across the restless sea, and its light seems all the brighter for the night having been so dark.

Esperanza and Alfred are still waiting up when I trudge back through the inn door at dawn.

"Violet—" Espie begins.

"I've got it," I tell them wearily. "I found it."

They both begin speaking at the same time, but fall silent as soon as I draw the bundled stone from my pocket.

"Are you—are you sure that's it?" Espie asks, concern pulling her expressive face into a frown. "Only I know you've had a shock, what with us failing to get hold of the deed earlier."

"I'm certain," I tell her. "Espie, look at me. I haven't taken leave of my senses. We've been looking for the wrong thing. Chasing after deeds made of paper, when it's a piece of Burleigh itself that's bound my House."

Pushing aside the torn strip of my skirt, I hold the stone into the light and take a look at it for the first time. Esperanza and Alfred bend to get a better view.

It's not much—just a fist-sized piece of broken masonry, the same warm color as Burleigh's walls, streaked with grey and with darker, rust-brown stains.

"Blood and mortar," Espie breathes.

"Yes," I say. "Quite literally. This is what's binding Burleigh. This is what my House needs back. Can't you feel it, reaching across the countryside toward the rest of itself?"

But my companions shake their heads.

"Well, I can. And what's more, it drew mortar out of my blood when I first touched it. What if—what if the reason Burleigh needs a Caretaker is that this missing piece is what allowed it to channel and control its own magic?" A sudden shock of recognition surges through me as I look down at the stone. I've seen this particular shade before, red and brown and grey all at once. Turning it over, I look at the stone's underside, and there it is—a place where a chip has been hewn off of it. A fraction of Burleigh's missing piece, taken for use in its Caretaker's key. To allow someone to channel the House's magic, as it no longer can.

"I think the key was made with a piece of this," I tell Alfred and Espie. "Which is why a Caretaker can safely work House magic, but Burleigh itself can't. What if Burleigh wasn't bound, so much as broken? What if that's what was done to all the Great Houses?"

Alfred's eyes are blazing, and I can all but see the gears turning in his mind as he tries to recall anything he's read that might support my epiphany.

"It's true they don't speak of deeds anywhere but in England," he says slowly. "In my Italian sources, it's always *cuore della cassa*— the heart of the House. In Spain they talk of *la fianza*, which means something more like a deposit, or a guarantee. An assurance of the

House's compliance. In France it's *le contrat obligatoire*—a binding contract or agreement, but I've also seen the rather more poetic *esprit de le foyer*—spirit of the hearth. I'd thought it was just semantics, though. The medieval chroniclers are known for taking rather a lot of artistic license. And nowhere outside of Europe has bound their places of power. The rest of the world left them free."

"We'd best discuss this on the road," I say. "We're running out of time, and I'm still afraid of Wyn trying to take things out of my hands, and giving himself up for Burleigh while I'm gone."

"Sit down," Esperanza orders crisply. "In ten minutes, we'll have the carriage ready. We'll change horses wherever we can, and won't stop for anything else until we get you back home."

✳28✳

BY THE TIME WE ROUND A BEND IN THE ROAD AND THE
Red Shilling comes into view, I'm exhausted by forced inactivity
and by constant, nagging fear. The anguished thrum of Burleigh's
heartstone, as I've come to think of it, saps my energy, too. But I
can't take it home—the moment I do, Burleigh and I will be at
odds. I'll have to get Jed and Mira off the grounds first. In the
meantime, there's only one person I trust to hold this unspeakably
valuable treasure.

Before the carriage has fully stopped, I'm out of it and through
the Shilling's back entrance.

"Frey?" I call out as I hurry down the narrow corridor, between
the storerooms and the kitchen and the public areas up front. "Frey,
where are you?"

"In here," she calls from her office. "Vi, is that you?"

Darting inside, I shut and bolt the office door behind me. Frey
raises an eyebrow. "How was Cornwall? Did you find what you
were looking for?"

"I found something else," I tell her, keeping my voice low. "But

I have to get home to look in on Wyn, and to get Jed and Mira off the grounds before I go back with it."

As I speak, I kneel at her side, taking Burleigh's heartstone from my pocket and holding it out to her. Frey peers down at it, a quizzical look on her face.

"It's not what you'd expected. Not what your father thought he'd find, either."

"No, it's a piece of Burleigh House. Frey, I can't go home and take this with me. I'm afraid the House won't understand. Burleigh's bound to kill me, as soon as I set foot on the grounds with this, and honestly I wouldn't blame it, even without the binding. The House needs to be whole again, and has no reason to trust people, when we're the ones who broke it."

"You want me to keep it safe, until you come back for it?" Frey says, guessing my request.

"Would you?" I ask. "If it makes you uncomfortable, you needn't. This stone is the most dangerous object in England right now. If the king knew I had it—but I have to get home—there's something the matter with Wyn—oh, how do I explain everything when I haven't got the time?"

She reaches out and cups my chin with one hand. "You don't, child. Give it to me. I won't speak a word about that stone until you ask for it again."

"Thank you," I tell her. "Esperanza and Alfred have been so good to me, truly they have, but Frey, I *trust* you."

"Go on, then." Frey rolls her eyes. "No need for a scene. Get home, and do what needs doing, then pick up your trinket and save that House."

I set the cloth-wrapped heartstone on her lap but she stops me when I've already got one foot out the door.

"Violet Sterling. Whatever goes on this next little while, try not to die. I'll never forgive you if you do—you're the best tavern girl I've had when you're actually here, and you'd be the devil to replace."

"I'll try," I say with a wry smile. "But I can't make any promises."

On the inside, my stomach is twisting into nervous knots. I half run back down the hall and burst out into the inn yard again, where it's begun to snow, though it's only the end of July.

"Violet, what—?" Esperanza begins from where she and Alfred are waiting for me next to the carriage.

"Going home, I'll be back," I call over one shoulder, already hurrying down the lane.

"She's got to stop tearing off like that," I hear Espie say to Alfred, and then I gather up my skirts and run.

It snows harder the closer I get to Burleigh House. Drifts blur the edges of the lane and I can't see more than a dozen feet ahead. I'm sure I'd be freezing if not for the fact that I haven't stopped moving. My breath smokes on the air, and finally the bramble gate appears amid the driving white, the thorns and vines already snaking back, opening the way for me.

Only once I'm through the gate do I slow to a walk.

"I missed you, too," I tell the House. "But where's Wyn? You've looked after him for me, haven't you? You haven't done anything awful?"

The ground beneath me rumbles ominously. Burleigh doesn't

like that at all, hearing me speak reproachfully to it. But fear has eaten away my softer and more sympathetic parts. It grows wicked and wild within me as I get far enough down the drive to make out Burleigh's shape through the swirling snow.

The jacaranda tree has lost all its leaves and blossoms. They lie in heaps on the ground around its trunk, filling the cold air with a sour scent of rotting vegetation. And my House. Oh, my House.

When I left, Burleigh was in ill repair. The guest wing was in ruins, and the rest of the roof needed patching, only growing worse day by day. Vines threatened to take over, and here and there, a windowpane wanted replacing. But my House, that looked poorly tended only a handful of days ago, is now a ruin.

Every window has blown out, and shattered glass mingles with gravel and snow on the drive, crunching underfoot as I draw closer. The roof has fallen in entirely, not just over the guest wing, and in places bits of the upper walls are already beginning to crumble. Ivy has been overtaken by wicked brambles. Burleigh would look almost frightening, were it not for the fact that I know it so well.

"Wyn?" I call, climbing the steps and pushing open the door. The corners of the front hall are choked with rubble. The four-lamp kerosene pendant has fallen from the ceiling and lies smashed in the middle of the floor. It's left a gaping hole in the ceiling above, through which I can see a patch of distant sky. Snow falls softly through the gap, mingling with twisted bits of metal and shards of lamp glass.

"Wyn?" I'm shouting now, picking my way through fallen masonry and leaving a trail of slush in my wake. "Wyn, answer me. Where are you?"

There's no sign of him, but when I push into the kitchen, Jed and Mira are there, nursing cups of tea and brooding under a great canvas tarpaulin that's been lashed down where the roof once was. They start out of their chairs at the sight of me, and in an instant, I've been engulfed by Jed's arms. It's even more like hugging a bear than usual, for in spite of the fire burning on the kitchen hearth, the room's still frigid, and he's wearing a greatcoat. Mira gets up and embraces me, too, and I stand for the briefest instant, safe and warm and loved.

I remember how this family was won for me, though. I ought not to have this by rights. It should be Wyn's, and I should've been the one who stayed behind, bound to the House as insurance against the coming end to its long dying.

"Where's Wyn?" I ask, pulling away from Jed and Mira.

A glance rife with hidden meaning passes between them.

"We're that glad to see you, Violet," Mira says. "We thought something might have happened to you as well."

"What do you mean, *as well*?" I ask, unable to keep panic from creeping into my voice. "Where is Wyn?"

"He's out in the family plot by the wood's edge, visiting with your father," Jed says heavily. "Here, take my coat, and just bear in mind he doesn't quite look himself."

It's snowing even harder now, but I know this land. I don't even have to think about the direction to head in or the path to take—my feet know the way.

I let myself in through the low fence that surrounds the cemetery, up against the looming woods. The nearby trees are still choked with brambles, their bare branches limned with streaks of dried mortar. And I see Wyn at once.

He's sitting in the snow with his back to Papa's plain grave marker. He's got on several bulky layers of tatty knit jerseys to ward off the cold, but the snow is thick on his untidy hair and his shoulders. As I draw closer, he looks different indeed—there's something gone wrong with his skin. It's an inhuman shade and texture, more like Burleigh's walls than anything else. And while there was never much softness to Wyn's appearance in the first place, what little there was is gone. He's all unrelenting angles and fierce symmetry, with eyes like the sparks cast off by flint and iron. I wonder if there's any warmth left to him at all, or if I would find him cold and unyielding as granite. None of that matters to me, though. Where there's life, there's hope, and I am unspeakably glad to find him alive.

"Wyn, what happened? I was only gone for a few days," I say. "What have you done with yourself?"

"It's . . . difficult," he answers, and the words somehow seem muffled, like the House showing me a memory. "I can't always tell now, where Burleigh ends and I begin."

I sit down at his side, wrapping Jed's greatcoat around me. "What did you do?"

"Vi, I know I promised I wouldn't, but—"

"You were going to finish the binding, weren't you?"

Wyn turns his face toward me for the first time, and somehow his flintlike eyes still retain their old, patient look. "I was. But Burleigh stopped me before the end."

He rests his head against Papa's gravestone. "Three nights ago, I finally got up the nerve to finish what your father and I started. To offer myself, everything there is of me, to Burleigh. So that it could carry on somewhere new, without you ever having to try your hand at unbinding it. I'll spare you the details, but it was dreadful, and it took hours, and then around midnight, Burleigh just . . . stopped. It was like one minute the House's whole attention was fixed on me, that crushing weight—you know what it's like—and then it just turned aside. I still don't know why, but it left me like this, and left Burleigh as you see it."

"That's right about when I found the heartstone," I say. "The House must have been able to feel it. Burleigh must want the stone back more than it wants a new start."

"Heartstone?"

Wyn straightens up and when I glance over at him, fear slams through me with a hideous jolt. Because where his expression and his eyes were his own before, now something indefinable in them has changed, and I know, just as I did after he worked House magic, that Wyn has gone from his body. This time, though, he hasn't left it empty. There's *something* in his place.

"Bring us the stone," a gravelly voice says, and I shudder, hearing it come from Wyn's mouth. It's like rock scraping against rock, and sets my teeth on edge. "Lay it on our doorstep and never come back, and because we have loved you, we will let you leave with your life."

". . . Burleigh?" I ask, forcing my fear down, as I've grown so used to doing. "Is that you?"

The thing that is no longer Wyn says nothing, just stares at me with opaque grey eyes.

"Burleigh, you know me," I tell the creature. "I can't just leave the stone, because if I do, you won't really be free. The binding has to be undone with blood and mortar, at your heart, just as it was made."

"We will *never* let another person set their blood into our mortar again," the creature says fiercely. "Not after being bound against our will so many times. Neither will we show you our hidden heart. We will take back what is ours for one shining moment, and break our binding, and die in power as we once lived."

"Think of the West Country," I beg. "You will ruin it if you stay this course. But I can make you whole, Burleigh, truly whole, and undo the wrong you've suffered. I would do that and more for you. Surely you know I would, my love."

The old endearment comes out forced and unnatural, though, because with Burleigh speaking through Wyn's body, all I feel is fear, and underneath it, something terribly akin to loathing. I have loved my House long and well, and I loved my father in spite of his stern ways. But to find that both of them have used Wyn as a pawn in this dangerous game is almost more than I can bear, because as much as I loved them, I love him, too.

"Would you, little girl?" Burleigh grates, and Wyn's cold hand rises to brush a finger against my jaw. I shiver, and try not to pull away. "Would you really? Don't you think after all these years, all these lives, we can look through those who dwell within our walls and see the truth in their hearts? You are no Caretaker. Your heart is divided. Would you truly unbind us, or use the power in our broken piece to unbind *him* instead? To force us to restore him?"

I take absolute care to ensure my face stays immobile, my hands motionless on my lap. It hadn't occurred to me that I might use blood and mortar and the heartstone to unbind Wyn, rather than the House.

But Burleigh leans closer to me and lets out a sigh like the rattling of small stones. "We see the war within you. The very blood in your veins is singing to us, and do you know what it says? *Treacherous. Treacherous. False.*"

I look at the creature before me, at Burleigh House wearing Wyn's body like an ill-fitting cloak, and all the distaste I feel fades to sorrow.

"Burleigh," I say. "You are vaster and older and more powerful than I will ever be, but I am still more than the sum of my parts. I contain multitudes, and I can fight for both you and Wyn. Remember that, when I unbind you—that I've been faithful, when you thought the worst. And I hope and pray that if Wyn's fate is tied to yours, freeing you will free him as well."

"He's ours," Burleigh rasps. "His blood willingly given, his bones willingly bound."

"He's not yours," I tell Burleigh. "He doesn't belong to anyone but his own self. And so long as there's one bit of him left, I will call him back and he will answer."

Swallowing the revulsion I feel with Burleigh's eyes locked on mine, I turn toward what should be Wyn, and take his face in both my hands. Pressing my forehead to his, I shut my eyes.

"Haelwyn of Taunton," I whisper. "Wherever you've gone, come back. I need you."

For a long time, nothing happens. The smell of cold stone is so strong, I think I might choke, and the ground rumbles beneath me, unsettled by my touch. The creature that is speaking for bitter, broken Burleigh makes an eerie noise, halfway between a hum and an avalanche.

But I don't let go, and I don't open my eyes until finally . . .

"Violet?" Wyn's voice says.

A small sound of anguish and relief escapes me, and I throw my arms around Wyn.

"I'm sorry, Vi," he says, and his arms are around me, too. "I'm so sorry. I didn't mean to go away, or to frighten you. It's just harder to hold on to myself now."

"No," I tell him. "You have no reason to apologize."

Brushing his untidy hair aside, I press a kiss to his forehead, and where my lips touch Wyn's skin, it warms, ever so slightly. He raises his head to look at me and our eyes meet, and he's *there*, the boy I know, fully present, with something in his gaze I've never seen before. But it must be in my eyes as well, that desperate longing I see in him, because all at once his mouth is on mine, or mine is on his—I don't know who began it. His lips part and mine eagerly follow, and it is intoxicating, feeling warmth spread through him again beneath my touch. I would give him all my heat, all my fire and determination and will, if it would only banish the mortar from his blood and the magic from his bones.

"I hate this," I tell Wyn when we stop. "I hate all of it. Why couldn't we have been born anywhere else? Why couldn't we have just been ordinary?"

For a moment, I'm afraid Burleigh will take hold of him again, to chastise me for unfaithfulness to my calling.

"This is what we're for, Violet," Wyn says, and there's a note of resignation in his voice that cuts me to the quick. "You're for the House, and I'm for you. I've known it since the first day I came here, though I didn't know that it would end like this. And maybe I wanted things to be different once, but now Burleigh won't let me finish the task I'm meant for and *that's* what I hate."

"What if we don't have to be who we were told to become?" I ask. "What if I don't want to put the House first always? What if . . . what if I want to put you first instead?"

I think of what Burleigh told me: that my heart is divided. That I will play my House false. And I'm honestly not sure what I'll do if I'm finally forced to choose between Burleigh and Wyn. All I do know that is that no one has ever unbound a Great House before, but I think it is my only chance to keep both my home and my heart intact.

"I still want what I was brought here for," Wyn says. "To save you, no matter the cost. To see you get out of this alive and well."

"Wyn, can't we save each other?" I ask.

He gets to his feet and helps me up. "I don't know, Violet. I suppose we can try, but I'm never going to stop wishing you'd just walk away."

I scowl at him. "I'd die first, and you know it."

"I do," he says. "And that's exactly what I'm afraid of."

❧ 29 ☙

LATE IN THE AFTERNOON, ESPIE AND ALFRED JOIN US. Wyn and I are in the study, which overlooks the front drive, and go out to meet them when they come through the bramble gate, on foot and unaccompanied. It's as if we've all decided not to comment on the state of the House, or of Wyn, though Alfred's eyes widen and I hear a sharp intake of breath from Esperanza. But I stand before them, holding Wyn's hand tightly, and Espie is the one who speaks first. She sets a valise down on the gravel next to her and smiles, though the expression's a little too bright.

"Do you have somewhere to put us up?" she asks offhandedly, as if she's just arrived at an ordinary country manor—the sort with a roof and windows and no destructive magic coursing beneath the ground. "Of course you'll probably be otherwise engaged tomorrow evening, Vi, and we'll go back to our rooms at the Red Shilling, but it'd be nice to get away from the crowds in the public room tonight. And perhaps you and Wyn wouldn't mind the company. Although if you'd rather be on your own, just say so."

"No, we'd be glad of the company," I say, glaring at a bramble that's creeping toward Alfred's ankles. It rustles and pulls away.

On our way indoors, I hang back behind the others and stop in the ruined foyer.

"Please don't be dreadful about this," I beg my House. "Please just let us all have one last pleasant night. I know you and I are at odds, but if you ever loved me, let me have this. I still love you, you know, whether you believe it or not."

A few sad white flowers blossom from a crack in the wall, drooping almost before they've opened. I reach out and pick the blooms, tucking them into the strands of my braid. That seems to pacify Burleigh, because the flowers flush with life, and outside, the sun comes out for the first time today. I run a reassuring hand along the wall all the way to the kitchen, where everyone has gathered. I feel loss and longing, pain and regret, through the tips of my fingers.

"I swear to you," I whisper, "everything will be alright. I'm not going to turn on you, Burleigh, just because you aren't the only thing I care for anymore."

The House is silent, as if thinking over what I've said.

And so, all of us within Burleigh's walls pretend that nothing untoward has happened, and that tomorrow I won't return with the heartstone, holding both Burleigh's and Wyn's fates in my hand. Mira sets about salvaging things to eat from the cupboard and pantry, with Alfred as her willing assistant. Jed and Espie sit at the table amicably chatting about crop rotations and land management, which leaves Wyn and me to wander the House, searching out the least damaged guest bedrooms.

"Should we each take one side of the hall?" I ask, after we've made our slow way up the stairs, having to choose every step among the brambles with care.

"No." He shakes his head decidedly. "Let's go together."

I'm glad of that. I want to be near him for as long as I can.

"I'm going to send everyone away tomorrow, of course," I tell Wyn as we search room after room that's been overrun by brambles. "I wish you could leave with the others—could get off the grounds and stay safe. Perhaps if you were gone, Burleigh wouldn't be able to finish what it started with you."

Burleigh is still entirely silent, giving me no sign of what it thinks about these goings-on. It's unnerving—more so than discontented rumbling or ill-tempered brambles would be.

"You're very noble," Wyn says with a smile, opening another door. "But things have changed since you first came home. I wouldn't leave now, even if I could."

I let out a frustrated sigh and Wyn bumps my shoulder with his own, gently. "Come and find me once you bring back the stone. One way or another, we'll finish this together."

We're still hand in hand when Espie's voice drifts up from downstairs.

"Vi and Wyn! Mira says it's time to eat!"

Stubs of candles illuminate the kitchen, set out at intervals along the table. Dinner is griddle cakes and applesauce but there's enough for everyone, and we are determined to be merry. Alfred reads pages from the newest bits of his monograph, which are rendered far less dry by Esperanza's acerbic commentary. Mira sings her Sephardic grandmother's old favorite, "Una Hija Tiene El Rey," which keeps Espie spellbound and beaming. I even let Jed coax me into showing off a string of birdcalls I learned while on the fens. Wyn watches everything quietly from his place beside me, but he smiles, and the candlelight softens his features.

When at last the candles begin to gutter and go out and we're forced to all part ways, the emptiness inside me that was filled for a few hours by warmth and light yawns wide again. I pace in the solitude of my own room for a few minutes, and then slip into the hall, pulling on a faded old dressing gown as I go.

Wyn's waiting outside as always, sitting on his makeshift pallet and reading as across the corridor, Burleigh replays the memory of Wyn's binding over and over again. It tears me apart to look as Papa sharpens a long, wicked knife, going first to the wall and cutting into Burleigh's skin. The House trembles, both in memory and reality, as mortar oozes from the edge of the cuts Papa has made. It clings, gritty and damp, to the knife's edge. Then Papa goes over to Wyn and I can't watch any longer.

"Do you want this memory?" I ask my own Wyn, who's just turned over a page. "Only it's a little grim."

"No, I don't want it at all, but the House likes to remind me of certain things," he says without glancing up. "I've got used to ignoring it. Don't watch this, Vi, it's not something you should see."

"Burleigh," I say sternly. "Stop that at once."

I'm not sure the House will listen, not after our strange and unsettling confrontation in the graveyard and its silence this afternoon. Burleigh isn't a certainty to me any longer, when once it was my bedrock. But the memory flickers and dies, and a wave of lilies of the valley ripple toward me. Their sweet fragrance fills the hallway and I sigh. Part of me wants to cling to the inevitability of who I used to be, to go into Papa's room, to run my hands along the scars that mar my House, and whisper to Burleigh that *everything will be alright, I'm here, I was born to be a Caretaker, you come before anything else.*

Instead, I walk over to Wyn, lilies parting before my feet. I settle down on the bolster and rest my head on his lap, and he puts his book aside.

"Can I stay with you?" I ask, keeping my voice quiet in the emptiness of the hall. "Please, Wyn?"

"Always," Wyn answers simply. I lie quite still for a while, staring at the debris-strewn floor, the cracked walls dripping mortar, the place near the main stair where the attic has caved in and a great beam rests slantwise, half of it propped up at ceiling height, its splintered end fallen into the corridor. So much has changed these last few months—once it was Wyn who'd take refuge in my room, feeling lost and ill at ease between the walls of Burleigh House. Now here I am, coming to him because he's the only thing in this place that grounds me. Only with him do I find a momentary sense of belonging, of surety, of home.

Wyn's hands move through my unbound hair. I shiver, though not with cold, and shut my eyes. Slowly, his undemanding touch and all the tension of the past summer overcome me. I'm half asleep when he speaks in a low voice, and at first I'm not sure if it's my own exhaustion that's muddled his words.

"*Fowles in the frith,*" Wyn recites. My heart jumps at the strangeness of his words, but slows again as I realize it's Wyn's own voice speaking, not Burleigh's harsh and gravelly tones. "*The fisshes in the flood, and I mon waxe wood—much sorwe I walke with for beste of boon and blood.*"

"What's that?" I mumble.

"Middle English verse," Wyn says. "It's what I'm reading. I read a great deal of it during the House arrest. And Burleigh thinks in Middle English sometimes."

"What does it mean?"

"The birds are in the wood," he answers slowly, "the fish are in the flood, and I must go mad—much sorrow I walk with, for the best of bone and blood."

"I don't know if I like it. It's sad."

"I know. But it's the one thing Burleigh and I agree on, most of the time."

"Say it again?"

He does, but before he's finished, I'm asleep.

The light is still thin and grey when I wake. I keep absolutely still, fixing this moment in my memory. Burleigh beneath me, anxious and brooding but quiet for now. Wyn beside me, so close I can feel the slow rise and fall of his chest as he breathes.

Then I get silently to my feet and take Wyn's book from where it lies on the floor beside him. It strikes me that in better times, he and Alfred might have become good friends. But these are the times we have, so I take the stub of pencil he's been using as a bookmark and scribble a note on the title page.

> *Wyn—*
>
> *I've gone to get the heartstone, because I don't want a fuss, and I don't want to say any goodbyes. I know you'll understand that. Could you get everyone off the grounds and out of the way first thing?*
>
> *I'll see you soon.*
>
> *Violet*

Leaving the book open to the note, I slip out the door. In my own room, I pull on my fen clothes and braid my hair and go down the main stairs of Burleigh House one last time, moving hesitantly among the brambles that slither up the staircase.

On the threshold of the front door, I pause.

"Will you wake everyone, once I've gone?" I ask. The House sends a soft-leaved vine climbing up the doorpost to twine around my finger and I sigh. Oh, Burleigh. Are we friends or enemies now? Why must you make it so hard for me to tell?

Outside, the snow is melting, leaving puddles and piles of slush everywhere. The air's mild and soft, like a day in spring, but there's an electric edge to it, a tension, as if a storm's brewing. I pull on a pair of gum boots before leaving the House, but mud spatters the hem of my wrinkled skirt, so that by the time I reach the Shilling I look like quite a vagabond. Fitting, I suppose, that I should look as downcast and desperate as I feel.

The Shilling's nearly abandoned at this hour but Frey's cousin Ella, who manages things from late at night till midmorning, is behind the counter, a cheerful yellow scarf wrapped around her tightly coiled black hair. I give her a halfhearted wave.

"Is Frey up?"

"Does she *ever* sleep? She's in the private dining room, balancing the books. Just ignore the placard, you can go right in."

"Thank you, El."

A little sign dangles from the dining room door, DO NOT DISTURB printed on it in decided capital letters. But I let myself in anyhow and Frey grumbles without looking my way.

"Can't you read? No one's allowed in here." Frey's got ledgers and small blank books and order slips and handwritten notes spread across the table, a fierce scowl on her face as she sorts out the business end of running the Red Shilling.

"It's only me," I say.

Glancing up, Frey leans back in her chair and tilts her head from side to side, stretching the tension from her neck.

"I needed a distraction; you've got good timing, Vi. You're not here for . . . what you left with me already, are you?"

"Yes." I nod. "I'd rather have everything over with, one way or another. There's no point delaying the inevitable."

Frey pulls the heartstone from her pocket with a sigh. "Here it is, then. I didn't like to leave it anywhere. It's hard to believe we've finally come down to this, isn't it?"

Though I ought to be going, I sit down next to her and stare at the heartstone. "What am I doing, Frey? I've got a lot riding on this—so much more than just the House, but . . . is it wrong of me to risk the West Country? To chance Burleigh ending up like Ripley Castle? I started out so certain, that I was meant to be a Caretaker and that Burleigh is more important than anything, but I don't know anymore."

"*I* know," Frey says. "And I haven't left Burleigh Halt. That more than anything should tell you I believe you're enough for this, Violet Sterling. If there was a doubt in my mind, I'd have packed up and left. Nothing personal, see, but I've lived this long in the world and I intend to live longer. But when you step back off those grounds having done what no one else could, not even your father, I'll be right here. He'd have been proud of you, George would. I hope you know that."

"I'm not sure." I gnaw at a ravaged fingernail. "I used to want nothing more than to be like him, but we've turned out to be very different people."

"That's why he'd be proud." Frey pushes the heartstone toward me. "He did a lot of things he regretted in life, your father. And I'm sure binding that boy ended up at the top of the list."

I glance at her sharply. "How do you know about that?"

"Esperanza, of course. Look, are you going to save Burleigh House and your beau or not? Because you can't sit here talking to me all day, I've got accounts to balance."

"Fine, I'm going," I mutter, taking the heartstone and dropping it into my own pocket. That feeling of brokenness, of pain and incompletion, is so strong when I pick it up that it's like being shoved, and I'm forced a few steps backward.

"Good, go on, then. I'm only going to cover so many of your shifts before I find a new serving girl, so don't dawdle while you're at it. And no, I'm not saying anything other than that; if you want pleasantries from me just you see that you get back here in one piece."

✤30✤

SO IT'S COME DOWN TO THIS: I'M AFRAID OF GOING HOME.
With Burleigh's missing piece in my pocket, I trudge across the
fields, clambering over low stone walls and wooden gates, because
meeting the others in the lane on their way into the village from the
House would be more than I could take.

And I am deathly afraid. My hands are slick with it, my belly
flips with it, my breath is quick with it. Fear, fear, fear that won't be
tamped down, no matter how hard I try. Instead I let it be. Let my
hands and knees tremble, and my breath quaver. I'm going home to
Burleigh House, which I've loved all my life. But it's Burleigh that
killed my father and may yet kill Wyn. That will surely try to kill
me when I set foot on the grounds with its missing piece in hand.
How one-sided the love I hold for my House has come to feel.

I am so caught up in my fear that I don't notice the faint sounds
of horses—the jangle of tack and occasional muffled thump of a
hoof. Instead, I push through the hedgerow opposite Burleigh's gate
and come out directly in front of His Majesty the king, backed by
two dozen mounted and red-coated soldiers.

"Hello, Uncle Edgar," I say, mentally scrambling to hide my shock and dismay, and hoping the words come across as easy and uncaring. "I've just been out for a walk. You haven't been waiting long, I hope? Though you are a few days earlier than I expected."

But the king's normally genial face is impassive and forbidding. "Did you really think I wouldn't notice you stealing from me? That as a deedholder, I don't have a sense for the Houses—*every piece of them*—and can tell when something's gone wrong? Because I've felt Burleigh declining all summer, Violet, and gave you a chance. More of a chance than you deserve. You took that opportunity, turned around, and robbed me."

"I don't know what you mean," I lie flatly, because there's nothing else I can do.

His Majesty raises a hand and snaps his fingers. Three horsemen in dark frock coats, not regimental uniforms, ride forward.

"These gentlemen are magistrates," the king says. "I assume you know what that means."

Three magistrates for a traveling court. Just like the one that sentenced my father.

"Violet Helena Sterling," Edgar Rex, King of England says, his voice clear and stern on the warm, soft air. "I hereby charge you with treason. And as Burleigh House is shortly to be burned, I recommend a sentence of hanging by the neck, until you are dead."

And then all hell breaks loose.

Enormous vines studded with thorns the size of my forearm explode out from the bramble gate. They twine around the delicate fetlocks of shying horses, and I hear the sharp report of cannon bones snapping. The lane is filled with foundering mounts and soldiers bound by brambles, unable to reach their powder or pistols.

Only the king remains untouched, but for once he's left witless, able only to stand and watch the destruction Burleigh has wrought upon his men in the blink of an eye.

I allow myself a scant second to watch, too, to marvel with a bitter sort of elation at the spectacle of Burleigh House acting with no regard for its bond. But the bare swath my House has cut through the gathered soldiers beckons, and already more killing brambles are clambering over the whole length of Burleigh's walls, turning them to an impenetrable hedge of thorns.

Gathering up my skirts, I run.

"Violet Sterling, set foot on those grounds and you're signing your own death warrant far faster than I can," the king bellows after me, but I ignore him. I hurtle across the threshold of Burleigh's gate and brambles snap back into place behind me, sealing me in, sealing everyone else out.

The sounds of screaming horses and shouting soldiers and the ranting king grow fainter at once. I stand stock-still, heart pounding in my chest, waiting to meet the same fate they have. Waiting for thorns to pierce my skin, for vines to tear at me, for the heartstone to drop from my pocket, leaving Burleigh almost, but not quite, whole. And then, the spectacular end. The West Country going down in flames or famine, in plague or flood.

But nothing comes. The chaos in the lane fades away entirely, replaced by birdsong and sunshine. All the snow of yesterday has melted so that Burleigh looks fresh-faced and inviting, as if we've just had an April shower.

It's the end of July, I remind myself. Inviting as this feels, it's wrong. All of it is wrong.

Every nerve in me sings. While the sun may be bright and the birds giddy in the trees, the overgrown lawns are still thick with thorns and thistles. The orchard drips not with meltwater but with mortarous blight. Oozing puddles of yet more wet mortar pockmark the path that leads to the desiccated wildflower meadow and the tainted woods.

I don't have time to linger over the ruins of the grounds. I need to find Burleigh's heart. House, my love, where have you hidden your most secret self away? I need you to trust me enough to show me where it is.

Burleigh's emotions are always strongest and clearest when I'm indoors, so I suppose that's where I'd better start. Hurrying up the front steps, I shut the door behind me.

"Wyn?" I call out, my voice loud in the preternatural calm. I lean against the doorway, thinking hard. There was nothing in Papa's ledger about *where* the House might need to be unbound, only mentions of his search for the deed. According to Alfred, a Caretaker should know where the House's heart is, but I've never been a proper Caretaker. I don't have the key to guide me, only my sense of this House. So it is once more down to me, and down to Burleigh.

As I stand and think, an eerie scratching and scraping drifts in from outside. Turning, I try to pull the door open an inch or two to see what's going on, but it won't budge. A tendril of vine snakes through the keyhole and I realize the front door has been sealed shut by Burleigh's inexorable, creeping fingers.

There are other doors, though, and countless windows. It's not enough to quicken my fear again—not yet. Intent on finding Burleigh's heart, I set off into the House's dark interior, intermittently calling for Wyn as I go. Where *has* he gone?

The halls are thick with ghosts—everywhere, pale blue memories gutter and glow, Sterlings that history has long forgotten still walking through Burleigh's ponderous mind. I open doors and run my fingers along walls and feel along bookshelves for hidden latches, waiting for some sense of rightness and surety, that yes, here is Burleigh's heart. Outside, the weather has shifted and a wind is rising—a dry, choking wind that rushes in through the shattered windows, carrying a fine and gritty dust that tastes and smells of mortar. I cough into my sleeve, and keep my arm up to shield my mouth and nose.

With each room I enter, the wind grows fiercer. It howls in the eaves, screams down the chimneys, gnaws through cracked walls, and rattles the last shards of broken glass in the window frames. The longer I stay out in it, the more I cough, until finally a fit nearly bends me double.

Briefly, I consider calling out to Burleigh, begging the House to stop. But it knows what it's doing, I'm sure. Whether this is an obstacle or a test or a warning, however, remains to be seen.

My chest burns and my head aches and spins, until as I leave each room, it takes me a moment to remember where I've come from, and which way I'm headed.

I search the study.

The conservatory.

The smoking room.

The drawing room.

The second-best parlor.

The kitchen.

The ballroom.

The dining room.

The breakfast room.

They all begin to blur together. Cracked walls. Encroaching ivy. Splintered floors strewn with rubble. And wind and dust everywhere, the sound and swirl of them overwhelming. The pain in my head is nearly unbearable, and each time I cough it feels as if my skull will burst. But I carry on, driven by that nagging sense that I've lost my way, or lost *something*, and must continue the search.

At last I climb the stairs in the front hall, reach the top, and sway on the landing. In my hand, there is a plain, uneven piece of rock, and when I look at it, it's as if someone's driven a knife through the base of my skull. I shut my eyes tight and wait for the pain to subside.

But I don't let go of the stone.

"Violet, what does a Caretaker put first?" Papa asks. The memory of his voice is so clear, even against the howl of the wind, that it's as if he's spoken from just beside me. I open my eyes and look down at the stone once more, and though the infernal aching of my head has driven the knowledge of what it is from my mind, I grasp the token tightly. There's something I've forgotten. Something tied to this bit of rock. Something I cannot find. If the wind would only die down for a moment, if my head would cease its pounding, I'm sure I could remember.

For now, exhaustion steers me toward my room, and the sanctuary of my bed.

I climb under the covers, pull them up over my head, and fall into a troubled sleep, still clutching Burleigh's heartstone in one hand.

* * *

"Violet."

It's hard to wake—sleep clings to me, and when I manage to open my eyes, pain bursts to life behind them. But once I manage to inch higher on my pillows, I can't help smiling in spite of it.

Everything is blissfully calm. Spring sunlight pours through my bedroom windows. A small fire snaps and crackles on the hearth. Mama and Papa both wait at the foot of the bed, and they fit together so well, her close to his side, him with an arm around her shoulders.

"Good morning, darling," Mama says brightly. Her voice sounds thin and far away. "Did you forget it's your birthday today? We've got a lovely breakfast laid out for you, and a whole day of surprises planned."

I rub at my eyes, because there's a strange, diffuse blue light swimming across everything—the windows and walls of my room, Mama's and Papa's forms, even the bedclothes. The only thing that seems entirely substantial is my own body. When I turn one of my hands over and open it, I find a broken stone resting on my palm. It tugs at my memory, and feels more important than such an insignificant thing ought to.

Papa comes over with a dressing gown and I step out of bed with a glad smile.

"Thank you, Papa." For a moment, I consider tucking the stone I hold into one of the dressing gown pockets, but an odd compulsion tells me to keep it close. So I wrap my fingers around it and smile at my father.

"Ready, my love?" he asks.

"Ready."

We walk together to the top of the steps, where Jed is standing by. Even Jed looks odd, though, lit by that same wavering light.

"Am I alright?" I ask him dully, because my head won't stop aching and though I've been told it's my birthday, I can't remember how old I'm going to be. "Everything seems so strange today."

Jed reaches out to pat my hand and I pull it back, not wanting to show anyone the token I hold. So he takes my other hand in his and I stifle a gasp, because his grip is cold as ice and my skin grows steadily greyer and more lifeless beneath his touch.

"Please let go," I beg. "Please. I can't bear it."

"It's just her usual trouble," Papa says to Jed with a shake of his head. Mama puts an arm around me, but she's careful not to touch my bare skin.

"Vi," she soothes. "Everything's fine. You're fine. Let's just have a lovely day, shall we? You know how anxious you get, and it's always over nothing. No one can make a mountain out of a molehill like you, darling."

My face heats and I keep my head down so she won't see the hot tears pooling in my eyes. It's true—I never seem able to manage my fears the way everyone else does. And I'm even afraid of letting other people see how panicked I can become. It stings to have my shortcomings cast up to me, when I work so hard to hide them.

Wyn is the only one who ever seems to really understand.

But at the thought of him, the nagging pain in my head doubles. Soon the fierce ache drives every other thought out, and I keep my mind a careful blank until it subsides. As the pain goes, it takes most of my recollections of Wyn with it, leaving only confusion in their wake.

"Is there someone missing?" I ask as Papa leads me into the kitchen. He and Mama are here, as well as Jed and Mira, but I can't help being ill at ease, as if we've left someone out and they may walk in the door at any moment.

"Silly girl." Mama brushes a kiss against my hair and for a moment my scalp freezes. "Who else is there? Mira, where do you want us for cake?"

I blink, and with a sudden, sickening wave of vertigo, find myself sitting out in the rose garden, on a checkered blanket with Mama and Papa. Mama hands me a china plate with a slice of white cake on it.

"Here you are, darling. Happy birthday."

Outside, it's easier to see the strangeness of the wavering light on their faces, the roses, the grass. I squint, trying to stare past it, and for a moment I catch a glimpse of the garden after nightfall, its rosebushes standing dead, the gravel pathways choked with moss and briars.

"I don't want the cake," I tell Mama, pushing the plate away. "None of this is right."

She looks at me and her porcelain doll's face saddens. "What have we done wrong? We're trying, Violet. How can we make you happy?"

But beneath her sweet voice, there's an eerily familiar sound. A grating quality, like brick rubbing against stone.

"I have to go," I say, struggling to my feet and swaying as my head pounds. "I have to find Wyn."

Mama frowns and I gasp at the starbursts of pain going off in my skull.

"Find who?" she asks.

"Wyn," I say through gritted teeth. "Papa's ward, the boy I grew up with who was supposed to be company for me. But we all know better now, don't we? We know it was more than company he was meant for."

"I don't know who you mean," Mama says, but there's a scream of stone on stone underpinning her words.

I walk away. My head is aching so badly all I want is to lie down, and I break into a sweat after ten paces, but I gather up all my flagging willpower and carry on.

"Violet Sterling, where are you going?" Mama calls after me. Her voice is barely human now, and when I glance back over one shoulder, she looks more like a stone angel than a flesh-and-blood woman.

Without answering, I walk faster, in through the kitchen where Mira's ghost watches me pass by.

"Violet Sterling," Mira repeats, "where are you going?" And as she speaks the words, vines burst from her mouth.

I clutch my broken bit of stone and hurry on through the House, heart pounding in my chest, pain rattling about beneath my skull.

"Don't do this, Burleigh," I choke at the foot of the stairs, which are thicker with brambles than ever, twining around the banisters and covering each step. But the thorns only seem to grow longer as I speak.

"Wyn!" I call. "Wyn, where are you?"

The only answer is the whisper and creak of yet more brambles growing up around the steps. Letting out a ragged breath, I scan the first stair, looking for a place to set my foot.

And I climb, step by step, searching for gaps in the thorns and tearing the skin on my feet and ankles to ribbons. When I look back the way I've come, each gap has widened, the brambles parting around a slick trail of blood I'm leaving on the stairs.

By the time I reach the landing, my legs are shaking so that I can hardly stand. But I don't have time to sit. What's more, I don't trust the House if I do. My head still feels like bursting and my wits are clouded. All I can remember is that I must keep hold of this insignificant bit of rock and find Wyn. As quickly as I can, I hurry down the hall to my bedroom and shut the door. It flies open again. Three times I shut it, and every time it refuses to close. With a sigh of frustration, I turn and cross the room.

Fire flares on the hearth, tall flames roaring upward and licking at the chimney. I ignore it and pass by, bent on reaching the linen cupboard, where vines are creeping from the floorboards and twining up the cupboard door as if to seal it shut.

Ignoring the sudden spike of pain in my head, I scramble for the door and grasp the knob before the vines are able to have their way.

The latch burns beneath my palm and I snatch my hand back with a hiss. Using a fold of my dressing gown, I try once more. Better. I wrench the door open before the vines can finish their work.

Wyn is sitting inside, arms wrapped around his knees.

"Don't, Violet," he says in a voice like heartbreak, and reaches for the door to pull it shut again. I wedge it open with one foot, because I have forgotten so many things but when I look at him, everything is a little clearer.

"I've been looking for you," I tell him reproachfully. "Wyn, we were supposed to find each other. I need your help. What *is* this?"

I hold the stone out, resting on the palm of my hand. "Why can't I remember what it is?"

Wyn pulls away with a groan. "Don't show it to me, Vi. I can't see that. It's too hard to hold on to myself when I'm looking at it."

For the first time, I slip it into my pocket. I can hardly remember Wyn, besides the fact that I need him at my side, and that everything in me says I'm safe with him. I know it with my bones and not with my mind. Perhaps that's why I haven't forgotten.

"Better?" I ask, and he nods.

I start forward, then hesitate, eyeing the vines that have stilled and wait, just shy of the door latch. What if this is exactly what Burleigh House wants? For me to take two more steps so it can seal me away forever?

"Can I come in?" I ask Wyn, and put all my uncertainty into the question. *Is it safe?* is what I'm really asking.

"Yes." He nods, and when I step forward it's as I feared. The door slams shut and I hear the sinuous rustle of vines as they jam the knob. But Wyn said it's alright, and even when I can barely recall our history together, I trust him.

The interior of the cupboard is pitch-black. I've never felt anything so like being buried alive, and my heart begins to race.

"Wyn, are you there?" The words come out ragged and shaking, and then I feel his arm go around me and my blood sings, because in this moment, sealed up within the walls of an incensed Great House, I'm safe.

"What's happening?" I ask him in a whisper. "I can't think. I can't remember. Nothing makes sense anymore."

When he speaks, he's so near that his breath warms the side of my face. He smells, incongruously, of warm rich earth, and it's an indescribable comfort in this place that is running to ruin.

"Violet Helena Sterling," Wyn says. "You're here to unbind Burleigh House, and Burleigh House is bound to kill you for trying."

Everything comes rushing back.

The king. The heartstone in my pocket. The House and me, struggling against one another. It hits me like a blow to the stomach, and I inhale sharply, tears pricking at my eyes.

"The House doesn't want to harm you." There's misery in Wyn's voice, and my heart breaks for him, caught halfway between himself and Burleigh. "It thought this would be simpler. That eventually you'd forget, and let the heartstone go, and we could all die together, when the last of the binding breaks or the king comes with his torches."

The sure and certain knowledge that Burleigh House has been in my mind, rummaging through my secret fears, tainting my perceptions of the world, acts on my spirit like slow poison. I can't think of it. I will lie down in the darkness and never move again if I let myself dwell on the wrongs and misfortunes and betrayals I've suffered on behalf of Burleigh in this life. And yet here I am, fighting for this stubborn, infuriating House.

"Death and freedom, all at once, and a tragic end to our story," I say to Wyn bitterly. "Is that all Burleigh can dream of? After thousands of years in this world, it can't bring itself to hope for more?"

"You know what it is to feel broken and rootless and betrayed," Wyn answers. But there's a rasp of stone behind the words, and I shudder. It's no longer him speaking, but Burleigh. "We've been wronged too often, Caretaker's child—even without the binding, we wouldn't gamble our wholeness on your goodwill."

Then all at once Wyn's voice is his own again, and he carries on speaking as if it had been him and not Burleigh talking all along.

". . . and if I set foot out there—when I catch the House's attention, it gets into me. Into my head. And I hate it, because we are one and the same. I feel the anger it feels, the wanting, the violence. Burleigh doesn't *want* to kill you for the stone, Vi, but that doesn't mean we won't if needs must."

"This isn't you," I insist. "Not the boy I know. There is no *we*, just you and Burleigh House. Hold on to yourself, Wyn—you'd never do me harm."

"Really?" It's strange and eerie, listening to Wyn's disembodied voice in the absolute darkness, hearing it grow less and less like his usual tone. "What have we ever been but bound, bound to put your needs before our own? We've never been free, Violet. Would you even recognize us, I wonder?"

He's mostly Burleigh again, wavering back and forth between the two moment by moment, and fear washes over me. I can't help but feel as if it's Wyn speaking to me, even when Burleigh's voice is the one coming from his lips.

"Couldn't I say the same?" I retort, falling back on Sterling stubbornness and indignation because there is nothing else left to me. "When have you ever known *me* to be free? Born on these grounds, shedding blood onto your soil every time I skinned a knee or pricked a finger. Told from the time I could speak that *you're meant to be the Caretaker, Vi, and a good Caretaker puts her House first.* You bound me yourself when I was five—I've spent more of my life with your mortar running in my veins than I have without it. You may be bound, but so am I."

"Give us what we lost," the voice says, and there's nothing of Wyn left in it, just the scrape of stone.

"I can't. Not like this."

Implacable fingers grasp at my arm and I jerk away, scrambling to my feet. But when I beat my fists against the cupboard door, the vines outside hold fast.

"Wyn," I plead, "stop this, please, you're frightening me."

For a long moment, all I can hear is the sound of my own rattling breath, a counterpoint to the inhale and exhale of whoever is here in the dark.

There's a snap like a small peal of thunder, followed by the smell of burning vines. The cupboard door flies open, and I'm blinded by noon sun, though I walked through the door on a moonlit night. Unforgiving sunshine shows my decaying room, the window seats littered with broken glass and slate roofing tiles, the bedclothes spotted with mildew.

Wyn stands in the shadows behind me. His skin is grey and rough as mortar, but his eyes are his own.

"There's something here Burleigh doesn't want you to find," he says, wincing as if the words burn his mouth. "Out in the back woods, past the trout stream. Everything's a muddle and I don't know what it is, but maybe it's what you're looking for. Maybe it's the heart of the House."

Already the grumble of stone is creeping back into his voice, and his eyes are glazing over with a film of mortar.

"Stay with me," I murmur, stepping closer and pressing my lips to his forehead, his jawline, his mouth. "Don't leave me, Wyn. I want you with me when all this is over. None of this matters without you—not Burleigh, not a Caretaker's key, not my name or my land or my legacy."

His eyes clear and fix on me. "Vi. There's no time. *Go.*"

With one last regretful look at him, standing half in shadow, half in sunshine, I gather my courage and bolt.

⋅⟫31⟪⋅

I WISH I'D PUT ON SHOES AFTER WAKING TO THAT FEVER dream of Mama and Papa. As I hurtle down the stairs, a dark and all-encompassing malice rises up through my bare soles. The House is unhappy, but I know who I am again. I know my purpose, and I will not stop for anything, not even Burleigh.

The sun hangs low on the western horizon as I burst through the conservatory door and wing my way across the rose garden. The light's lengthening preternaturally fast—I have no way of knowing how much time I've spent within the walls. The roses have resumed their dry, decayed aspect, now my mind is free of Burleigh's influence. The wildflower meadow lies dead and dying, too. Halfway down the well-worn path at its center, a thistle pierces one of my already damaged feet, but I keep going, ignoring the pain that jolts up my leg with each step.

The woods loom ahead, and there are still gaps in the wall of brambles surrounding them. I step through one open place, and am overwhelmed by a dreadful sense of unease, the sort of taut energy a wild creature possesses before taking its prey. It renews my sense of urgency, and I hurry along, twisted trees flashing by at the edge of my vision, reaching out to me with grasping twigs. I don't know if it's just the normal way of reaching branches or if the House is trying to slow me, but I don't stop to find out. Leaping over fallen trunks and low spots where fetid water pools on the ground, I head for Burleigh's heart, and for this journey's end.

My lungs burn and my legs shake by the time the trout stream appears as a glimmer through the trees. When the stream bank approaches, I gather myself without slowing and jump for all I'm worth.

The landing forces a yelp from me. Part of the thistle must still be lodged in my foot, because it feels as if I'm stepping on knives each time I shift my weight. But there's no time, no time. The pain in my feet is already matched by pain in my head. It blurs my vision and sets the forest spinning, and worse yet, dulls my wits.

I reach into my pocket and pull out the heartstone, gripping it tight. Let it remind me. Let it hold my focus.

Still, as the pain in my foot grows, I slow, and limp, and finally sit to pull the spines from my sole because it's silly to run when every step is an agony. By the time I've yanked all the spines free and wrapped the wound with a strip torn from my skirt, I'm not sure what I'm doing so far into the woods. It's foolish to wander so far from Burleigh, when the House has only ever looked after me and I've never wanted anything but to be together.

Getting to my feet, I've nearly decided to go back home, but then I see a figure moving through the trees near the edge of the grounds, starting and stopping as they go. With a frown, I walk toward them.

When I'm close enough to make out who it is, everything comes crashing back. I remember who I am once more: Violet Sterling, Caretaker by default of this ancient and vicious place, this House of terrible beauty, with its violent desire to be free no matter the cost. I am all that and more, since Wyn's life depends on my success. I've never been much of a one for games, but I've gambled everything on this endeavor.

And I haven't found my House's heart. Instead, I've found the Duke of Falmouth, His Majesty's dirty hands, burning my beloved Burleigh's forest. Falmouth strides through the back woods with a bucket of oil, dousing the trunks of twisted, mortarous trees. When a dry twig snaps beneath my feet, he glances up and gives me a wolfish smile.

"Miss Sterling. I caught a glimpse of you earlier but you were—how shall we say it—not yourself? Well done, Burleigh House, she looked absolutely bewildered. Ripley Castle never got nearly this far into the Ingilby girl's head."

The ground trembles beneath my feet and a breeze whips up, whispering angrily among the tree branches. It's heavy with the scent of damp earth and lamp oil. I cross my arms and glare at Falmouth, trying to make myself small and stubborn and thorny. "What are you doing here?"

"I'm here to finish this," Falmouth says, setting down his bucket and stepping into the path between me and the House. "It's so much tidier this way—we can't very well have you unbinding Burleigh, not even to save the place. Can you imagine if you succeeded? There'd be a general uproar, and people would be asking why every House can't be unbound."

"Why can't they?" I ask, belligerence weighting my words.

Falmouth shakes his head. "You know why. This isn't personal, Miss Sterling, it's politics—no one likes to give up power, and the Great Houses are power. His Majesty's power, and, by extension, mine."

"You're a villain," I say, and try to step around him.

But Falmouth stays in front of me, blocking the way. "Am I? Am I really? Look around you. There's only one villain on these grounds, and that's the House itself. Burleigh is already wreaking havoc in the West Country. Crops are failing—have already failed. Mortar's leaking out into the countryside and poisoning the earth. And what's this I hear about Burleigh and your father binding that boy? We've all hedged our bets, Violet. Your father took precautions should you fail. I'm taking precautions to ensure you don't succeed."

"If the king wanted to burn me alive with Burleigh, he should have just done it at the beginning of summer," I snap. Falmouth's under my skin, though I shouldn't let him nettle me. "Why wait all this time?"

"Oh, he had no intention of burning Burleigh with you inside the grounds," Falmouth purrs. "You're a bit of a blind spot for the king—I doubt he's even serious about hanging you. But I don't like the idea of the House damaging more of the land while you're in here, or if you fail—there's that little matter of the rents I'll be collecting when all this is over, you see. As per your agreement with His Majesty, the land in these parts will still be mine. So I took the initiative, and now I'll trouble you for that heartstone. Can't have you running back to the House and unbinding Burleigh while it's already ablaze."

I shake my head and glance past him at Burleigh, but he's blocking the way and the forest floor beyond the path is a sinuous tangle of brambles. Even if the way were clear, I can't leave him, not with the forest drenched in oil and ready to go up in flames.

Falmouth adjusts one of his cuff links fastidiously.

"The stone, Miss Sterling," he repeats.

"Never." I scowl at him.

"Very well."

He reaches into his jacket pocket. Light gleams on metal and by the time my mind's processed that it isn't a tinderbox in his hand, it's a pistol, the aftermath of a shot is already echoing through the air. Pain like I've never known splinters up my right leg and I crumple to the ground.

But I never let go of the heartstone.

The Duke of Falmouth walks over and stands above me, pistol still in hand. On his watch chain, I catch a glimmer of red—the bowstone of Burleigh House's key. It sickens me to see it in his possession, and I grasp the stone more tightly.

"You're a foolhardy creature," Falmouth says with a shake of his head. "Don't know when you're beaten, just like your father. I would advise you to lie very still, and hope Burleigh House thinks enough of you to hasten your end."

I watch through blurred vision, clutching the place where his shot lodged in my leg. Blood pours out over my hands, and it's coming far too fast, slicking my palms and pooling on the forest floor. I stuff the heartstone into my pocket to get a better grip, but it's not enough. Where my skin still shows through the scarlet stains, I can see myself growing paler.

Falmouth's footsteps retreat a little way, and I hear the striking of a match. Then the flare of flames, followed by a sudden, acrid billow of smoke.

"Goodbye, Miss Sterling," Falmouth says. "Pity about the House. I would have enjoyed bringing it to heel."

"Burleigh, I need you," I whisper, and the slur of my own words alarms me. "I know we're at odds, but I need you."

Everything in me stiffens as House magic rushes up from the ground and pours mortar through my veins.

"That's not what I meant," I gasp frantically. "Stop it, Burleigh, you'll kill me."

But the magic doesn't stop. I curl up on my side and stare at the leaves carpeting the forest floor, as with each heartbeat, blood rushes out of me and mortar rushes in.

⇥32⇤

I DON'T KNOW WHEN I'VE EVER BEEN SO COLD. BUT IN A way, it's a mercy because I can feel nothing else. None of the other pains—my splitting head, my torn feet, my bleeding leg—even register anymore. The trees waver and spin, and I glance down at the place where Falmouth's shot struck me, a handspan above the knee.

Mortar rimes the edge of the wound. It's already slowed the flow of blood, making it sluggish and thick. I watch as little by little, mortar seals my torn flesh altogether. As it does, the flood of magic pouring into me abates. I won't bleed to death, so long as I survive the mortar itself.

I never should have doubted my House.

Falmouth, still lighting fires nearby, grunts to himself, as if he's not sure whether to be put out or glad. I hear the sound of him fiddling with his single-shot pistol, the leaden clink of another ball entering its chamber, the little hiss of gunpowder being added.

Then there's a flurry of crackling dead leaves, followed by the sound of two solid things striking against one another. I struggle to push myself up on one elbow. Falmouth is on the ground, reeling, and just as he stood over me Wyn stands over him now, holding a splintered beam ready to strike again. And I can't tell who he is, the boy I know or Burleigh or both at once. All I know is that there is something strange and fearsome on his face that I have never seen there before.

"Stop it, Wyn," I gasp, to whoever's wearing the body of the boy I love. Veins of darkest grey are running through his already stony skin. "The House is bound never to take a life, and you're more than half Burleigh now. If you break another part of the binding—"

"Have you looked at him?" Falmouth's voice is bitter. He kneels in the bracken and glances up at Wyn. "Whoever he was, there's no coming back from this. He's not the boy you knew anymore— Burleigh's brought him to ruin, just like it will do to all the West Country if you unbind it, or let it have that stone. Do you know what I'm really doing here, Violet? I'm *saving* the countryside from you and Burleigh House. From the reckless foolishness of Sterlings, who believe this place can be better than it is."

I look at Wyn, and for a moment I see him as Falmouth does— as something made monstrous by Burleigh's power. As someone past the point of no return.

But it's only for a moment, and then my vision clears, and in spite of all his changes, I see only this when I look at Wyn: the friend of my childhood, and of my heart. Turning to the forest, already filling with smoke, and to the glimpse of the House between the trees, I don't see ruin, either. I see something worth saving, no matter how far it's fallen. No matter the things it's done.

In the end, I suppose this is my gift and my curse—that however Burleigh or Wyn may change, however much damage they inflict or suffer, they will always be lovely and worthy of love to me. And I will never stop fighting for them, or hoping for a world in which they are both whole and well.

I sit up, shedding leaves, and try getting to my feet, but my legs buckle. Once more I try to stand, and it does no good. I feel half made of stone myself, I'm so full of mortar, and somewhere inside me, the lead pistol shot scrapes against bone.

"She's going to die," the Duke of Falmouth says. "Why not make it quicker for her, Burleigh? You know this will only go one way— the girl was bound to failure from the start, as surely as you've been bound to the king and the boy's been bound to you."

"Shut up and don't move." However he may look, it's Wyn speaking, not Burleigh.

"Or what? You'll kill me and break your binding?" Falmouth retorts. "I don't think you'd dare."

Wyn ignores him.

"Violet, take out the heartstone," Wyn says.

Mutely, I obey. But the moment I do I begin to bleed again, as the power of Burleigh's missing piece leaches both blood and mortar from my veins. Wyn reaches out and places his own hand over the stone, still cupped in my palm.

I take in a trembling breath as warmth, rather than ice, spreads within me. I have never felt a magic like this before—one that suffuses my limbs with blissful well-being, and whispers of spring and rebirth. The lead ball works its way free of my bones, my sinew, my skin, and drops to the forest floor. The torn flesh left in its wake knits back together. Painstakingly slowly, a little of the ice begins to melt from my blood, mortar dripping from my fingertips and pooling beneath my feet.

Around us, too, the woods begin to green. Brambles recede. Bluebells carpet the ground in their wake and the nearest trees burst into summer life, hale and whole once more, except for those that are already in flames. I gaze on it all in wonderment.

"What is it?" I ask Wyn.

"House magic," he says with a smile. "The way it's meant to be."

Anguish gnaws at me, though, because while it's worked on everything else, the heartstone has done nothing for Wyn. Even as he smiles, there's an emptiness behind his eyes, and I wonder how much more magic he can do before Burleigh claims the last of him, and he becomes nothing but an empty shell for the soul of the House.

But then the Duke of Falmouth turns, and the pistol's in his hand once more.

"Alright, I've got to be going, so which of you is first?" he asks with that wolfish smile. "And if I shoot the boy, will anything actually happen?"

Wyn steps forward.

"Why don't you try it, and find out?" he says softly, standing only a few paces from Falmouth.

The duke raises his pistol, but as he does, Wyn raises a hand, too. Not quickly, not aggressively, not as if he's about to wrest the firearm away. Falmouth frowns as Wyn reaches out and touches one finger to his wrist.

That's all it takes. A torrent of killing magic roars through Wyn and into Falmouth. The duke sinks to his knees, shaking like a leaf on the wind. For a moment, a cloud of smoke hides him from view, but when the air clears again, I watch in horror as vines burst from his mouth, his eyes, his nose, his ears. He falls, and Burleigh's ravenous greenery consumes him utterly.

"Wyn," I choke, scrambling toward him. "Wyn, are you still there?"

He turns to me, and for the briefest moment, there's a familiar light in Wyn's eyes.

"I'm glad I was brave enough for you," he says.

Then the last of that light leaves him. When I reach out and brush a hand against his face, there's no feeling of waiting, of temporary absence. Not the faintest spark.

"Wyn, come back," I beg, taking his face in my hands. "It's Violet—please, come back to me."

But only Burleigh remains.

"He took it upon himself to break the binding," Burleigh says with Wyn's mouth, in its voice like shattering stone. "And there was so little of him left. We spared him for you as long as we could, Sterling girl. But in the end, he wanted to go."

"He's not—" I can hardly bring myself to speak the words. "He's not *gone*? For good?"

Burleigh makes no answer at first, and I can feel all the House's brooding attention pondering the question I've asked.

"We would rather not tell you," Burleigh finally says. "You are . . . very small. And perhaps more fragile than we'd thought."

"Answer. The question."

The creature before me, that is not my Wyn, and may never be again, hangs its head. "He is ours entirely now, Sterling girl—a part of us, and inseparable. But we are sorry we cannot give him back."

For a long time I keep entirely motionless, afraid even to breathe. Because I know the moment I begin to feel this loss, it will cut deeper than any thorn. Weigh heavier than all the world's mortar. Breed more damage than years of working House magic.

At last I glance over one shoulder to the edge of the woods. A wall of flame is eating away at the trees, flames hungrily consuming Burleigh's power and magic. But Burleigh can begin again, go elsewhere to take a new shape with the life Wyn's given it.

I hold the heartstone in my two cupped hands and the wide world beyond the grounds seems sere and empty. This could end now. I could leave, clamber over the wall, and disappear. Cast off my name, and the expectations it brings with it. In a way, the prospect is almost inviting. A fresh start. A clean slate. It's what Wyn always tried to convince me I wanted.

The truth is, though, I don't want any of that after all the things I've seen. After everything I've lived through, and all that I've lost. Nothing seems worthwhile anymore. Not the world. Not a life on my own. Not even Burleigh House.

But since the day I was born, I have been taught one thing. It comes as naturally as breathing to me, the knowledge that I am a Caretaker, and a good Caretaker puts her House first.

Before king.

Before country.

Before her life and her heart.

Now, at last, it's time for me to decide if I will break free of my bond, or fulfill the fate that Burleigh House and my father placed upon me. At the thought, something dark and bitter rises up within me. A wanting. A longing. A brooding desire, laced with vengeance.

I don't know if it's possible for Burleigh to return Wyn—for us to have another chance at becoming all the things we were never able to be, both on our own and together. But I do know this—if I stand at Burleigh's heart, with its missing piece in my grasp, I could bind it with blood and mortar to spend the last of its power and the final moments of its life at least *trying* to bring him back.

Rather than taking the few steps left between me and freedom, I slip the heartstone into my pocket and turn toward the House.

"Where are you going, Sterling girl?" Burleigh calls after me, but I make no answer.

The ground rumbles incessantly as I cross the field. The air is thick with smoke, and everywhere, brambles burst from the ground, slithering across the soil. Strange, light-on-water memories float above them—all the many ghosts of Sterlings gone before. Burleigh House itself is nearing absolute ruin. The roofless attics have all collapsed into the second floor, and bits of stone crumble from the remaining walls. Overhead, the sky boils with clouds, thick with unspent rain.

Inside the door I meet more ghosts. All of them drift silently through the remains of the House, like spirits leaving a dying body. And perhaps they are. I move against the flow of them, feeling nothing but a shift of cold air as they brush past me. They're all coming from the same place, moving down the main stairs like water over rapids and then splitting off in different directions as they reach the landing.

Stepping out of the way, I tuck myself into a secluded spot next to the stairs. And I watch the ghosts as I think, mind racing. The heart of the House. The heart of the House. Surely, in all the years

Burleigh and I have spent together, at some point it showed me a glimpse of its hidden heart.

With a start, I recognize one of the remembered Sterlings floating past. It's my grandfather, who I've only ever seen in an oil painting, and through Burleigh's eyes. My father's not far behind him, and the sight of them as they're remembered by Burleigh tightens my throat. They're not anxious or worried or wasted by House magic. Instead, they look calm, at peace, even happy. These aren't just ghosts, or memories, for surely my House has memories of people it hated—the king and all his predecessors, to begin with.

No, this procession of Sterlings is a parade of all the people Burleigh ever loved.

I stiffen at the thought, and at the sight of that procession of ghosts, all pouring down the stairs, all coming from the same direction. Taking the heartstone from my pocket and gripping it tight, I push back into the current of memories and begin to climb the stairs. The brambles choking the staircase have crumbled to ash that stains my feet as I hurry up the trembling steps. On the landing I see that while every door in the House stands open, one is shut. And every memory passes through it, appearing like figures passing through a cloud of mist.

Stopping outside Papa's room, I try the door. Locked. There's no roof left overhead, just the sky simmering with rainclouds. A crack forms in the wall beside me, yawning open with an inhuman groan.

"Burleigh," I say, knocking insistently. "Burleigh House, let me in."

The door stays locked.

"I'd never hurt you," I lie, forcing down not fear but the softer, gentler pieces of me. Because I'm still not sure what I'll do—whether I'll choose to unbind Burleigh, or bind it further in an attempt to bring Wyn back. I'm waiting for some sign or beacon, some undeniable sense of rightness to tell me *this, Violet. This is how you should choose.* "No matter what's happened before, if you let me in, I swear to unbind you. You've known me since the day I came into this world, Burleigh, and I've loved you just as long. Can't you trust me? Can't you hope for a world where you get more than a lonely rebirth, rebuilding on the bones of someone who never should have died for you? Let me set you free."

With a whine of rusted hinges, the door swings open. For a moment, I stand on the threshold, breathless and anguished. I almost hoped Burleigh would hold out. That it would shut me out and keep me from breaking its trust, and that would be all the sign I needed.

But the door is open, the way is clear, and I step one more time into Papa's bedroom, Burleigh's last and most faithless Caretaker, who stands on the verge of betraying her House.

The room is bare and roofless, and I pick my way around rubble.

"Have it your way, Violet Sterling," Burleigh says from across the room and I startle. There he sits, on the pile of moldering linens discarded in one corner, wearing the body that was once Wyn's. I swallow, and steel my nerves.

"Bind us or unbind us. Do what you wish," Burleigh continues, an almost sorrowful note in his shattered-stone voice. "The truth is, after all these years, we're tired. So tired, little girl. And it might be more than we could bear, to start over again. We don't have the strength of spirit or the force of will or the sense of purpose left for new beginnings. So do as you wish—have your way with us."

Through a window behind Burleigh, I can see the back woods. They're all ablaze now, and flames are beginning to lick at the wildflower meadow. Not long before they consume it, and come for the rose garden, and then start to gnaw at the walls as well.

I bite at my lower lip. Oh, Burleigh. How you break my heart. Whatever Wyn and my father did for me, I've never been anything but bound to you. And what shall I do, here at the end? Break my own binding—not one of blood and mortar, but of love and expectation and countless years of history—in hopes that I can buy Wyn a second chance at life? Or honor the bond between us, and give life to you instead?

"This is the right place, then?" I ask Burleigh. "Your very heart, where I can bind or unbind you?"

Burleigh shrugs, an all too human and Wyn-like gesture, and I wonder. He jerks his head toward the room's far wall. "Our heart isn't a place, Violet Sterling. You could have unbound us the moment you laid hands on that stone."

I glance over at the far wall in confusion and tears prick at my eyes. Because there it is, still carved into the plaster in tall and brutal capitals.

VI. My own, mortar-scarred name.

I have always been the heart of Burleigh House, though it is no longer wholly mine.

Smoke burns at my eyes and I don't want this, Papa. I'm not enough for it. How do I choose between two halves of myself? How will I live if from this moment on, my soul is split in two?

A good Caretaker puts her House first.

Before king.

Before country.

Before her own heart.

I kneel in front of Burleigh, choking on tears. Pulling my gutting knife from one pocket, I draw it across my palm. Blood wells up, bright and vital, full of life and still-unbroken promises.

"Give me his hand," I say to Burleigh. The House holds out its hand that once was Wyn's. But when I cut it, there's no blood left in these veins, only the gritty grey slick of mortar.

Putting my gutting knife aside, I take the heartstone out and set it on my own bloodied palm.

"Go on," I say to Burleigh, and the House fixes me with a devastating look. There are eight hundred years of pain and exhaustion and brokenness in those eyes that don't belong to it, and resignation, too. Right now, in this moment, Burleigh is entirely within my power.

Wyn's hand cups the top of the heartstone, my blood and Burleigh's mortar mingling together.

"Burleigh House," I say. "My name is Violet Sterling, last of my line, and my family has always served you well. By the blood in my veins and the mortar in your walls . . ."

Burleigh fixes his sorrowful, stolen eyes on me, and dear God, all I want is to see Wyn looking out from that face at me again.

". . . I unbind you. Be whole again, Burleigh. Be well again. Be free."

Rain slams into me from above as the clouds split apart. A great, earth-shattering roar of thunder shakes the skies, and the foundation of the House. Wind howls through the broken windows. And before me, Burleigh rises in power.

Blinding light radiates from the creature that is no longer Wyn and no longer the House I knew, either. I put up a hand to shield my eyes, and am struck by the sudden, irrational thought that perhaps this isn't Burleigh at all, but one of the seraphim Mira told me stories of on the fens. An angel of life or death, or perhaps both at once.

Everything around me is wind and thunder and light and rain.

"Remember this, Burleigh," I call out in a panic, my voice barely audible in the tumult. "Remember how I loved you. And if you can, give him back. Mend my heart again, as I mended yours."

There's no answer but the scream of wind and the growl of thunder. At last I'm forced to shut my eyes against the burning light and the driving rain.

When I dare to open them, the noise of the storm has grown bearable. Rain still pelts my skin, but I'm no longer on the grounds. Instead, I'm in the lane, my back to Burleigh's great iron gate, which has been restored to its prior form.

In front of me stands His Majesty the king and a regiment of soldiers, all of them soaked to the skin and looking like they've seen the dead rise up from their graves. Behind me, the House is swathed in a pillar of cloud and fire. The sounds of its restoration are a terrible and mighty thing.

I drop to my knees in the mud of the laneway, wrap my arms around my middle, and sob. I've proved myself the greatest of all Caretakers, and bought Burleigh House its freedom against all odds.

In spite of king.

In spite of country.
In spite of my own heart.
But oh, Burleigh. At what cost?
At what cost?

❊33❊

I DRIFT IN AND OUT OF SLEEP AS JED AND MIRA ARGUE with Frey at my bedside, tucked away in a little room under the Red Shilling's eaves.

"She's ours," Mira begs. "Let us take her home."

"That cot you've rented is hardly big enough for the two of you as it is," Frey says staunchly. "And it isn't home to Vi. You know where her home is. Let her stay here, in a place she knows."

Jed is the one who kneels beside the bed and takes my hand.

"Violet, my love. What do you think?"

I'm too tired to answer. And I don't care about any of it, or anything. I'm lost in the same fog they tell me still envelops the House, though it's been two weeks since I set Burleigh free.

In the end, I stay at the inn. Mira comes to sit next to me in the afternoons and evenings when Frey oversees things. The rest of the time, Frey herself keeps watch, sleeping on a pallet across the room. They're all worried, I know, but I can't summon the energy to take an interest or care. I sleep and sleep, waking only to take cups of broth or to use the chamber pot. Even the plate of autumn vegetables and stewed apples and warm bread that Mira brings me over Rosh Hashanah is not enough to tempt me.

Then one morning I wake to a robin singing outside the attic window, and realize the leaves of the branch he perches on have turned to gold.

"Frey?"

She's by my side in a moment.

"Are things alright, with the West Country? How will everyone fare over winter?"

Frey squeezes my hand. "There were plenty of folk expecting to starve, if you want the truth. But the day you walked out of that House, every apple tree in the West Country started a second bloom and every heifer and ewe dropped twins. No one's ever seen the like. The lambs and calves and apples have all grown up at a fearful rate, too—they started pressing cider last week, and the markets are full of stock."

"What about the king? He just . . . left, after I came out from the House. But before, he'd planned to charge me with treason."

"He's back at Hampton Court," Frey says. "Espie's gone with him, to make sure he doesn't get any ideas about renewing those charges. But I doubt there's any danger of that, not with the West Country in better shape than it's ever been before. If he laid a finger on you, there'd be riots in the streets. And I hear His Majesty's at a bit of a loose end, without Falmouth to manage things for him, but that Esperanza's taken over very capably."

"I'm sure she has," I say with a faint smile.

"Do you know what they drink to downstairs every night now?" Frey asks. I can feel myself flush under her close scrutiny. "To Violet

Sterling, the bond breaker, and to Burleigh House restored."

"And Burleigh?"

Frey turns, so I can't look her in the eyes. "Shut up tight, and showing no sign of opening its gate again. I'm sorry."

I don't ask after Wyn. I can't bring myself to speak his name. That wound is still too raw, and I'm not sure it will ever really heal. This is everything you once wanted, I remind myself. To see your House whole and well and free.

But inside me there is an endless sea, not of fear, but of grief, and I cannot push it back or confine it, no matter how hard I try.

At last, I find the will to get out of bed. And every afternoon I walk the scant mile to Burleigh House, though it takes me longer than it should to make the trip. I sit on the verge beside the lane and watch the meadow grasses go from gold to brown, the hedgerows sprouting red berries and gilded leaves. When the first frost comes and the afternoon air begins to bite, I wrap myself in a thick wool cloak, but I still make the journey.

Even now, with the walls impenetrable and the gate shut to me, I can't help being drawn back to my House.

Hanukkah comes and goes. But Mira's latkes and Jed singing "Maoz Tzur" in his deep bass voice are hollow joys this year. Christmas I keep with Frey and her son and daughter-in-law, who make the trip down from London. There's a tree in the public room of the inn and we sing carols with guests who happen to be traveling over Christmastide. Or rather, everyone else sings, and I stand mute, the music washing over me like a river parting around heartless stone.

When the holidays pass, I resume my vigil outside Burleigh

House, sitting with my back to the wall, dozing in thin winter sunshine, listening to the wind over the frozen fields.

And one day, one entirely ordinary day in mid-January, I wake from a fitful sleep outside Burleigh's walls and find a bluebell has sprouted between my fingers. I glance over to the wrought-iron gate and slowly, soundlessly, it swings open.

Getting to my feet, I walk over and stand on the very brink of Burleigh's grounds.

The House is visible again, all the mist that shrouded it burned away. It looks just as it once did, when I was a child. Warm stone. Leaded glass windows. Gardens dreaming of spring under their cover of frost. Wood smoke even spirals up from the chimneys, scenting the air. It looks and smells and *feels* like home.

"Wyn?" I ask, my voice carrying far in the cold and the silence. "Are you there?"

Only the birds in the hedgerows answer. And when I step away, I know I ought not to come back to Burleigh House again. I may be well enough in body, but so long as I keep returning, I will never be well in spirit.

When an early thaw hits, turning all the world to mud and sleet, I begin to think it's time to take my leave, not just of Burleigh House, but of the Halt as well. I wait tables as I try to make up my mind, and while most of my pay comes in the form of room and board, what coin I do get I put aside.

Frey's careful with me, watching closely, as if I've grown breakable since freeing the House. Perhaps she's right. Some days, everything seems fine. But others, I feel like a snapped reed, unable to stand on my own. I can't shake the temptation to slip out each night, after the inn has closed and the last of the evening's patrons wander home. To take the familiar north lane, until I reach the walls of Burleigh House. Once there, I run my fingers along smooth stone, returning time and again to the iron gate, where I stand on the threshold and speak into the hush of Burleigh at rest.

Wyn. Are you there?

Ash Wednesday is the day I settle on. It's before Purim this year, and I don't think I could smile through a celebration with Jed and Mira. I'll go back to the fens, I think, where life was simpler and where I knew my way. When I tell Frey, her eyes are kind.

"I understand, Violet. You'll write, though, won't you?"

Mira bakes as if there's no food to be had in Lincolnshire, and Jed whittles morosely, carving me little replicas of all the marsh birds. Though they've offered to come with me, I insist on going alone. They've made a life here again, renting a cottage at the edge of Longhill Farm, where Jed still day labors and Mira takes in washing and mending. I will not uproot them a third time on my behalf, though I'll miss them desperately.

I don't write to Espie to tell her that I'm leaving. She writes to me, though, to say that all of London is in a stir over what's happened with Burleigh House. There are riots in the streets after all, though I face no charges for what I've done. Everyone wants freedom for the remaining four Houses, now Burleigh's unbinding has proved a success, and they're not keeping quiet about it.

The last shift I'm to work at the Shilling comes at once too slowly and too soon. As always, I'm kept running across the tavern with trays of frothy mugs that smell of yeast and hops. I'm busy, at least, and it's a comfort. When I do manage a moment of self-reflection, I remind myself of this: the West Country is prospering. The weather has been just what it ought. Larders are full enough from the fall harvest to last two winters, rather than just one.

My House is well, as is the countryside. What more could a Caretaker want?

And yet.

Late in the evening, the inn door opens with a bang and a gust of wind that's still cold after dark. Shouts to close it come from the gathered farmers and I glance up to see a figure shutting the door. He crosses the tavern and sits at the long counter, where he sheds his coat.

"I'll be with you in a minute," I sing out. By the time I manage to get behind the counter with an empty tray, I'm breathless and red-faced.

"Can I help you?" I ask, and stop short.

"Hello, Vi," Wyn says.

For a moment we just stare at each other, and then he smiles. I'd nearly forgotten how a smile pulls his mouth up further on one side than the other, and how he squints just the slightest bit.

"Have you been well?" Wyn asks.

"Well enough," I say slowly. I'm not sure any of this is real. It seems too much like one of the muddled dreams I had last summer, while desperately working to free the House. But someone shouts for another drink, and my unconscious certainly never dwelled much on tipsy West Country farmers.

I turn with my hands on my hips. "Shut it, I'll be with you in a minute!"

"Sorry." I turn back to Wyn, still in shock. "And . . . and you? You're alright? Burleigh, too?"

"We are. It's taken a while, getting things sorted out, but both of us are well, and we're each of us in one piece, as you can see."

I steal looks at him in between polishing glasses. My hands are shaking, though, and I'm afraid of breaking something, so at last I set my rag down and give up the pretext of busyness.

"Wyn, I thought you were dead."

"So did I," he says frankly. "Until I realized there was clearly enough of me left alive to think it. And then I started coming back to myself, piece by piece. It took ages, though. I suppose even Burleigh unbound has a hard time working miracles."

Wyn smiles again, and my knees go weak. The florid-faced farmer calling for drinks is growing insistent, and I round on him to hide the tears pricking behind my eyes. "Harry Mason! Shut *up* or get it yourself!"

He grouses a little and hauls himself to his feet, joining me behind the counter, where he fiddles with the tap of the ale keg and mutters under his breath.

"Oh, stop it," I sigh, pushing him away. "Just let me do it."

When I've settled Farmer Mason with a full mug, I turn my attention back to Wyn.

"What—what will you do now?" I ask tentatively. "Where will you go?"

Wyn leans forward across the counter, resting his weight on his elbows, and is about to speak when Frey bursts through the back hallway door. I stifle a groan of frustration.

"Oh, blood and mortar, Violet," Frey says. "What are you still doing behind the counter? I think it's quite alright for you to end your last shift early if someone's come back from the dead."

"Are you sure?" I ask, and Frey rolls her eyes.

"Quite sure. Give me that apron, and go on."

Before I can blink, I've been unceremoniously hurried out from behind the counter, and then through the inn door onto the cobbled street.

"Goodbye," Frey murmurs. "I'm not going to make a fuss, but I wish you all the very best, Vi. And I think you'd better not change your plans. Leave this place behind you, but take that boy along."

The door shuts decidedly, leaving Wyn and me alone in the fresh nighttime air.

"In answer to your question, I thought I'd go wherever you go, Vi," he says at last. "If it's alright. The thing is, you've always come first for me. Before Burleigh House, or the countryside, or my own life. None of that's changed. I'm still for you, so I suppose we've just got to sort out who you're for, now Burleigh's unbound."

I'll never tire of it, hearing him say that I come first. But we walk, and my feet can't let their old habits go. Wyn and I are silent for a long time, carrying on side by side with a little space between us. It seems the only sound in the whole world is that of our booted footsteps.

By the time we reach the front gate of Burleigh House, my stomach is wild with nerves, though I'm not sure why. Wyn, who always knows when I'm anxious, reaches out and takes my hand. His skin is warm and soft and yielding, and a little frisson of sparks tingles between our fingers. Touching him feels uncommonly like magic— not the cold bite of mortar but a lush, living magic. A magic of our own making, that is full of beginnings, and possibility.

The iron-wrought gate opens before us, restored and free of bri-ars. Burleigh House lies at the end of the drive, a ruin no longer, every line of it gracious and inviting. A few lights already burn inside. The jacaranda tree sways gently, blooming in spite of the weather. It's all purple shadows and mystery in the moonlight.

I press a hand to the cool stone of the wall, and think of every-thing I've lost and won, everything I've given for this House that now radiates calm and well-being.

It's alright, Violet Sterling, Burleigh seems to say. *It's alright.*

Letting out a trembling breath, I turn to Wyn.

"I think—I think I'm for *me* now," I tell him. "Not Burleigh House. But sometimes I'm for you, too."

Wyn smiles.

"I was hoping you'd say that," he manages to get out before I kiss him.

Presently, he takes my hand again and we carry on past Burleigh's walls, into open countryside on the way to Taunton.

"Well, Vi," Wyn says. "Where are we going?"

"Did you know I own a cottage *and* a boat, in Lincolnshire?" I ask. "They're the only things in the world that really belong to me."

"I belong to you," Wyn says.

"Don't be ridiculous. We belong to ourselves. Have you ever been spearfishing?"

"No."

"It's not hard. I'll teach you."

"I would like that very much."

of Thorns who provided invaluable advice and encouragement—Bethany Morrow, Al Rosenberg, Steph Messa, Jen Fulmer, Hannah Whitten, Joanna Meyer, and Anna Schafer; to everyone at Triada US Agency who works so tirelessly on behalf of their authors, especially Uwe Stender, for putting together such a wonderful team, and Brent Taylor, for keeping track of foreign rights.

And on a more personal note, thank you, thank you, thank you to everyone who helped me navigate the labyrinth of writing a second book. This means you, Pod, and you, Steph, who made this idea a book in the first place. Truly, I have found my people. Thanks also to Ashley, my most enthusiastic cheerleader; to Mom, my one and only alpha reader/child-minder/laundry-folder/anything I need as I need it; to Tyler, who is the *best* partner I could have on this journey in every regard; and to my girls, who are the reason I do this in the first place.

If you're reading this book because you loved *The Light Between Worlds* and have been with me from the start, thank *you*. My readers mean the world to me—I cherish each and every word of encouragement from you that comes my way.

Last of all, it may seem a little silly to thank a House, but in this case it only makes sense. Thanks to Weymouth Manor, my ridiculous, rambling, good-natured home, that grows flowers beneath the snow in December, turns that one light on and off to say hello, loves us all, and can never *quite* bring itself to grow a vegetable.

ACKNOWLEDGMENTS

Much like a Great House, every book requires a small army to build and tend it. In the case of this one, I'm eternally grateful to Alice Jerman, the chief architect of Burleigh and Vi's story. She saw potential in this book, loved its magic, and cast the vision for what it could be. Alice, you push me to be better, and I can never write a scene now without having you ask in my head "But what are they *feeling?*" Thank you for your countless instances of help and insight and support.

None of my books see the light of day without input from the tenacious, brilliant, indispensable Lauren Spieller. She read this as the draftiest possible draft and helped steer it in the right direction. Lauren, I promise to try and write books with middles and plots provided you'll promise to let me think I'm right once a year (even if I'm actually wrong).

Thanks also to Clare Vaughn, my editor's assistant, who handles a lot of minutiae on the back end of publication and is a joy to work with; to Jackie Burke, my lovely publicist, who ensures readers hear about the books I write; to the early readers of *A Treason*